THIN SLICE OF LIFE

THIN SLICE OF LIFE

A NOVEL BY MILES ARCENEAUX

Thin Slice of Life

© 2012 Brent Douglass, John T. Davis and James R. Dennis

Library of Congress Cataloging in Publication Data:
Arceneaux, Miles
Thin Slice of Life / Miles Arceneaux
1. Title. 2. Fiction. 3. Mystery. 4 Suspense

Second Edition: January 2013
978-1-936205-84-4

Printed in the United States of America
Written by Brent Douglass, John T. Davis and James R. Dennis
Designed by Lana Rigsby, Thomas Hull, Carmen Garza and Jeffery Bleazard
Words and Music to "South Coast of Texas" by Guy Clark © 1981 Chappell & Co., Inc. (ASCAP)
All Rights Reserved, used by Permission of Alfred Music Publishing Co., Inc.

Stephen F. Austin State University Press
PO Box 13007, SFA Station, Nacogcohes TX. 75962
sfapress@sfasu.edu sfasu.edu/sfapress

**"THE SOUTH COAST OF TEXAS IS A THIN SLICE OF LIFE;
IT'S SALTY AND HARD, IT IS STERN AS A KNIFE."**

GUY CLARK FROM HIS SONG "THE SOUTH COAST OF TEXAS"

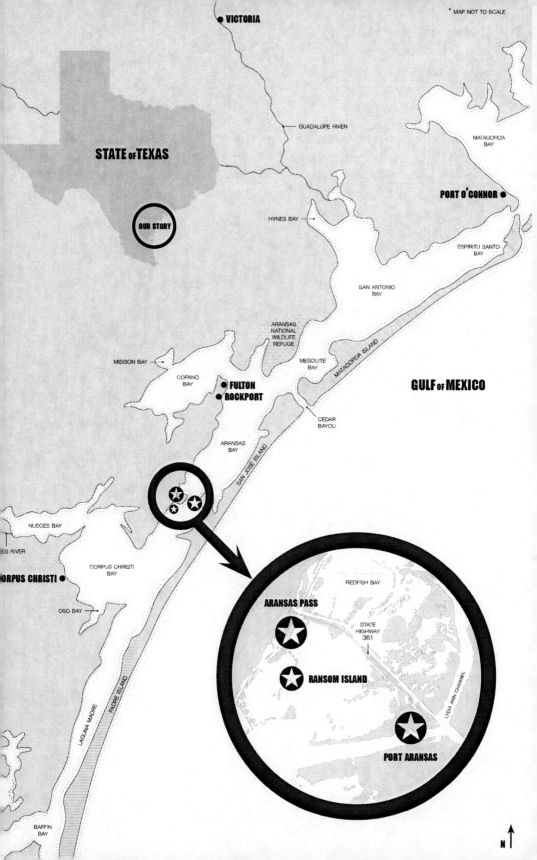

ACKNOWLEDGEMENTS

We would like to thank the wives, relatives and friends who have gone on the journey with us as *Thin Slice of Life* took shape over the past twenty-four years.

Mil gracias to esteemed authors Stephen Harrigan and Ben Rehder and acclaimed musician Marcia Ball for their forthright input and valuable suggestions.

Special thanks to Rigsby Hull and Jeffery Bleazard (our man in Shanghai) for their inspired design of all things Miles.

We gratefully acknowledge Stephen F. Austin University Press for their support and for the creative liberty they allowed us.

Finally, we are beholden to the rounders and ramblers, the troublemakers, ne'er-do-wells and raconteurs—and there are so damn many of 'em on the Texas Gulf Coast—that inspired many of the characters in this book.

—MILES ARCENEAUX

CHAPTER 01

OCTOBER, 1979

From above, the calm waters of the Gulf of Mexico reflect the deep blue of a bright October sky. A meandering seagull soars on a thermal updraft, alert for forage fish. From this height the occasional oil and gas platforms look like abandoned toys. Far off over the horizon the shoaling waters lighten to a translucent green as they rise to meet the dim humps of San José and Matagorda Islands.

Only one thing mars the vista: a column of greasy black smoke climbing into the flawless sky. The gull kites with the wind towards a steel-hulled trawler whose back deck is all but obscured by the billowing smoke and licking flames emerging from the engine room hatch. Markings painted on the rust-stained transom read *The Lazy Liz*, and underneath in smaller letters, *Fulton, Texas*, the boat's homeport. Men run aft bearing fire hoses and extinguishers, frantically battling the blaze.

Another vessel surges into sight, a pronounced wake marking its advance. It's another trawler, and it closes quickly on the stricken boat as maritime law and simple decency require. It's a fifty-eight foot gulf shrimper, the *Ramrod*, also out of Fulton. The *Ramrod* heaves to in front of the other boat, and the captain—it must be the captain, as no one else appears to be aboard—quickly sets the anchor and tosses over his own supply of fire extinguishers. He jackknifes his tall and lanky frame over the rail into the water and with long, powerful strokes swims to the bow of the burning vessel and clambers up the anchor line.

As it happens, the *Ramrod's* skipper recognizes the men on the *Lazy Liz*. They are Vietnamese, part of the postwar refugee population that has for the past few years been making itself felt in fishing communities up and down the Texas coast. The men nod at one another, too involved with the task at hand to exchange pleasantries.

But there is, nonetheless, a small shock of familiarity. Hardly surprising; the coastal Gulf waters are a small pond from the perspective of the fishermen, shrimpers and oystermen who work them. Everyone pretty much knows one another through greater and lesser degrees of separation.

The men on the stricken vessel know the curly-haired white man, too. His name is Johnny Sweetwater, from one of the old-line families of fishermen with deep roots in Fulton and its neighboring coastal town of Rockport.

Later, after the fire is quelled, the skipper of the *Lazy Liz* attempts to turn over the big diesels but his engines grind and refuse to catch. After a period of futile tinkering, the Vietnamese shrug their collective shoulders.

The Anglo captain, in a mixture of pidgin Vietnamese, Spanish and English maritime lingo, persuades them to let him fiddle with the diesels. He descends into the engine room and with a short but considerable expenditure of greasy, sweaty work, finally gets the big Cummins engines to crank over.

When he climbs up from below, the crewmen slap him on the back and congratulate him in the nasal singsong of their native language. The Vietnamese captain insists that he come inside and share a drink with them.

By dusk, with two bottles of rum down and a third bottle four fingers gone, Johnny excuses himself from the cigarette smoke-filled galley to check on his boat. Satisfied the *Ramrod* is holding fast to its anchorage, he strolls to the back deck of the *Lazy Liz* to observe the impending sunset and to enjoy the cool evening breeze. Leaning on the gunwale, out of view of his hosts, he focuses on a hatch cover located behind the cabin. He is just drunk enough to indulge an inborn curiosity to peek beneath the hatch into the holds.

He isn't sure what he sees in the dim light of the storage bins below deck, but he is sure it isn't shrimp. Half buried in the ice that normally blankets and preserves the catch, he sees several objects that are large, long and metallic, with stenciled numbers and identification markings visible even through the clear industrial plastic that protects them. *What the hell?*

The heat from the fire in the engine room has melted away much of the ice that was meant to hide the cargo. Whatever the objects are, Johnny quickly learns he isn't supposed to see them, because three crewmen scramble out of the cabin, yelling and shoving him away from the hatch.

The Vietnamese captain, observing the commotion, swears to himself and orders the men to sort themselves out and apologize. He slams the hatch shut and orders the men to go inside. "Take the rum," he says, thrusting the bottle at one of his underlings.

The crewmen apologize in their fashion and escort Johnny back into the crowded galley. The tension eases as the bottle begins to make the rounds once more. Johnny begins to tell an elaborate tale—illustrated with pantomime and many hand gestures—that seems to involve his brother Charlie, a Juarez *cantina*, two midget bullfighters, lots of tequila and several Mexican women of dubious reputation. Though they scarcely understand a word, the Vietnamese laugh uproariously, as much at the gusto of Johnny's vigorous recitation as at any literal interpretation.

As Johnny and the crew carouse, the skipper remains behind, unnoticed in the wheelhouse, where he picks up the ship-to-shore microphone and radios his employer and sponsor in Fulton. In terse sentences he recounts the fire, the intervention of the Anglo captain, and the inadvertent discovery of the *Lazy Liz's* secret cargo.

There is a short silence while the captain's master considers options. Finally, the word comes back across the crackling ether. The precise, ruthless tone of voice from the other end of the radio sends a chill down the captain's back.

Kill the man, says the voice. *Make it look as though he drowned. Leave the boat adrift. A missing man is easier to explain away than a missing vessel. Do it now.*

The captain replaces the microphone slowly and swallows. Instant obedience is hard-wired into the men who work for the man on the other end of the microphone. It cannot be otherwise. But this Anglo—he'd helped them out of a potentially catastrophic jam. And he is a fellow seaman, with all the universal bonds that fact implies. And the captain just plain likes him.

But all of that counts as nothing. Sticking his head into the galley, the skipper shouts for the biggest of the crewman to join him outside.

Not long after, Johnny Sweetwater finishes his bawdy shaggy-dog story and lurches to his feet, somewhat worse for rum.

"I'm sorry I can't stay for the cotillion, my little yellow friends, cause y'all know I love those little cucumber sandwich dealies." He sways side to side with the boat as he stands. "Say, boys, does it feel like the ground's moving?" One of fisherman rises drunkenly and offers to help the Anglo return to his boat.

Johnny waves him off and then, in his incipient Vietnamese, ceremoniously attempts to thank his hosts for their fine hospitality. The fishermen double over laughing at the effort. Johnny laughs with them and starts for the door.

"Well, so long, my hearties. Tell Miz Scarlett and them others I'll see 'em tomorrow at Tara. 'Cause tomorrow's another goddam *dia*, like they say."

Walking down the narrow gangway between the cabin and the rail, listing a little to port, Johnny never sees the looming figure behind him who steps out of a tool locker clutching a 48-inch pipe wrench.

The silent explosion of white light inside Johnny's head blows him off his feet and out of all rational thought. He vaguely registers the sensation of the rough deck planking abrading his cheek, although he could not have said what he was experiencing.

His eyes unfocused and unseeing, he feels himself ascending. *Flying?* he wonders vaguely.

The splash as his body lands overboard and the searing sensation of salt water in his lungs he notes only as distant phenomena. The back of his skull is crushed, his brain bleeding into his cranium, his heart and nervous system are running wildly, erratically and then not at all, the fading realization that something terrible has happened—all of these things he perceives as though at a great distance and of no cause of concern. He neither sees nor hears the *Lazy Liz* crank over her diesels and cruise away. The *Ramrod*, unloosed and untended, floats nearby.

The gentle swells of the warm Gulf waters bear him up and down in a gentle pendulum. Up and down and then up...endlessly up.

CHAPTER 02

The highway ahead shimmered in the morning heat and Charlie Sweetwater felt sweat pooling under his arms. Hot, humid air rushed through the open window, but the light had the slightest metallic edge that foretold the approach of autumn. His truck was a temperamental piece of crap and the A/C decided to quit working as soon as he hit the Chihuahuan Desert. Charlie and his brother used to call it the "Whore of Detroit" because they gave it all their money and it never loved them back. Years later, his brother had traded his interest in the truck for $75 and a pair of Tony Lama boots that needed new soles. But at least the radio still functioned.

Right now a static-laden Tejano polka scratched its way through the speakers. Charlie sang along for a verse and a chorus and then began talking back to the radio in Spanish to keep himself awake. 1500 miles of broken Mexican highway and arid South Texas brush country had taken its toll. He shifted uncomfortably in his seat and pushed the accelerator.

Charlie hadn't seen his hometown since his dad's funeral almost five years ago. That time, his brother Johnny had tracked him down in Cuernavaca and delivered the unhappy news over the telephone. This time, however, he'd sounded a hell of a lot more upbeat.

There was only one phone at the Playa Escondida Resort, the remote tourist operation that Charlie ran on the Pacific coast, but he happened to hear it ringing as he passed by the office cabana on his way to the reef for some spear fishing.

"Brother man!" Johnny shouted over the static. "I finally got through; I can't believe it."

"Hey, *hermano*. How the heck are you?"

"Terrific. Listen, I've got a proposition for you. How 'bout you get your ass out of Old Mexico and drive up here and see me in Fulton for a few days. I want you to meet somebody."

Johnny always liked to get straight to the point.

"You mean, like a girl?" asked Charlie, wondering if this time he'd be returning home for a wedding instead of a funeral.

"I'd rather keep it a surprise. Give you something to ponder on the way up."

There was a pause on the line as Charlie thought it over.

"Come on, bro,'" said Johnny, "I know you don't have jack-shit going on down there in lotus land. Besides, you haven't been back home in...I don't know how long."

Johnny was right. He had nothing pressing on his agenda, unless reef diving counted as an obligation, and he had no good excuse for staying away from his hometown for as long as he had. His lengthy absence hadn't been intentional; it had just become habit.

"Okay, Johnny. Why the hell not?"

Even through the static Charlie could hear his brother whooping on the other end of the line. "That's what I wanted to hear, 'mano! It'll be worth the effort. I promise."

"But why can't you tell me about this mystery chick? You're not getting married are you?"

"Have patience, little brother," he said. "Listen, I know it's a long drive so I'll look for you 'round the end of the week. I'm taking the boat out to the Gulf this afternoon—man, the shrimping has been outstanding lately—so if I'm not back in the harbor when you arrive, I'll be there soon after. End of the week. *Estamos bien?*"

Charlie laughed. "Yeah, we're good."

"Great. I can't wait to see ya."

"*Oye*, Johnny. You want me to bring you anything from Mexi..." but before he could finish his brother had hung up.

When Charlie finally reached the Fulton city limits he felt like a month of Judgment Days. But he recovered a little as he turned onto the familiar two-lane road that followed the edge of Aransas Bay. He was greeted by huddled stands of live oaks that bent in an arthritic pose away from the relentless Gulf winds, and by the pungent odor of decaying seaweed and dead fish that flavored the fresh sea air. Rickety wooden fishing piers, many still unrepaired since the last hurricane, jutted out from bait shacks that perched over the water (FRESH BAIT, LIVE AND DEAD read the hand-made signs).

The Texas coast was a blue-collar working coast, full of refineries, commercial fishing outfits and beer joints—a long way removed from the postcard vistas of Monterrey or South Florida. Many folks, try as they might, just couldn't conjure up an appreciation for the area's raffish, low-rent appeal, but Charlie recognized that the geography was woven into his DNA. Fulton had seen better days, but as far as hometowns went, Charlie had no complaints.

They had been quite a pair, the Sweetwater brothers. The girls rapturously referred to them as the "Sweets," but local law enforcement had other names for them—"little shitbird troublemakers" or "future defendants" being the most polite. Congenitally irreverent and frequently bored by small-town life, the Sweetwater boys were used to making their own fun. And growing up in Fulton, they'd had plenty.

Turning onto the crushed oyster shell road that led to the docks of Fulton Harbor, Charlie could see an agitated cloud of squawking seagulls hovering above the rigging and masts of the trawlers in the harbor. Somehow he wasn't surprised to discover that they gathered in a riotous mass directly over Johnny's empty boat slip.

Charlie pulled to a stop and watched a tan adolescent boy throwing handfuls of what appeared to be orange peanuts into the frenzied mob of gulls concentrated above him. Several groups of Vietnamese fishermen squatted on the decks of their weathered flathull shrimp boats, observing the scene without visible reaction. Johnny's mongrel dog, Ringworm, stood on the dock next to the boy, barking at the birds.

The boy saw Charlie and sat down on a sack of the orange pellets, his elbows resting on his knees, his hands cupping his chin, waiting, apparently, for Charlie to get out of the truck. The kid wore cut-off jeans and a faded T-shirt displaying a photo of *El Santo*, the Mexican wrestling hero.

Charlie stepped out of the truck and stretched his road-weary back, and then strolled down the pier toward the boat.

"*Buenos días*," said Charlie. The boy lifted his chin as a greeting. Ringworm walked up slowly and sniffed at Charlie.

"It's okay, boy. It's me." He cautiously reached down and let the dog sniff his hand. "Good dog." After a moment the dog recognized his scent and started romping around on the deck, wagging his ratty stub of a tail. Charlie knelt down and rubbed the mutt's belly.

"I'm Charlie Sweetwater," he said to the boy,

"I know," he said. "*Jew* look like Johnny," he said in hesitant English.

"He's my brother."

The boy nodded. He had olive skin, light blue eyes and a mop of curly brown hair that cascaded from under a Rockport Pirate's baseball cap. "I work with him on the boat."

Charlie looked over at the empty boat slip. "You do?"

"Johnny make me stay...this time. For the school." He cocked a thumb dispiritedly toward the Rockport-Fulton Middle School a few blocks away.

"*Vaya* Pirates," Charlie joked, but the boy didn't react. "Well ...he told me he'd be back around the end of the week. Maybe even today, you think?"

"*Jes.* Maybe."

"Hey, I have a question for you." The boy looked at him, waiting. "What in the hell were you doing just now...when I drove up?" He looked confused, so Charlie tossed a handful of imaginary peanuts into the air.

A cautious smile appeared on the boy's face. "That is food we sell for the birds. Johnny's idea," he added redundantly.

Charlie laughed. "Sounds like one of Johnny's crazy ideas."

The boy stood up and pointed to a label on one of the 25 lb. clear plastic sacks of orange pellets. It said "CAP'N JOHNNY'S SHRIMP-FLAVORED BIRD CHOW." There was a caricature of a squinty-eyed, pipe-clinching sea salt on there too, telling consumers that the pellets were "guaranteed," whatever that meant. There were probably twenty sacks stacked up on the pier.

Charlie grabbed a handful of the pellets and lifted them to his nose. "God almighty!" he said in disgust, tossing the pellets into the water. A mass of piggy perch instantly appeared and began nibbling at the pellets as they drifted toward the bottom.

"We not sell too much," the boy explained apologetically. "They are made of pieces of shrimps we put in a machine that Johnny bought from Judd Sprinkle. But the chow...it go bad too fast."

"So it seems," Charlie agreed. "Who does Johnny think will buy this stuff?"

"He say tourists and bird people buy it. But not so many we find out. Only the *gaviota*...the uh...."

"The seagull," Charlie said. If nothing else, his sojourn in Mexico had done wonders for his Spanish.

"*Jes*, the seagull. It is the only bird that like the shrimps chow. And Ringworm, he like it too, but his hair fall out from an *alergia* or something, and Johnny say he don't want a ugly dog."

Charlie looked over at the yellow mutt that was lying on the pier licking his balls. Ringworm looked like a cross between a dingo and a possum.

Charlie yawned and stretched. "What's your name, kid?

"Raul."

"Well, Raul. Where's a good place to grab a late breakfast?"

"Johnny like the Marina, on Key Allegro."

"Yeah, I like that place, too. How 'bout we go get us a taco or something while we're waiting for Johnny?"

CHAPTER 03

Charlie, Raul and Ringworm filed into the Key Allegro marina's combination cafe/bait-shop/and beer-joint. Seating himself at the bar, Charlie ordered three breakfast tacos, a Pearl beer, and a bowl of water for the mutt. They were alone in the cafe except for the sullen, muscular figure hunched over the griddle who began scrambling eggs and chorizo for Charlie's tacos.

Charlie looked around the empty room. "Is it always this crowded?"

"You're too fucking early for lunch. And too fucking late for breakfast."

Miguel Cantu Negron, the cook, bartender and bouncer, was not a man for witty repartee, having spent several years enjoying the hospitality of the Texas Department of Corrections. Two blue tears rolled down from his right eye, each one of the tattoos symbolic of a life taken. Despite all of his best efforts, Miguel Negron had not fully rehabilitated himself.

Miguel served their food and stood motionless behind the bar, looking at Charlie through hooded eyes. "Thanks," said Charlie, a little troubled by the dark-skinned man hovering over his breakfast. When Miguel didn't budge, Charlie finally looked up. "What?"

"You look like your brother," Miguel said.

"I get that a lot. I'm Charlie," He extended his hand over the bar.

Miguel looked at it for a moment then offered his hand as well. Charlie noticed markings across the knuckles. He took the large, rough hand and turned it toward him, palm down. Across the right, in dark blue ink, Charlie read the word VIDA. He glanced down at the other hand, which bore the inscription MUERTE.

Charlie stared at Miguel and nodded knowingly. "*El mundo es como un pepino: hoy lo tienes en la mano, mañana en el culo,*" he said deadpan, (The world is like a cucumber: today you have it in your hand, tomorrow in the ass). A brief laugh rumbled out of Miguel's chest, but he didn't smile.

The bell over the screen door rang, announcing the arrival of another late breakfast aficionado.

State Senator Llewellyn Cudihay wore a Panama hat, a pale blue guayabera shirt and tailored white cotton pants. His fifty-four year old face was red-veined and puffy. But upon seeing the cafe's other inhabitants, he straightened up, took off his hat and ran a hand through his mane of silver hair. It was an automatic gesture he made in the vicinity of potential constituents, even a quorum of voters as improbable as Charlie, Raul and Miguel.

Cudihay had represented the Coastal Bend, including Rockport and Fulton, in the Texas Senate for so long that he thought he was invincible, irresistible and Gawd's own gift to the democratic process. His critics—and they were legion—were amazed and exasperated how the perennial incumbent dodged prosecution and scandal year after year.

Almost every person in the district knew that the Senator was no Eagle Scout, but he brought home enough bacon to keep them voting for him. In return, he treated his district as his personal fiefdom and private hunting preserve.

Speaking of which, a pair of tits with a woman named Misty attached to them followed the Senator through the door. She was clearly *not* the esteemed Mrs. Cudihay, who languished in a modest rented bungalow back in Austin.

"Pinky" Cudihay fancied himself quite the ladies' man with ambitious young girls like Misty—the younger and hungrier these "personal assistants" were, the better. Around Austin, the insiders joked that every piece of legislation proposed by Cudihay bore the subtitle "An Unnatural Act of Congress."

Charlie Sweetwater finished off his tacos and feeling refreshed and revived, he jumped up and danced over to the jukebox. Doing his very best James Brown, Charlie sang, "I feel good/Na-na-na-na-na/

Like I knew that I would/Na-na-na-na-na-na!" He smiled at the selections on the juke and punched D9, D10 and G17. Charlie yelled out "Bingo!" and Ray Charles began singing "What'd I Say," as Charlie bobbed up and down in front of the Wurlitzer.

Cudihay looked over to Charlie in perplexed amazement that, finally, shaded into amusement. "Say, boy, come over here and talk to me and Misty."

Charlie looked at the Senator for a few seconds and then loped over to their table.

"Why the hell are you so jolly this morning?" Cudihay asked, smiling. "You get laid last night or somethin'?"

"Naw, just born with a song in my heart, I guess," Charlie answered, studying the Senator's blond companion who straddled the bar stool seductively. She wore a strapless orange sundress, very short. The front of her dress had slipped down a little, despite the considerable grip it had on her ample bosom. She followed Charlie's gaze and leaned over slightly to afford him a better view.

"Hah! Ain't nobody born *that* happy. Just dogs and simpletons. You're not a simpleton are ya?"

Charlie tore his eyes away from Misty's décolletage and laughed. "No, man. Not a dog either. To be truthful, I have achieved this enlightened state through years of meditation, spiritual probity and clean living."

"Somehow I doubt that," said the Senator, eyeing his new acquaintance skeptically. "What is it you do for this clean living anyway?"

Miguel set coffee, scrambled eggs, toast and strawberry jam on the bar and Charlie watched in horny fascination as Misty fixed her eyes on Charlie and proceeded to dip the end of her middle finger into the jam and then slowly slip the jellied finger into her mouth, sucking it up and down almost to her knuckle. "Ah...a little of this, a little of that," Charlie answered, distracted momentarily by the girl's culinary exhibition. "I specialize in beachfront property," he said.

The Senator pulled a flask out of his hip pocket and began to doctor his coffee. "You don't say? Goddamn, it's a great country, isn't it? Me? I'm a Senator in the sovereign state of Texas, charged by my constituents with the weighty responsibility of creating bills and apportioning money for programs that benefit the citizens in my district, which happens to include small business owners such as yourself."

Charlie pretty well had it figured out who and what Pinky Cudihay was. He even vaguely recalled voting for the man. "You don't say?" he responded.

"So tell me Mr....?"

"Sweetwater is my name. Charlie Sweetwater." He cocked an eyebrow and offered his hand. Cudihay grinned and took it while Misty studied Charlie with what he hoped was slow-blooming lust.

"So tell me, Mr. Sweetwater, how is the real estate bidness these days?"

"Uncertain."

"I hear you, brother. As you probably know, I've authored more than one bill in Austin that proposed to expand property easements along the Texas coasts...and if it wasn't for those damn open beach environmentalists, I'd have succeeded too."

Charlie pursed his lips and shook his head in mock dismay at the injustice of it all.

"I honestly don't know how a working man like you gets by," said the Senator.

"Well, to be honest Senator, I've had to supplement my meager income with an entrepreneurial idea that came to me one day in a flash of inspiration."

"Really?" purred Misty.

"Yes ma'am, a blinding flash."

"Tell me about this great idea, Mr. Sweetwater. I'm a big fan of the free market, especially in uncertain economic times such as these."

Charlie thought fast. "Well sir, after years of dedicated research and development, involving no small amount of personal sacrifice, I now market a product called 'Cap'n Johnny's Shrimp-Flavored Bird Chow.'" Miguel stifled a snort of laughter and continued scraping the grease off his grill.

"Bird Chow? You don't say? So tell me, who have you found to buy this, ah, remarkable product?" the Senator inquired, though he didn't really care. He poured another inch of whiskey into his coffee.

"Tourists mostly, and maybe a few gullible ornithologists. You throw out a few handfuls of my patented pellets and the birds just flock to 'em. I'll tell you, Senator, this stuff is selling like pussy on a troop train."

Charlie finished his beer and beckoned for another. He was on a roll. "It's a chance for folks to interact with the great congregation of bird life that we're famous for in these parts. Of course, most people come down here hoping to see a Whooper." (The area was the winter home to the only remaining flock of Whooping Cranes left on God's green earth.) "But they will generally settle for just about anything with wings."

The screen door swung open and a small pale man with chubby

features and male-pattern baldness peeked into the cafe. He was wearing a short sleeve button-down shirt and a fat necktie. "Oh, there you are, Senator," he said breathlessly. "I've been looking all over for you."

"What's the emergency, Neddy?" Cudihay asked irritably.

Edward "Neddy" Pomade was Cudihay's personal aide, responsible for keeping the erratic Senator on the well-planned agenda he prepared each and every day. His other duties included trying to contain, as much as possible, the brush fires caused by the Senator's perverse appetites, and to keep the Senator's frequent transgressions out of sight of his constituents and the "Goddamn Meddling Liberal Media." Neddy was fussy, tedious and obsequious—Cudihay couldn't stand him—but he wouldn't dare get rid of him.

"You're scheduled at the Kiwanis Club at noon, sir. You are the guest of honor."

Cudihay sighed, the responsibilities of his office clearly weighing on him. "A public servant's work is never done, folks."

He turned to his aide and said, "Gimme the list."

"Which one, sir?"

"Tonight's list, the list, goddammit. I'm gonna add a guest of honor or two." He turned to Charlie with a broad wink.

"I'll tell you what, Charlie Sweetwater; I'm throwing a little party over at my place this evening. It's a fundraiser to give me the chance to, ah, interact with my constituents. Why don't you come over, and bring about fifty pounds of that bird chow with you? Hell, we can serve 'em up as hors d'oeuvres if the guests get drunk enough."

"Uh, sir?" Neddy was eyeing Charlie dubiously. Cudihay held up a finger, a signal for his aide to shut the fuck up.

"Where do y'all live?" Charlie asked, looking more towards Misty than the Senator.

Cudihay flung his arm to point across the harbor. "Do you know where the old Key Allegro Inn was, before it burnt down?" the Senator asked.

"Yassah," Charlie answered.

"Well, we're right across the canal from there."

"Oh, you live in that big white house. The one that looks like Frank Lloyd Wright did a big ol' high-five with the guy who designed Trader Vic's? With the heliport by the side?"

"That's the one," the Senator smiled.

"Dang," Charlie mused. "Lifestyles of the rich and famous. What time do y'all want me over there?"

"We're gonna have cocktails at six and dinner around eight-thirty."

"That sounds just fine," Charlie replied. "I'll bring over some Beatles records and we can play 'em backwards."

"You do that," the Senator laughed. "Just don't forget them bird nutrients."

Charlie got up and motioned to Raul and Ringworm that it was time to leave. As he was about to step out the door of the Marina, he snapped his fingers and turned to the Senator.

"Say, Senator. Is it alright if I bring the dawg?"

Cudihay laughed again, and with a mouthful of scrambled eggs and picante sauce said, "You bring anybody or anything you want."

Charlie nodded. "Groovy."

———

CHAPTER 04

Charlie got bored waiting at the harbor for his brother so he decided to look in on another member of the family. Charlie glanced over at Raul, who was riding shotgun. (Ringworm preferred the bed of the pickup truck.) The boy was watching the bay as if he was expecting to see the *Ramrod* chugging toward Fulton Harbor any instant.

"Hey, Raul, you ever been to Shady's, over on Ransom Island?"

"*Jes*. Johnny take me there before."

"Then you know exactly where we're going."

A few miles outside of Rockport they passed by the abandoned Starfish Drive-in. Charlie recalled a faint childhood memory of sitting in his mother's lap in the family station wagon, watching the big outdoor screen. Johnny was sitting in their dad's lap and the car smelled like popcorn. Or maybe he'd just invented the memory and it became so familiar to him in the years after his mother died that he thought it was real.

Which reminded him of another memory that *was* real and that really did happen. One fall evening when he and Johnny were in high school they commandeered the Starfish projection room and replaced Walt Disney's *The Shaggy Dog* with a bootleg Ann-Margret film called *Kitten With A Whip*. All the moms in attendance were gratifyingly horrified, although the dads at the drive-in secretly thought Ann-Margret was the kind of smokin' hot babe who could give a hard-on to a cigar store Indian. The kids all wanted to see the anthropomorphized Disney pooch, not a sultry redhead starlet in a tight sweater. The Sweetwater boys thought they would end up in the prankster Hall of Fame.

When their dad, Dubber, returned from the Gulf, the football coach came to the house and asked him to please, for God's sake, please help him keep the boys out of trouble so they wouldn't get suspended from school...and therefore be ineligible for the upcoming district playoffs.

Dublin "Dubber" Sweetwater never remarried after the boys' mother died. Over the next fifteen years he tried his best to rein in his two wild-ass sons, but with little success. The task was made harder because he was often out in the Gulf trawling for brown shrimp for weeks at a time. In spite of everything, he got both boys through high school and then into the University of Texas in Austin. To everyone's amazement, both of them graduated. They stayed in school and got their degrees partly because "it was mama's dying wish," but also partly so they wouldn't have to stay in Fulton to help Dad out with the family business.

To the boys, shrimping looked like a sea-going road to Palookaville. They loved their old man, but couldn't help noticing that Dubber was stove up with arthritis at fifty, had lost part of two fingers in a winch accident and was usually about two good meals away from applying for food stamps. Piss on that. They had their own plans for the future.

But after their dad died, it was Johnny who elected to move back to Fulton and take over their father's shrimping business, even though Johnny had the most to lose—namely, a promising career as a landman for the Valero Energy Company and a lovely girlfriend from a prominent San Antonio family. She took one look at the rusty shrimp boats and the rough little town and said *adios amigo*. Johnny stayed and became a shrimper, and no matter how hard he tried to talk his brother into staying too, Charlie resisted. At the time he was having way too much fun drifting through an incautious assortment of schemes and opportunities in Mexico. Seeing the dilapidated old drive-in, Charlie felt sure that he had made the correct choice.

——

Just barely above water, Ransom Island rested in the middle of Redfish Bay like the exposed hull of a scuttled ship. In its day, the location was a fishing paradise and a lively hell-raising Mecca for G.I.s, Cajun oilfield workers, cowboys, shrimpers and fishermen of all kinds. That heyday—roughly from the late Thirties through the early Sixties—was still fondly and endlessly recounted by the survivors of the era.

Rupert Sweetwater had owned and operated Shady's Boat and Leisure Club since he purchased the small crescent-shaped spit of land shortly after Prohibition. He and his brothers constructed all of the buildings and piers themselves, and all three of Rupert's ex-wives helped him run the place—while they lasted. Ransom Island was not conducive to marital longevity.

But his fourth and current wife, Vita, had staked her own claim on the island and stayed on. She managed the books and practically ran the entire business, which was probably why this last marriage had survived so much longer than the other three.

But thriving it was not. Part Gilligan's Island, part Judge Roy Bean's Jersey Lilly Saloon, Shady's was in a deteriorating class by itself.

Charlie was an hour early for the next ferry and he and Raul were alone at the pier. Not many people found reason to visit the island anymore. All but two of the cottages were gone now, the rest carried away by Hurricane Celia in 1970, and the wooden fishing skiffs had rotted from disuse once motor boats became an affordable toy for most angling enthusiasts.

The railroad tie causeway, which once connected the island to the mainland, was long gone, fallen victim to channel dredgers and Intracoastal Canal traffic. Where once cars had thronged the causeway to attend the big dances at Shady's, now the increasingly infrequent ferry was the only means for automobiles or pedestrians to reach Ransom Island.

Charlie sat on the car hood gazing across the bay at the weathered buildings and piers of the scruffy island. When Charlie and Johnny were younger, their dad would allow them to spend part of their summers working at Rupert's place, outfitting the fishing parties, cleaning the daily catch, and doing odd jobs around the island. They slept on cots in the back of the bait and tackle store, and after they finished their daily chores they enjoyed the liberty to spend their time as they pleased. Those were raucous and generally idyllic summers for young boys. Under Rupert's watchful eye it was hard, though not impossible, to get into trouble on the small island.

The ferry finally approached and deposited Charlie and Raul on the far shore. They drove the short distance from the pier to the island's main building, a square one-story structure on pilings with a cedar shiplap exterior, a high-pitched corrugated tin roof, and a wide covered porch that wrapped around on three sides. Hanging next to the front door was a hand-lettered sign about the size of coffee table that said THE SHADY BOAT AND LEISURE CLUB in block letters. On the other side of the entrance was an oval sign that in bold red neon said simply, BEER.

Charlie climbed the steps to the entrance of his uncle's once-renowned bar and grill, carefully stepping over the liver-colored hound that sprawled out in front of the door. He paused for a moment on the stoop and then, like a gunslinger, swung open the rickety screen doors to Shady's and stepped inside.

"Well, I'll be gawd-damned! It's young Charlie, the black sheep of the Sweetwater clan." It was Jake Jacoby, a red haired, red-faced charter boat captain with an impressive beer belly and forearms as thick as pilings. He practically got his mail at Shady's.

"Hello, Jake."

"Hey, Vita! Come out here and see what washed up on the island."

Charlie walked across the worn plank floor to Jake's barstool and shook his paw. He nodded to some of the other patrons occupying the rusty stools around the long curved bar.

There was burly, full-bearded Tucker Adderly, a retired stock broker turned sailor; Pete Jackson, a master boat builder at the Lazzaro Shipyard in Rockport; and, of course, Juan Ezekiel Estrada Esquire III, a.k.a. John Graham. Juan had never had any visible signs of employment as far as Charlie knew. In fact, in the last twenty years Charlie couldn't recall seeing Juan leave his bar stool. For that matter, he'd never seen his beat-up '49 Chris Craft Constellation Cruiser leave its boat slip either.

He was pleased to see nothing had really changed at Shady's. Same electric Pearl Beer clock where one of the beer country's famous 1100 springs ran perpetually across the sign, same ancient Seeberg juke box, (Duke Ellington's "Satin Doll" was C-11), and the same jar of pickled pig's feet on the counter, with probably the same embalmed hooves floating like lab experiments in the unspeakable liquid.

Charlie noticed Bob Storey sitting at one of the metal card tables in a far corner of the room, chain smoking Prince Albert roll-your-owns and playing dominoes with his wife, Peggy.

"Afternoon, Mrs. Storey."

"Hello, Charlie," she replied. "Glad to see you've moved back."

"Oh, I'm just here for a visit....By the way, I like your new 'do.'" Her bleached hair towered up on top of her head like a conch shell. The last time he had seen her she had strawberry hair, shaped like a football helmet.

"Why, thank you." She patted the sculpted creation with her hand.

"How's your head, Bob?" he asked, grinning at the grizzled, wiry man and pointing a finger to his own forehead. It was widely known that Bob Storey was a killer. He was very proud of the fact that he had stabbed someone in a dock fight some forty years ago, even though it had officially been ruled an accident. But Bob insisted that it was a killing, fair and square.

Bob didn't talk much but he made sure people understood that he was a thoroughly dangerous man and was not to be trifled with. Years after the knifing, Bob had been the rigman and Charlie was working as the header on one of Dubber's shrimp boats. Charlie had accidentally dropped one of the heavy metal shrimp baskets on Bob's head as he was icing down the catch below decks, opening a three-inch gash in his forehead.

Charlie, seeing the insane blood rage on the self-professed murderer's face as he began to scramble up the ladder after him, sought his father's immediate intervention. "You guys quit screwing around," Dubber had told them. Bob had some temper. Over time, Charlie learned that the man was really harmless if you knew when to back off.

"Fuck you," was all Bob said.

Vita walked into the room wearing a baggy white cotton sweater and jeans.

"Hello, Awntie."

"Hello yourself, Charlie! Johnny said you'd be coming. How are you, darlin'?" she asked, wrapping an arm around his shoulder.

"Splendid, Vita. Couldn't be better."

She saw Raul and looked around for Johnny.

"Johnny's out in the Gulf," said Charlie. "When I talked to him from Mexico he said he'd be back in port by the end of the week. So I figured that while I'm waiting, I'd drop by and say hello."

"Well I'm glad you did. We haven't seen you in a very long time."

"Hey, Charlie," Jake boomed from down the bar. "I hear you're a big fancy beach resort tycoon now, down in Old Mexico."

"That's right, Jake. If being chief cook and bottle washer in a place with ten cabins, twelve hammocks and one *palapa* bar out in the middle of nowhere adds up to a fancy beach resort, then yeah, I've really made it big. I'm a rumor in my own time."

"Well hell, boy," Jake continued, "If you just want kitchen work in a fancy joint in the middle of nowhere you can get a job right here at the world famous Shady's." He roared at his own cleverness.

Vita arched her plucked eyebrows and looked at Jake. "Or maybe he could move down a notch or two and start his own two-bit charter boat service for high-toned rich pricks from Dallas." This caused Jake to laugh even harder.

"How far down the coast is your place, Charlie?" asked Tucker.

"Way down. Almost to Guatemala."

"Do they speak Mexican that far down," asked Juan, looking up from a sweating can of Falstaff, "or Indian?"

"Juan," said Tucker, "I think you're mixing up your languages."

"It's Spanish mostly," Charlie answered, "Although a lot of the indigenous people speak a Zapotec dialect."

"Speaking of Zapata..." said Juan, "...did y'all know there's a secret society called the Skull and Crossbones that dug up his head? They got it hidden in a shoebox at a frat house up East somewhere. Stanford, I think." (Tucker buried his head in his hands).

"Jesus, Juan," said Jake, "You screwed that story up six ways from Sunday."

"They use it for rituals and such," Juan added.

"I thought it was Pancho Villa's skull that got stolen," said Pete Jackson.

"Yeah, Pete, I think you're right." Juan agreed. "It was Pancho Villa. It's his head in the shoebox."

"You're a goddamned genius, Juan," said Jake.

Undeterred, Juan continued. "A lot of people don't know that Pancho Villa preferred riding a motorcycle in the Revolution, instead of a horse. He had a sidecar for ol' Zapata to ride with him."

"That's funny, Juan," Pete remarked. "All the pictures I've ever seen, he's riding a horse."

"Well of course he never rode his motorcycle around his men..." Juan answered, "...especially in battle."

Tucker decided to bite. "And why is that, Juan?"

"Because then he'd scare their horses!" Juan looked around him, as if the answer should be obvious to everybody.

Charlie smiled at Vita. Where else was he going to find this kind of entertainment? Vita returned his smile with a shrug and a rueful grin and pulled a beer out of the icebox for him. She pulled out a

Big Red, too, and handed it to Raul, ruffling his hair before she returned to the bar.

Charlie drank his beer. When there was a lull in the conversation he said, "So, driving up from Mexico this morning I heard on the radio there's a hurricane prowling around out in the Caribbean. Any of y'all know where it's going?"

The mention of an approaching hurricane never failed to change the tenor of conversation on the coast. It trumped almost every other subject of interest. No one seemed to think discussing millibar levels or Gulf Stream currents odd or inappropriate in any setting or on any occasion. Not in that part of the country.

Jake shifted on his barstool. Tucker began stroking his beard reflectively. Vita gave the standard answer. "God knows, Charlie... and he's not telling."

"This late in the season, I'm thinking it'll go north," said Pete.

"They say it'll be in the Gulf by tomorrow," said Jake.

"Rupert's bettin' it'll make landfall in Mexico," said Tucker. "Me, I think it's too early to say."

"Well, I hope your brother has enough sense to come in from the Gulf before long," said Vita.

Charlie nodded. "By the way, where is Uncle Rupert?"

There was hoarse barking and then a screechy baying noise from the front porch of the building. A deep, gruff voice almost as raspy as the hound's said "Shut up, Mingus, you fool dog!" Rupert filled the doorway for a moment and then spotted his nephew.

"Hey, Charlie! Welcome back to Shady's, boy." He lumbered over and placed his ham-like hands on Charlie's shoulders before embracing him in an affectionate bear hug that squeezed most of the air out of his lungs.

Rupert wasn't tall but his massive torso and Popeye forearms gave him a formidable appearance. He had prodigious ears, a bulbous nose and a large sandy-haired head that rested on a thick neck. Bright aquamarine eyes looked out from a weathered, deeply wrinkled face. Despite his craggy exterior and seventy-plus years, Rupert Sweetwater was still a ruggedly handsome and very vigorous man.

"I'm damn glad to see you, Charlie. Seems like it's been a hunnert years since you've been here."

"Yeah, it has been a while, Uncle."

"We've been speculating on the storm," Jake explained.

Rupert waived his hand in dismissal. "Aww, let it come. This place is a god-danged fortress." Vita rolled her eyes.

They chatted for a while, mostly reminiscing about old times, then Charlie got up to leave.

"Don't run off, nephew," said Rupert. "You just got here."

"We've hardly talked about what's been going on around here since you left," said Vita. "And you haven't told us a thing about your life in Mexico."

"Don't worry. I'll come back by. Johnny's probably pulling in to port right now, and I'd kind of like to be there to meet him. Besides..." he winked at Vita, "...I better catch that four o'clock ferry so I don't get caught in the famous Ransom Island rush hour traffic."

—

The *Ramrod* had still not returned, so Charlie dropped Raul off at the dock and drove to Johnny's house on Rattlesnake Point for a shower and to dress for the Senator's party: jeans, a faded burnt-orange T-shirt and a mint green leisure suit jacket he discovered in Johnny's steamer trunk. Before he left, he splashed a little Old Spice on his crotch.

Charlie drove alone to the Cudihay mansion. The huge white house sat right on the bay and confused architectural avant-garde with garish ostentation. Money and taste had never really been kissing cousins in Texas.

Cudihay met Charlie at the door, already much drunker than Cooter Brown. "Well, if you're not a sore for sight eyes," the Senator began. As Cudihay ushered Charlie into his home, Charlie could see that there were a couple of hundred people mingling on the manicured lawn.

Misty joined them at the entrance. She was dressed in not too much, like she'd thrown something on and missed. Charlie replied, "This is a lovely place you have here, Senator. It's just like my place. Spooky, huh?"

"Where is my bird feed?" Cudihay asked, a little too loudly.

"It's out in the truck. I thought I'd bring it in later just in case you run low on the appetizers."

"Say, boy," Cudihay put his arm around Misty, "do you know why God gave women ten percent more brains than cows?"

"No sir, I don't believe that I do."

"So they wouldn't shit all over the floor when you play with their tits."

Cudihay nearly fell down laughing. Charlie nearly fell down too, just for fun. Misty gave the florid-faced Senator a look that could have castrated a small bull. Hostess or not, her asshole meter was redlining where her erstwhile patron was concerned.

The Senator turned to Misty and asked, "Why don't you take Mr. Charlie to get a drink, and then show him around the place?"

Misty took Charlie by the hand, led him to the bar, and poured him the biggest, darkest glass of scotch he'd ever seen. She scooped a bottle of Russian vodka off the bar for herself and began the tour.

When they arrived in the master bedroom on the second floor, Misty bolted for a small wooden box under the bed. She took out a cold cream jar full of cocaine and offered it to Charlie. "Wanna bump?"

Charlie shook his head and told her that his cardiologist had warned him to stay away from blow until his triple bypass had completely healed. Misty jumped on the nose candy like a fat kid hitting the dessert buffet at Luby's. She washed the line of cocaine down with a swig of Commie vodka. Charlie opened one of the large windows that looked out across the water.

"What," Misty inquired, rubbing her powdered nose, "do you people do around here for fun?"

"Oh, mostly drink Pearl beer, fish ...philander." He watched her upraised behind appreciatively as she dropped to her knees and shoved the drugs back under the bed.

The full moon lazily hung over the bay. Leaning out the window, Charlie felt the cool sea breeze against his face. He smelled the barbecue and heard the drunken din of the party from below. Then, from behind him, Misty placed her hands across his chest.

"That stuff's good for you, you know" Charlie nodded towards the coke under the bed. "All the essential vitamins and minerals."

"I was brought up to believe your body is a temple," she whispered. Misty began some sort of obscene bump and grind against Charlie's backside. Charlie stared anxiously at the bay and noticed the Senator standing on the dock, looking up at the window...looking at him. About ten feet behind Cudihay, towards the bay, stood a pudgy man in polyester slacks and a Hawaiian shirt—the Senator's aide.

The Senator waved at Charlie. Charlie was just about to back away from the window when a rifle shot cracked across the bay and Cudihay's aide fell into the water.

Neddy Pomade was dead.

CHAPTER 05

The next morning Charlie rubbed his eyes and wondered if the disjointed images rolling around in his head were just a lingering bad dream. The specter of Neddy's soggy body being heaved onto a stretcher, the soaked shirt clinging to the folds in his doughy torso, stained by the blood, was still too vivid for comfort. Charlie vaguely remembered the honorable Senator standing in a pool of bright light talking to news reporters after the shooting. Hell of a party.

He raised himself off of Johnny's couch and searched the cabinet for some coffee. The weathered house on Rattlesnake Point was located about five miles from the harbor, perched out over the edge of Copano Bay on twelve-foot pilings. Johnny had bought it as a get-away house about a year before he moved back to the coast for good.

The architecture of La Casa de Sweetwater was sort of a random-access affair. The spavined sofa protruded almost into the kitchen. What passed for a living room could easily have been mistaken for a garage—a short-block V-6 engine served as an end table by the couch. Fishing gear in various states of repair hung on the walls next to a grouping of outdated calendars from a Rockport Mexican food restaurant. One of the calendars featured Pancho Villa on a white stallion (and not a motorcycle, Charlie observed). Marine charts, a tattered collection of John D. MacDonald paperbacks, and a well-thumbed copy of Heidegger's *Being and Time* comprised the Sweetwater library.

With coffee perking on the stovetop, Charlie wandered to the bathroom and stared at his unshaven face in the mirror. He stepped cautiously into the shower, and tried to remember if he'd attended other fancy garden parties where one of the guests was shot dead by a sniper. *Nope*, he thought. *Last night was the first one.*

He dressed in a hurry and drove to Fulton Harbor, where he was relieved to find the *Ramrod* resting placidly in its boat slip. Bright red stripes outlined the cabin and the gunwales; the windows were framed in a jaunty blue. The hull and deck had recently been white-washed with a fresh coat of paint and were blinding in the morning sun. Moored in the harbor among the drab Vietnamese bay boats, the *Ramrod* stood out like a parrotfish in an aquarium of mudcats.

Raul was already on the boat coiling a stern line.

"*Buenos días*, Raul. Is my brother up, yet?"

"*Hola*, Charlie," he replied with a toothy smile. His head still hadn't grown to fit his two front teeth. "No, he was not here when I come. Maybe he is eating at the marina."

Charlie started to step onto the boat and then he paused. "*Con permiso?*" he asked. If the kid had been working as Johnny's first mate, then he'd earned the courtesy.

"*Pase*," Raul answered shyly.

Most of the boats that lined the docks were bay shrimpers with high bows, low decks and flat-bottom hulls, good for maneuvering in the shallow depths of the coastal waters. But the *Ramrod* was longer than most of the bay boats, fifty-eight feet in length with a shallow draft cypress V-hull designed to operate in both the bays and the open gulf water.

When Charlie stepped onto the stern deck he looked around and whistled. "I'm impressed. I don't think I've ever seen the *Ramrod* looking so spiffy. You want to give me a tour?"

"*Hokay*, Charlie," he said brightly. "The bank give Johnny the money to make the boat like this, but he say we make the money back in the *golfo*, no problem. I think we do it too," he said over his shoulder.

In the galley Charlie noticed a half-eaten loaf of Buttercrust bread and some dirty dishes in the sink. Rumpled sheets covered two of the bunks and a slicker and a pair of paint-splattered pants lay on the third. His father's favorite gimme cap hung on a peg by the door, and next to it hung Johnny's battered straw cowboy hat, bringing to Charlie's mind the many trips out to blue water he had made with the two of them when he was younger. In the retouched landscape of his remembrance, the Sweetwater family at sea was as contented as a pod of porpoises. But following immediately upon these happy thoughts was another: *If Johnny tries to talk me into working this boat with him again, the answer is still no.*

Charlie and Raul emerged on deck and saw a uniformed Coast Guard officer standing on the dock behind the boat, waiting, it seemed, for them. Charlie approached the officer uncertainly. Raul slipped quietly back into the cabin, instinctively cautious around anyone wearing a uniform.

"Good day, Mr....?"

"Sweetwater. Charlie Sweetwater."

"You are related to Johnny Sweetwater, the captain of the *Ramrod*?"

Charlie felt a knot of fear forming in his stomach. "Yes, I am. He's my brother. What's this about?"

"Can you confirm that he took this vessel out to the Gulf some-time earlier this week?"

"He went out earlier this week, why?"

"Was he alone on the boat?"

"Yeah, he was alone. What the hell's going on?"

"Mr. Sweetwater, we discovered the Ramrod adrift yesterday afternoon, about sixty miles offshore to the southeast. We towed her here about an hour ago."

"Where is Johnny?" Charlie asked.

"He was not onboard when we boarded the vessel." The officer cleared his throat. "We presume that he went overboard."

"Overboard? I don't understand. Why...why do you presume that?"

"Well, sir, the vessel was not anchored when we found her. The outriggers were extended and although the nets were pulled in, there were fresh shrimp iced down in the hold. We think he might have fallen into the water accidentally."

Charlie's head was spinning as he tried to process this informa-tion. Falling overboard was a common job hazard in the shrimping business, where long, delirious hours, rough seas, slick decks and low gunwales led to many fatal accidents. But Johnny was so careful when he was at sea, he said to himself.

"Or it could be," the officer continued, "that he took a swim and the currents prevented him from getting back to the boat."

"A swim?" Charlie asked. "Why..."

"The ladder was out. It was hanging over the stern."

"No. Johnny was a strong swimmer. He could always get back to the boat, no matter how strong the current."

"The fact of the matter is, Mr. Sweetwater, that your brother is missing at sea. We don't know what happened to him or how he got separated from his boat, but we have one cutter, a helicopter and two spotter planes searching the grid where we think he might have gone in. We've been looking since we found the shrimp boat yesterday after-noon...about 2:00 p.m. Another fisherman recognized the vessel and called it in. We've issued a man overboard message on the emergency radio channel and we're monitoring the standard marine frequencies in hopes that another boat might help us find and rescue your brother."

"Maybe Johnny's on another boat. Maybe he ran out of fuel, or..."

"The diesels are operational, Mr. Sweetwater," said the Coast Guard officer. "Although we towed her in to port, we checked out both the engines and the fuel."

Charlie stood dumbfounded on the pier. The officer waited in silence, rotating his cap in his hand. Finally he said, "I'm sorry we didn't find you earlier, but we didn't know who, exactly, to contact. I've made a note of your relation to the...to your brother, so you'll have no problem getting updates from our dispatchers in Port Aransas."

Before he left, the Coast Guard officer handed Charlie a card with some telephone numbers and assured him that they would contact him immediately if there was any news. The officer drove away and Charlie stood on the dock, dazed. Raul came to the stern and looked up anxiously. He had been trying to listen from the cabin but was unsure what was happening.

"Where is Johnny?" he asked.

Charlie shook his head. "We don't know, *chavo*. They think he fell off the boat."

"Where, Charlie? *Donde*?"

Charlie waved his arm in the general direction of the Gulf. "Out there."

CHAPTER 06

Texas Ranger O.B. Hadnott cruised across the Copano Bay Bridge in the still coastal dawn. Because O.B. thought the prowl car radio distorted the focus necessary for clarity of mind and purpose, he drove in silence. He wondered why anyone would single out Pinky Cudihay, or any other particular Texas senator, for target practice, given that they all needed killin'. O.B. would prefer that Cudihay perish trapped in a burning whorehouse, fall overboard into shark-infested waters, or linger slowly at the end of a gangrenous limb.

The taciturn Ranger had a history with the oily, duplicitous Senator.

He had seen Cudihay's florid face in the news almost non-stop for the last twenty-four hours, promoting his sensational (and unfounded) theory that the assassin's bullet was likely meant for him, and not his "loyal, trustworthy aide—a dear friend...."

Still, O.B. needed no personal incentive to aggressively pursue his task. In O.B.'s mind, the bad guys had crossed a clearly marked line. Whoever the shooters were, their conduct posed a genuine threat to the State of Texas in that the sons of bitches had missed. These particular badmen, like most criminals, had a good idea but poor follow-through. O.B. had no use for a poor shot.

For over a century and a half the Texas Rangers had more-or-less honorably carried out the duties first assigned them by

Stephen F. Austin, acting "as rangers for the common defense...."

For the most part the Rangers, as agents answerable only to the Governor, had kept the faith, protected the borders, killed marauding Comanches and Kiowas, extinguished generations of Mexican *bandidos* and cattle thieves, put down small insurrections ("One riot, one Ranger") and generally prevailed over the bad guys in the course of ensuring the public safety.

Stephen F. Austin had never said anything about breaking strikes and busting unions, kicking in United Farmworkers organizers' ribs or killing Mexicans and South Texas Tejanos in wholesale lots back in the bad old days. All of which was also in the Rangers' historical portfolio. But nobody's perfect, O.B. figured.

For the life of him, Ranger Hadnott could not imagine a scenario in which an attempt on Pinky Cudihay's life threatened the public safety. Public sanitation, maybe. One thing, however, was for goddamn sure: That sniper, whoever he was, had conferred upon Hadnott the right to ask a lot of fucking questions.

And there were a lot of questionable plans afoot in the coastal jurisdiction of Ranger Company A. Department of Public Safety and US Coast Guard intelligence reports indicated a good deal of disquieting activity in the Coastal Bend area.

One gulf trawler had been reported missing for close to a year, while closer to home two smaller boats had disappeared almost within sight of the Matagorda Lighthouse, in fair weather and in relatively safe waters. So far no debris, bodies or clues had turned up. The owners of the smaller vessels were known to have engaged in small-time smuggling and other illegal activities. Anyone with half a brain suspected foul play.

More recently, a local fisherman had been reported missing at sea, and the local authorities were not hopeful he would be found...the damned fool. A West Texan down to the tips of his Lucchese boots, O.B. regarded any body of water larger than a stock tank with fear and disdain.

Within the last year, the Rangers had received reports from the Feds of significant purchases of black-market military armaments. Significant, said the reports, because the items were not the usual odd case of rifles or grenades, but were more sophisticated in nature—optical attachments for laser-sighted grenade launchers, high-powered infrared illuminators for long-range target sighting, and rocket-propelled grenades.

The recent shooting of the Senator's aide on Key Allegro and the Senator's subsequent braying on local television about "a heinous attempt" on *his* life was the last straw. The governor picked up the phone.

With no small amount of consternation Sergeant Hadnott received his temporary assignment to assist in the high-profile murder case down on the Texas Gulf Coast. His Field Captain in Lubbock told O.B. that he must possess skills especially suited to the case because Governor Bill Clements himself had requested Hadnott for the assignment. Then he admitted that the Sergeant's name had been submitted to the Governor by Ranger headquarters in Austin, primarily because the local Ranger was wrapped up in a bribery case on the border, and because Sergeant Hadnott's area in West Texas had such a light case load at present.

"So I'm being exiled to the swamps because I'm doing such a good job in my own jurisdiction?" O.B. Hadnott asked his Field Captain.

"Think of it as a vacation. I hear the Gulf Coast is real nice this time of year," the Captain had replied. "They say the redfish will practically fight to get on your hook."

"They also say a hurricane could be heading for the Gulf Coast, sir."

"Well, think of it as a change of pace then. How bad could a hurricane be, anyway? It's not like it's a tornado."

So Ranger O.B. Hadnott had been assigned to the case, if it could be called a case at all. "Figuring this sonofabitch out," Hadnott acknowledged, "is harder than nine kinds of Chinese arithmetic."

▬▬▬▬

CHAPTER 07

Later that morning Charlie and Raul motored the *Ramrod* across the harbor to the processing plant and offloaded the shrimp that was still iced down in the hold. Afterwards, the two of them tried to busy themselves on the boat while they waited for news about Johnny. Raul mended holes in the nets and Charlie cleaned up the cabin.

In the afternoon he checked in with the Coast Guard. There was no news so Charlie decided to walk around Fulton Harbor and visit with some of the skippers. Maybe Johnny had talked to some of them before leaving on his trip.

Charlie was surprised at the changes the harbor had undergone in his absence. Johnny had reported that Vietnamese immigrants started moving into the area about four years ago. Most were resettled refugees from the war and he said they'd taken to shrimping and crabbing like, well, like fish to water. But Charlie did not expect to find that the majority of the vessels in the harbor now belonged to the Vietnamese.

Since the bay—though not the Gulf—was closed for shrimping at present, almost every bay trawler was in port. Curious Vietnamese watched Charlie as he wandered among the slips searching for a familiar boat or face. Later he ran into Filly Martino, the captain of the *Sundown*. Martino explained that most of the boats had either been sold to the Vietnamese or, in the case of the remaining old-time captains, had moved to nearby harbors. He said he was thinking about selling too. The outriggers of Filly's rust-stained trawler were raised high, parallel to the mast, as if they were surrendering along with the captain. "Hope your brother shows up soon," he said in parting.

Jack Waggoner, who owned a couple of aging crabbing boats, was even gloomier. "Can't make a living crabbin' anymore," he said, adding that he was planning to retire as soon as the winter season ended. "No money in it. Too dangerous."

If the old-timers were taciturn about the pall that had settled over the Fulton docks, the Vietnamese fishermen that Charlie tried to chat up were almost mute. Not one of them wanted to talk to Charlie. "I'm starting to take this kind of personal," he told Raul.

The day ended with the sun exploding onto the horizon like an incendiary bomb, but Charlie and Raul didn't notice. The two of them spent an uneasy night tossing and turning in their bunks, thinking about Johnny and trying to avoid the most obvious conclusion.

43 | **07**

—

Charlie awoke the next day to the sound of conflict. He sat up in the top bunk of the *Ramrod*, untangled himself from the damp, rumpled sheet and then rolled over to his stomach to look out the open port-hole. Two slips down the pier, a group of Vietnamese were standing on the back deck of one of the bay shrimpers yelling at each other.

"Nice neighborhood, Johnny," Charlie mumbled. He rubbed his eyes and squinted at a sun that was already high in the sky. He'd finally fallen asleep just before sunup and had slept halfway through the morning.

Charlie hopped down off the bunk, slipped into his jeans and wandered outside. Raul had pulled down some of the trawling nets and had them strung out across the boat deck and onto part of the wharf. He was sitting on the pier mending some holes in a section of the heavy webbed netting.

"*Buenos días*, Raul."

Raul raised his chin in response. The angry Asian voices registered as a sort of dull background noise.

"Is there any coffee on this boat?"

"Johnny keep some in the kitchen under the, *oy*...." Raul scrunched his face in concentration, "the *gabinet*."

Charlie nodded. "Thanks."

The neighbors were still yelling at each other and Charlie observed them through the galley window as he filled a rusty pot with water and dumped in some ground coffee. Five people were involved and one of them, a thin, small-framed guy in a suit and wearing wire-rimmed gasses, jabbed his finger at a man wearing the same scruffy clothes as the other Vietnamese fishermen. Two stocky Asians with humorless expressions stood over the shrimper. The fisherman's wife cowered behind her husband.

Charlie placed the coffee pot on the stove and watched the two big guys shove the little shrimper guy down to the deck. The woman started crying and the two big guys laughed and climbed off the boat, followed by the skinny one with the glasses and nice clothes.

Charlie was lighting the burner when he heard Ringworm growl and then emit a sharp yelp. A moment later he heard Raul shouting frantically in Spanish, telling some "*pinche guey*" to let him go. Charlie flew out the door and saw that one of the big Asian guys had picked up Raul and was holding him over the water. Ringworm was limping but looked ready to lunge at the man.

"Hey, Hong Kong!" Charlie yelled, hurdling over the boat transom and onto the dock in one explosive leap. "What the *hell* is your problem?" He noticed the guy had kicked some of the netting into the oily water below the wharf. "You drop that kid in the bay and I swear to Christ you're going in, too...but *you* won't be coming back up." Charlie came by his hot temper honestly; his Uncle Flavius had been a brawler of legendary proportions.

The big guy dropped Raul on the pier, and then sized up Charlie as he moved toward him. Charlie could handle himself pretty well in a fight. He was lean and hard-muscled from years of reef diving, but this guy outweighed him by at least thirty pounds. Plus there was another man on the big guy's flank. Charlie looked around and picked up one of the netting tools Raul had been using, a pointed metal marlin stave, and held it calmly at his side. The thugs maneuvered around for an attack but the slight, bespectacled man yelled sharply at the men in their own tongue and they both stopped.

"I apologize for the behavior of my employees," he said. "Ho-Dac lost his temper when he tripped over the nets that are covering the pier. I assure you he would not have harmed the boy."

"Didn't look that way to me," said Charlie. Adrenaline still coursed through his body. *Who the fuck is this guy?* he wondered.

"I am Mr. Bao," the man said. "Nguyen Ngoc Bao. I manage the Sea-Tex seafood operation where you sold your shrimp yesterday, and I also manage many of the boats in this harbor."

He was wearing a white linen suit, the sort of suit made popular by South American dictators. Gold eyeglasses decorated his thin, weathered face. His oily black hair was thinning and his teeth were slightly discolored. He speech and bearing reminded Charlie somehow of the *ancien regime*.

Mr. Bao continued. "I have not seen you around these docks before. You are staying on the *Ramrod*?"

"I'm not sure it's any of your business." Charlie motioned for Raul to get back on the boat. Ringworm watched the men warily from the perimeter.

"Of course, I apologize, Mr.....it is Sweetwater, I presume?"

Charlie nodded suspiciously.

"I suspected so," Bao said. "You bear a striking resemblance to your brother." His overly-formal English almost constituted an insult in itself. Charlie disliked the little bastard on sight.

"How do you know my brother?" Charlie wanted to know.

"We have had business dealings together," he replied. "I have represented the Sea-Tex Corporation in the purchase of several of your brother's fishing boats." Charlie noticed that Raul was glaring hard at Bao.

"*Es verdad, chavo? Johnny ha tenido negocios con este cabrón?*" Charlie asked Raul, trying to confirm if what the Vietnamese man said was true.

"*Si Capitán, pero este hombre es muy mal, y le cay muy mal a su hermano.*" (Yes, but this is a very bad man, and your brother can't stand him).

"Mr. Sweetwater, regardless of what the boy may be saying about my relationship with your brother, you should know that he received a fair price for the boats and that he was not coerced into selling them to my corporation. I encourage you to verify this with the Rockport Bank, which assisted in the transactions."

"I'll think I'll just ask my brother," Charlie answered.

"Yes," said Bao. "Of course you can do that, too."

"In the meantime, if one of your *employees* lays a hand on this boy again, I'll string him up that flag pole." He gestured toward the Stars and Stripes that were snapping in the breeze at the harbor entrance. Charlie had no tolerance for bullies, and he was certain that Bao was the biggest swinging-dick bully on the docks.

Bao took a breath and seemed to gather himself. He clearly wasn't used to confrontation from anyone in the harbor.

"Good day, Mr. Sweetwater, I'll leave you to your...manual labor." He glanced over at Raul. "And may I remind you that this is a public dock, which you have completely blocked with your nets, and that there is a harbor regulation prohibiting the obstruction of the pier."

He looked at Charlie. "But because you are new here, and *don't understand* how things work, I will request that the Dock Master overlook this harbor violation"—he pointed to the mess of nets hanging off the dock—"and that he not issue you a citation." The emphasis Bao put on *don't understand* sent a little thrill of fear up Charlie's back. The man seemed to radiate menace.

Bao's guys kept glancing over at their boss, hoping he'd give them permission to pound the cocky Anglo into the mud like a dock piling. Charlie knew he should probably shut up now, but of course he couldn't.

"That's mighty white of you, Bao. Although it's funny to hear you call it a public dock, considering you act like you own it."

Bao forced a tight-lipped smile. "I will say good day to you now Mr. Sweetwater...before you say something you might regret."

Charlie couldn't resist a parting shot.

"Maybe my brother had business dealings with you, but you can forget about any of that with me. I hope you *understand*."

Bao paused but didn't turn around. Charlie watched him get into his car and drive away.

———

CHAPTER 08

The Coast Guard called off the search for Johnny Sweetwater after three days. Both Charlie and Rupert pleaded with the coordinator to extend the search and rescue mission, but to no avail. Due to the low statistical odds of survival, the case was downgraded from "active" to "suspended," pending further developments.

The authorities didn't say it, but the further development they anticipated was Johnny's body washing up on shore before sharks devoured it, or before it decomposed and sank to the bottom of the sea. The last thing Charlie wanted to do was sit on the boat and wait for a body to be found. But pretty soon people began stopping by the *Ramrod* to tell Charlie how sorry they were about what had happened.

Since the issue remained unresolved, the conversations were awkward and constrained. "Keep hoping for the best," said some. A few talked as if he was gone for good and they talked about how they "...sure 'nuff broke the mold after they made Johnny Sweetwater," and how Fulton would be a lot more boring without him, and how he was "old school one-of-a-kind, just like his dad."

Pastor Kelly came by and told him he would pray for both Charlie and Johnny, though he had given up on saving both their souls a long time ago. The irreverent heathen bastards had once smuggled an incontinent horse into his vestry. If Johnny had indeed drowned at sea, he would be glad to transfer the responsibility for his dubious salvation over to Jesus and the Heavenly Host.

After the Pastor left, Charlie spied a woman on the shore. She was sitting on top of a picnic table near the breakwater, watching him. Even from a distance he could see that this raven-haired girl was beautiful. She was dressed in a white, ankle-length dress that waved and billowed with the breeze. *Is she the one he wanted me to meet?* he wondered.

He started to walk over to her but he was intercepted by Rupert and Vita who were halfway down the pier, anxious to talk to him. After they hugged and conferred for a few minutes he looked up and the girl was gone.

The trio of Sweetwaters gamely spent the rest of the day on or around the boat, greeting the people that dropped by, taking turns checking with the Coast Guard to see if there were any updates. The family still had a lot of friends in the area and scores of people dropped by, although nobody quite knew what to say or what do with themselves after they arrived. Including Rupert and Charlie.

"Well hell, son," Rupert said, finally voicing their frustration, "I feel like a damned fool just standing around. You think we ought to take the boat out and look for him?"

Charlie had considered that option a hundred times already, but there was no telling how far the Ramrod had drifted before the Coast Guard found it, or when exactly he...when he what? Fell overboard? Jumped overboard? Was kidnapped by pirates? Was abducted by aliens? The search and rescue coordinator said their search grid encompassed over five thousand square miles of open water. If his body never turned up, they said, Johnny wouldn't be officially declared dead for seven years. The death certificate would read "death by misadventure."

"No, uncle. As much as I'd like to be doing something, at least people know they can reach me here if they find out anything about Johnny."

"What about tonight?" asked Vita. "You know you're welcome to stay over on the island."

"Thanks, but I guess I'll stay here," said Charlie. "I'd guess Raul wants to stay around here too." All day Raul had been sitting on a bench at the end of the pier, gazing at the water, Johnny's yellow dog sitting on his haunches beside him. "By the way, how long has that boy been working with Johnny?"

"Raul and Johnny were very close," Vita explained. "The kid snuck over the border and showed up here early last spring. Johnny was really trying to help him out. He even enrolled him in school last month, not that Raul liked it much."

"Yeah, he told me that was why he wasn't out in the Gulf with Johnny this last time out. Where does he live?"

"Until school started he lived on the boat," said Rupert. "Johnny said he was a hell of a hand."

"But when school started last month," Vita continued, "he started staying with the family of a friend he met at school—a real nice Vietnamese family."

"Hey, speaking of that, do y'all know a Vietnamese dude named Bao?"

"You met Bao?" asked Rupert.

"Yeah, yesterday morning. What's the deal with that guy? He acts like he's some kind of *cacique* or something around the docks. Walks around with a pair of goons and pushes around the Viet fishermen. One of the chunky bastards tried to throw Raul in the bay. It almost got ugly."

Rupert let out a deep breath. "Yeah, I've heard talk about him. He tries to put on the humble immigrant fisherman act, but I think he's got more going on than he lets on. I've heard a couple of his men refer to him as 'Colonel,' though I don't know what that's about. He seems to have a lot of juice with the mayor and the sheriff too. Johnny mentioned him a few times but he never seemed to want to talk about it much. He just said that he didn't like Bao and Bao didn't like him."

"I can see why," said Charlie. "The guy mentioned he'd bought some of Johnny's boats. Is that true?"

Rupert shook his head and grimaced. "The last few years were kind of tough for Johnny, businesswise," said Rupert. "I think your brother had the worst string of bad luck I've ever seen." Vita nodded in agreement.

"What kind of bad luck?"

"Well, let's see. There was that engine room fire that ruined the diesels and damaged the hull on the Ginny Jill over at the Conn Brown Harbor in Aransas Pass. Johnny couldn't afford the repairs so he had to sell her, to Bao. Or to a proxy for Bao, but it's the same thing."

"And the bank took the *Vale Madre* after he fell behind on the payments and they called the note," added Vita.

"Plus a whole bunch of other stuff," said Rupert. "A broken mast, equipment stolen off the boat, holes in the nets."

"So all that's left of the fleet is the *Ramrod*?" asked Charlie, incredulously.

"That's it. Seems like God or somebody just wanted to pound that boy flat."

Charlie shook his head suspiciously. "I don't know, Uncle." He looked up when he felt his uncle's piercing blue eyes on him.

"None of it never made no sense to me either, all that bad luck. And now this...I'm just getting a bad feeling about this, that's all."

"Spell it out, Rupert" said Charlie. He'd had a bad feeling growing in his gut as well—one that he didn't want to think about, much less talk about...not yet. "You think what happened to Johnny wasn't an accident?"

Rupert looked away and rubbed his earlobe. And then he forced a smile and said, "Let's give this some more time. You and I both know how Johnny likes an adventure. He probably woke up from a nap and found a boatload of Playboy Playmates fishing around the *Ramrod* and decided to swim over to join 'em for awhile. Hell, wouldn't you?"

Charlie forced a laugh.

For dinner they all nibbled on the food that friends and relatives had brought by during the day. The mess table was overflowing with platters of fried chicken, assorted casseroles and other covered dishes. The first thing people in Texas did when they heard about a family catastrophe was to start frying chicken. Charlie didn't have room in the small icebox on the boat so he helped Vita and Rupert load up their station wagon.

"You sure you and Raul won't come back with us?"

"I appreciate the offer, Vita, but we're fine here."

Rupert put a big hand on Charlie's shoulder, "We'll see you tomorrow, son."

After everyone cleared out, the harbor fell quiet again. Raul lay down in his bunk and went straight to sleep. Charlie sat in the captain's chair smoking cigarettes and wondering why he felt so goddamned guilty.

Johnny had made his choice to stay in Fulton and become a shrimp boat captain, and Charlie had made his choice too. In fact he couldn't wait to put the town in his rear view mirror once their dad's funeral was over. Johnny wanted him to stay and partner up in Dubber's fishing business. "Together, brother man," he said. "We'll take turns being Commodore. It'll be fun."

"Naw," said Charlie. "There's a flock of wild geese I've got to chase." So in the end, Johnny stayed and Charlie vamoosed. *Well, good for you Johnny*, thought Charlie bitterly. *Look where it got you.*

Charlie finally succumbed to his restlessness and quietly hopped off the boat, leaving a note for Raul on the table: "Couldn't sleep. Back before morning," he wrote.

CHAPTER 09

Charlie's old truck rumbled down the bumpy two-lane asphalt of Highway 35, past a couple of shipyards and a hulking carbon black plant that looked like some sinister Industrial Revolution throwback. He needed to get away from the boat and the harbor for awhile, needed a break from the black thoughts buzzing around in his head. For a moment he entertained an idea to just light out, keep driving till he dropped, get back to Mexico and his placid beach bum life. But maybe Johnny would show up in the next few days. *One way or another,* he thought morbidly.

He looked out the window at the dark bay, wondering if this was Johnny's idea of a joke. It was easy enough to imagine...just another one of Johnny's crazy pranks. He'd sneak in from the sea and show up at his own wake disguised as a beggar or an old man, like Odysseus, just to twist everybody's noggin a little bit. The thought buoyed him a little as he rolled through Aransas Pass, en route to the ferry that would take him over to Mustang Island and Port A proper.

During the short ten-minute ride across the ship channel, Charlie got out of his truck to watch the dolphins play in the ferry wake. He breathed deeply the familiar humid air and felt the salt spray wash over his face.

What there was of Port Aransas wasn't much. Never had been. Originally called Tarpon, after the indigenous trophy fish found offshore, the small town was best known as a Spring Break destination and a haven for sport fishermen and beach walkers. The place began as an expatriate Englishman's cattle and sheep station in the 1850s and its civic ambitions had never progressed much beyond that. As a connoisseur of offbeat, off-the-track locales, Charlie was a fan.

There were a few dockside seaman's bars, an antique two-story hotel called the Tarpon Inn, where the lobby was wallpapered with bright silvery tarpon scales, and a few restaurants specializing in the catch of the day—baked, broiled or fried.

One honky-tonk next to the harbor particularly beckoned: a tin-roofed building on pilings with swing-up hurricane shutters and a big deck. In a red-neon scrawl over the door read a sign: "Gatorhythms." Appropriately, a huge, hulking Day-Glo green alligator perched on the roof.

A relic from a long-since dismantled Mardi Gras float that had somehow found its way to tiny Port A, the jaw-gaping creation had ascended to the roof, seemingly on the wings of angels. Some of the bartenders at the club bragged about the humid young ladies they enticed into the interior of the creature for sexual capers. *It wasn't everyone*, thought Charlie, *who could say they'd fucked a Spring Break coed inside a giant fiberglass alligator.*

Charlie could hear a blues guitar wailing from inside and as he pulled into the potholed parking lot he was pleasantly surprised to see a familiar name on the marquee.

L.C. Hebert hailed from East Texas near the Louisiana border (the Cajuns out there, of whom there were many, pronounced the surname "Ay-bear") but he'd lately been making a name for himself in Austin, home to the most thriving music scene in the state.

Charlie had first seen him when the guitarist was on tour, playing in Corpus Christi. Johnny had dragged him to a small downtown club there and Charlie became an instant fan. Johnny took to sending his brother cassette tapes of Hebert's albums, and the fishermen, beach bums and scuba divers who made up Charlie's Mexico clientele soon became fans as well.

L.C. Hebert had busied himself for the past couple of years racking up critics' awards and some not-inconsiderable record sales by reclaiming the R&B charts from the disco swill that had hijacked the radio airwaves and the record store racks a few years before. He came to Austin from the inner-city wards of Houston, and he played what he knew: greasy, belly-rubbing rhythm and blues played to a shuffle beat, sauced with horns and spiked with bleeding, icepick-sharp guitar licks. T-Bone Walker, Bobby Blue Bland, O.V. Wright, Slim Harpo and Albert Collins were the faces on L.C.'s personal Mt. Rushmore.

And that was just what Charlie was in the mood for—thirty-six hours with little or no sleep notwithstanding. He'd once read a newspaper story about L.C. and the interviewer asked him to define the blues. "The blues is what gets you through," the guitarist replied simply, and that was what Charlie craved on this night—a soundtrack for some spiritual healing.

Charlie parked, paid his cover and slipped inside. He beelined for the bar and ordered a Dos Equis and a shot of tequila. His innate Sweetwater timing was impeccable—Hebert was just winding up his first set and he and the band had a half-hour break.

Charlie took his Mexican boilermaker outside and sat at a battered metal table by the dockside railing, troubled by thoughts of death and dark-haired women. Who was she anyway, that looker at the harbor today? And what was she to Johnny?

He lit a cigarette and pocketed his lighter, a Zippo embossed with the seal of the American embassy in Djakarta—a touchstone to another strange time and place. It was a gift from a Sri Lankan jewel smuggler he had met on an excursion to Cuernavaca. She was six feet tall, with a profile that would have stopped traffic in Paris or Milan, and she spoke with a languid sunset-of-the-Empire accent. Fluent in six languages, she had jet-black hair that reached to her waist, and smuggled star sapphires, rubies and emeralds past bedazzled customs officials on three continents. Or so she said. Their torrid and reckless affair ended when she absconded with his money and his passport, bound for an unknown destination (unknown, at least to Charlie and the Interpol officials who visited him shortly thereafter). Even so, he reflected, he'd probably do it all over again.

Charlie ruefully noticed the direction his thoughts had turned. He knew that one day he'd have to cut his dick off....

"CHARLIE SWEETWATER!" A dark, bestial hand, hairy down to the second knuckle, clapped down forcefully on his shoulder while another ham-sized fist seized his chair and pivoted him around to stare into the reeking face of *a monster!* Charlie jumped like a live shrimp.

"A close poi-sonal friend a mine!" the apparition rumbled. "Fancy runnin' into you here."

Smoke from a cheap cigar spiraled up around the man's champing jaws. An evil goatee grabbed for greasy sideburns. A black widow's peak stabbed between twisting, massive brows. There was a miasma of whiskey, Roi-Tan cigars, ice-blue Aqua Velva ("There's something about an Aqua Velva man..."), and the back alley spice of old perspiration hiding in the creases of his velveteen tracksuit.

Neon Leon Guidry poked Charlie in the breastbone with a fingertip that felt like the blunt end of a pool cue.

"Da last time I saw ya, you and yo' crazy brother was blowing up my crap game in Victoria. That old boy you was ribbin' was about to open you up with a straight razor. You wanna relocate to a hole in the ground, I got an uncle who's an undertaker over in Beaumont who can accommodate you, me."

"I was ribbing him, maybe," Charlie replied after his initial shock. "But Johnny was about to punch his lights out. He thought that 'old boy' was throwin' loaded dice, and he was right. It's a good thing you broke it up when you did. Johnny has what you could call a poorly developed sense of self-preservation."

The joke suddenly cut too close to home. Charlie saw something shift in Guidry's eyes. He'd heard the news, obviously. Charlie sought to change the subject.

"Damn, Leon, are you fogging for mosquitoes?" he asked, waving his hand in front of his face to ward off the toxic cloud of cigar smoke. "That thing smells like you set fire to your jock." Leon blew smoke in his face and laughed.

Hanging around L.C. Hebert meant rubbing up against his manager/booking agent/confidant and all-around cutthroat asshole, Henry Roosevelt Leonard Guidry III—"Neon Leon" to everyone up to and including his mama and his parish priest.

Leon Guidry was a foul-mouthed, unctuous, grasping, vengeful man, with two years in Huntsville Penitentiary on his resume and diamonds on his fingers. A lot of people thought Leon was as crazy as a rat in a coffee can.

Approximately the color of a light brown Italian loafer, Leon was (probably) part black, part Indian, part Cajun, part French, and part pirate. He himself didn't know, exactly, and no one else had the nerve to ask. Johnny used to say he didn't care what sort of Heinz 57 genetic cocktail Leon had crawled out of, he just hoped the villagers had hung the mad scientists and burned the lab after he escaped.

Guidry hooked a chair and sat down. He flipped his cigar butt over the rail into the bay. The merriment went out of his eyes.

"I'm sorry about yo' bruddah, man," he said solemnly. "Johnny is good people. A stand-up guy." Break time was over and the band was plugging in and tuning up. Leon stood up and headed back inside. "When he shows up you call me," Leon offered hopefully. "I'll get both of ya in on a high-stakes poker game I got going wid some highrollers from Corpus...first class chumps, every one of 'em. Be like shootin' fish in a barrel. 'Till then, you watch yourself."

As the band warmed up with Freddy King's "Hideaway," Charlie made his way back to the bar and ordered another round. He was out of smokes and he needed to think, so he got some change and went out to the cigarette machine in the alcove by the front door.

He was pulling the lever for a deck of Luckies when a voice came over his shoulder.

"You have a funny way of coping with loss."

Somehow he knew who it was before he turned around.

"I might say the same about you."

The slender dark-haired woman had changed from her angelic maxi-skirt and was in jeans and black boots. As she spoke, her shawl fell from her shoulder. She wore a silky, loose fitting blouse that revealed a slender neck and smooth bare shoulders. A delicate silver cross hung from a thin chain around her neck, almost disappearing into the vee made by her breasts.

She was quite tall for what Charlie guessed to be her Hispanic heritage, and her skin was light olive, appearing even lighter set against her dark eyes and sable hair.

"My name is Marisol Cavazos," she said, holding out a fine-boned hand. "I know your brother Johnny."

Charlie tried to think if he had ever seen her before. She had angular features, full lips, and watchful, almond-shaped eyes—he concluded that he had not. This girl, he would remember. *Delores del Rio*, he thought, *or the Aztec pin-up girl on the Mexican wall calendars at*

Johnny's place on Rattlesnake Point.

Charlie reluctantly released her hand. "Pleasure," he said.

She grabbed his elbow with surprising assertion. "Let's go outside. I need to talk to you about Johnny. And even though I love the music, it's hard to talk in here."

"The music, that's why you're here?"

"Why not? When misfortune touches you, the best response is to grab a handful of life. That's what the blues say, *verdad*?"

Charlie started to go back and grab a handful of cold beer but she wouldn't let loose of his sleeve.

"Come on, Sweetwater," she said, heading for the door. "The next round's on me."

They bought a six-pack of beer at the corner U-Tote-M and walked down to the boat basin. At length, they chose a finger pier and sat on the edge, dangling their feet over the dark water. Tugs and bulk carriers slipped silently up and down the ship channel on the other side of the stone jetty.

Charlie popped a top and took a long swig. "Okay, *señorita*, now that you've lured me away with your wiles...."

Marisol pulled a ring pull-tab off her own can of beer, held it up and sighted the moon through it. "There's a ring around the moon tonight. They say that means a big storm is coming."

Charlie looked up. "Yeah, I heard a hurricane is brewing out in the Gulf somewhere....So, we came out here to talk about the weather?"

She took a drink and patted her mouth lightly with the back of her wrist. "How close were you and Johnny?" she asked.

"Close, but we'd been closer. What can I say? You know how it can be between siblings."

"Not really. I'm an only child."

"Oh, well, it's a matter of knowing each other *too* well sometimes. But what do I know?" Charlie turned to Marisol. "Now it's my turn to ask you the same question...how close are *you* to my brother?"

"Close...and we were getting closer. I met him six months ago."

Charlie nodded. *So, she was Johnny's girlfriend.* "Lucky Johnny," he said.

Marisol ignored the remark. "Johnny spoke of you often. I think he missed you."

Charlie sat silently.

"Why did you stay away?" she asked.

Charlie shrugged. "No good reason."

"Johnny once mentioned that you two had a disagreement. What was it …if you don't mind my asking?"

Charlie did mind, a little. But what the hell. Sometimes it was easier to talk to strangers. "I wouldn't call it a disagreement. We just went different directions. He wanted me to help him work the shrimp boats after our dad died—take my turn at the wheel, so to speak, and I told him I wasn't interested."

"Funny how things work out, isn't it? Now they are both gone and it's your turn after all."

"That's a little cold…."

There was a tense silence and the more Charlie thought about what she said, the madder he got. *The hell with her.* He started to stand up and leave but the girl put a hand on his arm.

"Please!" she begged. "I'm sorry. What I said was very inappropriate."

Charlie let himself be guided back down to the pier. "He may not be *gone*, you know."

Marisol agreed. "I know that. I instinctively prepare myself for the worst—a defense mechanism I suppose." She took another sip of beer and Charlie let her go on. "I'd never met anyone like Johnny before," she confessed. "I'd never let anyone get that close to me before. It was just so…unexpected, falling for him like I did. And then…" she trailed off and he saw her eyes tear up in the lights of the harbor.

Charlie sighed. He decided to cut her some slack. She seemed genuinely aggrieved. Why should he be the only one allowed to feel lousy about Johnny? *The more the merrier,* he thought gloomily.

"It seems so…unreal," Charlie began, feeling that one telling deserved another. "I talked with Johnny only a few days ago. I was in southern Mexico…damn, it seems like a month ago."

"He told many stories about the two of you together," she said. "His stories made me want to meet you someday. Of course not like this."

Charlie smiled to himself, thinking of the tales that Johnny could tell. Goddamn they'd had some fun together.

"Are you staying at Johnny's house on Rattlesnake Point?" Marisol asked.

"Right now I'm staying on the boat."

"Johnny stayed on the *Ramrod* a lot these last few months. He said it was because he had work to do, but I think he was afraid that something might happen to the boat if he wasn't there."

"Like what?" asked Charlie.

Marisol looked at him for a moment, unsure. "He told you about Bao, right?"

"Bao? No, he never mentioned him to me, but I ran in to the guy around the docks yesterday. A real prick. What about him?"

She furrowed her brows. "This man had it in for your brother. I think he considered Johnny competition."

"I don't doubt it. Probably just another dispute over fishing territories." Having grown up in the commercial fishing business, Charlie had seen dozens of these dramas play out over the years, as more and more boats competed in smaller and smaller waters for less and less catch. Charlie said he was confident that Johnny could handle a fishing dispute at least as well as their dad could.

"Well, I think it's more than that," she responded, a little indignant.

Charlie waved his hand dismissively. "When Johnny shows up I'll ask him about it. Otherwise, it's not my concern."

Marisol set down her can and stood up. "How is it not your concern?" she demanded.

Charlie stood up, too. "Because it's Johnny's problem and he can handle it. And if he doesn't come back, which you seem to want to believe, then I guess we'll never know what happened....It'll be over. Life goes on. *Que sera, sera.* And all the other bullshit people say."

"How can you say that? It's your brother! And I *don't* want to believe he's dead. Anymore than you do."

They sat down again and sipped their beers. Finally Charlie said, "The Coast Guard called off the search today. We're hoping that somebody, a fisherman or a pleasure boat might see something or...find something."

Marisol closed her eyes tightly. She took a deep breath and spoke. "And if they don't...find anything, what will you do?"

"I'll go back to Mexico, I guess."

"You'll leave?" Marisol seemed shocked.

Charlie opened another beer. "Look, I have a life and a business down there," he snapped. He wasn't sure why he was taking his frustration out on this girl. But he couldn't stop. "It's not much of a life or much of a business, but it's mine, or part mine, anyway. I didn't want to be a shrimper after my father died, and if Johnny is...gone, I sure as hell don't want to be a shrimper now."

"But Johnny would want you..."

"...To see the error of my ways and develop a sudden affection for even longer hours and less money than I'm living on now?"

"No!" she flared, her eyes suddenly furious. Charlie felt a sudden tingle of fear at her abrupt ferocity. "He would want you to help him. Like he would help you if the situation were reversed. I have a friend in Rockport, he knows about this man, Bao. He told me that Bao is very dangerous, and that the word around the dock was that he hated Johnny. I came here to try and learn more, but before I got here he...." Her shoulders sagged.

"He disappeared."

"Yes," she repeated. "But I don't think he just...disappeared."

"Jesus, what is all this midnight mystery bullshit? Why do you have to introduce a boogie man into it? Right now nobody seems to know what happened. Maybe nobody will ever know what happened. And if it turns out he's dead, it'll be a goddamn shame, but I'll get over it."

Marisol jumped up and kicked her can of beer into the bay. "You..." she said fiercely, "...you think only of yourself. So run away to Mexico if you don't care to find out what *really* happened to your brother... what they might have done to him. Johnny was *familia*, but what the fuck, easy come easy go."

"What are you *talking* about?" Charlie said, genuinely mystified.

"I don't know much. But this man on the dock, Bao, the big *jefe*. I think he and Johnny had a fight or something. Last week, ten days ago, maybe. Then Johnny...."

"What kind of fight?"

"I don't know. My friend said he heard about them having a big argument down at the harbor. He said it had been building for awhile."

"Johnny had a sharp tongue and a wicked talent for getting under somebody's skin if he didn't like 'em. But...just because he had a beef with a guy doesn't mean...."

"Don't you want to find out what it was about?"

"What good would that do? It sure as hell wouldn't bring my brother back."

The girl plopped down on the finger pier once more, drained. Her voice was flat. "I...I don't know what to say. God, was I wrong about you," she said under her breath.

Charlie was overcome by confusion, exhaustion and emotion. He'd come to Port A to try and forget about the dread and suspicion in his gut, and now this girl insisted on talking about it. He decided to shut it down for the night. He wasn't thinking straight and he knew it.

"Alright, alright. Jesus. I'll talk to my uncle about this...maybe that friend of yours." But he was thinking *Please, God, don't let this turn into some hairball of paranoid fantasies. Uncle Rupert, this mysterious chica and her anonymous friend. Not exactly a winning hand to bet on.*

"Listen, I'm dead for sleep. I'll get a second wind, ask around. But I think all you crazy bastards have gone coastal. Too much salt air and skunkweed *mota*. Believe me, I know it when I see it." He gazed sadly down at the dark water below him. "Why would anyone ever want to kill Johnny?" he mumbled, more to himself than to her.

Marisol seemed to be calling a truce too. She looked up and nodded her head. Charlie could still hear strains of L.C. Hebert's music floating across the marina.

He reached down and pulled Marisol to her feet. She tossed the remaining beers carelessly into a nearby trashcan. One can caught the rim and popped out of the plastic holder, spewing foam when it fell onto the concrete bulkhead. She turned and walked away dispiritedly. "*Hasta mañana*," she said faintly.

Later, driving back to Fulton, Charlie struggled to clear his mind. Just following the white stripes on the highway was difficult enough. "*Hasta mañana*," he repeated.

———

CHAPTER 10

After the breakfast crowd cleared out, Miguel squinted out the window of the marina cafe and bar and spied a wavering vee of geese heading for the rice fields inland to feed. He plucked a toothpick out of the little toothpick deal by the cash register and stuck it in his mouth. He was starting to like this sleepy little town. A lot more than Houston.

Here, nobody from the Syndicato was hassling him to shake down a local mom and pop store or to smoke a gang rival. He didn't miss the mean streets of Space City, not even a little bit. Being on parole was boring, but not as boring as being locked down in the joint twenty-two hours a day. Much to his surprise, Miguel found himself acquiring a taste for the quiet life. But now a gangster of a different stripe threatened to fuck everything up.

He decided to pick up the phone and call his case officer.

"Hey, *chica*, you know Johnny's got a brother?"

"Yeah, I met him last night," Marisol answered from her room at the Surfside Inn in Rockport. "And I was *not* impressed. He's nothing like Johnny."

Miguel was thinking he was a whole lot like Johnny, but he didn't tell Marisol that. Miguel wasn't a big phone talker.

"Well, now that he's here, maybe he'll help us find out what happened to your *novio*."

"Not *us* Miguel. Never *us*." It was Marisol's professional duty, and her personal desire to keep her friend from doing anything to violate his parole. "Your only job is to stay behind that counter and keep out of trouble. And you can forget about Johnny's brother. He won't be any help on this. He's..." she searched for the right words, "...not interested."

"You sure you don't want somebody with some *huevos* to be, ah, interested?"

"Miguel," Marisol replied quickly. "You stay out of this!"

"Okay, okay...I wasn't sayin'...I was just sayin'."

"I mean it, Miguel."

Miguel Negron had not grown up misunderstood or with poor self-esteem. He didn't have "issues." He was a bad man who had done bad things.

He could live with that. Sometimes he did them for money, sometimes to serve a raw, unarticulated sense of frontier justice. That same rudimentary sense of fair play occasionally compelled him to do bad things for good reasons. Or even, rarely, good things for the right reasons. It balanced the scales a little he supposed. And sometimes he just liked fucking with people's expectations.

A restless child from far South Texas, he ran away to Houston at fourteen and spent the remainder of his misguided youth as a *pachuco* street fighter, boosting cars and selling weed. Miguel built up a small but useful reputation as a strong-arm guy and petty enforcer around Houston and Galveston. In that capacity, he'd drawn a seven-year manslaughter bit in the penitentiary in Huntsville for killing a dogmeat police informer. (Miguel claimed self-defense.)

Once inside, he made a quick, life-saving decision to roll with the Texas Mafia, the Chicano prison gang with cells in every prison in Texas and most of the Southwest. He kept to himself as much as possible, and tried to take a minimal role in the sadistic hazing of the new "fish" who appeared on the cellblock periodically. A beef with an Aryan Brotherhood redneck ended with the white trash peckerwood being pulled out of the grease trap behind the mess hall. The broken neck he'd incurred seemed redundant. Miguel never spoke about the incident and his habitual silence made him even more imposing to his fellow inmates.

By the time he'd come up for parole, Miguel had determined to work out a new path for himself, and the day he got out in 1979 he took a bus to his probation office in Austin and found himself sitting across a desk from...Marisol Cavasos.

Marisol, on the other hand, *did* have issues. She had grown up on the vast King Ranch of South Texas, the daughter of the unmarried schoolteacher who taught the children of the *Kiñenos*, as the multi-generational families who worked on the great *rancho* were called. She and Miguel had known each other as children. Once a week, after Mass, they were thrown together in Sister Teresa's Sunday school class in Kingsville, the small town that was founded by and designed to serve the ranch.

Marisol never knew her father, an itinerant surveyor who had passed through the ranch one summer many years ago. Only later did she learn about her mother's role as mistress to one of the titled Anglo heirs to the great estate—that is until the *patrón* discovered she was pregnant and ceased his affections altogether. When the close-knit ranch community came to realize that she fell into disfavor with one of the *patróns*, they kept their distance and withheld their companionship.

As a result, the young girl grew up in a quiet, shuttered house with a sad and lonely mother who instilled in her daughter a general suspicion and low opinion of men.

But Emilia Cavasos would make sure life was different for her daughter. When Marisol reached adolescence, her mother insisted that there be no more Spanish spoken in the house. "You're going to be able to make your way in the world," she said. "This country is too hard. I've watered it with tears for years, but it's still as hard as stone."

Emilia told Marisol of the big University in Austin, where, long ago, she had been the first *kiñero* to get a teaching degree. "It's full of smart Anglos," she said. "And some smart Mexicanos, too. The *rancho* is my life, but you deserve the world."

And five years later she left the vast and sheltered ranch and plunged into the pressure-cooker of university studies in Austin, but she never forgot or forgave the undeserved treatment suffered by her mother at the hands of the runaway dad and distant, philandering *patrón*. Despite the emotional baggage, Marisol grew up to be an uncommonly self-possessed young woman.

During school she labored as an unpaid intern for a state agency in the capitol. Simply by luck of the draw, she was assigned to the State Board of Probation and Parole. Her work did not go unnoticed and after earning her social work degree, the state promptly offered her a full time position as a Case Manager in the Corrections Division of the Texas Department of Criminal Justice.

Which was how she found herself, on a steamy summer day, sitting across a battered government-issue desk from Miguel Negron.

Although they had taken radically different paths after they left the South Texas brush country, the ambitious college graduate and the only-slightly rehabilitated thug renewed their unlikely alliance. It wasn't a friendship, exactly, but the Kingsville roots they shared were indelible and filled their past with the wistful nostalgia of childhood innocence.

As Miguel and Marisol worked through their assigned schedule of probation meetings, they found they shared a certain sly, fatalistic philosophy about life. That a murderer who had done a seven-year bit in the Texas Department of Corrections could still find the world a source of wry amusement seemed to Marisol to be little short of a miracle.

As for Miguel, Marisol awoke in him a paternalistic instinct he had never experienced. She was plenty smart and a tough cookie—he sensed that right away—and she didn't really need protection, but...he found himself in the unexpected position of wanting to help her somehow. Not that many of his talents were inside the law, but he'd find a way, someday.

That Friday afternoon in July, as the heat and humidity turned downtown Austin into a watery mirage, Marisol sorted through a pile of employment vouchers. She picked out one she had red-flagged the night before.

"*Oye*, Miguel, how are you at serving drinks?"

Miguel Negron, bored, sitting sideways and puffing on a cigarette, cut his eyes towards the young girl. "I stuck up a couple of liquor stores once," he said, dropping his eye in a lazy wink to let her know he was joking. Sort of.

"No kidding, tough guy. *Escúchame*, there's a job at a cafe and bar in Rockport, down on the coast. A marina, it says here. The qualifications seem...minimal."

Miguel didn't take offense. He knew his skill set didn't exactly cut him out to be a nuclear physicist.

"Last time I checked, guys with a jacket like mine couldn't hold a liquor license. Or even be in a place alcohol is served."

"Let me worry about that," she said.

"Why are you so anxious to get me a beach vacation?" he asked warily.

"If I have to check on you once a month, I'd just as soon do it in a place with a beach."

"I'd kinda had my heart set on Houston. I got friends there."

"That's what worries me," she said. "My job is to help you become a productive member of society, and help you keep your nose clean...and it's unlikely your Houston friends share my, um, zeal for your rehabilitation."

"How 'bout a bar in Austin then? I'm not big on small towns. I lived in one once, remember?"

Marisol flared. "*Híjole* Miguel! The only other jobs you match up for are cleaning out the grease traps behind Popeye's Chicken stands or unloading containers at the Port of Houston twelve hours a day." She pointed out the window at the brutal heatscape that was Texas in summer.

"You really want one of those gigs? In the summertime? This marina thing is easy, a day at the beach, like you said."

Miguel was a thug, but he wasn't stupid.

"So I pour beer and fry eggs and join the surf team in Bumfuck, Texas?" He pretended to ponder the matter, rubbing his jaw and nodding his head thoughtfully.

Marisol smiled to herself. "Cut the shit, Miguel. Go pack your inner tube and suntan lotion. Say hi to Flipper for me. Kiss a seagull. Get the hell out of here. I've got a hundred other guys in my caseload with real problems." She waved her fingers in playful dismissal. "*Vaya con Dios.*"

——————

CHAPTER 11

The next morning a representative from the Rockport Bank—from the company's parent bank actually, out of Houston—delivered some documents regarding the money Johnny had borrowed to upgrade the *Ramrod*. Charlie opened the official looking envelope and glanced over the papers. The bank was calling the loan. *Greedy bastards*, he thought. Then he remembered Bao and his comment about the boats he had purchased from Johnny previously, with the help of the same outfit.

Charlie saw that Raul was watching him examine the documents so he re-stuffed the envelope and tossed it nonchalantly onto the bench seat.

"Raul," he asked. "How did Johnny get along with these outlanders?" When Raul looked confused Charlie added, "The Vietnamese dudes. Our neighbors. Was he friends with any of them?"

"Most of them, they like him," said Raul. "He help them sometime with the *motores dieseles*. And he have some barbecues for them."

"Barbecues?"

"*Jes*. He say he do it to..." he pondered for a second, "...*para dar la lata al Coronel Bao*" (to piss off Colonel Bao).

Charlie laughed. "The guy's a colonel, too?"

Raul shrugged.

"Did it work? The barbecues?"

"Johnny think so. The *Coronel* don't like Johnny to make friends with his people."

Charlie grinned and looked at Raul with a glint in his eye. "*Oye, chavo...* my brother was wily...like a coyote! Why don't you put on some shoes and hop in the truck with me? We have us some important errands to run."

"*Que es un* errand, Charlie?" He'd seen that same coyote grin from Johnny before.

"*Es como un mandado.* In this case it's pork butt, some proper Pac Rim spices, noodles, and a shit load of Tiger beer, if we can find it. And maybe some other things, too. We're gonna have us a little *pachanga* tonight, Raul!" he explained happily, "In honor of my brother, Johnny Sweetwater. Shit, he'll probably show up himself. You know how much he likes a good party."

———

Meanwhile, Sergeant O.B. Hadnott sat in a metal folding chair, waiting impatiently for the sheriff to get off the phone. Without even looking up from the classifieds she was reading, a plump receptionist told him to take a seat. Buck would be with him in minute.

"So Corky drives the poor bastard down to Laredo," Buck Huckabee's voice could be heard clearly from behind his office door, "and takes him straight over to Boy's Town. 'Course, you know Willy, he ain't even been to an R movie before, much less a whorehouse. But that's where Corky takes him.

"So anyway, they go into some joint called the Pescador and proceed to get butt-lipped on tequila, dancing with the whores and everything. Corky says Willy was with one of the ugliest girls in the place. So Corky strikes a deal for Willy with the lady that runs the place, and the ugly girl leads Willy up the stairs to one of the rooms. And Corky says he's waitin' and waitin', thinking damn, maybe Willy's passed out or something, or maybe they're robbing him—you know that shit happens down there—until finally he decides to go up and check on Willy himself. Has to pay the *mamacita* lady another twenty bucks just to go up to the room...."

Ranger Hadnott sat erect in his chair, trying not to make eye contact with the receptionist who seemed oblivious to the conversation that could plainly be heard behind the door.

"So he says he opens the door and he don't see nobody in there at first, but he says he's hearing this loud yap! yap! yapping coming from a dog somewhere. He finally figures out it's coming from behind the bathroom door, so he opens it up and...." Ranger Hadnott hears Buck stifling a laugh... "and he says there's Willy, standing with his pants around his knees in front of this whore, who's sittin' on the toilet giving him a blow job!"

A pause. "Huh?" Another pause. "Well I don't know why she was sittin' there...I guess 'cause she had to pee or something...but anyway, listen, here's the best part....Barking like a sonofabitch is this little goddamn poodle dog, who so help me God, has been dyed pink!" More laughter. "And the fuckin' pink dog is hopping up and down on its hind legs behind Willy like some kind of freakin' circus dog, yappin' up at him while he's standing there gettin' the business."

Ranger Hadnott had had enough. He marched straight into the office of Aransas County Sheriff Buck Huckabee and pressed down the disconnect button, abruptly ending the call.

"What the...! You got a problem, Mister?" said Buck "Who the hell do you think you are?"

Hadnott leaned over the desk and, tapping the badge pinned to his shirt, spoke in a low, even and utterly forbidding tone. "I'm Sergeant O.B. Hadnott of the Texas Rangers, and I've got *official* business. You gotta problem with *that* sheriff?"

Sheriff Huckabee looked quickly at the badge then motioned for his guest to take the empty chair in front of his desk. Sergeant Hadnott remained standing.

"I'm here on special assignment from C Company up in Lubbock," Sergeant Hadnott continued, "and I need to see your file on the Pomade case."

Sheriff Huckabee took a long look at the tall man standing rigidly in front of his desk. The Ranger wore a gray Stetson, boots, pressed khaki pants and a starched white shirt with pearl buttons. His beak nose was peeling from a recent sunburn. The silver cinco peso badge with the five-pointed star gleamed on his breast above the pocket.

"I heard that a Texas Ranger was pokin'...I mean was doing some investigating down in my, uh, area," Sheriff Huckabee offered cautiously. "Is there anything in particular you're lookin' for? I might be able to help you."

"Just give me the file," answered Hadnott flatly.

While the sheriff searched the file cabinet for the case file, he tried to engage the Texas Ranger in some friendly shoptalk. "We thought we had some promising leads on this case but they turned out to be nothing. I'm beginning to think it could've been an accident, ya know?"

When the Ranger didn't answer, Buck launched into a convoluted theory about a stray shot from drunk and disoriented duck hunter from across the bay.

"But, nah," he said in conclusion, handing the file over to the Ranger, "I guess that theory won't work now that I think about it. Duck huntin' season doesn't start for another two months."

Hadnott took the manila folder from the police chief without expression and examined it briefly. "I need to borrow this."

"Well, ah, Officer Hadnott, that's my only copy there and..." he looked around the cluttered office, "...our copier's broke."

"I'll make copies of the documents I need and someone will deliver the file to you when I've finished," said O.B. "You okay with that, sheriff?" he mouthed the last word like it tasted of something rancid.

Buck Huckabee shrugged. "Suit ya self."

As O.B. cruised down Water Street in downtown Rockport he noted with some concern that businesses were boarding up their doors and windows with sheets of plywood. What kind of storm were they expecting, anyway?

He radioed the DPS station in Aransas Pass to verify that they had a Xerox machine. "Roger that, Sergeant," came the reply. "And you just received some information from Austin that looks kind of important. You might want to get over here and check it out."

As he drove, O.B. Hadnott thought about the sorry excuse for a sheriff he was supposed to count on for help on his case. The local police didn't seem much better. Two days on the coast and he already wished he were home, cruising the state, county and farm-to-market roads of the Panhandle. Down here in this mildewing coastal environment he was surprised to find that he longed (almost fondly) for the criminal types he had pursued on his West Texas turf for most of the past twenty years. Any cattle rustler, bank robber or other miscreant that had the misfortune of being pursued and nabbed by Ranger O.B. Hadnott generally did time in one of the state's many correctional facilities. This rural, mostly solitary police work suited O.B. to the T.

He was content with his life in West Texas and could not imagine living anywhere else. Especially not the Gulf Coast. He hated the humid, clotted air, the *mañana* sense of indolence, and he was unsure what to make of the incomprehensible racial stew of black, white, Cajun, Tejano and Asian coast dwellers, and the fatalistic sense of helplessness that the implacable ocean imparted to them all. He regarded with superstitious dread whatever might lie under that ocean's green swells. And what was worst of all, he felt like nothing was under his control.

When Hadnott arrived at the DPS station, everyone in the office was gathered around a small television. At first O.B. thought they were watching a ball game, but as he approached the group he saw they were focusing intently on a weatherman who stood in front of a satellite map. The TV man pointed at a massive swirly white stain sitting on the edge of the Gulf of Mexico. Another map appeared with a small winged symbol superimposed over the south central part of the Gulf. The symbol reminded O.B. of some kind of farm implement, but the weatherman called it Lana. Little white dots traced Lana's path over the top of Cuba and across the map of the sea. The dots seemed to indicate that the ominous looking thing was starting to turn south, towards Mexico, which is exactly what the weatherman was saying.

"Thank God for that," someone said.

"Too early to tell," answered another.

"No matter where it goes, we're still gonna have some long days and nights in front of us," remarked an officer.

"Have we received the disaster plan yet?" asked another.

"No, not yet," answered the first. (It turned out that the disaster plan for Hurricane Lana was the same as it had been for every other blow for the past fifty years—first cover your own butt and then advise everyone in the affected area to run like a bunch of spotted-ass apes.)

"Afternoon, gentlemen," said Hadnott. "Ma'am," he said to the female dispatcher, touching his fingers to the brim of his Stetson and dipping his head.

The group greeted Sergeant Hadnott amiably, although there had been a lot of idle speculation about the Texas Ranger since he'd showed up at their office the day before yesterday. It was hard to get a read on a guy who talked as little as O.B.

"Y'all said there was some information for me?"

O.B. read through the faxes from Austin—background information on a list of potential suspects whose names had come up in his initial interviews with local citizens and law enforcement (excluding Sheriff Huckabee, of course)—and one POI report really grabbed his attention. Shortly thereafter he left the DPS station, waving perfunctorily to the small covey of gray uniforms still huddled around the T.V.

CHAPTER 12

Neon Leon Guidry paused on the cracked cement sidewalk in front of the He's Not Here Bar & Grill, on an anonymous side street in Houston's teeming Fifth Ward. As he opened the door, the late afternoon sunlight cut a swath of gold across the liver-colored carpet. A June bug fluttered in and smacked against the fake mahogany veneer that covered the walls.

Warm weather, which in Houston meant all the time except for about four weeks around the Advent season, endowed insects and plants with frightening avidity. People grew torpid in the heat, but the lower orders thrived. The June bug bounced off the wall and fell to the carpet, where Leon unknowingly dispatched it with one step of his coconut-and-wheat-colored wingtips.

The door swung shut behind him, plunging the empty barroom into dimness. Leon strolled past the makeshift bandstand, behind the wet bar and through the kitchen. Outside, rush hour traffic began to pile up and down the length of Elgin Street.

A wizened black man sat in a cubbyhole kitchen, shelling shrimp. "Help you, Cap?" he asked. Leon bustled through without answering.

Behind the kitchen, a short foyer lined with the same worn carpeting led to a private office. Leon knocked perfunctorily and stepped into a miasma of cigarette smoke, cheap cologne and stale beer.

For a moment he stood on the threshold and gazed flatly at Senator Llewellyn "Pinky" Cudihay.

"I'll be go ta hell, Lou-Ellen. I heard about ol' acquaintance be fo'got and all dat, but I haven't heard from you much since you dedicated yo' life ta public service" (Leon pronounced it "soi-vice"). He eyed Cudihay's bespoke linen suit and fancy two-toned shoes. "Shit, bein' a man of da people looks like a pretty good gig...."

Cudihay stomped across the room to an ice chest and pulled out a dripping bottle of Jax beer. He didn't offer Leon one. His opinion of his old running buddy's sarcastic repartee hadn't improved with time.

The He's Not Here ice chest, adorned with the bar's logo (a dated caricature of a tough-looking mug in a fedora and double-breasted suit with his hands raised as if to say "What can I tell ya?"), did duty as a beer chest, wine cellar and occasional crawfish condo. Cudihay, more accustomed to the elegant bars and bistros of the four-star hotels lining Lamar and Travis streets downtown, seemed almost comically out of his element. Guidry noticed, and wondered. And worried.

The Senator had called him out of the blue, said he wanted a place where they could meet and he wouldn't be recognized, and Guidry suggested the run-down gin mill in inner-city Houston near his office and recording studio. It didn't get any more off the radar than that.

Leon hadn't seen Pinky Cudihay in quite awhile, but they shared a vivid and turbulent history that Cudihay—in his current role as a blue-chip state senator—was in no mood to advertise. Guidry noticed right away that there was the sense of something unhealthy lingering around Cudihay—the absence of the man's characteristic whiskey flush, a sort of deflated bonhomie, a scent of mortality.

"Been reading any papers besides *Billboard* and the *Racing Form* lately?" Cudihay asked, taking a deep swig off his beer.

"Well, yeah, da *Wall Street Journal*. I gotta keep track of my portfolio. But it seems like I mighta seen something about you recently on the six o'clock news. Some party dat got out of hand...."

"It was out of hand alright. I goddamn near got shot!"

"As I heard it, someone did get shot."

"Ah, yeah, and that's a tragedy," Cudihay said as he shook his head in melodramatic dismay. "But here's the thing—I think maybe that bullet was meant for me."

Leon Guidry couldn't help it. He roared with derisive laughter.

"Jesus Christ, Lou-Ellen, you haven't changed. Even when you was a saxophone player out on Highway 90, playin' for tips and backseat blowjobs, you still thought your shit smelled like Chanel No. 5. I think bein' a political big-shot in a linen suit is a step down for you."

Cudihay's expression didn't change. "Yeah, Leon...I think it is. I got my eyes set on bigger things. Always have. I outgrew you and all those shitholes we used to play, just like I outgrew a white-trash neighborhood in Beaumont and the family that came with it. I like my linen suits and my big car and my top-shelf pussy and all the things that come with bein' a big shot. You're right about that."

"So why call up a lowlife like yours truly? Me bein' outgrew, and all?"

Cudihay snapped the cap off another beer. "It's a funny thing, Leon. Even big shots need help once in awhile, and that help can come from some funny places. Things have been a little shaky for me, lately. The Senate Ethics Committee is looking into some of my business interests, the goddamn red-hot reformers and those pinkos at the *Texas Observer* have been spreading mendacious lies about my record, and there's a punk-ass assistant district attorney—a 'crusader!'—in Victoria County that's gonna run against me in the primary. I needed to change the subject. Needed to make a splash. Get my name in the papers in a big way."

Guidry leaned back in his chair. "Don't tell me...."

"There's a guy, I know. He's a businessman, connected up and down the coast with shrimpers and shipping and what all. A Vietnamese guy named Bao, Colonel Bao. Upstanding guy, far as I can tell." (Cudihay's eyes were suddenly shifty, Leon noted.) "But he deals with some rough old boys. You pretty much have to if you're gonna make out down there."

"Yeah. I heard of da guy," said Leon.

Cudihay nodded. "So I had a thought. I throw a party and something...happens. Dramatic, you know. A big picture window facing the bay and a couple of guys with a jon boat and a deer rifle. A shot from the dark in a crowded party, my big picture window goes crash real nice, I'm back in the news. Just a stunt—lots of broken glass, nobody hurt. We'd have us a laugh about it."

"Well, it made the news alright," Guidry said as he twisted the cap off his beer bottle. "And for all the wrong reasons. What the fuck happened?"

"Bao said his guy missed," Cudihay said tiredly. "The boat was bobbin' up and down in the swells, I dunno. Just flat fuckin' missed, man."

"Is that *his* story?" Neon Leon asked disgustedly. "That it's hard to get good help these days?"

Cudihay sat puddled in silence, the desultory breeze from the limply revolving ceiling fan stirred a couple of hairs on his pompadour.

Finally, he spoke up. "Bao didn't tell me nothin' and I didn't ask. If those two boys in the jon boat are gonna end up baitin' some Viet crab traps, I don't wanna know.

"The hell of it is," said Cudihay with a wan smile, "I did get a nice bump in my poll numbers. Neddy would've been happy with that, I guess."

Guidry stood up and pulled a soiled handkerchief from his breast pocket. He walked over to the ice chest, swirled the handkerchief around in the slushy ice and water, and ran the cold rag around his face and neck. He suddenly felt tired to the bone.

"And this guy, Bao is your idea of a good-ole-boy constituent?"

"Not hardly," replied Cudihay. "Our relationship is a little more... complicated. What has me worried was his story sounded like bullshit. More and more, I've started thinking that shot was a warning."

Leon looked skeptical. "Ya' mean he'd blow a guy away in public just to *warn* ya? Man, you're blowing smoke up yo' own ass."

Cudihay cast a speculative eye on his old running buddy. "We were both too old to fight in Vietnam, but how much do you know 'bout that war, Leon?"

"Just stories I hear," Guidry replied. "Talked to a few vets. Why you askin'?"

"I knew some guys who went over and came back, too. And they told me there was always a Colonel Bao in the picture somewhere. There've been guys like him over there ever since the Chinese rolled down to kick ass and take names a jillion years ago."

The Senator sucked on his beer. Number four. Not that he was counting.

"Guys like Bao...middle-management facilitators or freelance entrepreneurs, if you want to be charitable. Or, hustlers and gangsters and flat-out bandits, if you want to remain in the truth's company.

"Guys like Bao ran the country for the French, and made sure they got rich doing it," Cudihay said. "And then for the Japs during the war, and then the French again. By the time Lyndon Johnson decided to turn Southeast Asia into an American Dream theme park—fuckin' don't ask me why—Bao and guys like him were entrenched.

"We bailed out, but by then it didn't matter. Bao just changed uniforms and greeted the North Vietnamese at the gates of Saigon with open arms. He and his cronies kept the trains running, as the saying goes, and nobody was too goddamn particular about their pedigrees. I've heard he had ties with those guys in Laos, the Meo tribesmen, who turned him on to muling raw opium out of the country on CIA airplanes. I heard he sold exit visas to South Vietnamese big shots out the back door, and then turned around and sold the big shots out to the new regime, collecting from both ends. I heard lots of things."

Leon held up one palm to stop the flow of narrative, turned abruptly on one heel, yanked open the office door and walked down the hall. He fished a crumpled twenty dollar bill out of his pocket and handed it to the cook, a toothless man the approximate hue and circumference of a tarred wharf rope. "Hey, T-Bone, go get us a bottle and some ice. An' a half-pint fo' yourself."

"Sure t'ing, Cap," the old man said, and disappeared.

Leon waited until whiskey was swirling in his waxed paper cup before asking Cudihay, with some asperity, "How do ya know all of this shit?"

Cudihay took a long pull on his own glass. His face flushed slightly.

"How do I know?" he asked rhetorically. "I goddamn well made it my business to find out once Colonel Bao and I..." Cudihay's lips made an involuntary moue of distaste, "...became better acquainted."

Outside, the sun had disappeared over the shimmering coastal plain, and the evening sky was turning a deep violet. Out in the front room, Leon heard the wheeze of the jukebox and the rattle of dominoes as the night's contingent of time wasters filtered in. None of the regulars intruded on the meeting in the back room.

"Is he really a colonel?" Leon asked.

"Oh, yeah," said Cudihay as he rooted around in his drink. "Full bird colonel in the South Vietnamese army. I dunno if he bought the rank at a Saigon garage sale, or if it was a payoff or he capped a real colonel and helped himself to the uniform. But one day he was strutting around in the Tet parade, and all his goons were decked out as sergeants and lieutenants and such.

"None of that made a shit to the North Vietnamese, though, and when the NVA tanks started rolling into the parking lot of the Saigon Hilton, I reckon Bao had to re-evaluate his political priorities pretty dang quick. The trail breaks down, but he must've started doing business at the old store, only this time as a *muy rojo* Commie-gook.

"But something musta went wrong....Maybe he bribed the wrong comrade or forgot to bribe the right one. But he had to scamper. And now he's here, just another sucker for the American Dream. Like Texas needs one more outlaw."

The Senator had been blissfully ignorant of all this history the day Colonel Bao first approached him at a fundraiser in a Corpus Christi resort hotel. Cudihay had glad-handed his way into a glassy-eyed stupor before ducking into the men's room for a little pharmaceutical pick-me-up. And when he came out of the stall, snuffling like a hog after a truffle, Bao was just...there.

He introduced himself in a voice so soft and self-effacing that the Senator had to lean forward to hear him speak: Nguyen Ngoc Bao, a recent arrival to freedom's shores, and the titular head of the recently-incorporated Sea-Tex Maritime Association. Cudihay had no way of knowing that Bao had in fact arrived on freedom's shore two years previously, on a false visa, with a dead man's name on his passport and the sort of attitude for his adopted home that a crocodile reserves for a poodle.

Bao continued his spiel as the Senator's nose twitched in self-induced anesthesia. "We are," said Bao, "a small but growing group of local parties who are interested in obtaining equitable working conditions for all of the commercial fishermen in the Costal Bend." He said. Smiling.

Cudihay smiled back blandly. But behind the smile, his mind churned. *He's organizin' the slopes*, he thought, with something he only dimly recognized as wonder. The brand-newest, hardest-working, fastest growing slice of a gumbo coastal populace—an exploding voter demographic in the heart of Cudihay's district that would stretch halfway down the 21st century....

If he's gonna fuck me, he's gonna have to buy me dinner and drinks first, the Senator thought, regarding the man with his own Cheshire-Cat grin.

Sure enough, as though on cue, Bao's smile widened, and the hand that a moment before had held a business card now extended a fat envelope.

"I felt damned embarrassed," Cudihay confessed to Neon Leon Guidry almost two years later. "Like I'd been caught playin' pocket pool in church."

Leon snorted into his drink in amusement, or contempt, or both. "I didn't think ya had it in ya to be embarrassed, me. Da last time I paid attention to dat lunatic asylum in Austin, a crazy chicken farmer was passin' out $10,000 checks on the floor of the House. Not even Huey Long would have stood for such shit as that."

Cudihay shrugged extravagantly. "As you know, Brother Guidry, the Vatican has yet to canonize the first legislator from our Great State....But even so, Bao is something above and beyond politics as usual. Still, I didn't give the little bastard another thought for months...."

Actually, it was four months and seventeen days later before the Colonel rematerialized like bad juju into the Senator's life. Cudihay was taking the private elevator from the Senate office wing to the underground parking garage under the Capitol when, at the last moment, a slender hand inserted itself into the gap between the doors, and Bao slipped into the car, like smoke.

He smiled but sparingly during his brief conversation with the Senator, but that smile, when it dawned, was redolent of Alpine meadows, frolicking puppies, lemonade, and the Ten Commandments.

"I'd gotten the kiss when I took his money," said Cudihay, as Guidry nodded in unsympathetic understanding. "Now I had to stand still for the fuckin'. Bao knew about the controlling interest I had in Maddox Exploration. Shit, I thought I had that thing hid so well a Catahoula cur couldn't sniff it out. But he knew."

" Maddox Exploration?"

"They're that crowd that bid to slant drill a gas well about a thousand feet from the Whoopers' refuge out at Aransas. The Park Service and the Army Corps of Engineers were like to shit a brick, but they were led to consider this country's energy plight in these tough times."

"An' who led 'em to da light, I wonder?" mused Leon.

Leon Guidry ordinarily enjoyed the attention span of a mosquito when the subject did not involve music, money or poontang. But he found himself captivated, about one-third good drunk, and just a little scared as the tale unspooled. He wondered just how far events, happenstance and the Senator's outsized appetite would propel his old pal into this maze whose walls were money, political muscle, threats, and power. It was a high-stakes game, and Leon suddenly didn't feel like he wanted to be dealt in.

He and Llewellyn "Pinky" Cudihay went way back, to when Pinky was a kid fresh out of Beaumont High who thought he had a way with a tenor sax, and Leon himself was a pompadoured hustler who had barely scraped the bayou mud off his suede shoes. "How'd you get strapped wid' a name like Llewellyn, anyway?" Leon asked one time.

"Aw," said Cudihay, "Mama gave all the good names to the dogs."

Leon himself came from Vinton, just across the Sabine River from Beaumont. The stateline town was the ancestral home of Guidrys both black and white, and most shades in between. As a youngster, he made a small packet booking bands like Cookie and the Cupcakes, the Boogie Kings, and Little Whisper & the Rumors into VFW dances and car lot openings and, later, into border roadhouses like LouAnn's, the Big Oaks and the Texas Pelican Club.

Pinky couldn't play saxophone worth a flying *chinga*. But he struck up an acquaintance with the older boy based on a mutual fondness for the blue light joints that dotted the state border, and that promised action a lot more interesting than Pony League Baseball could offer.

It wasn't a friendship exactly—more a mutually-advantageous system of exploitation—but whatever it was, it endured through whiskey hangovers, cockfights at Jay's Lounge, whorehouse marathons (and subsequent cases of crabs and the clap), and Cudihay's morbidly obsessive quest for money and status and the respectability he thought they conferred.

Leon never fooled himself into thinking that money equated with respectability; he just thought of it as a passport to a bigger world and better options. With that in mind, Leon kept hustling and the paydays got bigger. Soon, he was booking bands on a nightly basis at joints between Corpus Christi and Lake Charles. The seat of his honky-tonk empire eventually migrated from Vinton to Houston.

As for Cudihay, as he moved into the political realm, the Senator-To-Be found it expedient to have a clandestine friend with access to large bundles of untraceable, frequently replenished cash money.

Leon was a handy connection in those early scuffling days. But they drifted apart as Cudihay found himself hanging around a better class of crooks. That was all right with Leon; he had his own fish to fry with his string of juke joints, his floating backroom crap games and the burgeoning career of L.C. Hebert.

When the Seventies finally dawned, Leon had improbably hustled himself into near-respectability. And Pinky Cudihay was finally in show business, or at least the carnival Midway of politics.

"...He never let on how he knew," the Honorable Senator was

exclaiming. "But goddamn it, he knew! There wasn't any bluff in him. Hell, I don't even think they have poker in Vietnam. He didn't say another word; just got off the elevator.

"Two weeks later, he was on the books for an appointment, right between the Scout troop and the Veterans of Some Fuckin' War or Other. He came in, hat in hand, and gave me the poor mouth about the assignment of shrimping permits in Copano Bay and a whole other grocery list of stuff, and might I know somebody on the Land Commissioner's panel on coastal management?"

"Lemme guess," said Leon with a widening smile.

"What, that I chair that panel? Well, no shit."

It went on from there, as the level in the whiskey bottle declined: a payoff here, a regulatory sidestep there, even some discreet blackmail and intimidation. What began to really bother Cudihay was that not all the favors had to do with shrimping or the Vietnamese community. Once, Bao asked for the patrol schedules of Coast Guard patrols up and down the Coastal Bend. Another time, a little indirect pressure was brought to bear for a favorable hearing by the State Parole Board on behalf of a felony lifer whose name Cudihay did his best to instantly forget. The convict drove away in the backseat of Bao's Lincoln Continental.

The sleazy and cynical little kickback scheme with Maddox Exploration would not have served to keep the Senator on the short leash through all of these machinations. But plenty of dirt, both personal and professional, had attached itself to Cudihay's coat tails over the years, and Bao had an unusually adept nose at sniffing it out. Over and over, the Senator's pitiful refrain repeated itself like a foghorn honk: "I dunno how he knew...but he knew!"

Dumb bastard, thought Guidry. *I know. Bao knows the same way colored folks have always known what was going on up at the Big House. Known whatever they needed to know to survive, and sometimes even prosper. Slopes or niggers, they're still furniture to the white folks hatching their plans in what they fancy is secret. We watch from the shadows and listen from around corners. And we know.*

He shook himself out of his reverie. Cudihay was looking at him expectantly, as though it were his sole purpose on earth to make sense out of the Senator's ethical train wreck of a life and near-death experience. Neon Leon shook his shaggy head. "So...'Splain it to me, Lucy. Why drag me into this?"

"Well, because I hadn't seen you in forever. And you are, God help me, the only one I can talk to about this. And because you owe me for pulling that jealous husband off of you in Lake Charles before he could fillet you like a grouper. Because maybe you're connected in that part of the world and you can help me find a handle on Colonel Bao."

Guidry shook his head. "You got an over-inflated idea of my, ah, connections down there. I knew a guy who knew dis Colonel, but he ain't wid us no more. And I know a couple of bookies, an' a few ol' boys in da Bandidos an' maybe a local wiseguy or two. I dunno if I could help you out wid yo' boy. Even if I wanted to."

"Leon, believe it or not, it took a lot to pick up the phone to call you. You're one of those guys I was trying to keep off my books, to be honest. But all I'm asking is if you can...ask around, maybe? That little yellow fucker is up to something down there in Fulton and I need to know what it is. And I want *him* to know that I know it, too."

The pathetic part of the story was the unstated fact that the esteemed Senator from the great and glorious State of Texas really *did* have nowhere else to turn. None of his cadre of flunkies and ass-kissers and semi-legal bagmen could help him as much at this moment as a coonass hustler with whiskey stains on his shirt.

"If it came out that I had put someone up to a publicity stunt that ended up as a murder, my ass would be cooked. That's what I meant about a warning. Bao wants to make sure I stay on the porch."

"C'mon, Lou-Ellen, no one would ever believe it. No one would print it."

Cudihay laughed morbidly. "Hell, it doesn't have to be in the paper. One time Lyndon Johnson was in a tight race and he told his number one boy to start spreading the rumor that his opponent was making time with the barnyard animals. The flunky said no one would ever believe the man was a sheep-fucker. Lyndon just laughed and said, yeah, but let's make him deny it." He sat still for a minute. "That's politics, son."

"Well, you got any ideas what dis Colonel's into these days? Besides your half-assed schemes?"

Cudihay paced the carpet in small circles, swirling his glass so that the liquor mirrored his progress. "I'm not exactly sure," he said at length. "Bao's been buying parcels of land between Palacios and Port A, but never in his own name. He's been using blocs of Sea-Tex stockholders—most of whom are populatin' local cemeteries, I imagine, to register the deeds. I looked, and Sea-Tex itself is incorporated in the Cayman Islands. There's no paper trail I can find.

"A lot of the holdings are up around Matagorda Bay, over near those Maddox leases that Bao's so fond of waving in my face. Hell, he even insisted I get him the service contract on one of the bay drilling platforms we control. Anyway, there's some good anchorages up in there, and lots of sloughs and bayous where boats can slip in and out without attracting a lot of attention. Mebbe he wants to set up the Viets with their own shipyards and slips...."

"What, fo' shrimpin'?" interjected Leon. "I heard dis Colonel plays kinda rough, but dis bidness of takin' shots at people in public view— man, dat's a liddle too Mardi Gras for words." Leon's stocky body had puddled in his club chair until his chin had settled on his chest.

The Senator nodded. "I know, but...I dunno. That sumbitch thinks he's got my pecker in his pocket and *that*, ol buddy, is why I need you right now."

The two men talked sporadically for another twenty minutes, mostly about old, but not necessarily good, times.

Finally, Leon sighed and said, "I'll ax around, me. But...you know how it is. No promises." He shook his head. "You a sad sight, Lou-Ellen. I like you more when you're an asshole. You seem mo' human, somehow."

Cudihay said, "I got to hit it. I've got a committee meeting at seven a.m. sharp tomorrow. How 'bout a lift?"

Leon settled his sweat-stained straw porkpie on his head and heaved himself laboriously to his feet. "Naw," he said after some small reflection. "I'm gonna go out ta Gilley's. Dat band of mine, da Crawfish Cowboys are playin', and I wanna catch dat lyin' bastid who's givin' me a short count on the door."

The two slipped out through a back door and into an alley behind the barroom. A yellow streetlight cast urinous beams down the oil-slicked pavement. The pair did not shake hands.

"Watch out for fallin' rocks," said Cudihay in parting.

Neon Leon kept walking. His voice floated back over his shoulder. "You do likewise, Lou-Ellen. You do likewise."

CHAPTER 13

Bruce Lee's chiseled torso had been striped with blood by Han's razor-sharp Bear Claw prosthetic. Anyone in the harbor watching the film could plainly see that Bruce was really pissed off now. After an almighty fight in Han's chamber of mirrors, Bruce emerged victorious, avenging his family and restoring honor to the Shaolin temple that trained him. The large gathering of Vietnamese fishermen cheered, whistled, and clapped with enthusiasm.

As army helicopters swooped in on Han's secret island to finish off the bad guys and the credits began to roll down the screen in Vietnamese, Charlie concluded that his party had been a monster hit.

He couldn't believe his good fortune in finding the classic Kung Fu reel at a small AV shop in Corpus Christi. The vet who owned it had brought the film back with him from 'Nam and agreed to rent it out, along with a noisy projector, for a very reasonable fee. Who cared if the Hong Kong Chinese dialog was dubbed over with English—it had Vietnamese subtitles! A not-to-be-missed cinema event for every Vietnamese citizen in Fulton.

Charlie and Raul had improvised an expansive movie screen by rigging a borrowed spinnaker sail over the main mast and outriggers of the *Ramrod*. The projector sat on a makeshift table made from a stack of crabtraps and a piece of plywood. The shrimpers-cum-cinephiles sat on gunwales, cabin roofs, cleats and boxes, or just squatted on the surrounding docks.

Earlier, Charlie and Raul cooked and served thirty pounds of skewered pork barbecue and countless bowls of rice noodles with fish sauce. Charlie had made a point to shake hands and ask the name of every guest that came by his boat. One of the neighbor kids, a young man named Sammy Nu, helped him prepare a sign in Vietnamese announcing the free barbecue and free movie: "Brought to you by Your Friend and Neighbor, Johnny Sweetwater."

Before the movie, Marisol dropped by unexpectedly and sampled a plate of food. "Not bad," she told Charlie. She observed the gathered Vietnamese families that were eating and chatting around the boat. "I think Johnny would approve." She was also thinking she might have to reassess her opinion of Johnny's younger brother.

Later, Charlie spied Bao's tan Lincoln Continental idling in the parking lot across the harbor. Standing in front of the barbecue grill he raised a long spatula and waved hello to the darkened windows of the car. He took a juvenile pleasure in getting Bao's goat. When the car drove away, Charlie patted Raul on the back. "Guess he doesn't like barbecue."

"Or Kung Fu movies," Raul answered.

—

Late that night Charlie and Raul were sleeping soundly in their bunks when Ringworm growled. Charlie opened his eyes and listened intently, hearing only the soft rustle of palm trees near the parking lot and the creaking and groaning of the wooden boats in the harbor. He was about to close his eyes again when he glimpsed a shadow pass by the curtain. He sat up quickly and slid silently off the bunk. Raul breathed rhythmically from the darkness of the bottom berth.

Charlie unlatched the cabin door and pushed out slowly. He stood still in the cool evening air and listened again. Maybe the shadow came from someone walking down the finger pier, or maybe, he thought, it was just a breeze from the open galley window that rustled the curtain. Ringworm was nowhere to be seen. The dog usually curled up next to the winch under the main mast. Charlie decided to walk once around the boat and then go back to bed. It was too chilly outside to be wandering around in boxer shorts.

Just as he rounded the corner of the pilothouse a sleeved arm grabbed him around the neck and shoved him into the gunwale, arching his back out over the bay. Charlie deflected the man's other arm, which swung around to strike him. He quickly twisted out of the neck hold and pushed off from the attacker.

The two men squared off on the foredeck and Charlie realized the guy had a knife in his hand. Belatedly, he realized that blood was dripping down his side where the blade had grazed him in the initial attack. A cold chill of terror ran up his back. He hated a knife.

Both men had their arms extended in front of them and they crouched in a wrestler's stance. The intruder feigned a few thrusts with the knife and then rushed in. Charlie lunged back at the man to shorten the distance between them and caught his arm before the knife could cut him again. As they were grappling on the deck Raul appeared around the corner.

"*Que pasa...!*" he began, but he froze in fear when he saw the two men fighting.

"Run, Raul! Get the hell out of here," Charlie yelled. Raul disappeared for a few seconds and then reappeared.

"Raul!" Charlie struggled to shout. He was breathing heavily as he and the attacker wrestled for position. *Damn, but this fucker's strong,* he thought. "Raul, I said...."

"No, Charlie!" he screamed.

Charlie managed to push the attacker against the forward mast cable but as he released one of his hands to punch at the man's face, he tripped on the anchor rope and stumbled backwards. The man broke from Charlie's grasp and moved away from the guy-cable, preparing to lunge again, but before he could attack, Ringworm's yellow shape flashed across the deck and latched onto the man's arm. He howled in pain and the knife dropped to the ground. Charlie staggered his opponent with an uppercut to the jaw, knocking him against the gunwale. Charlie rushed him again and drive-blocked him over the edge of the rail into the bay.

At the same moment he heard the splash, Charlie heard the rumble of the engines and looked up to see Raul's face in the pilothouse.

Much to his surprise the boat started moving forward. *How did he unloop the lines so damn fast?* Charlie wondered. A moment later the roar of the diesels drowned out Ringworm's frenzied barking and the clamorous banging of the Viet trawlers as the wake of the *Ramrod* created a small typhoon in Fulton Harbor when the boat tore flat-out through the jetties into Aransas Bay.

CHAPTER 14

The next day Charlie Sweetwater reclined in the gimbal-mounted captain's chair with his bare feet propped up on the *Ramrod's* wheel, thinking dark thoughts. A steady breeze ruffled his sun-bleached hair as he took a long drag at a Mexican Delicado cigarette and gazed out at the Gulf. Drifting a hundred miles offshore, he dipped and rolled with his boat as it eased over the endless indigo-blue swells.

His eyes had been fixed on the southeast horizon, the direction the hurricane would approach from if it didn't veer off to Mexico or Florida, or languish and downgrade to a tropical storm. Or maybe even turn around and boogie back to Africa. Hurricanes this late in the season were rare, and no hurricane he'd ever heard of had survived to make landfall on the Gulf Coast after mid-October. Let alone two days before Halloween. *Still*, Charlie thought, *there's a first time for everything*.

He'd been listening to the chatter of the shrimpers all morning. Having heard nothing regarding Johnny or his whereabouts, Charlie began to accept the possibility that his brother was never coming back.

He winced as he reached up and switched the radio to the maritime weather channel—the flap of skin his attacker had detached from his side had been fastened back into place with a squirt of

Krazy Glue from the tool locker, but the wound still seeped into the bandage, leaving a bright red stain on the gauze.

"Who was that man?" Raul had asked repeatedly as the *Ramrod* blasted through Aransas Bay, headed for the Lydia Ann Channel and the Gulf.

Charlie tried to think of some answer that wouldn't scare the boy until he realized that was ridiculous. Raul had watched the man try to fillet Charlie like the Catch of the Day.

"He had to have been one of Bao's men," Charlie said tightly, still shaken. He clasped the boat's wheel in an adrenaline-fueled grip. "The Colonel wants to up the ante. Or scare us to death. I'm not sure."

"*I'm* not scared!" said Raul. "Not of that *pendejo* asshole!"

Charlie pursed his lips and nodded. "Whatever you say, kid," he answered.

But today, he had bigger fish to fry. He moved from the pilothouse to the galley where his charts were laid out on the mess table and waited for the monotonous voice of the maritime channel to drone out the latest coordinates of Hurricane Lana. Charlie carefully charted the storm's current location, size and general direction, and then factored in its wind speed and barometric pressure.

He sat up straight and looked again to the southeast. Nothing to cause alarm as far as he could tell. Partly cloudy skies and a warm southeasterly breeze at 12-15 knots. The only telltale signs of the tempest that raged in the middle of the Gulf were the gradual deepening of the ocean swells, and the bands of high altitude cirrus clouds that pointed their delicate icy fingers back at the violent winds that blew them ahead of the storm.

"What are you gonna do, Lana?" he said aloud. "*Hija de puta.*"

He walked to the small cramped sleeping quarters where he leaned his elbows on the top bunk and looked out the open windows toward the stern of the *Ramrod*. Raul was on the back deck, stripped to the waist, his skin tanned to a coffee-colored brown. He was leaning over the edge of the boat intently studying a fishing line in the water. Ringworm lay on the deck nearby with his back legs splayed out behind him.

Charlie could see why his brother liked the boy. Twelve hours ago they were attacked by a knife-wielding assassin, and now the kid was happily fishing off the back of the boat like he didn't have a care in the world. They'd finally had a chance to talk. "How did you get here,

Raul?" he had asked him. "And why in the world did you end up with Johnny?" *Of all people*, he could have added.

The boy gave Charlie a bright smile and then disappeared into the cabin and returned with a tattered pair of tennis shoes and a faded postcard. "I walk!" he said proudly, lifting the grubby Adidas up by the shoestrings.

"*Bueno*, okay, I only walk from Matamoros. And," he continued, "I have this." He handed Charlie the postcard. On the front was a black and white picture of a cowboy sitting astride a giant jackrabbit. It said "Greetings from Texas." The card was addressed to Guadalupe de la Rosa in Tampico, Tamaulipas, Mexico.

Charlie vaguely recalled the name, remembering that it belonged to a pretty young prostitute that Johnny had fallen for at the Tamyko Pagoda, an upscale whorehouse in Boy's Town outside of Nuevo Laredo. The two brothers made the trip to the *Zona de Tolerencia* many times during their high school and college days. Charlie remembered that Johnny sometimes went to Nuevo Laredo by himself just to visit Lupe de la Rosa on her days off. Now Lupe's kid was returning the courtesy, dropping in on her mother's favorite gringo.

Once Charlie got the boy to open up (switching to Spanish helped), Raul recounted how he had been living with his grandparents in Tampico. His mother had died in a car wreck shortly before he left for Texas to search for "Juanito" Sweetwater, the man she spoke of so fondly when he was a young boy.

He also described the tense relationship that Johnny had with Colonel Bao. Johnny apparently suspected that Bao's business interests went beyond fishing. "Bao not know how to catch a shrimp if it jump up and bite him on the ass." Raul said in English, paraphrasing Johnny. The kid still thought that one was pretty funny. "He had a big fight with Bao," he continued, switching back to Spanish.

"About what?" Charlie had asked.

Raul shrugged. "I couldn't understand what they said, but I could hear Johnny inside the fish house, yelling...and then he started fighting with a man that works for Bao. I don't know who won, but Johnny had blood on his shirt when he came out of the building."

Raul didn't know what other uses Bao had for his boats, but Charlie had a pretty good guess. He wandered outside to the built-in icebox and searched around in the slush for a Dr. Pepper, thinking about outlaws and buccaneers.

Jean Lafitte, the infamous gentleman pirate of the last century, found Charlie's slice of the Texas Gulf Coast ideal for the smuggling and plundering that helped make him a rich man. After the U.S. government kicked him off of Galveston Island in 1821, Lafitte reputedly based his operation out of San Antonio Bay for several years until he finally disbanded his business, liquidated all of his assets except for a few fast ships and sailed to Mexico, where he met an unknown fate.

As kids, Charlie and Johnny spent months looking for a buried treasure that, according to legend, Lafitte hid in a thicket of trees near Live Oak Point, cached for his eventual return. Charlie was a great admirer of Jean Lafitte, and as an ardent student of the successful pirate's life and times, he recognized in Bao another ambitious smuggler when he saw one.

Bao was no romantic swashbuckler, though. From Charlie's observations so far, he saw he was a leech and a gangster. He shivered, remembering the feeling of the knife blade slicing along his rib cage.

A loud cry outside sent Charlie running from the cabin to the stern of the boat. Raul had one foot planted against the back rail, his fishing pole bent almost double from the pressure on the line.

"*Jesus Cristo,* Charlie! I have caught the Moby's Dick!" shouted Raul. Charlie peered over the stern into the dark blue water and spied a large creature straining against the line forty or fifty feet below the surface, madly trying to shake the hook from its mouth.

"What did you use for bait?" Charlie asked.

"Shrimps," replied the boy through clenched teeth.

"It's probably a big-ass ling, or it could be a shark. Do you need help?"

"No, Charlie. I fish it out myself," puffed Raul as the creature made another dive, causing the reel to shriek like an electric drill as the line rushed out. Charlie could see other fish in the water, small sharks, bonito, jackfish and barracuda, all darting around below the surface. The desperate struggle of the hooked fish agitated the other fish around it. Raul slowly pumped his catch up to the ocean surface, reeling in quickly each time he lowered his pole and then using all his strength to raise it up again.

After a thirty-minute battle Raul, sweating and heaving, had the fish up against the back of the boat. It rolled onto its side, staring blankly up at the sky, more exhausted than the boy from the struggle. Charlie snared the fish around its tail so as not to injure it and then he hoisted it onto the deck with a heavy splat.

"*Mira, Capitan!* That is a big mother fish, no!" It was a six-foot ling. Ringworm sniffed at the fish cautiously.

"No doubt, *chavo*. If I had a camera I'd take a picture," said Charlie.

"*Verdad?* No one will believe me when I tell them," said Raul. "But I think he make a good meal. We eat him, no?"

"Nah. Ling is a pain in the ass to cook. And I don't know about you, but I'm sick of eating fish. If we don't get us some store-bought groceries real soon—some food that we don't have to scale, gut or shell—I swear I'm going to start talking like Flipper." Charlie did his best imitation of the movie star porpoise and Raul laughed until he had tears in his eyes.

When he stopped laughing, Raul asked the question he had been wanting to ask all day, "The hurricane, Charlie. Is she coming here?"

"Hard to tell, Raul," said Charlie, recognizing the apprehension in the boy's eyes. "These things have a mind of their own. But one is out there for sure and we'll keep a close watch on it. Meanwhile, they say the fishing is fantastic before a big storm, so I suggest you throw this big guy overboard while he's still alive and then see what else you can pull out of the water. *Bueno?*"

"*Bueno, Carlito.*" Raul held up his palm to give Charlie their special "Sweetwater secret handshake" which involved three different kinds of handclasps, a palm slide and a finger snap.

——————

CHAPTER 15

O.B. Hadnott had never been in a shrimp processing plant before, but he was told he could probably find Nguyen Ngoc Bao there.

The retail seafood store, located street-side in front of the tin warehouse called the Sea-Tex Fish Company, seemed empty when Hadnott walked through the door. The small room had two long horizontal glass counters where the fresh seafood was artistically laid out on beds of ice like an undersea buffet. He gawked at the harvest: shimmering Spanish Mackerel and platter-sized flounder with pairs of eyes awkwardly poking through their flat leathery heads, blue crabs with red-tipped claws, and a half dozen bright pink snapper with startled expressions.

O.B. had never realized so many strange, alien creatures existed out there under that green water. Catfish and crappie caught at the end of a bamboo pole in a West Texas stock tank marked the extent of Hadnott's aquatic adventures. Just then a girl rose up from behind one of the counters, surprising O.B. She had been stooped over a large cooler on the floor.

"You want fish?" she asked O.B.

O.B. stared at the girl in wonder. She had long black hair that was wrapped in a thick plait reaching almost to her waist. He observed that she was short and slight but very well put together, and that she seemed elegant and feminine even as she whisked a strand of hair from her face with a heavy rubber seaman's glove. *This is one beautiful woman*, O.B. thought, with what he hoped was only a professional appraisal.

"You buy fish?" the woman repeated.

"Uh, no ma'am. No I...I'm here looking for someone." She stared at him quizzically. O.B. continued. "His name is Nguyen Ngoc Bao," he said, struggling to pronounce the name that up to now he had only seen written on official reports, including the one just faxed to him from Ranger headquarters in Austin. He pronounced it *"Nee-gwen Nee-gock Bay-o."*

The girl smiled. "In Vietnamese, the name pronounced *Win Noc Bao*," she corrected. "Like bow-wow...you know, like talks the dog." Then her face hardened. "He not here. Gone from office."

O.B. was glad that he could understand this girl's English. He had felt like a fool a few days earlier while trying to question the Vietnamese fishermen about Neddy Pomade's shooting. They'd looked at him like he was a goddamned Roswell space alien. "But he does work here, right?" he asked.

"I not know. I only work here part time, and my job now is put fish in ice box so it not go bad if we lose power because of storm." She impatiently heaved a mackerel into the cooler.

O.B. forced his eyes away from the girl and looked around the room. "Where are the shrimp?" he finally asked, conversationally. Now it was her turn to look confused. He motioned toward a black-board on which FRESH-CAUGHT SHRIMP was printed in chalk.

"Shrimp in back. Coming off boats," she replied, nodding toward a heavy door. Hadnott could see people moving around through the small window in the door.

"The boats are out fishing even with a hurricane coming?" he asked.

"Coming in from Gulf. Sometimes that when shrimping is best," she said, returning to her task.

"Maybe the shrimp don't want to get caught in the storm so they jump into the nets on purpose," he added, allowing one side of his mouth to move up almost imperceptibly. O.B.'s version of levity.

"You ever been in hurricane?" she asked with exasperation.

"No ma'am, I can't say I have."

"Nothing funny about it."

O.B. reddened in embarrassment. "Is there anybody back there who might know Mr. Bao's whereabouts?" he asked, reassuming his official character.

The girl stopped grabbing fish and turned to O.B. "You want to look for Colonel Bao in back, you go, okay. I not stopping you."

"Colonel? Then you do know Mr. Bao," O.B. answered.

She looked sharply at the tall officer. Who the hell was this sunburned cowboy with the huge white hat and clunky boots? Nobody dressed like that around the harbor.

"Okay. Mr. Marlboro Man, why not you go back and look for him, you know? Just pretend we do not even talk so you not make trouble for me. You come in and you walk right by me, okay? Now, I have work to do." She grabbed a forlorn-looking tripletail by the nose and tossed it into the cooler.

When it was clear the girl wasn't going to look up again, O.B. self-consciously ambled to the door and entered the processing plant.

He was met by a powerful odor of shrimp and fish and his nostrils flared in response. In front of him twenty or so Vietnamese women raked wet, brownish shrimp off a noisy conveyor onto a long table where they were deftly ripping the little crustaceans' heads off, two shrimp heads at a time, and then throwing the headless bodies into slatted wooden crates filled with ice. A big bearded man in gray coveralls and rubber boots weighed the shrimp that fell into a big oblong pan from another cranking conveyor that, O.B. surmised, led out the back of the building and down to the holds of the shrimp trawlers. A few of the Vietnamese women sneaked glances at O.B., looking in the noisy processing plant like the proverbial fish out of water that he was.

Finally the bearded man turned around and saw him. "Yeah?" he yelled, over the din. "Whataya need?"

"I'm looking for Mr. Bao," Sergeant Hadnott yelled back.

The bearded man shook his head no. "Not here. Out of town." He looked at the Ranger momentarily then resumed weighing the shrimp and making notes on a yellow pad before he dumped the glistening load onto the conveyor that would lead to the creatures' ultimate decapitation by the busy Vietnamese hands.

Unfazed, O.B. surveyed the big room. Oily black nets hung from one section of the warehouse smelling faintly of tar. Coils of rope and all sizes of shackles, turnbuckles and J-hooks were arranged on shelves in another area. It was as foreign looking to O.B. as a tack room on a West Texas ranch would have seemed to one of the Vietnamese headers.

O.B.'s eyes followed a narrow staircase that led up the side of building. Through the dirty window of an upstairs office he saw motion behind a desk—someone talking on a telephone.

The Ranger ascended the stairs and at the top of the landing a burly man who had been dozing in a folding chair sprang awake. He stood up quickly and grabbed Hadnott by the arm. The Ranger stopped and looked down at the rough hand that was wrapped partially around his biceps.

He raised his eyes and set them on a flat, tough-looking oriental face. "You mind removing your hand from my arm, before I do it for you?"

They glared at each other for a few seconds until the man, his eyes flitting back and forth between the Ranger's face and the badge pinned to his shirt, slowly released his grip. O.B. straightened his sleeve and turned to go to the office. He knocked once and walked in uninvited.

A slight, bespectacled man bent over an unrolled chart laid out on a large cluttered desk. He spoke in Vietnamese on an old-fashioned black telephone. He quickly sized up the tall lawman standing in the door of his private office and hung up the phone. He rose from his chair and greeted his guest with a forced smile.

"Good afternoon...officer?"

"I'm Sergeant Hadnott from the Texas Rangers and I was hoping to be able to talk with you for a minute. You would be Mr. Bao?"

"Yes, that is correct," he answered, still smiling. "Please take a chair." He motioned to a ladder-back chair sitting next to a dented filing cabinet. O.B. grabbed the chair, moved it to the desk and sat down. He placed his Stetson on his lap.

"What is it that I can do for you, Sergeant Hadnott?" Bao finally asked.

"Well, it looks like we've managed to get through the hardest part already," he said.

"I don't understand, Sergeant."

"Just finding you here, in your office, after so many of your employees said you were out of town."

"Ah. I apologize for that. I must admit I gave my staff strict instructions not to disturb me. As you might imagine, I have a most urgent desire to locate and call back to port the boats that belong to the Sea-Tex company. Very dangerous, these storms."

At that moment the short wave radio began to crackle. The sing-song patter of Vietnamese emanated from the radio and Bao reached back and lowered the volume.

Hadnott noticed a couple of dusty CCTV monitors sitting on the work space lining the wall, tucked between rows of marine catalogs and three-ring binders. Black and white images of water and grass and an occasional road sequenced one after another on the video monitors. O.B. could not tell where the video signals came from, but they weren't from the harbor or the Sea-Tex building. He speculated that Bao must have one hell of a powerful wireless transmission system.

"You're the owner of the Sea-Tex Company, Mr. Bao?"

Bao smiled again. "I am afraid not, Sergeant Hadnott. This operation is part of a large holding company headquartered in Houston."

"A holding company?"

"Yes. Gulf Port Industries, Inc. is the name of the company. Regrettably, I know very little about them. My correspondence with them is limited to registered mail and the occasional telephone call."

Sergeant Hadnott pulled a pen and a notepad out of his pocket and scribbled a few notes. "And your position in the corporation?"

"Being a Vietnamese immigrant, I was hired to manage the company's small fleet of boats here in Fulton which, as you may have noticed, are increasingly manned by my countrymen. I am a hired hand, as you might put it here in Texas, working from the neck down." Bao beamed at Hadnott from across the desk.

O.B. reciprocated with a thin smile, but he was thinking what an accomplished liar this smug little so-and-so was. The research from Ranger Headquarters revealed that the Sea-Tex and Gulf Port businesses were effectively owned and operated by Mr. Nguyen Ngoc Bao through a shell corporation in the Cayman Islands. His control over the operation lay buried deep in the records, and it was a very sophisticated set-up, but the State Comptroller's office had said that there was no doubt; Bao called the shots and ran the show.

"And how many boats are under your management, Mr. Bao?"

"I am happy to say that Sea-Tex now operates seventeen trawlers out of the Fulton area," he answered proudly.

Another lie, Hadnott thought to himself. Austin had traced over fifty-seven boat registrations to Bao's organization. They were registered in every port on the Texas coast from Freeport to Port Arthur to Port Isabel. Some registrations with Gulf Port connections had even turned up in Louisiana.

"I see." He made a notation on his pad. "You've been very busy since you arrived here in United States. When, exactly, did you arrive, by the way?"

"It was in the spring of 1976. Shortly thereafter I received my American citizenship." He pointed to a framed document proclaiming him to be a citizen of the United States of America. Next to the certificate was a black and white photo of Bao standing next to a shrimp boat. O.B. observed a military insignia on the sleeve of the shirt he wore in the picture. "And yes, I am happy to say that I have been very busy."

"Your first boat?" O.B. asked, motioning to the photo.

"Yes. That is correct. I named her the *Texas Rose* in honor of my adopted state," Bao answered, testing the Ranger's patriotic predisposition. *Just one of the boys, officer. Call me Tex. God bless John Wayne.*

"What was your occupation in Viet Nam, Mr. Bao, before you came here?"

"Ah, Sergeant, such a long time ago. I come from humble roots, a small fishing village in the Mekong Delta area. It is an area not unlike the wetlands here on the Texas coast. Through the efforts of your government, I resettled to these shores and started a new life. For that opportunity I will be ever grateful."

"But you were in the military, too" noted O.B., nodding his head toward the photograph.

"The ARVN recruited heavily from the peasant class," Bao replied. "We had no choice in the matter."

"Right," said O.B. Headquarters had tracked down a handful of American liaison officers formerly stationed in Saigon who confirmed that Bao had been a full colonel in the South Vietnamese secret police, reputedly notorious for his brutality and his illicit side businesses. The report said that the CIA's folder on Colonel Bao was over three inches thick, covering all manner of questionable activities performed during his "service" to his country.

"Funny," O.B. continued. "I could have sworn I heard one of your employees refer to you as Colonel."

Bao ignored the remark. "Please pardon my curiosity Sergeant

95 | **15**

Hadnott, but what is the nature of your visit to my office? Is there a question about my immigration status? Because I can assure you that you will find everything in order."

Sergeant Hadnott decided to cut to the chase. He had little patience for verbal sparring. "As you no doubt know, there was a homicide last Saturday night in Key Allegro. Have you or any of your employees heard anything or do you know anything regarding the shooting of the victim, Mr. Neddy Pomade?"

Bao regarded the Texas Ranger carefully. Perhaps this law enforcement officer was different from the "go along, get along" police types he had dealt with in Fulton.

The Colonel knew nothing of the modern Texas Rangers and up to this point he had assumed that their glorified reputation was just a Hollywood façade—a fanciful and romanticized indulgence, like those Beefeaters at the Tower of London. He was surprised they still existed. Nonetheless, his instincts told him to watch his step with this one.

"I read of this in the paper," Bao replied. "And I would not know anything about that unfortunate event. Speaking for all of my employees, I can say that we...how do you put it here?... we do not *run* in that crowd. Key Allegro might as well be on a different continent than Fulton Harbor as far as we Vietnamese are concerned. We do not meddle in their affairs...in any way," he added, looking brazenly at Hadnott.

The Ranger dug in his wallet and pulled out a business card. "Nevertheless, if you do hear something, or if you do come across any information that might help us, I would appreciate it if you would give me a call." He held up the Aransas Pass DPS card and then tossed it on the table.

"One more question Mr. Bao, so you can get back to your fishing business. There have been reports of illegal smuggling activities in these waters. Do you know if any of the employees in your fishing fleet might have observed anything of this nature?"

"I try to keep close watch over all of this company's investments, Sergeant. I hire the boat captains, I supervise the outfitting of the trawlers and I carefully chart the productivity of each boat. We are a seafood company. And *our* business is to harvest shrimp, fish and crabs. I can assure you that none of my men would be involved in...smuggling activities."

"I just asked if they might have seen or heard anything, Mr. Bao."

"No, Sergeant Hadnott. They have not. They would have told me. There are no secrets around the docks."

"Of course not," O.B. said tonelessly. The Ranger rose from the chair and placed his hat back on his head. "Mr. Bao. Thank you for your time. I assume I will be able to reach you here in case I have any more questions?"

"Possibly. Possibly not. If the hurricane changes its course and passes close to Fulton, then I cannot promise I can be reached here."

"Oh, yeah, the hurricane," O.B. repeated. "I guess that could change the situation."

"They usually do, Sergeant."

"Well, good day Mr. Bao," said O.B, turning to leave the office.

"Colonel," Bao said tersely.

"I beg your pardon?"

"It's *Colonel* Bao...*Sergeant*."

A tight-lipped smile formed on Sergeant Hadnott's face. *Twenty South Vietnamese colonels and a major wouldn't equal one Texas Ranger you skinny little pissant*, thought O.B.

"Good day...*Mr.* Bao."

O.B. walked out, scowling at Bao's bodyguard as he went. He exited the building through the fish market but the pretty girl behind the counter was gone. He wouldn't have noticed her anyway because his mind was busy figuring out how he was going to pin the lying immigrant gangster's ears back. Hurricane or no hurricane.

━━━━

CHAPTER 16

The following day, after breakfast and another chart reading, Charlie switched off the radio and surveyed the horizon. It was overcast and gusty but not stormy yet. He and Raul took advantage of the relative calm and spent several hours doing minor repairs and adjustments to the boat. The rising ocean swells were increasing so he and Raul lowered the stabilizers to moderate the pitching.

By lunch, Charlie's battery had run down. He was exhausted. Only six days back and he'd been stabbed, witnessed a sniper take out an aide to a Texas Senator, gone toe to toe with Fu Manchu, and been affronted by an attractive Woman of Mystery. He decided he needed a nap.

"Listen up Raul, your job is to stay tuned to that radio while I catch forty winks." Raul looked puzzled. "While I sleep," Charlie amended. "Wake me up if you hear them say anything about the storm changing directions. Or in two hours, whichever happens first. *Comprende?*"

Raul nodded, a serious expression on his face.

"That would be three o'clock. You got it?" He gestured toward the clock in the pilothouse.

"*Sí, Charlie.*"

"Okay, I guess you and Ringworm are in charge now," he added, softening his tone a bit. "Permission to pass out, First Mate de la Rosa?"

Raul laughed and saluted. *"Adelante, Charlie."*

Charlie climbed into the bottom bunk, closed his eyes and immediately fell asleep.

—

Earlier that morning, Miguel Negron turned on the lights in the Key Allegro Marina store/restaurant/cocktail lounge, fired the burners on the stove, and started a pot of coffee. He enjoyed the early mornings before the regulars arrived. It afforded him time to mull over such thoughts as meandered onto his personal *tabula rasa.* He flicked on the radio and listened to the weather report. Hurricane Lana had entered the Gulf and was changing directions every few hours, heading everywhere from Vera Cruz to Mobile, Alabama. Landfall was a meteorological crapshoot. He looked out past the cafe area through the front window towards the crimson east. *Red sky at morning, sailor take warning. Now why the fuck did I think of that,* he wondered idly.

Within minutes the red sunrise changed to orange and then to a disturbing saffron color. The sickening glow filled the entire building and the interior of the room. Miguel, who had ridden out Hurricane Beulah in the county jug in Brownsville, had a bad feeling about Lana. *If I blow away to Cuba, I'm gonna have Marisol's ass,* he thought.

The last thing he wanted was a change in the weather. Or any kind of change for that matter. For better or worse, Fulton and the Key Allegro Bar & Grill had started to feel like home to him.

Later that afternoon Marisol dropped by the Marina to discuss Miguel's hurricane evacuation plan—there were procedures to be followed whenever a parolee left town or his job. Up until now the hurricane swirling offshore had been something of an abstraction to Marisol, but the empty boat basin and boarded-up buildings she passed on the way to the Marina underscored the urgency of the impending situation and caused her to worry. A savage storm was out there in the Gulf...and maybe Johnny was out there, too. In the back of her mind she harbored the faint hope that someplace, somehow, he was still alive. She also worried briefly for Charlie and Raul, who day before yesterday had unexpectedly disappeared from Fulton Harbor, presumably on the *Ramrod*—headed for safer environs, she hoped.

But Miguel wasn't planning to go anywhere.

"I'm stayin' here, *chica*," he mumbled. He was holding a half-dozen roofing nails in his mouth and was about to hammer a 4x8 piece of quarter inch plywood over one of the restaurant bay windows. It was a modest little business but he had been charged with running it. That meant protecting it from fire, storms, looters or any other threat. Mother Nature be damned, that bitch.

"It'll be dangerous," Marisol warned.

Miguel snorted. "Right. I'm shakin' in my boots."

"The weather report said the barometer is going through the basement; everyone with any sense is getting as far away from here as they can get."

"This morning they said it was going to Mexico."

"That's what everybody thought. But about two hours ago they got an update from one of those hurricane hunter airplanes. The storm buttonhooked back north, and it looks like it's taking dead aim for Fantasy Island here."

Miguel either didn't hear or didn't care what his friend and parole officer had said, so Marisol reluctantly picked up a hammer and bag of nails and began helping him button up the building. Balancing on a ladder, struggling to holding down a sheet of plywood in the rising wind, she remembered the punch line to one of Mark Twain's favorite shaggy-dog stories: "Gawd help the sailors at sea on a night like this."

—

Charlie landed face down on the floor and it took him a second to realize that he had been thrown there from his bunk. He grabbed at the doorframe and tried to pull himself to his feet. The boat pitched violently and Charlie suppressed a strong impulse to panic when he looked out the door at the roiling sea, gray and menacing in the twilight. The dog stood unsteadily in the middle of the galley, watching Charlie with worried eyes.

What the hell time is it? Charlie wondered, trying to surface from a fog of deep sleep. He stumbled into the galley, cursing as he banged into the mess table. Raul was curled up fast asleep in the big captain's chair, his Walkman earphones wrapped around his head. The clock said it was almost 7:00 p.m.

"Holy shit!" Charlie gasped.

Charlie switched on the short wave unit over Raul's head and the loud crackling, as the radio settled into its frequency band, nearly caused the boy to fall out of his chair.

"Start the engines and head up into the wind, Raul," Charlie said in a low voice. He took a reading on the Fathometer to gauge his location in the Gulf from the depth of the sea. The *Ramrod* had drifted further southeast.

"*Lo siento*...I mean, I am sorry Charlie. I...I don't know what...."

"Forget it," Charlie said without looking up. "Make sure everything is secured outside." Raul scrambled out of the wheel room. "And be careful on deck!" he yelled after him.

No nonsense now. The wind had picked up considerably and it had begun to rain.

As the ever-steady voice of the marine weather channel began broadcasting the status of the storm, Charlie grew pale. The pallor deepened as he finished plotting the coordinates and calculating the size, speed and direction of what the radio voice now called an "extreme" hurricane. Glancing at the barometer, he saw that incredibly, the pressure had dropped an inch in the last six hours to 28.5.

"We're sitting on the edge of the freakin' hurricane," he said out loud. He hollered for Raul to come inside the cabin. "Raul," Charlie struggled to keep his voice calm, "the storm has changed directions and picked up speed. We're going to have to try and beat it home. Get the life jackets out and let's put 'em on, then we'll pull in the stabilizers and secure all hatches, windows and doors. *Entiendes*?" Raul nodded. "It's going to be rougher than all hell on the trip back."

He didn't tell Raul that in a very short time Lana had not only changed its track and speed, but had also mushroomed into a full-bore hurricane that was bearing down on them at approximately fifteen knots.

Charlie plotted the shortest distance to port and found his options discouraging. The closest harbor was Port Aransas to the southwest, but to get there he would have to cross into the path of the rapidly advancing front of the storm.

Too risky, he decided. If he had enough fuel he could head up the coast to Pass Cavalo. Charlie checked his fuel gauge and frowned. That would be cutting it way too close, and he couldn't risk being caught close offshore or in open water with no power.

The only other choice was a narrow passage called Cedar Bayou, the elusive, winding cut that sliced through the barrier island of Matagorda. It lay almost directly in between the first two options and offered the shortest distance to shore. It was usually inaccessible but Charlie recalled fishing the cut at high tide a time or two with his brother. A rising storm tide increased his chances that the narrow cut might be passable, but only a little.

He'd have to risk it. If Jean Lafitte could do it in a two-masted schooner, thought Charlie, then by God so could he. But to get there would require running his vessel wide open in heavy seas to reach the cut in time.

Raul reappeared in the cabin, wide-eyed and soaked to the bone. His life jacket was open and most of the buttons on his flannel shirt had been ripped away by the wind. "Do I use the sea anchor, Charlie?" he asked anxiously.

Charlie thought for a moment. The anchor would help keep the vessel stern-on to the heavy seas—less chance of getting rolled by a wave, but.... "No, Raul, it'll slow us down too much, and we have a long way to go." He glanced over at the boy, who looked like he'd been keelhauled. "You and the dog better keep inside the cabin from here on out," he said. But Ringworm had already found refuge under the mess table, wedging himself between a box of nautical maps and the bench seat.

The first couple of hours were the worst. They encountered waves that Charlie estimated to be at least twenty-five feet high—waves that crashed over the boat and completely engulfed the pilothouse in green water for a few horrifying seconds. Howling gusts shook the cabin violently and Charlie wondered if the wind might rip the structure off the deck and carry it up and away.

When the black night came he couldn't see the surface of the sea or anything else outside of the windows. Walls of water washed over the boat and blew by in solid sheets, and rare glimpses of his bow were obscured by airborne streaks of foam. He was especially fearful that a rogue wave would appear out of the darkness and hit them abeam, rolling the vessel over entirely.

Raul stood next to Charlie at the helm, clutching the front console, his legs bent to absorb the shock as the *Ramrod* pitched and reeled against the sea. He frequently looked over at the captain's face, which was bathed by the lights of the instrument panel. Charlie stood at the wheel gripping the polished wooden knobs, staring intensely into the darkness. He did not seem to Raul to be afraid.

Raul wanted to be brave too, mostly to prove he was tough, but also to redeem himself in Charlie's eyes after his blunder earlier that evening. Charlie hadn't seen him hurl his Walkman into the sea after he was sent from the cabin to secure the decks. He should have kept alert. He should have concentrated on the boat, he told himself. In truth, Raul was terrified of hurricanes, but he was more afraid that he would be sent back to Mexico. He wanted desperately to prove to the new captain that he was a worthy first mate, come hell or high water. Especially high water.

Eventually, gradually, the violent winds began to slacken and the monster waves to diminish, and after six long hours they were able to punch through the leading edge of the hurricane. Charlie estimated that they would make landfall around first light, which would put them in Mesquite Bay at least an hour or two before the cyclone. Then he could motor into the relative safety of the Victoria Channel, a man-made barge canal that cut thirty-five miles into the mainland, where he could tie up the boat and ride out the hurricane.

—

CHAPTER 17

A gloomy, blustery dawn revealed the inconspicuous landmarks that marked the entrance to Cedar Bayou. As an unofficial passage (not even a passable passage according to most), no official markers indicated the narrow cut that divided Matagorda and San José Islands. But Charlie recognized the shape of some high dunes near the channel and located the exposed rigging of a sunken trawler that marked the entrance to the bayou. Charlie and Raul could see huge waves thundering onto the shore, rushing right up to the base of the sand dunes that normally rested a hundred yards back of the surf.

Charlie knew that if he miscalculated his approach to the mouth of the channel the *Ramrod* would run aground and be flipped onto the beach. If he wanted to survive he would have to thread the needle and be damn careful about it.

"Are you ready for this, *chavo*?" Charlie asked Raul. The young boy eyed the ill-omened mast of the wrecked boat that revealed itself between the mountains of water that lay before them, wondering what had happened to the crew of *that* boat. He looked away, shrugged, and raised his hands, palms up, in the classic expression of Latin fatalism, as if to say "It is in God's hands," or perhaps more appropriately, "What fucking choice do we have?"

Charlie grabbed the wheel of his boat, clinched his teeth and pushed the twin throttles forward. The boat pitched violently in the massive swells and he struggled to keep the bow heading up into the narrow slot that pierced the barrier island. They flinched involuntarily when the horizon vanished from their view as the boat dipped into a trough of water, and then their breath returned when the soggy shore reappeared once again, a little closer than before. Twice they felt the keel of the boat slide across a sand bar, but within minutes (an eternity) they traversed the split and were slowly and carefully piloting the *Ramrod* through the winding Cedar Bayou channel.

Charlie slapped the console with his hand. "Still a hell of a boat!" He looked at Raul and winked. "Pretty nifty, eh *hombre?*"

"*De veras, Capitán,*" said Raul smiling. He exited the cabin and retrieved the long bamboo sounding pole from below decks so he could help the *Capitán* navigate their boat through the tricky stretch of water. Johnny's brother had *cojones* alright—just like Johnny did. He braced himself against the rail on the bow and began pushing the long pole into the muddy white-capped water, sounding the depth, grinning the entire time.

Once they were safely out of the snaky bayou and into Mesquite Bay, Charlie turned the wheel over to Raul and went back to inspect the outriggers, mast and cables. He looked back at the giant storm, and through the hazy daybreak he could make out a towering wall of cumulonimbus clouds poised at the edge of the Gulf, dark purple where the wall met the sea, and then a menacing gray all the way up to their billowing silver tops. The dog reappeared and relieved himself near the scupper hole, and then he sat down next to Charlie and looked up at him reproachfully.

"Scared the pee out of me too, Ringworm."

It was gusty and getting rough in Mesquite Bay as they approached an imposing oil and gas service platform en route to the Victoria Cut. The platform was fastened to a forest of heavy creosote pilings in the middle of the bay. On the roof of the metal building that capped the platform a long row of seagulls strained against the offshore gale. Padded pilings lined the loading dock on the lee side of the structure and a steel mesh staircase climbed up to the corrugated tin structure on top.

"Raul?"

"*Si, Capitán!*"

"What were you planning to cook us up for breakfast on this fine fall morning?" Stress always produced a ravenous appetite in Charlie, and after the previous night's run to shore he felt like he could eat an entire feral hog.

"All we have left is that snapper fish I catched yesterday. And a can of some colored greens," Raul responded.

"Collard greens, and an old stinky fish. That's what I thought. With the hurricane coming, it could be a couple of days before we find a store that'll be open for business."

Charlie strained his eyes to read a recent-looking sign that had been posted on the structure. The sign said SEA-TEX CORPORATION. TRESPASSERS WILL BE PROSECUTED TO THE FULL EXTENT OF THE LAW. *Great*, he thought. *Bao's outfit.*

"Raul, let's you and me see if anyone left some grub around before they closed up for the storm. They're bound to have a can of beans or something stashed away. I'll pay the proprietor back later. He'll understand," he said hopefully.

Raul regarded the platform dubiously and cast a fearful eye behind him at Hurricane Lana, which was ripping up the sea not so far away. He wanted to move as far away from the storm as he could. The last thing he wanted to do was stop at *this* place. He'd seen the Sea-Tex sign too.

Charlie carefully motored up to a cluster of thick pilings and Raul threw a wide loop over the top of the tallest post and wrapped the other end of the line around a cleat on the bow. Charlie emerged from the stern with a pair of rusty bolt cutters he dug out from under the sacks of bird chow that still lay molding in the lazaret.

"Ease out another twenty feet of line and hang loose for a few minutes," Charlie yelled. "I'll be right back."

As Charlie began his ascent up the catwalk steps, pausing briefly to cut a heavy chain that secured a wire mesh door, he realized he was being followed by a camera that was encased in a heavy metal housing bolted to the building. The camera panned and tilted to follow his every movement. Charlie waved at the camera, opened his mouth and pointed inside to signify (Charlie hoped) that he was hungry, then he pointed to the building above him, smiled and flashed the camera a peace sign before continuing up the steps.

On top of the platform, Charlie clutched the handrail and bowed his head to the wind while he walked around the heavy reinforced structure looking for an entrance. He tried to peer through the darkened windows but they only reflected his face and cupped hands. He found a sturdy steel door and used the bolt cutters to snap the stainless steel padlock, but a deadbolt still secured the door. Using the tool like a crowbar he inserted the tip into the jamb and began to pry.

"This is gonna cost me some change," he said aloud. He almost fell backwards when the door finally gave way with a loud crack. He leaned over the edge of the rail and gave the thumbs-up sign to Raul, who waved warily from the boat.

Charlie entered the room and looked around. The place looked like a small wellhead operation but he was surprised how clean and neat it was. Other bay rigs he'd seen were littered with dirty coffee cups, old magazines and greasy rags and tools.

He noted the thick pipe tubing that housed the drilling shaft, piercing the center of the room like a fire station pole. A large diesel generator and a couple of Uninterruptible Power Supply units rested against the wall, and numerous valves, gauges and other apparatus jutted out of the pumping equipment in the middle of the room. But it felt wrong to Charlie—too clean, too meticulous.

Surveying the room, he noticed a shortwave radio station and a row of covered consoles and cabinets against the wall. He untied the heavy canvas tarp that blanketed the console, hoping to find an icebox or a pantry. His eyes widened as the unfolding tarp revealed multiple TV monitors adjoined by a computer keyboard and several control panels. He peeled off the remaining cover and stood back to assimilate the elaborate system of electronic equipment that lay before him.

The computer terminals and control consoles were equipped with buttons, switches and meters unrelated to this type of drilling operation. Metallic maps, studded with small LEDs, were built into the console, depicting the surrounding topography. Charlie marveled at the setup.

"I wonder what this mother does when you fire it up?" he asked aloud. He located the thick power cable, connected it to the power source and started flipping levers on the console. When he found the right switch the system purred to life and a dazzling array of lights began to blink on, accompanied by beeps and clicks.

"Bingo." As he studied the console he wondered why Sea-Tex (and

Bao) would install an expensive system like this out here, on a gas rig, in the middle of Mesquite Bay.

He was amused to discover that several familiar vistas appeared on the monitor screens as the video images locked on line. One screen displayed the cut leading into St. Charles Bay. After several seconds the picture switched to a northern field of view, exposing the upper reaches of the same bay, and then the screen changed abruptly to a shell road that led to a small dock.

Black and white video images of the surrounding bays continued to flash across the TV sets while small red lights blinked on and off across the electronic map board when the corresponding cameras switched onto the monitor screens. Charlie realized that the wind was beginning to blow the white caps off of the waves in most of the pictures.

"Time to split," he mumbled, but he remained transfixed in front of the monitors, mesmerized by the high-tech tour of the coastal bays. Out of the corner of his eye, Charlie caught the image of the *Ramrod* on a monitor screen. He tried a joystick on one of the keyboard controllers and was pleased to find that it controlled the pan-tilt unit that was mounted on the rig.

He enjoyed playing with the camera until he saw that the *Ramrod* was pitching alongside another boat below. It belatedly occurred to him that someone had simultaneously been watching *him* when he climbed up the steps to the shack.

"Shit!" he yelled. It was a crew boat, probably belonging to the rig, and to Bao. Charlie dashed to the thick glass window on the lee side of the platform. Two men rushed up the steps of the catwalk carrying automatic weapons.

Bounding to the busted door, he wedged a metal chair under the doorknob and frantically searched the room for a more substantial barricade. He ran to a heavy steel filing cabinet and, with strength fueled by fear and adrenaline, dragged it into place next to the chair. The men began shoving on the door with their shoulders.

Charlie looked for another exit but found only the one entrance. The men banged against the door with their bodies and the file cabinet began to nudge away from the wall. Charlie struggled to gain control of his thoughts.

"There has got to be another way out of here!" he screamed inwardly. "Think!" He picked up a metal folding chair and hurled it into the glass window, hoping to shatter the glass, but the chair bounced off and skittered across the room. Then his eyes fixed on the steel pipe casing that disappeared into a hole in the floor. He ran to the bolted trap door, slid back the latch bolt and pulled open the heavy-hinged cover. His eyes followed the sleek eternity of pipe that plunged vertiginously into the salty water below and then even deeper, he imagined, through hundreds of feet of mud, shell and rock.

Charlie sat on the edge of the precipice and contemplated the ridiculous options he had before him. As the metal filing cabinet crashed against the floor and the door flew open, he quietly slipped through the hole and free-fell fifty feet into the shallow bay.

At first Raul didn't know what he saw dropping like a heavy anchor through the middle of the platform's metal structure. He had hidden in the wheelhouse after the crew boat roared up beside him from the northwest. He had not seen the boat in time to sound his horn and warn Charlie. Peeking through the bottom of the window, Raul had seen two of the crewmen leap onto the mooring platform, and he'd seen their guns as well.

Leaning over the *Ramrod's* starboard rail, out of view of the crew boat, Raul saw Charlie's dripping head pop out of the water and he indicated to him that there was another man on the crew boat.

Charlie nodded and swam out to the line that secured the *Ramrod* to the piling. Removing a pocketknife from his belt scabbard, he struggled to grab the line that alternately disappeared into the bay when the bow dipped into the trough of a wave and then snapped taut, twelve feet out of the water when the next wave lifted the boat back up.

Charlie caught the line once but it was yanked from his hand before he could get the blade on it. He flinched when he heard the muffled pops of a low caliber handgun and the *zip* of the bullets entering the water near his head. The shots continued as Charlie dove under the water and Raul ran into the wheelhouse to crank up the engines.

When the gunman realized the shrimp boat next to him was manned, he fired into the wheelhouse with his revolver, shattering the port windows. Raul peeked through a porthole and saw the man on the boat trying to stabilize himself on the rocking deck as he reloaded his gun. Raul stood on his tiptoes and caught a quick glimpse of Charlie wrapped around the taut line like a night crawler on a hook.

Seeing the gunman aiming again at Charlie, Raul slammed both engines into reverse and spun the wheel hard to port, causing the stern to lurch toward the crew boat. An extended outrigger swept across the stern, knocking the gunman to the deck and smashing into the cabin.

At the same moment, Charlie managed to saw through the line at its maximum tension point and the freed line whipped him violently against the bow of the *Ramrod*. Dazed from a head wound after being catapulted into the boat, he managed to maintain his grip on the frayed tail of the rope. He dangled alongside the hull, his knife clenched between his teeth, as Raul desperately attempted to disengage the *Ramrod's* outrigger from the shattered window frame of the crew boat cabin.

Raul pivoted the trawler away from the crew boat and Charlie climbed over the gunwale as bullets began to rain down on them from the top of the rig. Charlie topped the bow and sprinted down the port side of the boat, diving for the open hatch of the lazaret. He could hear the dull thud of the bullets as they buried themselves into the wooden deck around him.

Raul overcorrected his turn and the *Ramrod* slammed against the crewboat. Charlie grabbed two sacks of bird chow and hugged them next to his body for a flak jacket and then sprinted for the cabin. Two slugs entered the smelly sacks of feed and one grazed his thigh before he could reach the safety of the cabin structure that shielded him from the gunmen above—but not the one on the crewboat. Charlie froze when he found himself looking down at the face of the man with the handgun, which he now pointed directly at Charlie's head.

"You're dead," the man said. Charlie stared across the gunwale at the bearded Anglo. Only a few yards separated the two men.

Without warning Charlie heaved the two sacks of chow over the rail. The man tried unsuccessfully to dodge them and they caught him square in the chest. He fell backwards in a heap and the sacks split open, sending the orange pellets scattering up and down the deck. Charlie took the wheel and reversed the diesels until they cleared the stern of the crew boat, and then he pointed the *Ramrod* for the mouth of Mesquite Bay and slammed the throttles forward.

Looking back over his shoulder, Charlie could see that the crew boat had busted loose from the pier and was blowing away from the rig. A great commotion of sea gulls had set upon the boat like a swarm of harpies, scarfing up Cap'n Johnny's Bird Chow pellets that had spread over the deck. The man on the boat flailed at the birds, trying to make his way back to the wheelhouse so he could retrieve his crew, who stood on the pier screaming at him to return. Charlie figured he had maybe a five-minute head start before the faster crew boat caught them again.

They barreled toward a narrow cut in Bludworth Island, heading for the Intracoastal Waterway. Raul looked over at Charlie's bleeding head and thigh. "Are you okay *Capitán*?"

"I think so," said Charlie, still panting from fear and exertion.

"Are you still *hongry*?" Raul asked, stone faced. Charlie's pursed lips broke into a broad smile.

"If it's not my mouth that gets us into trouble it's my stomach. *Verdad*, Raul?"

"*Así es*, Charlie."

Charlie laughed loudly and lightly punched Raul in the shoulder. "That was one *hell* of a job steering that boat back there, Raul! *Bien hecho, hombre!*" Charlie shook his head in disbelief. "Goddamn!"

The *Ramrod* entered the Intracoastal and Charlie gunned his engines, turning northeast towards San Antonio Bay. After a few minutes, he steered sharply into a small protected inlet called Ayres Dugout, shielded on both sides by tall scrub-covered spoil banks that partially obscured the boat.

"They will probably think we're heading the other direction, back towards Fulton," said Charlie. "As hard as it's raining, I don't think they'll be able to see us in here."

"Who are those guys, Charlie?" Raul asked.

"I don't know. I think they're part of Bao's group." Charlie had to shout over the gale.

"Why are they trying to kill us? *Por qué?*"

"I don't know that either Raul. Trespassing, I guess. Hell, I don't know. I'm going to go up on the roof and keep watch. You stay here in the wheelhouse and keep your eyes peeled, too. These bastards mean business."

———

CHAPTER 18

As gale force winds went from shrill soprano to basso profundo and storm swells rose by the second, Senator Llewellyn Cudihay staggered into the Key Allegro Marina Cafe, considerably the worse for wind and weather.

In spite of his misfortune, he seemed otherwise full of piss, vinegar and what Marisol judged to be an extravagant amount of cocaine and scotch for such an early hour.

O.B. Hadnott sat alone in a corner of the bar, his chair tipped back and his boot heels cocked in valiant repose on a nearby table. He either didn't notice the politico's chemically fueled condition or didn't choose to. Mostly, he tried not to let on that he was scared shitless. He deeply regretted his decision to drop in on the Marina to interview the convicted felon that HQ told him worked there. *Magnificent fucking timing, you moron,* he thought.

Wherever Cudihay had gotten his nose powdered, he wouldn't be going back for more any time soon. He owned close to a million dollars' worth of real estate just two hundred yards away, but it might as well have been on the moon. The rain, as all could see through the door which opened briefly to admit the Senator, howled sideways in sheets, and the wind rocked the few cars in the parking lot like baby cradles. With difficulty, Miguel wrestled the door shut and battened it down. Whatever happened now, they were on their own.

Cudihay spied Marisol in the lantern light and homed in on her like a Scud missile.

"Well, *Señor* Negron, how 'bout a Bloody Mary, *por fa-vor*," said the Senator loudly, throwing a twenty on the bar, "I want to be sure and tip sufficiently. Knowin' your history, and all. What is it, five guys you killed? You're a regular Billy the Kid."

"Two," said Miguel.

"Huh?" asked Cudihay, blinking at the bartender's terse reply. Outside, the wind notched itself up another dozen decibels.

"I have killed two men," said Miguel. "So far."

The implied threat sailed over the Senator's head like a laughing gull. He staggered across the room as another surge of wind and water shook the building. He set the glass in front of Marisol. "Here ya are, little lady. Ah bet you never been served a drink by a real murderer before. But don't you worry; the Governor made me an honorary Texas Ranger, jus' like Sergeant Whatnot over there. Ah'll defend your virtue. Up to a point, that is."

Marisol pushed the glass back toward the Senator. "Drink it yourself. Maybe it will keep your mouth busy with something besides talking."

"I can think of a few other things I could do with my mou...."

Just then, the entire building seemed to tilt on its axis as a massive surge of wind or water—it hardly mattered which—slammed into the storm shutters. The building actually rocked on its pilings, and the shelf upon which the kerosene lantern was perched collapsed. It rolled down the bar, trailing a flaming spume of lantern fuel. Then the light went out.

"Gawd!" bellowed the Senator from somewhere nearby, speaking for them all. O.B. Hadnott overbalanced himself and went Stetson-over-tea-kettle onto the grimy floor. Marisol yelped and the rest of the bar's denizens lurched for something stable to hang on to. She thought disjointedly back to something Johnny once said: "Lord, I don't want the ham or the cheese—I just want out of the sandwich...."

Miguel Negron righted himself first and began slapping wet bar towels on the patches of flame.

The wind got louder, entirely drowning out the idiot static on the shortwave and the ship-to-shore. Not that it mattered. Anybody still at sea at this point was beyond the power of speech or prayer.

—

Charlie squatted atop the cabin roof, squinting at the bay through the pelting rain. He noted that unbelievably, the wind was increasing. Unless the hurricane had dramatically changed direction again, it would make landfall somewhere nearby. It was like it had followed them in from the Gulf. Like it was hunting them. *Is it possible to piss off a storm?* he wondered.

Bao's crewboat was out there hunting him too, and Charlie felt like a jackrabbit hiding from a predator close on its scent. He resisted the urge to bolt for half an hour until a particularly violent gust of wind-driven rain finally sent him scrambling down the ladder.

"The hell with this cowboy and Indian shit," he hollered at Raul, "Let's get outta here! We still might make the Victoria Channel before it's too late."

Back in the cabin he glanced at the fuel gauge—nearly empty. Frowning, he checked the barometer. The reading was so low he refused to believe it at first. He thumped it several times and it stubbornly remained at 28 inches. The hurricane was sitting on them now. "Holy shit," said Charlie. "Raul!"

"Sir?"

"Where is your life vest? *El chaleco salvavidas*?"

"I...I don't know what happen to it. I think I take it off this morning."

"Never mind," said Charlie, realizing that his was missing too. "Just get in the cabin. Where's the dog?" He noticed Ringworm was standing at the boy's feet. Both of them were looking up at him anxiously. Charlie took a deep breath. No need to scare the boy any more than he already was.

The bay was getting meaner and Charlie motored as best he could through the narrow Intracoastal Waterway toward the open waters of San Antonio Bay. Twenty more miles to the Victoria Channel and he would be out of harm's way.

Raul was the first to spot the silhouette of the crew boat in the driving rain. The boat was heading directly toward them. Charlie spun the wheel around and reversed direction. He headed straight back for the reef-infested shallows of Ayres Bay hoping to lose the crew boat or run them aground. He navigated almost by instinct through the tricky waters—waters too shallow to be passable at normal high tide.

With the crew boat still behind them, Charlie struggled to maintain control of the *Ramrod* as he motored on through the interconnected bays, moving further and further away from Victoria Channel. For a few minutes he lost sight of them and decided to risk circling back through the Intracoastal to make one last run for the channel before the hurricane sank his boat.

"I think we lose them, Charlie," Raul shouted hopefully.

"Maybe," Charlie answered. "Here, take the wheel. I'm going to get a better look from the stern. Hold on tight, boy." Charlie gave the wheel to Raul and braced himself for the wall of water that engulfed him when he went out on deck.

At first he couldn't see anything behind him. Then gradually, through the waves of rain, he made out the faint outline of the crew boat. *Somebody taught that sea captain the ropes*, thought Charlie. In the safety of the deeper water, the powerful crew boat was gaining on them. Charlie couldn't believe they were still after him.

"Sons of bitches!" he screamed. It wasn't just about pursuing Charlie anymore; they were running for their lives, too. He figured these guys must be shit scared of Bao, because nobody would take these kinds of risks in a killer storm unless a threat of a death worse than drowning figured into the equation. As he clung to the mast and considered his options he noticed the bundled trawling nets straining to free themselves from the rigging. He ran into the wheelhouse and reached over Raul to pull down the twin throttles, reducing the engines to half speed. Raul looked at him like he was nuts.

"They're still behind us. You just maintain this speed and keep our present course, straight down the channel," he said. "I think I can throw a serious hitch in their get-along. *Comprende?*"

"No, sir," said Raul.

"Just keep her in the center of the channel," said Charlie pointing directly toward the tip of the bow with his fingers. He dug around in the toolbox and removed a large pipe wrench, which he waved in the air like a war club. Raul wondered if Charlie meant to throw the heavy tool at the other boat.

Charlie laughed maniacally and then exited the cabin into the raging storm. He clutched the rail and carefully inched his way back to the solid wooden fishing doors secured in racks on either side of the boat. The doors served to submerge the nets and spread them in the water when they trolled the sea floor for shrimp. Without them, the nets floated behind the boat in a tangled mess slightly beneath the surface of the water. Charlie disconnected the nets from the doors and the nets unfurled behind the outriggers like a mane, attached to the boat only by the thick black cable that ran through the eyes of the outrigger and spooled around the massive winch that Charlie controlled with a three-foot lever.

Charlie let out some cable until the nets fishtailed in the water behind the *Ramrod*. Steadying himself, he grabbed the lever with both hands and squinted intently, looking for the vaporous outline of the crew boat. Visibility was almost nil and he waited for a break in the sheets of rain. Finally, the bow and front cabin of the crew boat materialized in the channel less than 150 feet away. Charlie slammed the winch lever over and the cable began spinning off the spool. The nets disappeared into the water and Charlie waited.

They had spotted Charlie. One of the men crawled on his belly onto the bow of the crew boat. Charlie could see that he held a rifle.

In the next moment, Charlie wasn't sure whether it was the nets fouling the crew boat's propellers, or the sudden explosive gust of wind that staggered the man as he rose to his knees to fire his gun. Whichever it was, the boat lunged, the man lost his balance and then abruptly vanished off the deck into the consuming waters. The boat began to fade into the gray swirling background and just before it disappeared from view, Charlie glimpsed its hull turn obliquely to the wind, veer into a spoil bank and then roll over.

Soon after the crew boat disappeared, Charlie turned his full attention to saving his own boat from the hurricane, which by now was crashing full force into Matagorda Island and churning its way through the bays, over the Blackjack Peninsula and across the Aransas National Wildlife Refuge.

He cut the cables and staggered back to the wheelhouse. In the tempestuous waters he struggled to control the boat's course through the bay. The wind-driven rain blasted through the shattered port window, drenching the instrument console and sending torrents of water through the cabin. The wind alternated between a slow plaintive wail and a low moan, a sound that nearly unnerved Charlie. Nevertheless, he managed to run his boat up into a narrow land cut just inside the boundary of the Aransas Wildlife Refuge.

Ultimately, he had to relinquish control of the *Ramrod* after a savage explosion of wind pinned her to a grassy bank by her outrigger and began to pummel her with wind and water. Charlie cut a section of line and fashioned a half-hitch knot around Raul's belly and then tied the other end around his own waist. Without forewarning, he grabbed Raul and jumped off the listing deck onto a bank of tall grass blown flat by the force of the wind. Ringworm jumped after them.

Less than a mile away, in a lull between gusts of wind, Charlie could see the outlines of the four-story concrete and steel observation tower that rose above a thicket of live oaks in the distance. Built to allow bird watchers to scan the refuge for Whooping Cranes and other avian rarities, it now looked like the only man-made object anywhere around capable of withstanding the storm's fury.

With Raul close behind him, connected by the coarse rope, the two started the slow, nightmarish journey toward the tower. They crawled on their hands and knees through the mud, shell and salt grass, gasping for air between the sheets of rain and bay water that traveled parallel over the surface of the marsh like they had been blasted from the barrel of a water cannon.

Some of the wind gusts lasted almost a minute and forced them to lie flat on their bellies in the mud, gripping the shrubs and clumps of grass to prevent them from being torn loose from the land. They continued, inch by inch, toward the tower, the only place Charlie could think of that might save them from the rising water and the sea surge that would soon rush like a rip tide over the littoral, sweeping up everything in its path. Somehow the dog managed to stay glued to Charlie's lee side, creeping along beside him through the salt marsh, his belly low to the ground.

When they finally reached the tower, they witnessed a storm surge that rose so fast that floodwaters literally chased them up the sloping cement pathway that led to the observation deck on top. The tide rose to eighteen feet above normal and forced them halfway up the ramped building before it stopped. Survival-minded rattle-snakes and water moccasins also sought refuge on the tower ramp, and Charlie and Raul had to fend them off with branches and sticks. An alligator attempted to share the tower with the dog and the two humans but eventually disappeared beneath the churning water to burrow into the mud below.

They settled in three-quarters up the ramp, slightly below the treetops and partially protected from the stinging water that sailed through the air above the oaks. Lying flat against the concrete ramp with their hands gripped tightly around the iron bars of the railing, the two responded to the hurricane onslaught in their own distinct ways.

Raul prayed desperately to the Holy Virgin of Guadalupe and to Michael the Archangel, patron saint of storms, to deliver them safely from the tempest. He made them a hundred promises that he fully intended to keep, if only he could survive to see one more day.

Charlie raged back against the calamity with primal screams and curses, barely audible even to himself over the din of the storm. He taunted the hurricane with challenges and insults to its parentage until he was hoarse.

Ringworm huddled between them, closing his eyes to the stinging rain. Deep down, both Charlie and Raul realized that Hurricane Lana wasn't listening. The storm was a primeval force, devouring light and sound, rationality and language—it didn't care whether either one of them lived or died.

After several hours the winds abruptly ceased. Finally trusting their senses to accept the stillness and silence, Charlie and Raul climbed to the observation deck at the top of the structure. Incredibly, a few minutes later, the late afternoon sunlight illuminated the surrounding area. They could see hundreds of birds floating above them in the still air. Below, swirling muddy waters covered everything but the leafy tops of the live oaks, which were a dark luminescent teal in the extraordinary light. The purple curtains of the hurricane encircled Matagorda Island and Charlie and Raul's concrete fortress. The *Ramrod* was nowhere to be seen.

"*Ya, Charlie?*" Raul asked. "It is over?"

"No Raul, only half over. *Estamos en el ojo*...the eye. There will be more to come." Charlie figured that the storm would rage until well past dark—long night ahead.

In the same moment, Charlie and Raul saw, or thought they saw, some movement in the water several hundred feet away. They realized it was a body, drifting on a large piece of wood. Charlie glanced down at the muddy brackish water below, which receded quickly as the storm surge drained out onto the wide coastal plain. Then he looked toward the southeast, the direction the fierce winds would come on the back side of the hurricane. He started down the ramp then turned back toward Raul. "It's the Christian thing to do, right?"

Charlie swam, and then waded in chest-deep water to get to the half-drowned man, keeping a wary eye out for snakes. He recognized him as the same man who had attempted to kill him just hours before—the man on the crew boat that Charlie had knocked down with the bird pellets. He was a muscular Caucasian man that appeared to be in his mid-forties. On his upper arm was a tattoo of a snake wrapped around a dagger. Charlie noticed with a shudder that the man's hand was nailed to a hinged wooden cabin door with a sixteen-penny nail. He lifted the man's head and looked at his bearded face.

"You alive?" he asked.

The man cracked open an eyelid and forced a weak smile when he recognized Charlie. "I guess that depends on you, friend," he said in a hoarse whisper.

"Where are you hurt?" Charlie asked, looking over the man's body.

"My legs are broke...and something's busted inside too," he said. "You kind of threw us for a loop back there in the chan...," he coughed violently and both of them noticed the blood that frothed from his mouth.

Charlie dragged the raft back to the cement tower, the man's legs trailing lifelessly behind him in the water. When they reached the ramp Charlie knelt down and looked the man in the eyes. "What's your name?"

"Sonny."

"Sonny, I'm going to have to take that nail out. The boy and I can't get you up the ramp if we don't. Why did they do it?" He nodded at the hand spiked to the door. "Why did they nail you to this thing?"

Sonny lifted his head and gave a wan smile. "They didn't do it. I did. Can't swim with my legs broke...didn't want to pass out and drown...no life vests on board, so I pegged myself to the cabin door before I lost my boat." He cocked his sodden head at Charlie "What the hell did you sink us with, anyway? Rope?"

"Nets."

"I'll be damned."

Raul held the man's free arm to the floor and Charlie put a foot on the door to hold it down, and then used all his strength to yank the hand and the nail out of the waterlogged wood. He pulled the nail on through by the head. The man did not scream but after a moment his eyes rolled back in his head and he passed out. Charlie and Raul carried the broken, unconscious body up the ramp and sat the man against the railing.

After a few minutes, Sonny regained consciousness and observed the two men sitting against the rail. One of them, the older one, rested his arms on his knees, gazing out at the sea. The other one, the dark-skinned boy, sat with his head against the rail, his eyes closed. They were scratched and bruised and their tattered clothes hung on them like Spanish moss. An ugly yellow dog had crawled into the boy's lap.

"Why did you fish me out of the water when you saw who I was?" he asked. Charlie regarded the man calmly and shrugged his shoulders. Sonny continued. "You know how to handle a boat pretty good, Sweetwater."

"How do you know my name?"

The man ignored the question. "I can appreciate a good captain when I see one. I piloted a gunboat in Nam." He coughed hoarsely, his breathing labored. "That's where I met Bao." Charlie straightened up, listening closely. "You two be careful," said Sonny. "The Colonel is one mean motherfucker."

"Don't waste your strength talking," said Charlie. "We'll get you out of here as soon as this little blow is over, then we'll take you to a hospital."

Sonny started to chuckle but winced instead. "I'll be dead before morning and you know it, friend," he wheezed. Racked by another fit of coughing, he passed out again. Charlie propped him upright against the wall and trickled some rainwater into his mouth. He cut a section of the rope he had used as a lifeline and tied the unconscious man to the rail so the storm would not take him. In a few moments nothing but the metal rods of the ramp rail would separate them from the vicious onslaught of wind and rain, but it was safer than the turbulent waters that swirled below them.

Charlie and Raul stood and braced their hands on the wall facing the Gulf. They both sensed the passing of the eye at the same time. The sun disappeared into a haze and it grew dark. A southwestern breeze began to bathe their faces and they involuntarily tensed up as they watched the sinister inner wall of the hurricane approach, quickly devouring the land and seascape to the south and southwest.

Soon it consumed the last lingering light of day as well.

Charlie grabbed a few lengths of rope and wrapped them around the rails next to Sonny and pulled Raul close by his side. The winds strengthened and they braced themselves for the savage bite of the storm. The rain assaulted them unmercifully. Charlie clutched the cold wet railing with Raul and the dog curled up beside him.

At one point during the ferocious tail end of the hurricane, the dying boat captain regained consciousness and leaned over to Charlie. He grabbed Charlie by his ragged shirt and pulled his ear close to his bloody mouth. He spoke earnestly and continuously for several minutes, pausing now and then to suck in a labored breath. Charlie's head never moved from the man's shoulder until Sonny stopped speaking and soon afterwards stopped breathing as well.

Raul crossed himself while Charlie shut the dead man's eyes and laid his head on the pavement. Then Charlie, the dog and the boy hunkered down together next to the wall, forming a tight impenetrable scrum, and waited for the hurricane to pass. Sometime during the night the winds loosened the knots that held Sonny's body to the rail and the storm carried the body out to sea.

———

CHAPTER 19

"...power is in the process of being restored in the affected coastal counties. According to a representative of GCP&L, repair and cleanup efforts are being hampered by the many roads either damaged or washed out entirely by the Category Four hurricane, and by the high water that remains in many low-lying inland areas." Channel Ten newscaster Walter Furley read through the news, looking as bedraggled as the inhabitants that watched the dusty 26" TV mounted in the corner of Klein's Cafe in Rockport.

"In a hastily-convened press conference at the Aransas County courthouse, State Senator Llewellyn Cudihay urged the governor to relay a request for immediate federal disaster relief for the afflicted area." The camera switched to a clip of the Senator standing on the courthouse steps in an immaculate, tailored summer-weight suit worth a month's pay of nearly any of his constituents. Someone in the Senator's office in Austin had tossed a suitcase onto one of the first National Guard helicopter transports out of Camp Mabry.

"I have faith that the abiding compassion of our leaders in Washington will soon extend itself like a munificent blanket of succor over these storm-tossed multitudes," said Senator Cudihay with a pompous flourish.

Miguel looked up from the plate of waffles that he was wolfing down with alarming speed. "*Mentiroso*," he growled. He was in a real hurry to get back to his own restaurant. He had grudgingly agreed to accompany Marisol to Klein's so she could get to a working phone and check in with her supervisor in Austin.

Klein's Cafe was one of only two establishments in town that had a generator and working communication. But Miguel didn't want to call anyone, and he didn't care what had happened to the rest of the area. He worried only about himself, the Marina and their mutual well-being. He eagerly accepted his self-appointed role as guardian and protector of the property.

"Protection from what, exactly, Miguel?" asked Marisol, who sat across the table, nursing a tall mug of coffee.

"Looters."

"But we ate and drank everything in the place yesterday. What on earth would someone...loot?"

Miguel ignored the question and kept eating.

Marisol sighed, and reflected. Even now, she could not quite recall getting off the skinny Key Allegro island and making her way to Rockport that crazed morning. The winds had abated somewhat by dawn, and the fact of the sunrise itself seemed an incredible miracle. She and the rest of the Marina refugees emerged cautiously. Across the small bay, Rockport looked like a smashed wedding cake.

Everyone soon learned why no help or further companionship arrived before the storm reached its height. The small bridge to the mainland had crumbled before the onslaught of a panicked weekend skipper who had tried to gun his fifteen-foot tall cruising yacht at full throttle under the twelve-foot bridge. "Do the math," Miguel had muttered. Marisol had talked Miguel into scrounging up a skiff and paddling them across Little Bay so they could make their way over to Klein's.

The newscaster droned on: "The National Hurricane Center rated Lana as an 'extreme' Category Four storm, with top gusts of over 155 mph. The eye of the hurricane crossed the mainland at dusk yesterday, making landfall on the Aransas National Wildlife Refuge. On the local front, National Guard troops are arriving to augment the local sheriffs' departments to re-route traffic and discourage looters." Miguel looked up and gave Marisol an "I told you so" look.

"...Property damage is visibly extensive and could run up to a billion dollars. Human casualty figures are still rolling in, but it appears that so far, the toll in lives and injuries is expected to be light—thank God for that," he added.

Marisol was more intrigued by what she overheard from the muddy storm survivors that had staggered in that morning and who were exchanging their stories around the tables in the cafe. They told more "truth" about the hurricane than all the facts, statistics and aerial pictures combined.

One of Key Allegro's wealthier inhabitants had surfaced after the blow to find a flat-hulled crab boat afloat in his Olympic-sized pool. Someone else described how he saw an Assembly of God church in Aransas Pass demolished, while just 100 feet away, in Jimmy's Just Beer icehouse, drunken revelers in the midst of a Halloween hurricane party sang Bobby "Boris" Pickett's "Monster Mash" twenty-two times in a row, blissfully unscathed.

Instant karma, Marisol thought.

People were already calling the October 31 storm "The Halloween Hurricane"—a name that was sure to stick after horrified townsfolk said they witnessed a flood tide swamp the town's oldest cemetery, sending a macabre parade procession of coffins floating down a downtown street.

Miguel mopped the syrup on his plate with a piece of toast and stood up to leave. He stuck his tattooed hand into his back pocket to retrieve his wallet and Marisol stopped him. "My treat," she said. "A small token of my appreciation for the fine hospitality at your restaurant last night."

"It was my pleasure," he deadpanned.

—

Over on Ransom Island, the interior of Shady's was dark, dank and gamy. Vita half-expected to see the Creature From the Black Lagoon sleeping off a bender in the corner. Only faint slivers of sunlight found their way into the old building by way of the boarded-up door and windows and from beneath the floorboard cracks. Empty liquor bottles, beer cans, pitchers and glasses occupied every raised horizontal surface, while the floor was covered with sleeping bodies strewn around the large room like toys discarded by a messy and petulant little boy.

Vita walked through room surveying the damage. She had survived three hurricanes here, and although she could remember rowdier parties, she couldn't remember one any stranger than the one that had started yesterday morning and raged on long after Hurricane Lana had run inland.

In addition to the hurricane party regulars, seven Vietnamese families were coveyed up in a group in one corner of the building. Their makeshift hammocks and privacy curtains crisscrossed the rafters, windowsills and tables, forming a bizarre Third World mobile.

The families had been fishing in Redfish Bay when the fast-approaching storm prompted them to seek refuge at Shady's. They had hauled all of their personal contents from their boats into the main building and now the colorful fabrics and strange family heirlooms, precious objects from a recent, yet now very distant past, added an exotic flair to the rustic barroom interior. Vita hoped that their boats, which for most of them constituted both their homes and their livelihood, had outlasted the hurricane.

Stepping over several sleeping bodies, Vita made her way to the front door. Tucker Adderly lay on the welcome mat just inside the front entrance, clutching a beer can in his big hands. It rested on his ample belly and rose and fell with the peaceful rhythm of a pump jack, right in time with his prodigious snoring. Tucker loved a good hurricane party better than dove hunting and Southwest Conference football. He'd taken pains to trailer his sailboat inland, kiss his disbelieving wife and then speed back to Shady's against the steady line of evacuees.

Juan Estrada was still planted on a barstool like a mound of wet clay, his face flattened against the tile bar top. Bob and Peggy Storey slept on a pair of pushed-together domino tables. Vita vaguely recalled Bob announcing to all and sundry that he would personally maim the shit out of anyone who encroached on his improvised bed.

Mingus, Rupert's liver-colored hound dog, sat near the door waiting forlornly for somebody to open it so he could go pee.

Vita stooped to pet the dog and then grabbed a claw hammer and began tearing at the three-quarter inch plywood that had successfully barricaded the door from the storm. Tucker opened one eye to observe the clatter then closed it again.

"Don't get up, Tucker," she said. "As soon as I air out this gymnasium I'll serve you breakfast in bed."

"Do I hear the voice of Saint Vita?" Tucker whispered from the floor. "Healer, Provider and God's Best Bartender?" Vita wrenched out the remaining nails in the plywood, unbolted the double doors and threw them open, letting in a flood of bright sunlight. He moaned and sat up against the wall rubbing his bloodshot eyes. "I feel like I've been eaten by a wolf and shit off a cliff."

"Really pathetic, Tucker," said Vita, as she stepped out onto the deck to observe the condition of Ransom Island in the light of day.

"I need a cup of coffee," he groaned.

Vita paid him no attention. She was taking stock of the property. The flood tide had receded and she saw that most of their island was still visible and had not been reclaimed by the bay, a slow but inevitable fate for many of these small nubs of sand and shell, but a process hastened by the massive torrents of water driven over the islands by a hurricane. Apparently, The Shady Boat and Leisure Club had indeed dodged another bullet. She noted that the high water mark had reached the top step of the stairs, which climbed up eight feet from the soggy ground. All manner of debris clogged the landscape—small skiffs, Styrofoam ice chests, crab traps, old tires, at least one dead cow and tons of seaweed. Most of the island's dock pilings poked above the water, but Vita had no doubt the storm had stripped away the dock planking and finger piers. She sighed, thinking of the work that lay in front of her.

Of course it was a borderline miracle anything remained in place at all, she reflected. If the tide had risen another few feet, Shady's could have been forced off its pilings and floated away. Vita had witnessed entire homes wash out to sea. Or, equally horrifying, if the building had held fast to its mooring and the water had continued to rise, it could have turned the beer palace into a gruesome underwater mausoleum.

Both scenarios were sobering and Mrs. Earl Rupert Sweetwater firmly resolved to experience her next hurricane in the safety of a San Antonio Riverwalk hotel room, watching reports on the Cable Network News channel—with or without her husband.

Vita found a cigarette in her blue work shirt and lit it with an official Shady's lighter, which featured a topless hula girl on the cartridge. In the calm following the storm, Vita allowed herself to indulge in a few dark thoughts and a blue mood. But only until she finished her smoke, she promised herself.

She heard Mingus barking his hoarse, gravelly bark at something moving amidst the wreckage on the western shore. She strained to make out the two shapes picking their way through the shallow pools and piles of refuse left by the storm. The tall figure had a T-shirt wrapped around his head in a turban, and held a long paddle in his hand like a staff. The shorter one wore a gimme cap and wielded a shorter paddle, which he swung around idly, occasionally stabbing it to the ground to pop a beached Portuguese Man-o-War or to poke at other random objects he encountered as he walked. A yellow dog followed on the heels of the boy. Mingus stopped barking and ran to them, wagging his tail.

"Charlie Sweetwater," Vita said under her breath. "...and his motley crew."

Charlie and Raul approached and stopped in front of Shady's, looking up at Vita on the stoop. "What's it gonna take to finally wash this place away?" Charlie asked.

Vita smiled broadly and descended the steps. "You two look terrible. Where on earth did you come from? Where did you weather the storm?"

"With the Whooping Cranes over at the Refuge," Charlie began, and then seeing Vita's puzzled look said, "I'll tell you our story if you tell me yours. After coffee and breakfast maybe? Raul and I could eat a bucket of tits."

Raul giggled and Vita playfully slapped him on the back of the head. "You're always welcome here, even if one of you could stand to have his mouth washed out with soap," said Vita. "Come on in. You guys look like you need a nurse more than a fry cook. Is the leg bad?" Vita pointed to Charlie's bloodied thigh bandage, which he had fashioned from a pair of ratty Hanes jockey shorts.

"Nah. It only hurts when I walk," said Charlie.

"OK, breakfast first, then I go to work on you guys," said Vita.

Inside, bodies began to stir and someone was attempting to boil water on the gas burner. "How did y'all get on the island?" Vita asked as the two entered the door of the honky-tonk.

"Found us a washed up skiff in the flats next to...." Charlie paused just inside the entrance. "Good God, Vita! This here's the real disaster. You running a leper colony now, or what?"

Tucker Adderly, still on the floor in the safety of the shadows, held out his hand to Charlie. "Alms for the poor."

"Tucker!" Charlie laughed. "You look like dog shit. Get up, man!

Vita said she'd fix us all breakfast."

"Did I say that?" asked Vita, making her way toward the kitchen.

"Saint Vita will feed the multitudes and turn salt water into wine," Tucker affirmed. "She delivers babies into the world. Verily, she is a giant among us." Tucker started trying to struggle to his feet.

"Looks like she throws one hell of a party too."

"Verily," said Tucker.

Charlie heard an infant crying somewhere in the Vietnamese encampment. "Did you really deliver a baby last night, Vita?"

"The Chu family decided to name their new son Shady," said Vita. "We are so honored."

Charlie laughed. "Shady Chu. Ain't that a bitch?"

He waved at the Vietnamese families who were unstringing hammocks and gathering their kids and belongings, recognizing quite a few of them. "Jesus, Vita, you got half the Vietnamese fishing industry staying with you."

"Nowhere else to go yesterday," she replied.

Charlie yelled to the group, "I counted seven trawlers still tied up safe and sound to their moorings at the Ransom ferry dock." He held up his hands and showed them seven fingers. "Seven boats." An instant confusion of voices followed as the fishermen discussed and speculated on this piece of news. Perhaps they were still in business after all.

"Where's Rupert?" Charlie asked Vita.

"Check the bathroom in the back room," Vita answered. "That's where I left him this morning. He wasn't feeling so good." Walking by the bar on the way to the kitchen, she tapped Juan Ezekiel Estrada Esquire III on the shoulder.

"Juan, hon, you're going to have to remove yourself from my bar so I can try and make some breakfast." Juan Estrada lifted his head and looked around, confused. A bottle cap was stuck to his cheek.

Vita started shouting out orders to some of the guests regarding their immediate instructions for the preparation of breakfast. "Pete, you start the generator and get your sons to fetch some fresh water from the tank! Juan, clear the bar! Tucker, you want coffee so bad, why don't you get up and make us some? And Peggy, if Bob promises not to stab any of our guests, he can cut up some potatoes for hash browns. We've got a passel of hungry folks here."

Raul spotted a couple of Vietnamese boys that he knew from Fulton

Harbor. He approached them and they began to quietly share their tales.

Charlie found Rupert on his knees in front of the toilet, his chin resting on the porcelain seat. He didn't look at all well. "You okay down there, Rupe?" he asked.

"Yeah, fine, fine. I'ze just down here gettin' a drink," he replied. Rupert turned around and grinned. "Charlie? How the hell are you?"

"Good. I was feeling sorry for myself, 'till I saw you. But I feel better now. Thanks."

"Don't mention it," said Rupert, slowly getting to his feet. "That was one mother-scratchin' hurricane party. And a hell of a hurricane, too." He lumbered to the sink and stuck his entire head under the running water until it was soaked.

Charlie looked for a towel and not finding one handed him a t-shirt from the bed. "You're out of towels."

"Oh yeah, we had to use them for the nativity last night." He toweled off his head and sat down to put on his pants.

"I heard about that. I didn't know y'all knew anything about birthin' babies."

"Hell, I didn't either. But Vita gets the credit...and the mother, of course. I just took orders. How's my place look from the outside?"

"Better than it does from the inside. You've got a new channel cutting through the northwest end of the island, and you're going to have to build a new boat house and re-deck all your piers, but other than that it looks like you survived another one."

"Radio said Port Lavaca got hammered pretty hard," Rupert remarked as he dressed.

"Port Lavaca, Palacios, Seadrift. I'd be surprised if Port O'Conner has a building left standing," said Charlie.

Rupert finished dressing and took a long look at Charlie, caked blood on his forehead, a scarlet crescent under his ribcage, a bloody rag tied around the thigh wound, cuts and bruises all over his arms and face, and a filthy turban on his head. "Goddamn, son. Did you decide to tie yourself to a mast and watch the hurricane up close?"

"Something like that. We spent Friday night out in Gulf. Let ourselves get clipped by the edge of the storm. And yesterday we spent the afternoon being chased around the bays by one of Bao's gunboats. We ended up spending the night in the observation tower on the wildlife refuge. It was pretty rough."

Rupert was silent for a moment, letting this sink in. "The boy was with you?"

"Yeah. Johnny's dog too. I'm going to see they both get a merit badge for it."

"Lose your boat?"

"Last time I saw her she was pinned down in a marsh gettin' the bejesus beat outta her by the storm. Don't know if she made it or not."

After a pause Charlie said, "Rupe, we could sure use a place to hole up for a day or two, me and the boy. Things have kinda gotten outta hand."

"No problem," Rupert replied. "You gonna tell me about it?"

"Breakfast first, heavy shit later," said Charlie as he walked out the door and ran into Vita. Vita grabbed Charlie by the arm and began questioning him about Raul's condensed version of their experiences and Charlie repeated his mantra, "Breakfast first, heavy shit later."

———

CHAPTER 20

By midday, with the help of the guests, the interior of Shady's began to resemble its old self again. A hung-over but otherwise enthusiastic work detail removed the plywood from the windows, bagged up bottles and cans, and cleaned off the foul smelling storm slime from the front entry steps and the support pilings. They scrubbed the kitchen clean and hosed down the dance floor. Someone turned on the jukebox to drown out the gasoline-fired generator.

The Vietnamese families were in high spirits because all of their boats had survived the blow and the new baby boy and his mother were getting along just fine. By afternoon the water had receded to about high tide level and a cool breeze began to freshen the air, which was still heavy with the smell of the storm. The men took turns using Rupert's radio to verify the whereabouts and condition of their homes, boats and relatives.

Fed, bathed, doctored and slouching in a folding chair on the sunny side of Shady's veranda, Charlie popped the top to an ice-cold can of beer and felt the golden liquid flow down his throat. "Peppy and Refreshing!" said the Pearl beer sign on the wall. He listened to the hum of Shady's voluntary work crew, chattering and laughing inside the building, and he marveled at their allegiance to his uncle's decaying fish and beer palace.

Hundreds of stories contributed to the Shady's myth. The fishing was legendary. Old timers recalled catching tubs full of speckled trout around the island. The music and dancing was always eventful. Bands as diverse as Bob Wills' Texas Playboys and Duke Ellington had played there to energetic mixed crowds. Shady's had never discriminated on the basis of color or economic status. All paying customers were treated equal, and if someone didn't like Shady's particular brand of populism, then Rupert or one of his brothers would help that person find the door.

Charlie guessed that the caretakers and patrons of the Shady Boat and Leisure Club sensed the importance of this accumulated history and of their part in that history. Thus, the compulsion that occasionally prompted them to defy all good sense and flock to an island square in the path of a hurricane, each one knowing he might be there to witness the literal end of something—each one ready to go down with the ship.

After a couple more beers, Charlie permitted himself to slide away from the sharp edge that the experiences of the last forty-eight hours had honed on him. His senses numbed a bit by fatigue, sunshine and alcohol, Charlie permitted himself to relax on the stoop. As long as he didn't move his battered body or entertain any thoughts, everything was wonderful and the world indeed looked level. He lowered his eyes to half-mast and indulged in a delicious indolence. Johnny the Mystic had called this state "beervana." A barrage of disturbing thoughts buzzed at the edge of his mind but he shut them out long enough to slip into a restless sleep.

Late in the afternoon, Rupert and Vita pulled two more chairs out to the deck and sat down next to Charlie. Vita handed him a tall glass of fresh squeezed lemonade.

"For your health," she said.

"Well, I do believe we made some progress cleaning up this mess today," Rupert remarked, mopping his neck with a bandana and looking out at the island.

"Sorry I played hooky today, Rupe," said Charlie.

"Don't worry about it, son. We've had plenty of help."

"What are they saying on the shortwave?"

"Well," Rupert began "...the towns north of here got hammered—it's as bad as you said it would be. Corpus, Aransas Pass, Port A...they fared a lot better. Lots of buildings and trees are down but no deaths reported, yet.

"Jake Jacoby radioed in this morning. He says Rockport and Fulton got hit pretty bad too, but his boat made it through okay. He anchored it out in Little Bay. Says he spent a hairy night holed up at the Marina restaurant over in Key Allegro."

"He'll try and make it over here in the morning," added Vita.

"Any news about Johnny?" Charlie asked, although he was less hopeful with every passing day. A week had passed since they called off the search.

"No, Charlie. Nobody's seen or heard anything."

There was a lull in the conversation and Charlie could tell they were waiting for him to talk.

"Well," he said, looking over at his aunt and uncle, "...y'all wanna hear another hurricane story?"

"Damn skippy," Rupert answered.

Charlie moved his chair around to face them and calmly recounted his tale from beginning to end, from the Johnny Sweetwater barbecue and subsequent attack at Fulton Harbor, to beaching the *Ramrod* on a muddy shore somewhere near San Antonio Bay, to the chilling conversation with Sonny on the wildlife observation tower. He tried not to leave anything out. Rupert and Vita had provided him refuge in their home and he wanted to serve them up the whole enchilada. *Besides*, he thought, *somebody else needs to know...just in case.*

"...and that's the straight and the skinny of it," Charlie concluded. "I wish I was making it up."

"So he's running guns and dealing drugs," said Rupert, reflectively. "Can't say I'm surprised. This Bao plays kinda rough, don't he?"

Vita shook her head in disbelief. "For heaven's sake, Charlie, why would anybody want to start killing people to protect a smuggling operation? Half our customers have smuggled something in their boats at one time or another. Rupert, your poppa ran guns to Mexico during the revolution. But it was never like this...was it?"

"Vita," said Charlie, "I think there's some really big money involved here, and the guns have gotten a little more...*serious* since then. Sonny mentioned 'Stingers,' and 'TOWS' and 'LAWS,' light anti-tank something-or-other. And he's selling these toys to just about anybody with the money to buy 'em: unfriendly governments, rebel forces, drug dealers, you name it."

"And he thinks you're in the way," added Rupert.

"Evidently," Charlie confirmed. "Sonny says Bao's convinced I'm trying to home in on the smuggling business...and that I'm bent on sabotaging his. This guy Bao, he's coming from a whole 'nuther place than the rum runners and small-time smugglers you're talking about, Vita."

Rupert nodded. "Sounds like he's built quite an operation, what with that high tech outpost in Mesquite Bay and him hiring an ex-Marine and such. And apparently he'll do anything to protect it."

"No kidding," Charlie agreed. "And on top of that, I kicked sand in his face in front of his own people over at the harbor."

Rupert chuckled. "I wish you'd have called me for your dinner and a movie deal. That was a good one."

Vita shot a disapproving look at her husband, and then addressed Charlie. "But I don't understand. You haven't even been here a week and Bao tries to kill you? That doesn't make any sense to me."

"You're right, Vita. But I think he might have had it in for Johnny too, and when I showed up...."

"He figured you came to join forces with your brother," Rupert concluded.

"Something like that."

"But why would he think you're on to his smuggling business?" Vita asked.

"I don't know, Vita. Maybe Johnny knew something, so Bao figured he'd passed the info along to me. Maybe he's paranoid. Before Bao's guy died on the tower he mentioned that his boss is really wound up about an upcoming deal with some big-time players from Mexico. Said the Colonel wasn't trusting anybody with the details, not even the goons in his inner circle."

Rupert whistled and shook his head. "Damn, son. You've sure 'nuff stepped in it, haven't you?"

At that point Raul stepped around the corner of the building. He stared at Charlie with worried eyes.

"Hi, Raul," Charlie said, cautiously. "How much of this did you hear, *chico*?"

"All of it," he replied. "So if we don't go from here, Bao will kill us?"

"No, Raul. Not if we're careful."

"Charlie," said Vita gently, "It might be a good idea if you two did go away for awhile. Let things cool down. For your sake *and* the boy's."

"It might be a good idea for Raul, Vita, but I'm not sure I'm ready to leave just yet. Bao can go to hell."

"He's got a point there, Vita," said Rupert. "The youngster doesn't need to get involved. He's got family in Mexico he can stay with. But somebody's gotta stand up to this son of a bitch, Bao."

"Good gracious, Rupert!" said Vita, incredulous. "Have you lost your senses? This isn't some Western movie...."

"Nobody is sending me nowhere!" Raul blurted out, nervous about a conversation that kept referring to him in the third person.

"This is my home *también!* I come here all the way from Tampico with nobody's help and I come back the same way if somebody try to take me there."

"Nobody's talking about sending you back to Mexico for good," Charlie explained. "Just temporarily. It's just too dangerous here, for now."

"Dangerous!" yelled Raul. "*Y antes no fue peligroso,* Charlie? I was with you all the time out there. We are both shot at, we both get chase, and we beat those guys and we beat the hurricane together, *recuerdas,* Charlie? You remember?"

Raul stood rigid and defiant on the porch, challenging Charlie with bright blue eyes.

"You're right, Raul. You're not going anywhere. We're a team, right?" Charlie smiled. "I musta lost my mind for a minute."

"You've all lost your minds!" screamed Vita. "What are you going to do, Charlie? Challenge Bao to a high noon shootout on Fulton Beach Road? Maybe a duel? Let Raul act as your second so he can watch you get shot in the back as you pace off your steps? Bao doesn't play those kinds of games and he doesn't play fair. He'll order you dead and that's that. You tell me, Charlie Sweetwater, what exactly are you planning to do?"

"I don't know yet, Vita," he murmured. "I still don't know."

"I do know you'll need some help," said Rupert. "This here's our home too. And it ain't right what's going on."

Vita assaulted Charlie and Rupert with a furious and frightened look. "*Merde!*" she screamed, stamping her foot down on the deck and then storming away.

The door slammed and the three figures sat in silence on the veranda, keeping their own counsel. In the fading light they watched a frigatebird work the calm waters of Redfish Bay until the sun dropped out of the sky and finally disappeared into a rosy haze on the western horizon.

CHAPTER 21

Col. Bao dropped a ship-to-shore radio microphone on a metal government surplus desk and sighed with fatigue. The storm had ionized the atmosphere, and wireless service remained spotty. His head buzzed with static and garbled half-legible conversations.

The Colonel had been up for most of the previous two days, and now he was worrying about his fiefdom in the wake of the storm. He sat in the office of a warehouse he owned in Sinton, far enough inland to be spared the worst of the storm's flood tides and winds.

According to both of the faiths—Buddhism and Catholicism—in which he had been raised (and had subsequently discarded), everything happened for a reason. But Bao's head was sloshing with a lack of sleep, too much coffee and poorly suppressed anger. Master plans, if any, seemed remote to him.

God—or Buddha—knew how many of his boats had been wrecked. The big outfits like Gulf King had sent their fleets running northeast to New Orleans and Mobile once the storm's path became irrevocable. But the small boats in his fleet would have been in nearly as much danger in the open Gulf as if they had stayed put. Bao had ordered his captains to run their craft back up into the bayous and estuaries and hunker down. But he harbored no illusions that all of his trawlers, shrimpers and workboats still had their gunwales above water. One boat in particular, a boat bound for Mexico, he feared had been caught out in the storm. Almost two days and it still had not reported in.

Of the men who crewed those boats, Bao spared not a moment of concern. Men were meat, and meat could be replaced. But cargo, especially precious cargo...Bao lit another cigarette and exhaled noisily.

Most of his surveillance cameras were inoperative, and his Sea-Tex office on the Fulton waterfront was probably without power, or worse. Of his other command center, on the platform out in Mesquite Bay, he had no word and less hope. The crew boat out of Port O'Conner that he'd sent to the water-borne post after the intruders had been discovered had not radioed in after the storm.

Col. Bao was, in the idiom of his adopted country, not a happy camper. He was exhausted; his finely-tuned web of legal and illegal operations might be in tatters, and his people were out of touch (and therefore out of his control). And he could smell his own sour reek.

A knock on the office door ushered in one of Bao's functionaries. Behind him, the Colonel made out the hulking figure of Senator Cudihay. Bao snubbed out his cigarette and beckoned Cudihay inside.

The Senator was dressed in a crisp tropical weight suit the color of young wheat. He was, in addition, shaved, neatly coiffed and sweet smelling. Bao, whose own office plumbing had been contaminated with brackish seawater and backed-up sewage, wore a sweat-stained work shirt and soiled khakis. He looked like a common dockworker. And he hated it. Looking at Cudihay's plantation-owner figure, he hated it even more.

"You've been a popular boy," said the Colonel evenly. Cudihay crossed his legs (plucking at the pants seam to preserve the sharp crease as he did so) and made himself comfortable. "I'm afraid your halo and angel wings don't show up so well on television."

"Ah'm a man of the people," Cudihay replied with satisfaction. "And the more piss-poor, jammed-up, strung-out and fucked-over people get, the better I look to 'em. Nothin' like a man's house getting blown away to make him appreciate his elected officials. They know I can make those state and county bureaucrats jump when I holler froggie."

"And I suppose you will manage to make a dollar or two out of their plight," Bao said.

"I think there is an excellent possibility of that," Cudihay said with a smirk. "Did I mention I've got a cousin out in East Texas who owns a lumber mill? He supplies plywood and framing lumber for every lumberyard and hardware store in the surrounding three counties. I deep-sixed some environmental riders on the last budget bill so he can clear-cut a bunch of that good Big Thicket old-growth timber. In turn, he gives me a consideration out of every ton of lumber he sells. You think they're not gonna sell a lot of building materials around here these next few months?"

"It seems like a gamble," Bao said. "What if this hurricane had gone a different direction?"

"Shit, I don't know. I guess we'd of had to pass some county zoning that required every household to have a wooden tool shed, a rose trellis and three ping-pong tables on the property. Aren't you a betting man, Colonel?"

"Yes," said the Colonel, inhaling his cigarette down to the filter. "And thanks to your storm, my bets are all in jeopardy. I'm afraid we're going to have to put our regular agreements in abeyance until I can re-capitalize and re-organize. I fear I have lost a significant amount of inventory and perhaps workers as well."

"Well, so what?" queried Cudihay. "Put in for disaster relief, same as everybody else."

"That will not suffice," Bao said. "It is true that I have a legitimate business structure that will require compensation with insurance money and disaster relief, as you say...." He steepled his fingers and leaned forward across his desk, thrusting his raptor's profile towards Cudihay, who involuntarily flinched. "But...."

Cudihay stirred in his seat, a rivulet of sweat forming on his brow. "But..?"

"My other enterprises—from which you have benefited—require your personal assistance."

Cudihay's eyes narrowed. "I don't recall any 'other' dealings, Colonel."

Bao snapped his fingers and his goon stepped out of the shadows and pulled Cudihay's jacket down over his shoulders, effectively pinning the Senator's arms. The Colonel shoved his desk aside, planted a deck shoe against Cudihay's chest and kicked the pinioned man across the room onto his back, chair and all. Cudihay's head rang off the concrete floor. He squealed with terror.

Bao stood over him, puffing and gasping. In an effort at regaining composure, he lit another cigarette with a shaking hand.

"Listen, you fat…." Bao added a word in Vietnamese which Cudihay guessed—correctly—translated to "motherfucker."

"When I was in Saigon, I settled my accounts with parasites like you with a bullet. You and your predecessors leeched off this community for years before I arrived. Now my activities—from which you have squeezed the usual extortionate kickbacks—are in a shambles, and at a very inopportune time. A project is coming to fruition which will demand all my attention and resources."

Cudihay had no idea what Bao was talking about, but he had never seen the Colonel lose control like that.

Unseen hands picked up the Senator's chair and squared him up roughly in front of the desk. Bao had resumed his seat—thank Gawd—and puffed on his cigarette. He reached into one of the lower drawers of the desk, brought out a bottle of cognac and poured a healthy jolt into a plastic go-cup with a Larry's Tackle Town logo on the side. With two quick gulps, the cup was empty. Bao poured a slightly smaller shot, sat back and shook his head, absorbed for the moment in thought while he regained his composure.

Cudihay had never for one second imagined he might be offered a drink. He considered himself lucky to still have a tongue with which to taste one.

Bao remained silent, wreathed in cigarette smoke. Cudihay tried to unwrinkle his wadded-up tan linen suit coat.

He had no way of knowing that Bao was at least as scared as the Senator. Scared for his life, in fact. The hurricane could not have come at a worse time for the Colonel.

Smuggling up and down the Texas coast had given him a base of operations and a certain degree of economic autonomy. It also broadened his circle of acquaintances, as such enterprises are wont to do. He found he could make a truly vulgar amount of money stealing guns and munitions stateside and selling them south of the border to *narcotraficantes* and radicalized disaffected would-be revolutionary Communists in the jungles of Southern Mexico and Central America. Bao wasn't interested in loosening the shackles of the oppressed masses or empowering a bunch of pre-Columbian Maoists. He was a businessman.

Which was why he zeroed in, like a heat-seeking missile, when a well-connected family in Mérida approached one of Bao's lieutenants with an offer to open a franchise, as it were, on the family business. The big *jefe*, Sanchez, flew up to Fulton himself to discuss the deal.

Mexican brown heroin had just begun to find its way up to Texas and the Southwest. Before now, smack had flowed south to the border states from the Mafia suppliers in the East and Midwest. Not that there had been much of a market for it in Bao's corner of the universe, except for some luckless junkies in the inner-city wards of Houston and Galveston, or a few Texas tenor sax players who shot up in homage to Charlie Parker.

But Bao could spot a market on the come. Times were tough, and marijuana wasn't getting folks where they wanted to go any more. Cocaine was the white folks' drug, good for getting Spring Break sorority girls horny and punching a hip ticket at an uptown party. It struck Bao as a frivolous and silly drug. Speed also had a niche but it used people up before they could become long-term customers.

Heroin hadn't reached the tipping point in South Texas yet, but a certain percentage of Vietnam vets had returned home with a habit they'd acquired on R&R in Bangkok or Manila. The same stuff perhaps, Bao reflected, in which he once dealt.

Well, the New World was full of opportunities, and Bao was ready to jump into bed with the Mexicans. In fact, the foreplay was already over, but the fool delivering the first shipment full of Stinger missiles and machine guns never made it to his destination. Bao thought back to the first of what seemed to him an endless succession of calamities.

The first expedition began inauspiciously when the engines to the *Lazy Liz* caught fire out in the Gulf and the captain invited that meddlesome white fisherman onto his boat (that meddlesome *dead* fisherman, he amended). Later, when a Mexican coastal patrol spotted the boat near the Yucatán coast, the skipper dumped his cargo and ran home like a scalded dog. Cargo he was supposed to have exchanged for the first shipment of Mérida Brown. In retrospect, a jail cell in a Mexican prison should have been the least of that captain's worries. The fate Bao visited on the hapless underling when he returned was far worse.

"Well, *que lastima*, shit happens," said Sanchez from his Yucatán compound. "But it is not my problem, Colonel. It is yours." From Sanchez's perspective, the distribution plan was still sound, the groundwork had been laid, and the pieces of the machinery had already been put in place, so in the interest of making a show of faith and gaining a territorial foothold in South Texas, he decided to forgive the Yucatán screw-up (for now) and front Bao twenty kilos of pure black tar heroin. "I know that this time you *will* make it right, Colonel...won't you." It was not a question.

In fact, the remaining kilos of the oily, roux-dark blocs sat packaged in two 55-gallon drums labeled "marine fuel" just ten feet away from where Senator Llewellyn Cudihay was sitting and sweating.

Keeping the drugs company in the barrels were banded stacks of hundred-dollar bills, his profit from distribution of the merchandise so far. Not a lot, but Bao needed every cent he could get his hands on. It was time to go all in—in two days time he would pay the Mexicans for the initial load, make the down payment on the new, larger shipment of high grade smack, and deliver the drugs to a Houston gang contact for subsequent distribution. The gambit would cement his position as the *jefe* of the Gulf Coast heroin trade, and make him a hefty profit to boot.

The fact of the matter was, though, he needed more capital. And quick.

The Vietnamese gangster was under no illusions where he stood. The latest down payment for the drugs, in the form of arms and cash was supposed to be halfway across the Gulf. But then that hurricane—that *fucking* hurricane—had probably sunk his boat, and otherwise waylaid his plan. He had no way of knowing the fate of his boat and crew, but he suspected the worst.

The Mexican narcos might overlook one goat fuck like the dumped cargo, but to miss the second payment, too—so what if it was caused by an act of God? —would put Bao on their shit list. Any further complication would result in Bao being strung up by his *cojones* and gutted like a feral hog. He would have done the same in their place.

Sure enough, his Mexican confederates were none too pleased about the delay, but Sanchez said fine, since Bao seemed to be incapable of making a delivery to the Yucatán via boat, then he'd fly up to in his own plane and make the exchange in Texas. "I'll call you with the rendezvous point," he said. "And by the way, Colonel, we will expect to receive the *entire* payment...and all in cash."

Bao needed money fast—liquid funds, *muy rapido*. In fact, his life depended on it. All day long he had heard Cudihay boasting on the radio and television about the vast resources at his command. Search and rescue money, reconstruction money, money for the Coast Guard, the highway patrol, the disaster relief crews. Kickbacks from cronies. Torrents of money, all flowing through his hands if you believed the bloviating shitweasel. He'd preached the same gospel to Bao's face just minutes ago.

Bao looked at Cudihay—sweat-soaked, jittery, with an expression like a virgin at a prison rodeo—and saw his lifeline.

That Cudihay teetered on his own razor-thin financial precipice, Bao had no conception. Nor would he have cared.

The Senator would save his life, by God. Or he would fucking kill him.

"Llewellyn." He spoke sharply, and Cudihay's head jerked abruptly. He extended a pack of cigarettes towards the Senator and dug the brandy bottle back out of the drawer.

"Llewellyn, you have incurred a debt to me. You've made me lose my temper, and that's not something I do lightly, especially in front of my men. I am depending on you to help me redress this loss of face."

The unlit cigarette hung in the middle of Cudihay's fat face. The plastic cup of cognac shook tremblingly in his hand. "Repay...a debt... to you?" stammered the shell-shocked Senator.

"Yes." Bao leaned forward. "Let me explain to you how we will proceed...."

———

CHAPTER 22

Charlie hitched a ride back to Fulton on one of the Vietnamese shrimp boats and Raul remained on the island—but only after making Charlie swear to two saints, the Mother Mary and *El Santo* (the silver-masked wrestler) that he would come back for him the next day.

In Fulton, the afternoon light that lay on the land had a crystalline, preternatural clarity. In the aftermath of the storm, it was a beautiful day. Down by the breakwater, the Viet hands at the Sea-Tex Fish Company wandered around the rambling, steel-sided building wondering what to do and where to start.

On a vacant lot next to Sea-Tex, a Vietnamese family had rigged a lean-to, and cooked what looked like noodles and fish soup, ladling it out to the Sea-Tex workers and their Fulton Harbor friends.

Charlie's stomach went into overdrive as he smelled the aromas drifting from the makeshift kitchen. He bee-lined over, miraculously discovered a soggy dollar bill in his torn, stained shorts, and got a quart-sized tin can of soup redolent of lemongrass, broth, shrimp, lime, sesame oil, and some Oriental spices he couldn't guess at. He slurped it all down without benefit of a spoon, and went back for more.

Half a dozen Vietnamese kids ran around the vacant lot, playing grab-ass, splashing through puddles and rooting around in the detritus the storm had tossed up. They seemed to be having a marvelous time.

One boy, the approximate size and shape of a fireplug, scrounged up a waterlogged Nerf football and was tossing it to anyone who looked his way. As Charlie wandered by, the kid hauled off and drilled it at Charlie's torso. Not expecting the toss, he didn't get his hands up in time, and the ball hit him in the chest with a thump and a squish of seawater.

"Dat!" a woman called the boy from the soup kitchen. The boy grinned merrily, picked up his ball and trotted away.

"Nice catch." Charlie turned around, and there was Marisol, straddling a brand new bicycle, looking at him and shaking her head. She wore one of Johnny's flannel shirts, faded jeans and a pair of huarache sandals. Her dark hair was tucked up under a red bandana. A woven net grocery sack hung across her shoulder like a bandolier, bulging with unidentified goodies. She looked impossibly romantic, like she was on her way to join the rest of the rebels up in the hills above the capital.

"You're okay?" said Charlie. He was relieved to see her safe and sound.

"Yes, I'm okay," she replied, smiling.

Marisol pointed at the cut on Charlie's forehead, the blood stains on his shirt and then the bandage around his thigh, just visible under his khaki shorts. "What about you?" she asked.

"Ready for the scratch and dent sale...but okay," he replied.

"And Raul?"

"He's fine, too. He and Johnny's dog are staying with my aunt and uncle over on Ransom Island." Charlie realized his ears were humming. His over-amped nervous system was trying to process seeing this vibrant, smiling girl in the midst of the wreckage and devastation. Seeing his goofy Loony Tunes-style grin, Marisol responded with an inner smile of her own. She'd seen that same grin on Johnny's face before.

"I was afraid you two were caught out at sea," she said.

Charlie made a dismissive gesture. "Well, yeah, we were. It was interesting, but no big deal."

"*Ay, que hombre eres!*" she clapped in feigned admiration. "No big deal, huh? Then where's the boat? I didn't see it in the harbor."

His spirits sagged noticeably. "I dunno. I hope that when I find it, I find it semi-intact. What about you?" asked Charlie. "I see you didn't have the good sense to evacuate either."

"No, I guess I didn't. I spent the night at the Marina on Key Allegro. Somehow that rickety old building didn't fly apart during the storm. A few times it almost did. Miguel did a good job keeping the holes plugged and the fires out. Last night I stayed at Johnny's place. I hope you don't mind."

An uncomfortable silence followed. Charlie concentrated on a Caracara hawk soaring on the updrafts, searching for meat, live or dead. Strangely, he did mind. Was it jealousy? Charlie was confused by the muddle of feelings he was having. "No, I don't mind," he lied. "Stay as long as you want. Hell, it's probably more your house than it is mine."

"Thank you."

"So who did you liberate the bicycle from?" he asked.

"The window of the bicycle store was broken. This one was out in the street. It was, you know, public domain. All very above-board and legal."

"So couldn't you have taken a page from Johnny's book and hotwired a Cadillac or something? I could use a ride right now."

"One look at you in a Cadillac and the police would shoot you on the general's principle."

"Oh yeah," Charlie replied playfully. Her occasional malapropism was endearing. "... and what about you? They'd take you for my Meskin *bandida* accomplice."

"Ha. They would think I am a beautiful and exotic woman of color who accidentally found an unwashed thug in my Cadillac. And of course, they would be correct."

Charlie thought about it. She was probably right. Goddamn it. He smiled back at Marisol.

"I'm afraid you're on your own," she said. "Besides, you have your own transportation." She gestured toward the harbor and sure enough, Charlie's vintage pickup improbably sat high and dry on the crushed shell parking lot, surrounded by downed tree limbs, telephone cables and trash. "Maybe you can give *me* a ride?"

Charlie reflexively patted his pants pockets then realized he'd left his keys on the *Ramrod*. "Left the keys on the boat. Could you at least hotwire my truck for me?"

"Like I said, you're on your own. I boost bicycles, not cars." She smiled, re-mounted her bicycle, and pedaled away toward Rattlesnake Point, a solitary figure gliding through ruin. Over her shoulder she said, "I'll be seeing you around, yes?"

"Yes," Charlie yelled back, then when she was out of hearing, "I sure as hell hope so."

——————

22 |

CHAPTER 23

"If you watch the horizon, you won't puke." Jake Jacoby spoke matter of factly from the flying bridge of his forty-two foot Bertram. O.B. Hadnott slumped over the rail, staring forlornly at the four-foot swells undulating beneath him. He squinted up at Jake and nodded, then proceeded to throw up over the side again.

"Sorry 'bout the delay," Jake continued, "but it looks like they've just about marked off the wreck. We should be able to get outta this chop and be on our way anytime now."

It was early afternoon and Jake Jacoby and O.B. Hadnott had been idling for over an hour just outside the jetties of the Corpus Christi Channel near Port Aransas. The Coast Guard had discovered a sunken trawler and they were diverting any vessel over twenty-five feet into the Gulf to ease the congestion. After the hurricane, lots of freighters were returning to port in Corpus Christi after running north and east to evade the storm. Their ponderous shapes dotted the horizon for miles, a shadowy archipelago waiting to proceed through the channel and into Corpus Christi Bay.

Apparently, one unlucky shrimp boat (Bao's boat, loaded with bundles of cash and illegal arms, though no one knew it) had been caught out by the hurricane. Jake figured it had tried, and failed, to make it to the safety of Conn Brown Harbor in Aransas Pass during the storm. One of the wrecked trawler's outriggers protruded from the water, surrounded by a wide ring of Coast Guard warning buoys marking the wreck.

"How far to the island?" O.B. managed to ask.

Jake fished a toothpick out of his teeth. "'Bout five miles as the crow flies. But we might have to wind around a bit to get there. Say, you want some crackers or a 7-UP or something? Might make you feel better."

O.B. shook his head. He watched a school of blue-green fish eagerly gobbling up the previous contents of his stomach. "What the hell kind of fish is that?" he wheezed, tilting his head toward the feeding frenzy churning the water beneath him.

"That'd be the Horse-eyed Jack," said Jake, not even looking over to verify. "Eat just about anything."

O.B. closed his eyes, revolted. He tried again to mitigate his continuing Gulf Coast misery by remembering the simple satisfaction of hard, dry, high plains ground. Instead, his thoughts returned to the long, wretched night he'd spent at the marina restaurant or bar or whatever the hell it was supposed to be.

O.B. had never really considered his own mortality until that night, not even when he'd had to confront armed criminals in the line of duty—a situation where he had at least some measure of control. But the thing that assaulted the little pier and beam marina was like a malicious beast. It pounced on the building and pushed and clawed all evening and most of the night to get inside.

When morning came and they shoved the heavy jukebox away from the door, and pried the plywood loose from the frame, O.B. momentarily forgot his manners and pushed out in front of everyone, bounding outside into the open air. He recklessly scrambled over the damaged pier connecting the building to the slimy, mud-covered parking lot and planted his feet on solid, if soggy, ground.

He realized now he had probably looked pretty silly, standing there defiantly on the crushed shell pavement in his filthy khakis and waterlogged boots, glaring back at the battered bar & grill, silently daring anybody to make a smart-ass remark. But the refugees that followed him out looked nearly as shaken as he.

O.B. met Jake Jacoby out in the parking lot.

"You know," Jake said casually, as he strolled up next to O.B. and scanned his eyes over the ragged island, "I always thought a hurricane would somehow *clean* the land, you know? With all that wind and water and such. But, son of a bitch! Look at this! It leaves the most god-awful mess. It'll take months to clean the mud and trash off this island." He turned and faced O.B. "I'm Jake Jacoby." He offered his hand and O.B. grabbed it like a lifeline.

The Sergeant helped Jake retrieve his boat—it had been lashed between six pilings in a cat's cradle of long lines that helped it rise and fall with the storm's surge. Jake then helped the Sergeant make his way back to Rockport and, eventually, the Aransas Pass DPS station. The two men struck up a friendship of sorts and the next day, O.B. took Jacoby up on his offer to accompany him to Ransom Island.

"There's a guy over there," said Jake, "the uncle of the man that's missing at sea. You'll like Rupert...and you might learn something, too."

So far, all O.B. had learned was that he had no tolerance for seasickness. O.B. vomited over the side and watched his notepad fall from his pocket and disappear in the swirl of water and fish.

At long last, the Coast Guard began to direct the boats through the restricted channel and Jake motored on towards Redfish Bay. Within minutes the calm waters rescued Hadnott's truant equilibrium and soon after, restored his will to live.

—

O.B. Hadnott crested the denuded spoil bank on the windward side of Ransom Island and found Rupert Sweetwater and Juan Estrada struggling to drag what looked to be a twelve-foot tall knight in armor out of the shallow bay towards a pickup truck parked on the beach. Rupert, stripped to the waist and wearing a beige pith helmet, was holding the tin giant's armored legs under his arms, while the shorter, younger man had the colossus' arm draped around his shoulder, the helmeted head resting stiffly against his cheek. It looked as if the two were helping a drunk find his way to bed.

"Well, I still think it could be the real deal," the short man said, straining against the weight of the armor. His longish, dirty blond hair was slicked back in a greasy 50's pompadour. "The storm mighta stirred this old fella up from one of them Spanish galleons that sunk out here way back when."

"Could be, Juan," said the other. "There was probably lots of twelve-foot tall knights from the Middle Ages came over on boats with the sixteenth century explorers." He paused to catch his breath for a second and let some of the water run out of the leaky heel of the foot. "And I understand they favored wearing heavy armor when they sailed around in these bays, on account of its buoyancy. This armor mighta belonged to ol' Cabeza de Vaca's older, taller brother. You know, Bill Russell de Vaca."

Juan paused as well, trying to remember when the Middle Ages occurred in history. Unsuccessful in this, he tried a different tack. "Maybe it come from a museum that got flooded out in Corpus."

"Yeah. Or maybe it washed into the bay from the front of that Knight's Rest Motel in Aransas Pass, and the storm tide pushed it over here."

Juan stared down at his feet, buried in the brackish mud. This explanation apparently registered as he clearly recalled the giant pair of armored knights that for years had guarded the sad entrance to the roadside tourist court a few miles away. Okay, so maybe he hadn't salvaged a priceless museum-quality antique, but he could sure add this splendid specimen to his own ever-growing collection of junk. "You think they'll be wantin' their knight back?" he asked.

"I won't say nothing," Rupert promised, as he looked up to see O.B. Hadnott squatting on his haunches on top of the spoil bank. "Afternoon," said Rupert.

"Afternoon," replied Ranger Hadnott. "Need some help with that?"

"We 'bout got it now, I think." Juan and Rupert struggled a few more feet and dumped their load on the sand. It sounded like they'd dropped a loaded toolbox.

Ranger Hadnott descended from the sand bar and offered his hand. "I'm Sergeant O.B. Hadnott, with the Texas Rangers."

O.B shook Rupert's hand, noting the firm handshake.

"I'm Rupert Sweetwater, and this is Juan Estrada." Juan nodded suspiciously. He was worried the Ranger might make him return his newfound prize.

"That's one fine conquistador you got there, gentlemen," Sergeant Hadnott observed.

Rupert smiled and looked down at the tin giant lying face down on the ground. The legs sprawled out awkwardly on the beach and the arms, one reaching forward, the other bent back, suggested a clumsy

Australian crawl. The knight seemed to be attempting to escape back into the water. Juan reached down and pulled a wad of seaweed off the helmet. He peeked inside the visor and a blue crab rushed out of the head and scurried back into the bay. Juan jumped back, alarmed.

"All kinds of things wash up on the island after a hurricane. Today we've found two dead cows, a pink Amana refrigerator, a Boston Whaler and a Texaco filling station sign," Rupert said.

"Don't forget the Kon Tiki mask," added Juan, regretting having spoken as the words left his mouth. This Ranger might have the authority to confiscate every treasure he had collected in the aftermath of Lana, a storm that was proving to be particularly bountiful for him thus far.

Over the years, Juan Estrada had amassed a remarkable collection of random artifacts that washed up on the island or that he had scavenged from the mainland. He had filled his wreck of a boat from bow to stern with all manner of haphazard items ranging from old radios to rusty outboard motors to moldy comic books. He had cleared a narrow path from the cabin door of his old Chris Craft all the way back to his cramped sleeping berth in the bow. He'd hollowed out small enclaves to make room for a 19 inch Magnavox television set, a rusty two-burner stove, a 1963 RCA turntable, and his prized collection of warped Don Ho records. All the comforts of home.

"Y'all gonna load that knight in the truck?" Ranger Hadnott inquired, nodding at the rusty blue Ford.

"Planning on it," said Rupert.

"Lemme give ya a hand then," the Ranger replied.

—

Seated at a quiet corner table inside Shady's, Rupert and O.B. Hadnott sipped on RC Cola and talked about hurricane parties and the weather. O.B. couldn't get his head around the notion that somebody would host a rip-snorting bash in the middle of a deadly storm. On purpose. Having endured just one of these storms, he felt pretty confident in thinking that this behavior was downright crazy.

"I think that's downright crazy," he said.

Rupert chuckled. "Yeah, my wife would probably agree with you."

Vita snuffed audibly from behind the bar.

"Well, enough about the weather, Mr. Sweetwater."

"Rupert. Please call me Rupert, Sergeant."

"Okay, Rupert," O.B. was ready to get down to business. "Mr. Jacoby tells me that you're a relative of the man that was lost at sea. I'm sorry for your loss."

"Johnny was my nephew. His dad was my youngest brother,"

Sergeant Hadnott was about to ask him about the relationship between his nephew and Bao—another one of Jake's suggestions, when Rupert spoke again.

"...And I don't think it was an accident."

"That's a bold statement, Mr. Sweetwater...that contradicts the official Coast Guard findings."

"I know, Sergeant, but I don't believe that's the whole story. I think Johnny got himself tangled up with a bad *hombre* over in Fulton and that it might have had something to do with his 'accident'."

"The bad sort you're referring to would be Colonel *Noo-gwen Nook Bay-o* from Fulton?" Hadnott asked, struggling to remember the way the beautiful Vietnamese girl had pronounced it.

Rupert drew a deep breath. The Ranger had mangled the name, but they were talking about the same guy.

"That's right, Sergeant. I'm sorry you missed Charlie, Johnny's brother—he's had his own troubles with the Colonel—but I'll be glad to tell you what he told me. And after you hear what I know about Bao and the rest of it, you can go talk to Vita over there, and then to Jake, and then to Tucker and Pete—they've all got information to offer. Or, we can save you some time and all of us just talk it out together at the bar. Then you'll get the whole ball of wax all at once."

Vita stood behind the counter, polishing the same beer glass over and over, keeping an anxious eye on the Ranger and her husband. Vita wasn't sure what sort of bombs her husband might be ready to throw.

Jake Jacoby and Juan Estrada sat on the other side of the horse-shoe-shaped bar with Tucker Adderly and Pete Jackson. Hadnott noted that nobody had uttered a word, other than him and Rupert, since the two had taken their seats at the table.

"We're all mighty interested in this thing," Rupert continued.

Against his better judgment, O.B. Hadnott consented to join the other Shady's regulars at the bar. It wasn't the way he did things back in Fisher County, but this was unfamiliar territory and he needed some help. His encounters with the sheriff and the Rockport PD had made it clear he was on his own...especially in the wake of a hurricane.

As the huge wooden ceiling fans clacked lazily from the rafters, the Shady's gang related to Ranger Hadnott everything they knew or thought they knew about Colonel Nguyen Ngoc Bao and his nefarious activities on the Coastal Bend. They talked about Johnny and his ongoing row with the Colonel. They recounted Charlie's version of the knife attack in Fulton Harbor and his run-in with Bao's men at the service platform in Mesquite Bay. They repeated Sonny's dying words to Charlie the night of the hurricane. Having lost his notepad in the Gulf, Ranger Hadnott took notes on Shady's bar napkins.

The Sergeant was intrigued, but not surprised by the story. From the moment he met Bao his gut had told him the man was a bad piece of work.

Race or nationality didn't matter. Hadnott had known a lot of white-trash peckerwoods who held themselves the same way: stick-up men and union busters and badass felons. The way they came on, daring you to try them. Bao had had that same *give-me-your-best-shot* arrogance, that "fuck you" hardcase bravado. It came off him like a pheromone reek.

Hadnott wouldn't be surprised if Bao was behind Johnny Sweetwater's presumed death and probably lots more besides. Maybe even the shooting of Neddy Pomade. But it would take more than freewheeling chatter from some well-meaning barflies to make any sort of case.

After the group brought the Ranger current, Rupert turned his big palms up and asked the question. "So there it is Sergeant Hadnott. Now, what are we gonna do about it?"

"I thinking maybe we should go visit the Colonel as a group," ventured Pete, the boat builder. "You know, show him that it ain't him against one, but him against a whole community."

"Yeah," said Tucker. "Like a friendly reminder that if he attacks one of us he attacks us all. Kind of a NATO, collective defense thing. A Three Musketeers deal."

"*We're* not going to do a blessed thing," Vita interjected. "Let Officer Havenot here do his job. Him and his merry band of Rangers. It's what we pay our taxes for, isn't it?"

Vita glared defiantly at the line of surprised faces staring at her on the other side of the bar.

Formidable woman, thought O.B. And she had a good point.

"Vita," Rupert said carefully, approaching his wife like a cowpuncher approaches a spooked remuda.

"Don't even try," she shot back, "to justify a face-off with that cold-blooded..." she searched for the word, "...criminal! It'll just get somebody else hurt or killed. And y'all aren't a lynch mob, no matter how tough you talk. Three Musketeers, my eye."

Rupert looked over at the other guys, searching for some support. Instead it was Ranger Hadnott that spoke up.

"Mrs. Sweetwater is right, you know." Vita's scowl moved from her husband to Hadnott, then softened when his words finally registered.

"This is police business and although you fellows have all been a big help—a real big help," he stressed, "the Department should probably handle it from here." O.B. spoke in his official voice. "Mrs. Sweetwater said it herself—it's what we get paid for."

"With all due respect, Ranger, you can't keep a group of law abid'n citizens from making a social call on Mr. Alleged Offender." Jake Jacoby was smiling when he said it, but his eyes weren't.

"I don't cotton to vigilantes, Mr. Jacoby."

"That idn't what I said," Jake replied.

"And that's not what we are," added Tucker Adderly, heatedly.

"Hold on a minute everybody," Rupert raised his paws to indicate a truce was in order. "Listen, Sergeant Hadnott...Jake and Tucker are right. We aren't plannin' to string up any Vietnamese gangster," he glanced warily at Vita. "We're just kicking around some options. You gotta understand that everybody here is kinda partial to this little corner of the world we live in, and we've got family involved. We can't just sit back and wait for another *accident* to happen. There's gotta be something we can do to help out on this thing."

Vita relaxed a bit when the tough-guy rhetoric took a more civilized course.

"You hadn't seemed to mind our help so far, Ranger," said Tucker.

Hadnott pondered the situation for a few seconds. "You folks have been more than helpful, and for that I thank you. I really mean it. Any new information that you turn up, I would be much obliged if you would get in touch with me." He began to fish a DPS card from the Aransas Pass station out of his wallet.

"I'm a Honorary Texas Ranger," Juan Estrada declared abruptly to no one in particular.

Everyone turned to look at Juan, who seemed to be absorbed in an attempt to peel the Lone Star beer label off a sweating longneck bottle.

"A Texas Ranger? What do you mean, Juan?" Rupert asked patiently, as if he were talking to a third grader. The group waited for Juan to answer. Jake guffawed. Vita looked exasperated. O.B. wondered what in the hell this Gulf Coast greaseball was taking about.

"Yeah, I got me a certificate and everything," Juan continued.

Rupert continued. "Whereabouts did you get your Ranger, um, appointment, Juan?"

Juan looked up, seeing six heads turned in his direction. He stammered, "I mean it was long time ago. It was just a Junior Ranger certificate."

"You mean from those stupid cereal box tops?" laughed Jake, his eyes wide.

"Well. Yeah," Juan replied defensively. The room burst into laughter and Juan reddened.

Rupert came to the rescue. "I remember those promotions. From Kellogg's I think. Seems like just about every boy in Texas was a Junior Ranger at one time or another." He looked over at Jake. "You weren't a Junior Ranger, Jacoby? When you was a boy? You're about the right age." Jake's laughter trailed off and then stopped. "And what about you, Pete?"

Pete rubbed his crew cut and smiled, nodding his head. "Like a good Ranger, I'll be brave, honest..." he drawled, knitting his brows in concentration. "I can't seem to remember the rest of it."

"Obedient...," continued Jake, somewhat sheepishly, "brave, honest and obedient."

"...and always keep my eyes open for danger." O.B. Hadnott finished the Junior Texas Ranger's official pledge. He shook his head and smiled, momentarily nostalgic. He had tacked his official Junior Ranger certificate to his wall back in Fisher County. He looked up and saw the amusement in everyone's eyes. "Hell. I was a boy just like any other boy in this state. But y'all know this ain't some kid's deal. It's something for the proper law enforcement agencies to handle."

"Just you, a couple of guys from the DPS office and the eminently qualified Sheriff Huckabee?" Tucker asked.

"I can handle it," Hadnott began, then he corrected himself. "The law can handle it."

"You know," Rupert began, "I can't believe I'm saying this, but

Juan here's made a good point." Juan looked up from his beer, surprised. "Although nobody in this room doubts the abilities of Sergeant Hadnott here, or of any Texas Ranger for that matter, it seems like I remember reading somewheres that the Rangers have the authority to utilize ordinary citizens in the pursuit of their duty."

Juan, encouraged by Rupert's acknowledgement of his good point, felt he had more to offer. "Fred MacMurray, in that movie he did in '49 about the Texas Rangers, he recruits some local cowboys to help him when he goes after that gang of cattle rustlers. Gabby Hayes plays the ranch foreman that rides with him to get back them cows. I think Joe Yuma was the name of the cowboy."

An awkward silence followed as Juan went back to the task of removing the Lone Star label from the sweaty bottle.

"Exactly, Juan!" said Rupert. He turned to the Ranger. "It's no different than you lettin' us help you get the bad guy here. We're just looking out for what's ours."

Vita had been getting antsier by the minute listening to this new drift in the conversation. "Well aren't y'all just the bravest cowboys that I've ever seen?" she drawled with a mock Southern belle accent. "It makes mah heart flutter." She held her hand to her forehead and pretended to swoon. Then her hot Tabasco voice re-asserted itself. "Nobody has any proof that Bao's killed anybody or smuggled any guns. Until there's some *proof*, you boys have nothing. You provoke a fight with Bao and you don't have any idea what a man like that might do."

Rupert looked at his wife. "But, Vita, we do know what Bao might do, and he's the one doing the provokin', not us."

"Gentlemen," Hadnott interrupted, "Once again, the lady's right. Until we get more information to support the allegations against Mr. Bao, we have no legal grounds to take action. Right now what I need is information." He looked at the faces around the room. "I'll say it once again. If y'all would let me know if you hear anything new related to my case, it would be very helpful." Ranger Hadnott gathered his bar napkin notes and got up to signify the conversation was over.

"And if you get information that concerns the case, and the safety of my nephew Charlie?" asked Rupert.

"And the boy, Raul?" added Vita.

O.B. Hadnott considered the question carefully. It wasn't customary to involve civilians in these types of cases but, what the hell, the Rangers had more flexibility than just about any law enforcement officer in Texas. "Then I'll call you. That's a promise." He turned to Jake. "Mr. Jacoby, could I impose on you once again to drop me off on the mainland? Maybe those waves have calmed down some."

Jake nodded. "Sure thing, Sergeant Hadnott. I ought to be getting my boat back to Rockport before dark anyway. The swells usually lay down a bit in the evening." He couldn't help an evil grin. "But I'd let Vita set you up with some Dramamine all the same."

As they walked out the door, O.B. turned around and said to Juan, "Gabby Hayes plays a judge in the McMurray movie, not a ranch foreman. And the cattle rustlers appear in *The Texas Rangers Ride Again*, which came out four or five years later. Anthony Quinn plays the ranch foreman Joe Yuma in that movie."

Ranger Hadnott stared closer at Juan's dirty blond duck-ass haircut, the blue veins popping along his red Irish potato nose and his bloodshot blue eyes. "*Amigo*, are you sure your name's Juan Estrada?" he asked with a rare smile.

Juan plastered his wet beer bottle label to the bar and shrugged. "Change your name, change your life," was all he said.

O.B. placed his Stetson on his head and walked out the swinging doors of Shady's, doing his level subconscious best to look like John Wayne at the end of *The Searchers*, walking off the homesteader's porch into the wide open desert.

———

CHAPTER 24

The sun shone down on the tangle of wreckage, stinking mud, dead fish, swamped boats and roofless ruins that had once been the quaint twin bayside communities of Rockport and Fulton. Coast Guard helicopters and watercraft ferried the displaced and dropped off supplies. National Guard soldiers from San Antonio and Austin wielded chainsaws, removing downed trees and telephone poles. Portable generators drove power tools and jackhammers as people worked to clear away the jigsaw puzzles that had once been homes and businesses.

A few intrepid establishments had opened their doors to help people affected by the storm, which included just about everyone who hadn't had the good judgment to evacuate. Like Charlie, for instance, who stood patiently in a long line that had formed that afternoon in front of a damaged and windowless Rockport Bank, waiting his turn to be ushered into the bank by a gun-toting National Guardsman. The upbeat storm survivors that waited with him shared their stories and the food and drink they'd brought with them. They were all caught up in a conflicting jumble of emotions that included relief (I'm still alive!), gloom (But my house is gone!), excitement (I found my skiff in a tree!) and edgy exhaustion.

When he'd finally worked his way up to the gaping entrance of the bank, Charlie realized he had lost his wallet in the storm. He was lucky that a bank VP recognized him in the muddy lobby. "Hey there, Charlie. Long time no see. Sorry to hear about your brother. Have you had any word?"

"No news," he answered.

The VP appraised Charlie's bruised and battered body. "I'm glad to see you survived the hurricane. Looks like it whupped up on you pretty good."

"Split decision. Lana won on points."

"How about the boat?"

"I'll find out tomorrow. I had to leave it, um, anchored out near Ayers Bay, between here and Port O'Conner," he answered, remembering that the bank still owned most of the *Ramrod*, and that the sons of bitches wanted to take it back.

"Well, I hope she's okay," said the V.P. earnestly. (Maybe he didn't know his bank had called the loan, thought Charlie.) "Let me show you back to your security box."

Alone in the private viewing stall, Charlie opened the lid to the long metal box and sorted through the family's accumulated valuables, such as they were.

There were some antique wooden fishing lures, a diamond wedding ring—his mother's he assumed—and a few black-and-white photos of the family. Charlie studied a photo of his parents standing on the seashore, ankle deep in the surf. Johnny was knee high and holding on to his mother's hand. He was smiling and looking down at Charlie who squatted in the sea foam letting the sand and water rush through his open fingers.

Charlie found the letters of incorporation for the business and discovered that Johnny had the foresight to adequately insure the shrimp boat—a requirement no doubt insisted on by the bank's tightass loan officer, God bless him. Of course his brother hadn't prepared a will. Who writes a will while they're in their thirties? It didn't matter anyway, he supposed, since without a body it couldn't be probated for seven years. He was about to lock up the box when he spied another envelope with a Corpus Christi Memorial Hospital logo in the corner.

Inside were two lab reports analyzing some blood specimens collected on September 16, 1979...apparently from two separate subjects. The report had various numbers and letters describing the blood but Charlie couldn't make heads or tails of the data. There were no names on the report and he began to wonder if the data described some hideous family blood defect that had killed his parents and his brother and was lurking in his own veins waiting to kill him too. *You're getting too paranoid for you own good, hoss*, he thought.

A typed letter addressed to Johnny Sweetwater from Dr. Harold Holmes, the same doctor that had attended his mother during her illness, put those grim speculations to rest.

Dear Mr. Sweetwater,

We have completed the blood work that you requested. As I mentioned to you in our conference last week, the HLA test detects the presence or absence of human leukocyte antigens found on the surface of white blood cells in a blood sample. These HLA-B27 antigens are proteins that help the body's immune system differentiate between its own cells and foreign, harmful substances. Everyone has an inherited combination of HLA proteins in their white blood cells, which create very distinctive HLA markers for every person, almost as unique as a fingerprint.

The tests were rather conclusive, and if you would like to come by my office again, I will gladly provide you with a full clinical analysis of the data. In regards to your specific question regarding the paternity of the boy, Raul de la Rosa, I can tell you quite confidently that you are almost certainly the boy's father. The test results support this finding with approximately a 95% probability.

Congratulations and best regards,
Dr. Harold H. Holmes, M.D.

Well, thought Charlie, *I'll be dipped in shit.*

CHAPTER 25

After leaving the bank, Charlie wandered toward the harbor in a daze, thinking about the newest member of the Sweetwater family. He wondered how he'd missed the obvious blood connection when he'd met the boy the first time. In his mind he began to compare line of jaw, the epicanthic arc of eyelid, the curve of neck, and the delicate flowering of ear—not to mention the blondish hair the kid kept stuffed up under his ball cap. Raul was a darker, skinnier version of his dad.

That the boy had taken it upon himself to walk from Matamoros to Fulton—over two hundred miles of rough, thorny brush country—believing that somehow he would be able to find his assumed dad from a scribbled address on a five-year old post card, was right in line with Johnny's impetuous trips in the other direction, to Mexico, where he had courted and impregnated the boy's mother (a sporting lady) in Nuevo Laredo thirteen years ago. Both father and son acted out of an outlandish optimism and a reckless disregard for convention and good sense.

Yep, Raul fit snugly into the Sweetwater family mold. His natural ease at sea somehow brought the equation full circle. *Tio Carlito,* he thought. Shit. He recalled the fuddy-duddy old fart from the *My*

Three Sons television show. Ol' Uncle Charlie.

At the harbor Charlie was astonished to discover that Charlotte Plummer's, a venerable old seafood restaurant jutting out over the water, was open for business. Hungry enough to eat the giant squid from *20,000 Leagues Under the Sea*, he entered and sat at a booth near the entrance. Without looking at a menu, he ordered a mug of beer and a Fisherman's Platter, which consisted of fried everything, plus buttered Texas toast and a tiny bowl of watery coleslaw. The American Heart Association had not designated his menu selection as "heart healthy." For Charlie, however, it was just what the doctor ordered.

The restaurant was about half full—mostly locals, but also some Red Cross workers, half-exhausted from the arduous storm cleanup, a few insurance adjusters in short sleeve shirts and clip-on ties, and a large table of very vocal out-of-towners freshly arrived from Dallas to check on their toy boats and their ticky-tack second homes. The windows and storm shutters were open to admit the late afternoon breeze.

A pretty Vietnamese waitress brought him his beer, apologizing that it wasn't cold. "Still no power for beer cooler," she explained.

As he waited for his food and sipped his rodeo-cool beer he gazed out the open window at the boats in the harbor. The slips were beginning to fill up again as the shrimpers returned to port. The berth where the *Ramrod* docked was conspicuously empty. He noticed with a start that his truck was gone too.

"Son of a bitch," he said, leaning out the window, anxiously searching the parking lot for his lemon-yellow pickup. "Son...of...a... bitch," he repeated.

When he pulled his head back inside the window, Marisol was standing in front of his booth.

"Speak for yourself," she said. "You lose something?"

"Yeah, my boat, and now my truck."

Marisol giggled. "I don't know about the boat, but your truck is in the parking lot."

Charlie looked out the window again. "No. It's not."

"The restaurant parking lot," she cocked a thumb toward the door. "I borrowed it this afternoon. It's right outside."

Charlie blinked, and then sat down. "Borrowed it?"

"I hotwired it, like you suggested. Miguel showed me how. Anyway, it's easier than I thought it would be. Just run a wire from the battery positive to the coil, and *voila!*"

"*Voila*, you're now a car thief," said Charlie. "And you an officer of the court, sort of."

Marisol had changed out of the Patty Hearst attire she had on that morning and wore a sleeveless white cotton shift. Her coal black hair was tied back loosely with a fat piece of yarn. She was the most gorgeous car thief he'd ever seen.

"Don't be such a *mamón*," she said laughing. "My car is still stuck on Key Allegro. I can't get it until the bridge is repaired. Mind if I sit down?"

"By all means. I ordered enough food to feed the Pirates of the Caribbean."

"I can't believe this place is open," she continued. "I thought Klein's over in Rockport was the only game in town."

"Well, there's no power here, so if you had your mind set on a cold beer or an iced drink, you're out of luck."

The petite Vietnamese woman came over to take Marisol's order. She pulled out her order pad then noticed she hadn't brought Marisol a menu yet.

"I'm sorry. I forget menu," she said, apologetically.

"That's okay," said Marisol. "I'll just have a shot of tequila. Herradura if you have it." The waitress carefully wrote down the name of the drink and left.

"So," said Marisol, "you tell me about your day and I'll tell you about mine."

"You first," said Charlie.

She shrugged. "Not much to tell, really. Since phone connections are spotty, I went by the Coast Guard office in Corpus Christi today to see if there was any news. With all the road detours it took me half the day to get there."

"What'd they say?" Charlie had to lean over the table to hear. The table of over-moneyed drunks was getting louder and filling the restaurant with their gab.

"No new developments. No reports whatsoever regarding Johnny." Marisol's shoulders sagged. "When they realized who I was, the staff kept looking at me with those pitying eyes...as if I didn't understand the long odds of finding him."

"Sometimes it feels better just to do something," said Charlie.

The waitress arrived with Marisol's drink. "Sorry if wrong," she said. She set down a large juice glass filled to the brim with the tequila. She explained that she normally worked the kitchen, but since so few of the regular wait staff had shown up she had been asked to fill in as a waitress.

"You're doing just fine," Marisol said encouragingly. The waitress smiled. Charlie ordered another beer and watched the waitress walk away.

"Now that's a drink," said Charlie appreciatively.

She held up the big glass and thrust it forward. "*Salud.*"

They clinked glasses and Charlie drained his beer. "When Johnny called me down in Mexico he mentioned that he really wanted me to meet someone, like he had some important news to tell me or something. Were you two, you know, engaged?"

"Not that I know of," she answered. A faint smile appeared on her face as if she were imagining a now unattainable future with Johnny. Her smile disappeared. "No. I think he would have mentioned something like that to me before he invited somebody down for the announcement."

"You might have said no?" teased Charlie.

"Why even think about it?" she said tersely.

"Sorry," said Charlie. "But that clears something up for me."

The waitress returned with the beer and the platter of food. Charlie stared at the pile of deep-fried lumps stacked high on the plate. Suddenly he wasn't so hungry any more. The drunks at the big table raised their collective voices a few decibels higher. Marisol looked over at them, irritated.

One of the men there, a burly fat-faced man in an oversized Izod shirt with a popped collar and a NASCAR cap, brayed for the waitress to bring them another round of drinks. But the Vietnamese waitress was already coming through the kitchen door laden with food orders precariously balanced on a tray.

"No-no-no, Missy! Take the food back. We want another round of drinks first, chop-chop." As she returned to the kitchen with the tray of food he addressed the others at his table. "Goddamn boat gook prob'ly doesn't understand a word I said. Hey, that reminds me. Do y'all know how you fit five hundred Vietnamese into a matchbox?" He paused for dramatic effect. "Just tell them it floats."

The other four couples laughed at the joke. NASCAR's wife laughed the hardest of all. Marisol turned around and regarded the table icily. "*Groseros*," she mumbled.

After a few minutes the waitress returned with a new tray of drinks. As she tried to sort out who had the Cuba Libras and who had the Seven & Sevens, the Richard Petty wannabe attempted to imitate the girl's accent.

"Sank you velly much fo Cuba Ribra, mamasan. After drinkie maybe we go boom-boom? You likey, mamasan?"

Marisol looked over at the manager who studiously ignored the whole situation. The waitress returned to the kitchen and the conversation shifted to another subject—a color commentary on how "the trouble-making niggers" were making the Dallas Cowboys the laughing stock of the NFC East.

"You just watch, Henry. One of these days they'll even put a gook player on the team." Everyone laughed some more. "Imagine some scrawny little Vietcong in a Dallas Cowboy uniform. Texas will have gone to hell. Nothin' but spooks, spics and slopes playin' for America's Team."

"Assholes," Charlie growled. Marisol's eyes narrowed with a look of ancient Aztec malevolence.

When the waitress returned a little later with the tray of food the whole restaurant was tense, wishing the drunks would leave or that the manager would step in and put an end to the harassment. When she got to the red-faced drunk and began to set down his platter of Redfish Veracruz, he seized her arm and pulled her down, whispering something in her ear, his tongue roaming around freely. Her face flushed and she dumped the entire tray of scalding fish and tomato sauce on the man's lap and slapped him hard across the face.

Marisol looked urgently at Charlie. "You better do something," she told him in a low, edged voice, "or I will."

He slid out of the booth as the fat-faced man screamed obscenities at the waitress, who defiantly stood her ground next to the table. The big drunk slammed the serving tray onto the table and stood up, fish and salsa sliding down his crotch. He clutched the woman's blouse and pulled his beefy arm back to punch her when a man flew out of a back booth and grabbed the drunk's wrist with one big hand, and the back of his red neck with the other hand.

"What the hell?" Out of the corner of his eye, the drunk saw a tall man with a white pearl button shirt and a sunburned face. O.B. Hadnott.

"Let go of the lady," O.B. told the drunk in a gritty monotone. Ice was in his voice. Hadnott hated blowhard drunks and he couldn't abide anyone who would throw down on a woman, drunk or sober. Especially this particular woman—the same woman he'd met in Bao's fish market.

He changed his grip to a policeman's come-along and leveraged NASCAR's forearm up in between his shoulder blades. The intense pain had a wondrously sobering effect.

"Okay, okay," he finally replied, releasing the woman's blouse. "I wasn't gonna do nothing. It was just an automatic reaction, that's all. That fish liked to burnt my pecker off!"

"You'd hardly miss it," O.B. told him. "I want you to sit down in that chair, and stay sittin' down after I let you go. Then you're gonna apologize to the girl for what you've been saying and for what you were gettin' ready to do to her. Do you understand me, mister?"

The man nodded yes. One eye was fixed on the cinco-peso Ranger badge on Hadnott's shirtfront.

"I can't quite hear you," O.B. said, deftly twisting the man's arm around behind his back an inch higher.

He winced. "Okay, okay. Jesus, I'll sit down."

"And the apology?" O.B. insisted, twisting the arm a little higher up his back. From his booth, Charlie noticed one of the other drunks had grabbed an empty beer bottle and held it beneath the table.

"I...I'm sorry, lady," the drunk stammered. But his piggy little eyes were full of rage and drunken bravado. It wasn't over; in fact, the fun was just starting.

When O.B. released the man all hell broke loose. NASCAR turned around and threw a roundhouse punch at O.B.'s head. The Ranger ducked and jabbed him hard on the nose sending him flying backwards into a big sea aquarium tank. The glass aquarium busted to pieces and live fish, crabs, an octopus and even a small stingray splattered all over the floor of the restaurant.

One of NASCAR's pals behind Hadnott picked up a beer bottle and rushed the Ranger, but Charlie was out of the booth and on the man in a flash, slamming him upside the head with his forearm. The bottle shattered on the floor.

Hadnott punched another would-be attacker and sent him sliding across the floor, where he found himself sitting at Marisol's feet next to her booth. She promptly poured the tequila into the man's eyes and used both feet to kick him down onto the floor. The man lay on his side in a puddle, shrieking in pain. *"Pendejo,"* she said to him.

Charlie scrambled over a chair and leapt from a table top onto the back of another one of NASCAR'S friends, who was about to bring a chair down on the Ranger's head. The momentum of the flying tackle sent the two men tumbling into a row of out-of-town diners at an adjacent table. Three stunned State Farm insurance adjusters scattered like bowling pins across the linoleum.

Women were screaming, bodies were flying and live fish were flopping all over the floor, when O.B. stood up on a chair and bellowed, "Everybody hold it!" Incredibly, the free-for-all stopped and a room full of astonished faces looked up at the source of the thunderous voice.

"Now listen up!" he shouted. "My name is Sergeant O.B. Hadnott of the Texas Rangers," he pointed to his badge for all to see, "and this little scuffle is officially *over!*" He scanned the room with fierce eyes.

A few people staggered up and brushed themselves off. A group of terrified Red Cross workers sidled out the rear emergency door. Sergeant Hadnott looked over at NASCAR, covered in red sauce, sitting in a heap under a pile of broken glass. "You!" he demanded. "You need an ambulance?"

"I think you broke my nose," he replied morosely.

"You'll live," the Ranger said dismissively. He located the Vietnamese waitress.

"Ma'am. Are you okay?" She nodded quickly.

One of the redneck's wives piped up. "You saw what that slant-eyed bitch did to Buster! I want to know what you're gonna do about it."

"What I'm gonna do is charge ol' Buster with assaulting a peace officer. You want me to add your name to the report?" he asked the woman. The woman's mouth shut with a snap.

Two police cars arrived almost instantly and Sergeant Hadnott picked up his Stetson and walked through the restaurant pointing fingers at those he wanted the officers to arrest. As they hauled off the drunks, O.B. removed his hat and spoke briefly with the Vietnamese waitress, making sure she was okay. Then he came over and stood in front of the booth where Charlie and Marisol were sitting.

"Are you going to take us to jail, too?" Charlie asked the Ranger.

"No, I expect not. Thank y'all for the help a while ago."

"Our pleasure," Marisol replied. Noticing the twinkle in her eyes, O.B. didn't doubt she'd thoroughly enjoyed her part in the ass kicking.

"But since we're all here together," O.B. continued, "I wouldn't mind having a word with you, if you don't mind."

"Sit down, Sergeant. I'm Charlie Sweetwater," Marisol scooted over to sit with Charlie while the Ranger slid in across from them.

"Pleased to meet you. And you are?" he asked, looking over at Marisol.

"I am Marisol Cavasos. A friend of the family."

O.B. tipped his head. "Nice to meet you, too."

"Thank you," she smiled. "I appreciate what you did for that waitress. That man had no right to treat her that way."

"No Ma'am, he had no right," he said, thinking, *If that son of a bitch woulda hit her I'd a snapped his neck.*

"I believe we had the pleasure of each other's company at the Marina the night of the hurricane, Miss Cavasos."

"That's right! I remember you now." Then she continued reflectively, "Although I don't remember much after the lights went out, and then the wind and the rain..." she shook her head. "I couldn't think about much more than surviving the night."

"No ma'am, me neither," O.B. responded, not too proud of his own borderline panic attacks during the storm.

"Well, now that we know that you are a bona-fide Texas Ranger," Charlie said, "what would you like to have a word with us about?" He was instinctively suspicious of peace officers...or any public official, for that matter. Living in Mexico for five years hadn't helped much.

"Mr. Sweetwater, I had a long talk with your uncle this afternoon at Ransom Island. He and his wife and the rest of the boys over there gave me a lot of information about the dealings between you and Mr. Bao.

Charlie and Marisol exchanged glances. "I suppose Bao's the reason you're down here on the coast then?" Charlie asked.

"Might be," said Hadnott. "There's quite a few things I'm looking into. I suppose you heard about Mr. Pomade's murder last week."

"Of course I did. It's a small town. I was at that party, too."

O.B. raised an eyebrow. "You a friend of Cudihay's?"

"No, I provided comic relief, I expect. I was pretty fried after making a long-haul trip from Mexico and...I guess I just wanted to twist off a little bit."

"Sergeant, have you talked to Bao yet?" asked Marisol. She wanted to cut to the chase.

"I visited with the Colonel a few days ago," he said, "over at Sea-Tex, before the storm."

"He's a charming guy, isn't he?" said Charlie.

"No. I don't think so." O.B. didn't recognize or acknowledge irony. "Ms. Cavasos. Why do you bring up Bao? Do you have information that links him to a crime?...or to Mr. Pomade's murder?" asked the Ranger.

"No, no I don't. Not for that. But if Rupert and Vita told you all about Bao, then I guess you know he's not exactly a model citizen."

The Ranger didn't respond but pulled a handful of scribbled on bar napkins from his shirt pocket and began to study them on the tabletop. The officer nudged the napkins and re-arranged them as though they would reveal, Ouija-like, all the answers.

The three of them talked for half an hour about Bao, and about Charlie's adventures in the bays. The Ranger took new notes and crosschecked with Charlie and Marisol the information he'd received from Ransom Island. He was especially interested in Sonny's mention of a big deal going down with the Mexicans. Reports from HQ, corroborated by the Houston PD and their paid informants had discussed a large shipment of heroin that was scheduled to hit the market, soon.

As the light dimmed, Charlie realized that the three of them were alone in restaurant. But in a moment the pretty Vietnamese waitress reappeared, coming straight over to their booth. She had changed out of her waitress uniform and was obviously preparing to leave. When O.B. Hadnott saw her he tried to stand (out of courtesy), but his long legs banged against the table, upsetting glasses and rattling crockery.

"Don't get up, Mr. Ranger," she said. "I remember you from other day, at Sea-Tex...my other job, and I see you again here, two times already, in restaurant. You always watching me."

O.B. blushed like a schoolboy. He'd thought he was being pretty darn covert, observing her furtively over his coffee. But he just couldn't help himself. She was just so goddamn pretty.

"I want to thank you for what you do tonight," she said.

O.B. tried to speak but no words escaped his mouth.

After a few seconds Marisol tried to jump-start the Ranger's vocal cords. "Why don't you ask the lady her name, Mr. Hadnott?"

"Uh, yeah," he mumbled, his sunburned face turning an even deeper shade of red. "Ma'am..." he began.

"My name is Trinh An Phu," she said, interrupting, "but here in America I am called Trinny." She held out her hand and O.B. Hadnott reached over and held it briefly and very gently. Trinny smiled at him. "You not such a rough and tough guy with the ladies are you, Mr. Marlboro Man?"

O.B. tried to think of a response to this but his mind went blank.

"I like that, okay?" she chirped. "Thank you again for tonight. Maybe I see you again?"

O.B. nodded mutely. The girl turned and walked away briskly, her purse slung over her shoulder, her long plaited black hair swishing behind her. O.B. watched her walk across the room and exit the restaurant.

Charlie and Marisol cleared their throats and tried not to smile.

"I think she likes you, Sergeant Hadnott," said Marisol.

"Naw," O.B. replied, "She's just..." his voice trailed off and he began to study his big hands as they fiddled with the saltshaker. He noticed grains of white rice mixed in with the salt. *Why would they put rice in with the salt?* he wondered to himself.

"No?" Marisol asked brightly. "Then why did she leave this on the table?" She picked up a Charlotte Plummer bar napkin with a phone number written across it in bold blue ink, and under the number, the name TRINNY in caps.

O.B. glanced at the napkin, surprised—how did he miss that?—then his eyes returned to his hands, which seemed to belong to someone else. Once again he felt the blood pumping into his head, flooding the capillaries in his face. He shifted in his seat and struggled to focus.

"Mr. Sweetwater, Miss Cavasos," he said. "I want to thank y'all for your help." Ranger Hadnott was anxious to wrap up the interview. The Vietnamese girl had thrown him off his game. "And I would really appreciate it if y'all would call me if you have any additional information that you think might be pertinent to the topics we discussed this evening. I'll just leave you my card..."

O.B. dug in his pocket for a DPS card, and not finding one he pulled out his pen and began to fumble for something to write on. Marisol held another bar napkin in her fingers, smiling.

"Here, Sergeant," she said, "Use this."

O.B. almost smiled as he wrote down the main switchboard number for the Aransas Pass DPS. "Dang things come in handy, don't they?"

He handed the napkin to Charlie and then Marisol handed Trinny's number to Officer Hadnott, who stuffed it in his pocket without looking at it.

"Goodnight," he said, rising from the table and placing his hat on his head. "Mr. Sweetwater. Ms. Cavasos. You two be careful."

After Sergeant Hadnott left, they got up to leave, as well.

"Who are we supposed to pay for our supper?" Charlie asked no one in particular as he looked around the empty and darkening restaurant. "And for the floor show, too?" The swinging doors opened and an old man in a filthy apron came through with a plastic tub. He started picking up dirty dishes from the empty booths. Charlie recognized him.

"Hey, Chucho!" he yelled across the room. "Do we pay you for this fine plate of fried fish that you cooked up for us tonight?" Charlie's appetite had returned, but his Fisherman's Platter had gone flying at the first punch.

The old man shrugged his shoulders. "You can pay or not pay. I don't care. Charlotte pays me to cook."

Charlie pulled a twenty-dollar bill from his pocket and threw it on the table. Heading for the door he said, "There you go, Chucho. You can call it a tip for the cook or you can give it to the management. Your choice."

Chucho waved without looking up from the dirty platters he was stacking.

Outside, Charlie and Marisol stood on the veranda in the waning light. The yellow pickup sat alone in the parking lot. With its protruding headlights and oversized silver bumper and grille, it appeared to grin sardonically at Charlie.

"Told ya," said Marisol.

"You want to go with me tomorrow to search for the *Ramrod*? Jake is taking me and Raul out on his boat."

"No thanks, Charlie. I've got some things to do in town. I could sure use your truck, though."

"Well, you and Miguel are apparently the only ones that know how to start the sonofabitch anyway."

"Hey, all us Chicanos are born knowin' how to boost a car. Didn't you know that?" she said, smiling.

Charlie smiled back. "You know, I'd heard that. You think you might be able to boost me over to the ferry, then? I guess I'll stay at Rupert and Vita's again tonight."

"I've got a better idea," she said. "You haven't eaten dinner yet and neither have I. And I've got jambalaya on the menu tonight at the Chateau Sweetwater. You interested?"

Charlie felt his pulse increase slightly. He tried not to let his mind leap too far ahead. She probably just wanted to grill him some more about Bao. "I am interested," he replied. "Barroom brawls make me ravenous."

"Okay," she said merrily, "but first let me show you how to go about stealing your own ride."

———

CHAPTER 26

Neon Leon Guidry moved like a Mardi Gras float through the dim lights that lent the Cloak Room a sepulchral air. Leon wore a shocking pink Hawaiian print shirt, crumpled white linen slacks, and a sweat-stained porkpie straw hat. The legislators and lobbyists who inhabited the deep booths turned to stare at Leon as he meandered through the happy hour crowd. A cheap cigar clenched in the corner of his mouth emitted a cloud of acrid smoke.

"Shoeshine" Jesse Miller, the doorman who had guarded the portals of Austin's premier political watering hole for years against just such riffraff, approached Guidry. "Can I help you...sir?" he asked, with only the thinnest veneer of politeness. A nearby bartender watched Jesse; if Jesse surreptitiously raised two fingers, it meant "call the cops." The bartender's hand was poised to dial.

"Thanks, Cap," Guidry rumbled. "Ah'm lookin' for one of yo' public soivants. Short little fella in a $300 suit. Big diamonds on his fingers. Prob'ly feed your baby to a dingo for a nickel."

Jesse Miller's mask of imperturbability did not shift a millimeter. That don't narrow it down much in here, he thought. But he replied with perfect finesse. "Ah, yes sir, Senator Cudihay said he would be expecting someone. I should have guessed. Please follow me."

The doorman led Leon to a smoky back corner of the bar. The tables were empty, except for one, at which sat Llewellyn Cudihay and an owlish-eyed young man who looked about fifteen years old. Cudihay had two cigarettes burning in an ashtray and a highball glass full of Cutty Sark in front of him. His companion sat staring slightly cross-eyed at four glasses of his own, the ice slowly melting in each. Apparently, he wasn't used to the pace of "conferences" with the Senator.

"Thanks for coming," Cudihay said effusively, rising up to pump Leon's hand as though pimping for votes. Guidry shook his head; some things never changed.

"Force a' habit, Leon," said the Senator, plopping his bulk back down in his chair. "Take a pew, Brother Guidry. Have a drink."

"Naw, I don't think so. I got ta make this short. L.C. Hebert is playing Soap Creek Saloon tonight, and I got ta meet him for sound check in an hour."

"Yes, I think I read about that," the Senator said. "You might have finally picked yourself a winning racehorse, Leon. Going to be a big show. Maybe I'll bring my sax, come sit in."

"L.C. would kill you, Lou-Ellen. An' if he didn't, I might. The last time you sat in at one of my shows, you got shitfaced and invited a waitress an' the guitar player's wife to play 'Escaped Convict and the Warden's Daughters' out in your limo. It cost me two large to keep dat club owner and my guitarist from skinnin' you like a nutria."

The Senator's pink face flushed. But only just a little.

"Yes, well...people in public life tend to have outsized appetites... But it's really L.C. I wanted to talk to you about, Leon."

For once, Guidry was surprised. He struggled to keep from showing it. A Texas senator shouldn't even acknowledge the existence of a black guitar player; it didn't fit. The only black people Cudihay took an active interest in were of the shapely female persuasion.

"You wanna autograph, Lou-Ellen?" asked Guidry, puzzled.

The Senator exhaled a lung full of smoke and leaned forward, the bonhomie gone from his eyes. He seemed to be staring inward, like a doctor contemplating the best way to deliver bad news to a patient.

"Yes, Leon, that's exactly it. I want an autograph."

Guidry suddenly felt wary. He cut his eyes toward the young man at Cudihay's elbow, who thus far had not uttered a word.

"Who's your prom date?" he asked.

The Senator favored the boy with a smile. "This is Robbie Mack. His daddy has been an invaluable supporter over the years. Robbie Mack is in the first year of law school over at the University. He helps me with some legal research and, uh, preparing documents." His smile positively twinkled.

As though Cudihay had pushed a coin into a slot, Robbie Mack leaned over, opened a briefcase at his feet, and removed a file, which he handed to the Senator.

Whatever is in that file, thought Neon Leon to himself, I'm gonna just hate it.

"I need an autograph, Leon," said the Senator, all business once more. "But not L.C. Hebert's. Yours." He pushed the file towards Guidry.

Guidry opened the file. It was a real horror show, all right.

On top was an indictment form, addressed to the grand jury of Travis County, undated. Neon Leon's name was neatly filled in. The signatures of the District Attorney and the State Comptroller were missing, but Guidry had no doubt that Cudihay could easily arrange for those oversights to be corrected. The document was a gun, loaded and cocked.

"Seems you haven't been paying your sales taxes to the Great State of Texas, Leon," said Cudihay sadly. "All the shows your acts have played in the state, all the concerts you've promoted, all the albums you've consigned to record stores.... There's a felony-sized chunk of change that the taxpayers are owed. By you."

Guidry sneered. "Dis is a chickenshit beef if I ever seen one. Fo' one thing, my taxes were paid. It's on file. Fo' another, I think the State a' Texas has better things ta do than to chase around one coonass bidnessman."

The Senator took a substantial gulp of whiskey and patted his mouth dry. "I feel almost certain the appropriate tax records will turn up missing, Leon. Robbie here is energetic, but somewhat disorganized. He doesn't always put things back where he found them.

"And yes, the state puts lots of priorities ahead of you. Almost all of them, in fact. But right now, I don't have that luxury. If I choose to call in some favors, I can have this taken to a grand jury...and, by the way, enjoin you from working in the state while your case is being considered. Down here, we empanel grand juries for six months. What would six months out of business in Texas do to your livelihood, old friend?"

You know goddamn well what it would do, you graverobbin' mother-fuckah, Leon thought to himself. But all he said aloud was, "Is dis all ya got?"

By way of answer, Cudihay nodded to the file. Leon turned over the next sheaf of documents. He sighed.

It was a copy of an old Fort Worth Police report.

The Senator shook his head. "That was a bad scene, Leon. Pistol-whipping two men in public. I think one of them had to eat soup through a straw for six months. Unlicensed firearm, felony assault ... the Fort Worth cops would love to clear this one."

"Dat was da Thompson brothers," Leon responded heatedly. "Dat was nuttin' but a goddamn shakedown."

Leon was putting up a good front, but it was about two-thirds bravado. Inwardly, he quailed from the ferocity of Cudihay's assault. They had never been in-the-trenches buddies, exactly, but the Senator was threatening the sort of Technicolor ruin and carnage that Leon could hardly imagine inflicting on his worst enemy. Broke, busted and maybe even looking at a stretch with the big stripes in some TDC shithole....

"Are we clear on this, podna?" the Senator asked, without responding to Leon's mea culpas.

"*Hell*, no," Guidry replied. "Maybe if you was to explain why you're coming down on me like I was Jack de Ripper..."

"Robbie Mack, would you excuse us for a minute?" the Senator asked. The young gofer gathered up his papers in a messy pile, crammed them in his briefcase and bid Guidry a slurred, Scotch-scented goodbye before caroming off the edge of the table and making his untidy exit.

"Now, then...."

Cudihay's voice was stripped of almost all inflection.

"I wanted to impress on you the seriousness of my situation," he continued. "There is someone who...requires a sum of money from me. He made himself clear to me, and I want to make myself clear to you. We go way back, but if you don't come through on this, I'll bury you deeper than King Tut."

"So where do you want my auto-graph, Lou-Ellen? I could make some suggestions, me."

"Here's what it is, ol' buddy. Someone who is in a position to... insist on things...needs an infusion of cash to make up for, ah, losses he suffered during the recent unfortunate turn of weather down on the Coast. You remember us talking about him.

"It's cash that I can't beg or borrow, or leastways have people see me doin' it. I already got the Senate ethics committee and that ambitious prick from Victoria County that's gunning for my seat lookin' over my shoulder at all that hurricane relief money I'm doling out. I need a banker who steps light. And you're a damned old Fred Astaire when it comes to your money. L.C. Hebert is your slot machine, paying off big time. There's enough sugar in that bowl to give me a taste. Now fix me up something good and we can forget all this recent unpleasantness and go chase some pussy."

Leon had to laugh. "I love your rebop, Lou-Ellen. Somethin' tells me dat Colonel Bao customer's got your ass in a sling. You really are scared of this guy, aren't you?"

Senator Cudihay took a swallow of whiskey. An amber thread snaked out of the corner of his mouth and down into his shirt collar. He looked at Guidry, however, with stone-sober eyes.

"Right down to my socks," he said. They talked some more. Or, rather, the Senator talked and Guidry listened.

Neon Leon sleepwalked his way out of the Cloak Room and out into the fading light of day. Numbly, Leon backed his big Chrysler Imperial out of the parking lot and headed west past the edge of town towards the neon roadhouse lights of Soap Creek Saloon. And it was there, watching L.C. Hebert weave his bluesman's spell, that he had an idea.

———

CHAPTER 27

"So I told you about my day. Now you can tell me about yours." Marisol said conversationally as they pulled off the Fulton Beach Road to let a Red Cross convoy roll by.

Charlie looked at her blankly. His adrenaline high had disappeared since the fight and he felt himself fading. He hadn't fully recovered from the hurricane ordeal or his wounds, which were beginning to hurt like hell. He felt like a nickel's worth of dogshit.

"Oh yeah, sorry, I'm kinda wiped out right now." Charlie yawned and rubbed his eyes. "Well, now that you mention it, I did find out some interesting news. I was going through the family heirlooms at the bank today—in the safe deposit box—and I ran across some blood tests from the hospital in Corpus."

"Blood tests? What were they doing there?"

"Johnny had 'em done. For him and for Raul...not that long ago either."

"Yeah, and...?"

"And it turns out that Raul is Johnny's biological son. The doc that wrote the report said the results were 95% conclusive. The mother is most likely a girl from Nuevo Laredo that used to work in a...um...a social club he used to frequent down there. Of course that was a long time ago," he added quickly. "Johnny hadn't seen her in years. Raul said she died in a car wreck earlier this year. "

The convoy passed and Charlie crept back onto the blacktop, driving slowly to avoid the limbs and other detritus the storm had deposited there. Marisol sat quietly. Her lover had fathered a whore's son. Hell of a late Christmas present.

Charlie looked over at Marisol to see how she was taking the news. He supposed she was wondering how long Johnny had known about all this before he died, and why he hadn't told her about it. But Charlie was wrong.

"This changes everything for you, doesn't it, Charlie?"

"For me?" He wasn't sure what she meant.

"Johnny's probably not coming back...and the boy doesn't have a mother. And Raul flat refuses to go back to Mexico, not that there's much of a life for him there. He's depending on *you* now. You're practically his closest relative. Like a father to him."

It took a moment for Charlie's brain to register all this. Finally he shook his head vigorously. "Whoa, whoa, whoa! Me? Like a father? I can't take care of that boy! And *I* sure don't have a problem returning to Mexico."

His voice faded as an indecipherable expression crossed Marisol's face. It might have been anger. Or exasperation. It was hard to tell in the dim light of the pickup.

They left the main road out of Fulton and drove in silence, skirting the southern shore of Copano Bay. Charlie turned at a sign marking Rattlesnake Point and followed it to a smaller, barely visible road paved in oyster shells. The low coppery sun gleamed off the puddles of standing water, casting the truck's shadow behind them in a black and angular shape.

The storm had rocked and rolled the house considerably. The lean-to shed at the end of the small pier was gone, and the pier itself listed drunkenly into the water, nearly all of the crosspieces stripped from the joists. The winds had uprooted a mesquite tree in the yard, and Charlie could see some hand-formed shingles were missing. But the roof still clung to the structure, the storm shutters had remained bolted shut and the wind hadn't detached the water tank at the side of the house, which meant that the gravity-fed water system probably still worked. At least to the extent that it had ever worked.

"How do you like Johnny's Better Homes and Gardens' show-piece?" Charlie asked with attempted levity.

He awaited a response, but Marisol only walked silently towards the front door. She fished around on a tiny shelf over the transom, removed a key and attempted to unlock the door with trembling hands.

The interlude of silence bothered Charlie out of all proportion.

Now the walls between them rose back up and Charlie felt the familiar onset of befuddlement, which promptly did its usual clumsy two-step with desire. *Is she pissed at me?* he wondered, clueless.

The inside of the shack smelled like a gypsy camp: mildew, fish, old grease, brackish water, and generic Gulf Coast funk. There were no lights—there was no power.

In lieu of electricity, providence offered up a multitude of rat-chewed candles and a couple of propane lanterns. No radio and no TV, but an old, paint-spattered jambox still functioned (once Marisol found some batteries in a kitchen drawer). Charlie found some old cassettes on a bookshelf: *Kind of Blue*, by Miles Davis; *20 Golden Hits*, by Ernest Tubb; and a tape of Chicano hits by Los Tigres del Norte and Little Joe y La Familia. But the cassette player didn't work and when Charlie tried the radio on the jambox, all it conveyed was news about the storm and the demented ravings of an evangelist somewhere down around Eagle Pass talking about "Gawd's will." He switched it off.

Marisol and Charlie unbattened the storm shutters, allowing the prevailing Gulf breezes to freshen the air. Walking across the room, Charlie stumbled over a stack of *Texas Highways* magazines and stooped to pick them up. He was exhausted nearly to the point of hallucination. His balance was suddenly a moment-to-moment thing and his arms seemed to have grown unusually long. Vertigo nibbled at the edges of his vision. Tension, fear, too many cigarettes, little sleep and less food—all had him on the ropes.

As for Marisol, she looked nearly as fresh as a spring wildflower, goddamn her. Two lines were chiseled between her brows, and her generous mouth was set in a firmer line than usual, but other than that, her vitality seemed nearly undiminished. "You set the table," she told Charlie, "I'll cook."

Charlie pulled a dusty-smelling sheet from a closet, and placed it on the dining table, which apparently also had served as a fly-tying table and a workbench—a vise was attached to one end. There was a small adjacent bedroom, but Charlie was reluctant to venture into it. Just the sight of a bed might jerk him into oblivion, like a piggy perch on a hook.

Marisol rummaged around in the kitchen behind him. "Let's see what we can whip up in this here *cocina*," she mumbled to herself.

She lit the lantern and lifted a beat up Styrofoam cooler onto the old linoleum countertop, and from it she began to withdraw miracles. A package of rapidly-thawing shrimp. Some rice and assorted vegetables. Coffee (coffee!). Some garlic and chilies. A can of milk. A bottle of Haitian rum (glory!). White wine. More candles and other sundry goodies materialized.

Setting the shrimp in the sink to finish thawing, she rummaged in the cupboard and found some cooking oil and a coffee can of miraculously-unmoldy flour. "*Bueno*," she said, and began to chop onions and celery and garlic and chilies.

Charlie leaned a hip against the counter and watched her work.

"You never did get around to telling me how you met Johnny," said Charlie, conversationally.

"The Marina."

"The Marina?"

"Yep," she replied impatiently, blowing a strand of hair out of her face with a quick puff. "He happened to be there when I was having a parole meeting with Miguel."

"He brought you here often?" Now that he was inside Johnny's house, Charlie felt the need to reconstruct some kind of memory of his brother and his life before he disappeared.

"Of course he brought me here," she said without looking at him. "This was his home."

Charlie could almost imagine Johnny sitting at the table, sipping on a beer and watching Marisol cook, just as he was doing now.

"But Johnny always cooked," she said, bluntly, evaporating the tableau Charlie had imagined. She lifted the long butcher knife and pointed it at him. "And *I* watched."

Charlie took this as a hint that she wanted him to help, so he began rummaging around in the cabinet above the sink, searching for a skillet. Marisol set down the knife and pushed the cabinet door closed. Charlie backed away as she reached down and grabbed a heavy cast iron skillet from under the sink, slamming it down heavily on the burner.

"I can handle it," she said irritably. "There's no room in here for you." Abruptly she stopped working and placed both hands on the counter. She gazed broodingly out the kitchen window at the crepuscular light, her face as dark as the bay.

"Dang. I can't even help out in my own kitchen?" Charlie asked facetiously. He wasn't sure what to make of the mood that had come over this girl.

"It's not your kitchen," she said heatedly, without looking at him. "It may turn out you own the building, but this home is not yours. You don't deserve to claim it."

"What's got into you, Marisol?"

No response.

"You're kind of a chickenshit without your butcher knife, aren't you?"

Then she did look at him.

"I would not be talking about chickenshits if I were you."

"Why the hell not?" he answered.

She picked up the knife again and he watched the blade flash in the lantern light as she deftly sliced, chopped and minced. Brown hands on a silver knife. Flour was beginning to brown in oil. Marisol stirred the roux with short, angry strokes.

"Why the hell not?" Charlie repeated. He felt like his head was beginning to fill with hot, greasy smoke.

Her voice floated back over her shoulder as though from a great distance. "You don't seem burdened with an excess of courage, Charlie," she said sadly. "I think Johnny knew that about you. You are his brother, and in some ways so much like him. But he swam in life's river, while you have barely stuck your toe in the water."

"What a bunch of existential horseshit," Charlie snarled. His hands shook, and his tongue felt so thick he could barely articulate words. "Just where does some Tex-Mex tootsie get off with some kind of half-bright..."

"Psy-co-log-ical insight?" she said mockingly. "Maybe I'm a *bruja*, Charlie, and I can read your mind. Maybe I'm being a bitch. Or maybe I'm just calling you on your bullshit. I just...expected more from you," she added quietly.

Charlie found it hard to focus. He was infinitely tired. "Like what?" he mumbled.

She stirred the vegetables into the darkened roux. "How well do you think Johnny knew you?" she asked.

"Not worth a goddamn, I guess, according to you."

"I think he knew you *too* well."

"What the hell does that mean?" Charlie demanded.

"After your dad died, Johnny asked you to help out with the family business, and he told me you said no. But he defended you and said that the boats and the business, staying here in Fulton, was a choice, not an obligation. He didn't begrudge your choice to move on. And he didn't bother you with details of his feud with Bao, because he knew what your response would be. You couldn't be bothered.

"But now, it's more than that, isn't it? There are obligations. Johnny has a son—a son with no home, and no father. But to you, Raul and the boat, Johnny's *accident*, they are only an *inconvenience*... No jumping into the river for you."

"Jump in the river?" He was rigid with anger. "I carried Raul through a fucking hurricane! And I haven't exactly backed down from Bao."

She shrugged, and now her eyes were hot, too. "As for the storm... you were there; he was there. You both survived. That was just *fortuna*."

The vegetables and shrimp steamed fragrantly in the pot. Somewhere in the back of his mind, Charlie felt his stomach growl with hunger as the savory aromas permeated the room. But fury and embarrassment crowded the sensation out.

"And your fights with the gangster Bao..." she continued, "they are just...reckless. You have a temper, and you aren't scared to react to danger. Big deal. Johnny was like that too. But I'm talking about something else."

"What the hell *are* you talking about?" he said, his voice tangled with exasperation.

"Don't you realize it was Raul that Johnny wanted you to meet? He wanted you to meet his son...." She turned away and extinguished the flame under the pot. "Johnny had the courage to commit to something. To the family business. And to Raul. You don't," she concluded.

Charlie's mind roiled in tired confusion. "I don't have a thing to prove to you."

"No, *nada*," she snapped. "But I hoped you might just be capable of one brave thing. I never thought it was too much to ask until now." She waved her hand at him, dismissively.

He reached out and caught her wrist.

Afterwards, he could never quite reconstruct events. She pulled back—or did she? Somehow, they both turned in counterpoint and wound up with her arm twisted between them, pressed against the wall of the tiny kitchen.

Her breath was smoking with heat, her eyes—as Charlie could see from two inches away—sparking with emotion. His own brain synapses popped and crackled like a fistful of Black Cats.

He started to step back, but her free hand caught the back of his head and pulled him forward. As their lips met and their bodies swayed back, they took a step and stumbled backwards over a kitchen chair. Toppling from a great height, they fell until they landed on the couch in the tiny living room.

Charlie didn't get up—he couldn't. She was on top, their limbs tangled up like the Devil's own garden hose.

Shadows fell down around them.

"One brave thing..." somebody whispered in the dark.

They moved with the slow and drunken deliberation of exhausted dreamers, and afterwards Charlie was never entirely certain he had not imagined the whole thing. He felt so tired, so far gone on the ragged edges of emotion and sensation that their movements felt like an abstraction. And when she leaned over him, her dark hair sweeping across his face, even the landscape of dreams was blotted out.

As their bodies entwined, he tasted the ocean. *Ah yes...that
again*, he thought distantly. For days, he had been immersed in the
salty, funky, humid emulsion of the Gulf. Air and water and Marisol
seemed to dissolve into one another in a sort of elemental essence. It
was a hallucinatory revelation.

They lay together on the couch in silence, holding each other
tightly. Later, against his will, he fell exhausted into sleep.

Feeling adrift and a little disconsolate, Marisol arose from their
embrace. Far from certain about her own motives, for a moment she
felt a fresh sense of completion and resolve. But at the same time, she
recognized the impulse for what it was—a bad idea. Sleeping with
Johnny's brother wasn't going to solve anything.

"One brave thing," she said quietly, and she did not know if she
addressed the words to Charlie or herself.

She heated up a bowl of the jambalaya on the stove, extinguished
the lantern, and ate outside in the moonlight, out on the deck overlooking the water. She was naked, but the breeze kept the mosquitoes
back under the bushes. After her meal, she lit a Delicado cigarette
she had filched from a pack in the kitchen, and sipped from a glass
of Barbencourt rum. She smoked in silence and stared out across
Copano Bay at the distant silver line that delineated the water from
the sky.

CHAPTER 28

Leon Guidry regarded L.C. Hebert with some misgivings. The two men sat in a corner booth of the coffee shop of the Austin Motel, where L.C. and the band were staying.

Hebert, in turn, regarded Neon Leon with equanimity. His manager/lawyer/record company president/booking agent and general all-pro fixer obviously had something on his knotty little mind. L.C. knew there was a certain amount of social discourse to dispense with before they got to it. They'd been chatting about this and that for the better part of an hour; it wouldn't be long now.

"...So I was walkin' wid Michelle an' Angela down Telephone Road last Sattidy, an' yonder comes Lyle Mentone, you know dat sorry bastard, him?"

"Yeah," said Hebert, sipping a cup of coffee. "He told me one time I ought to switch to bass—two less strings to think about. Talk about a waste of skin."

Leon snorted cynically and said, "He looked wasted awright. When I saw him up close, he looked like he'd taken out about forty feet of guardrail. Musta been a long Friday night.

"Anyway, me an' Michelle an' Angela were strollin' along, an' he does a double-take when he sees us. 'Man,' Lyle says, 'You got one woman too many...'" Leon paused, savoring his punch line. L.C. made a little rolling motion with his hand to move things along.

Leon chuckled—not a pretty sound. "I said, 'Hey, Lyle, it's okay...I got two dicks'."

L.C. Hebert laughed appreciatively. Michelle and Angela were his cousin and sister-in-law, respectively, but of course that didn't matter to Leon. They were both fine-looking women, and L.C. could only speculate on their reaction to Leon's Noel Coward-esque bon mot.

Leon had some funny blind spots, he thought. He'd publicly mortify his friends and kinfolks without a second thought, fuck a rock pile on the off chance there was a snake in it and pistol-whip anybody who jacked him around. But he went to Mass every Sunday, kept five abandoned pug dogs in his two-bedroom shotgun house near the Gulf Freeway and seemed—so far, at least—constitutionally incapable of blindsiding any musician once he had taken him or her under his wing.

Guidry himself wasn't so sure about that last part anymore. He had spent the previous night chewing over his conversation with Senator Cudihay while L.C. finished playing to a packed house at Soap Creek Saloon.

Cudihay needed a big wad of untraceable cash, needed it quick, and evidently couldn't get it elsewhere. It wasn't a typical shakedown. The Senator had looked pasty and desperate when he braced Leon in the Cloak Room. Scared people made Leon nervous. You couldn't predict what they'd do.

Leon hated bush-leaguers. Give me a stone-cold gangster any day, he thought. *Lou-Ellen, you may be a stud duck in the political trenches, but you're in way over your head on this shit.* In the meantime, he could see his client had run out of patience and small talk.

"Well, L.C.," he said haltingly, "I wanna see if you're happy wid our arrangements. You got a Grammy nomination now, the phone's ringin' like crazy, mebbe we're all gonna get real busy real soon. I was thinkin', we might wanna talk about, ah, uppin' the ante on some things, ya know?"

"Hey, Leon," Hebert replied, "I hate paperwork. You book the gigs and pay the band. My management contract is with you, and my recording contract too. You keep track of my royalties, and that's cool. I trust you been payin' my taxes to the state and the feds—you damn well better be. You keep me and the band on an allowance—a per diem, I guess you call it—and that's enough for me. I just like to have a little whip-out on hand when I want it; I always thought those big flash rolls were for punks, ya know?"

L.C. leaned back in the booth and spread his hands. "So, I dunno, man," he said with a small smile. "The ante already seems pretty up there to me."

"Well, I was thinkin'..." Guidry began, suddenly hesitant. "...Ah, what I thought I might do, ah, is take a loan—an advance, really—against some of your future royalties. Get liquid, you dig? Get a big chunk of change together an' put together a national tour. Hit da coasts. Book some studio time. Mebbe look at hirin' some more horn players like we been talkin' about.

"I t'ink you got a lock on this Grammy, and when you win it, there's gonna be a lot of heat and light on you. We gotta be ready to take advantage of it. Your whole catalog's gonna get a big bump in sales. We gotta press up some more of da older albums, be ready to meet the demand. Hell, who knows, maybe Columbia or Atlantic might decide to license the damn things and put 'em out themselves. Hey, a major label, podnah! We'd be fartin' through silk."

L.C. Hebert lifted his fork and drew the tines slowly through the busted yolk of fried egg on his plate. He swirled the cold coffee in his cup. "Advance against royalties, huh?" He said slowly, raising a skeptical eyebrow. "Big chunk of change, you said."

Guidry seemed in a hurry to wrap things up. "Well, yeah, podnah, it's bidness, y'know. Paperwork an' shit. I typed up a letter of agreement last night..." he reached into the inside pocket of his seersucker jacket and pulled out a folded sheet of motel stationery "...an' if you wanna sign this, I'll draw up the real thing when I get back to Houston..."

Hebert held up a palm, gently, but the gesture shut Neon Leon up as effectively as a noose around the neck.

"This ain't you, Leon," L.C. said quietly. He looked into Guidry's perpetually bloodshot eyes. "This ain't you."

"Wadda you mean?" he replied.

"It ain't like you to be so obvious and...clumsy. You a hustler, Leon, but not a stupid and ham-fisted one. You tend to be more, ah, oblique." (Leon blinked. He wasn't sure what "oblique" meant, but he was pretty sure the word had never come up in his conversations with L.C. before.)

Hebert leaned forward and propped his chin on his folded hands. He peered intently at Leon.

"You can't take an advance against my royalties, Leon, 'cause they go straight into a tax-deferred escrow account. You can't press more copies of my old albums because you've got pallets of my old stuff sitting in wholesalers' warehouses all over Texas an' Louisiana, and you've been writing 'em off on your taxes as returned inventory. The feds would be all over you like a duck on a June bug if you dropped another ten or twenty thousand units all over the landscape. And you can't license my catalog to a big-shot label, 'cause all of my masters—in case you've forgotten—revert back to me five years after the release of every album."

Leon Guidry—there was no other word for it—gaped. His jaw literally dropped, in a way it hadn't since he was twelve years old and he'd first seen fourteen-year old Mary Lou Broussard naked.

He stared at L.C. Hebert as though the young man had suddenly started speaking in tongues.

"Another thing you oughta know, Leon..." L.C. was enjoying himself in his laid-back way, Guidry couldn't help but notice "...I been doin' a little, ah, private audit of your books since six months after we started workin' together. You're on the road a lot, I gotta key to the office, and, well, those filin' cabinets of yours aren't exactly Fort Knox."

Leon barely managed to get his voice working. "Audit?"

L.C. smiled. "Yeah, Leon. Somethin' you didn't know—the little colored guitar player once took an undergraduate degree in accounting at Prairie View A&M. Scary, huh?"

"Goddamn terrifyin'. Where do you get off sneakin' behind my back, lookin' at my books, you little bastid?"

"You can stand on any corner in Texas and swing a bushel basket and fill it up with broke-down, busted junkie musicians. I'm not gonna be one of 'em. You've always taken a little cream off the top, Leon. I don't think you can help it. It's your nature, and I think you'd be all knotted up if you couldn't skim something offa someone.

"But that's okay. I understand that. That's the price I pay for you havin' my back, takin' care of the day-to-day, keeping the assholes at arm's length from me, and protectin' my interests. I can let some cream slide. Call it a little extra off-the-books commission."

The twinkle of amusement went out of L.C.'s eyes. "That's why I don't understand this. It's...inept. And insulting."

He unfolded his hands and spread them in a gesture of inquiry.

"So, c'mon, podnah. What's really goin' on?"

Leon felt...sheepish. He couldn't quite put a finger on it. A sense of absolution, maybe. L.C. was letting him off the hook. There was the sense of a weight sliding off his shoulders. Or maybe he was finally cocking an ear towards, God help him, the better angels of his nature. Christ, maybe the nuns back in school were right; there was a conscience in there somewhere.

He leaned back and lit his first cigar of the day. "Well...lessee... you remember our mutual friend, Lou-Ellen Cudihay, that fat white man who used to come sniffin' around at the gigs?"

"The Senator didn't exactly make himself scarce when there was whiskey and women floating around."

"Don't I know it. Well, last night he called me to meet him, an'..." Guidry laid it all out—the flushed and nervous politician, the outsized threats, the abrupt ultimatum....

"Sounds like someone's puttin' the squeeze on him," L.C. observed.

"My very thought, and I know who" Leon agreed. "I'll tell you one thing, podnah—I ain't gonna sit still for a tax beef or anything else in that bastard's bag of tricks. But right off, I can't see what to do about it.

"Well, lemme think...." L.C. said. "Lemme think on it...."

As L.C. Hebert pondered, Leon Guidry did some thinking himself. *I think*, he mused to himself, *I gotta change da lock on dat office.*

CHAPTER 29

O.B. scalded his tongue when he sipped the coffee that Melba, the sole proprietor of the Palm Harbor Marina, had just handed him.

"It's a little hot, honey," said Melba with a big smile.

The marina was empty except for Melba and the Ranger. Melba had long auburn hair, an attractive if somewhat weathered face and an athletic figure that looked like it had gone over its share of hurdles. She was starting to make O.B. very nervous.

The less O.B. responded to Melba's conversation, the more she seemed to be interested in him. That confluence worked against O.B., because by nature he did not waste a single word.

Through the window, O.B. spotted a boat motoring toward the jetties that formed the entrance to the Palm Harbor canal. He seized the moment. "I think that might be my man," he announced a little too loud. He stood up quickly and reached into his back pocket for his wallet.

Melba laughed. "No charge, cowboy," she said. As he headed for the door she added, "I didn't mean to scare you off." O.B. walked out the door with what he fancied was dignified deliberation.

The boat belonged to a crabber, so O.B. sat on a wooden picnic table under a tall sable palm and waited for Rupert Sweetwater's motorboat to arrive. Rupert had called him a couple of hours ago and asked him to meet him at this marina. He said he had some information that might help him in his case against Colonel Bao. "I could sure as hell use it," O.B. had told him.

As O.B. watched the bay he puzzled over another conundrum, namely what to do with the phone number still burning a hole in his front pocket. He removed his hat and placed it on the table, then removed the square cocktail napkin and read, for the hundredth time, Trinny's note. And for the hundredth time he rehearsed the things he would say to Trinny if he ever worked up the nerve to call her.

She had been on his mind since he'd first seen her behind the counter at the Sea-Tex fish house and then later, at the restaurant. As he went about his daily business she crowded into his thoughts more and more, and at the most unexpected times.

He imagined her with him when he ate his solitary meals, when he went to buy his frozen dinners and soda pop at the store, when he witnessed a flight of pelicans gliding in a graceful line over the bay. He knew he shouldn't indulge in such schoolboy daydreams, but he liked the way they made him feel.

Things were getting slippery, the longer he was away from the iron certitudes of West Texas. He felt adrift, literally, the more he marinated in the salt air and foreign, tropical sun. He also knew he was venturing way out of his comfort zone, which rested somewhere between stoic abstinence and a gloomy pessimism regarding all things romantic.

O.B. wondered what life would have had in store for him if he hadn't become a Ranger: if he had stayed back in Rotan, working on a pipeline crew or driving an oilfield service truck like his dad, living in a glorified line shack. No wife or, worse yet, married to one of the dull and beaten-down Bible-thumping West Texas harridans who sucked the joy out of every day.

He thought of his boyhood friend, Buddy Ruff—on his third wife and working on his third heart attack, the last he'd heard. He thought of the commitment he'd made to the Ranger life, one he honored, yet at times seemed like one long series of stakeouts, drafty apartments, solitary holidays and cheap motels like the one he found himself doing time in now.

In truth, he had always been mystified by the female sex and he knew his experience in this area was woefully undeveloped. Yet his thoughts kept returning to Trinny, without any clear understanding of the reason. What would be the reaction, he wondered, if he showed up back in the High Plains with her on his arm? Astonished at his own audacity, he began to consider something he would have considered unimaginable only a week ago.

The women back home who had once set their sights on the quiet, rugged-looking Texas Ranger had all but given up on O.B. Hadnott. "His heart's broke," they said. "He was jilted by his first love," they whispered to each other.

All true enough, but O.B. never talked about that, not to anybody, not even to Buddy Ruff. O.B. felt pretty sure he'd never have to think again about the events of that raw winter night back in Odessa, when he was still a young DPS officer doing his time on the roads of West Texas. That is, until department orders sent him down to the Gulf Coast to investigate a case involving, of all people, Llewellyn Cudihay.

It so happened that for a few dizzy months in Officer O.B. Hadnott's young life, he had been in love.

Nadine Thaxton worked as a secretary in the vehicle license division of the Midland-Odessa Dept. of Public Safety office. She was buxom, boisterous and almost a natural blond. O.B. had secretly admired her for months and finally a friend inside the Department set them up—a double date at the Coronado Bowling Lanes with another patrolman and his girl.

To O.B.'s eternal wonder, Nadine took a liking to him and the two got along famously. As their courtship progressed, he even allowed himself to imagine a future that included a Mrs. O.B. Hadnott, a modest country home where they could both settle down, and maybe, who knows, even some little Hadnotts to carry on the family name. Junior Rangers, so to speak.

O.B.'s West Texas dream progressed according to plan until a certain freshman state senator who made frequent trips to the area happened upon Nadine one afternoon at a Dairy Queen in Odessa. The legislator was in Odessa for work related to his position on the Interstate Oil and Gas Commission.

Not particularly wise to the ways of the world, but wanting to be, Nadine was quickly taken in by Senator Cudihay's polished line of bullshit. For several months, O.B. was oblivious to the side action that Nadine was getting with the Senator until, before his very eyes, Cudihay snatched her from his life.

A group of local investors, flush with money and certain that the oil boom in West Texas would last forever, chose an unlikely and impractical location for the Oil Patch Restaurant, which they somehow wedged into a galvanized double-wall steel drum storage reservoir. The converted sludge tank was, for a few years at least, an upscale steakhouse (at least for Odessa), frequented by what passed for local high rollers and big wigs. A spiral staircase wound around the inside of the circular tank, leading patrons from the ground floor restaurant up to a members-only cocktail bar that formed a curved elevated platform hanging out over the kitchen and part of the dining area. From this vantage point, Cudihay spied O.B. entering the restaurant with his lovely date. In spite of the nasty blue norther that was blowing dust and snow sideways across the plains, the Oil Patch was full of patrons.

Fueled by a considerable amount of Wild Turkey, Llewellyn Cudihay watched as the young highway patrolman removed Nadine's coat and scarf and ceremoniously pulled out a chair for her at a table. He'd saved up a month's worth of patrolman's pay for the night out.

The visiting Texaco executives and local big wheels that sat at the table swapped jokes and laughed and slapped each other on the back, but Cudihay only half listened. All his predatory attention was focused on Nadine. Slipping around and sneak-fucking was new to Nadine, but old hat to Cudihay. In his drunken bravado, he decided to go public with his new conquest. Screw these Dust Bowl yokels and, in particular, screw the gangling young highway patrolman who was cramping his style.

After the two lovebirds sitting below had received their drinks and ordered dinner from the waiter, Cudihay made a phone call from the bar. Within five minutes the headwaiter approached O.B.'s table and informed him that he had received a message requesting that Trooper Hadnott contact the DPS office immediately. O.B. excused himself and walked to the pay phone located in a foyer area near the restrooms. As O.B. dutifully dialed an office that was not expecting his call, Cudihay grabbed his coat, made quick apologies to his party for having to leave, and headed down the stairs.

The young officer spoke impatiently with the department switchboard, trying to figure out what couldn't wait until he was back on duty the next day. His confusion increased when he looked back across the room toward his date and saw a portly stranger in a fancy blue suit leaning over *his* table, whispering in his girlfriend's ear.

The switchboard finally connected Trooper Hadnott with the ranking DPS officer on duty and O.B. turned to the wall, straining to hear the sergeant over the noisy din in the restaurant. When he turned around again, the man in the blue suit was holding Nadine by the arm, hustling her towards the exit. On their way out the man slipped a bill to the headwaiter, who rushed to hold the door for the couple as they left. The man in the blue suit said something close to Nadine's ear and she threw back her head and laughed out loud. A clear, lusty, musical laugh. O.B. could hear it from the other side of the restaurant where he stood, dumbfounded.

When it finally occurred to him what was happening, O.B. Hadnott strode to the entrance, his brows furrowed. Standing outside the restaurant in the swirling wind, he caught a glimpse of a white Caddy screeching out of the parking lot onto Grandview Avenue. The car fishtailed on the slick pavement. Sleet slanted down through the cones of light formed by the street lamps and, for a moment, the light illuminated the interior of the Cadillac just enough for O.B. to see that Nadine was scooted up close to the driver, her head resting on his shoulder.

That was the last he saw of Nadine Thaxton. And, up until this week, Llewellyn Cudihay.

A short time later, Rupert's small Hunter came into view and O.B. carefully squared the Stetson on his angular head. He quickly stuffed the bar napkin into his shirt pocket and his hand moved to the cinco peso badge on the other side of his chest. He fiddled with the badge for a moment, making sure it was pinned on straight and then he stood up resolutely.

You had better focus on your investigation, Olin Brady Hadnott, he scolded himself...*before the damn thing gets away from you.*

Two Vietnamese men rode with Rupert in the boat. Rupert tossed a line to Officer Hadnott as he sidled his boat up next to the bulkhead. To keep the boat from scraping the concrete, O.B. sat on the ledge with his boots on the gunwale of the Hunter.

"My friends here don't wanna tie up at the public dock," Rupert explained, nodding toward the marina. "Too many eyes, and we don't know who they might belong to."

The older Vietnamese man appeared to be about sixty or seventy. He wore loose, paint- and grease-stained khaki pants and a mostly white undershirt. A wide-brimmed conical straw hat was held tight over his head by a piece of string cinched up under his chin. He had the leathery look of commercial fishermen everywhere. The younger man, a boy really, wore a Texas A&M T-shirt and a baseball cap. Rupert sported a battered beige pith helmet and a long-sleeve work shirt.

Rupert cut the engine. "You meet Melba yet?" he asked, smiling.

"Yep." O.B. answered.

"She invite you to run off to Vegas for a little blackjack and maybe a visit to that Elvis wedding chapel they got?"

"Um," was all the Ranger could reply. He'd had a feeling Melba would play him like a hot quarter slot if she got half a chance.

Rupert laughed again. "She's not the bashful sort. Vita gets about half jealous ever time I have to come by here for something. Anyway, thanks for meeting us here. Sergeant Hadnott, this is Nu Dang, and his nephew Sammy."

The two men didn't look up at the Texas Ranger. "Mr. Dang doesn't speak any English, but his nephew does. I've known Nu Dang since he came here from Vietnam four years ago. Started out with nothing but an aluminum skiff and some homemade nets and now he owns free and clear one of the finest shrimp boats in the harbor. The *New Hope* is her name. He used to be my biggest seafood supplier until Bao forced him into selling exclusively to Sea-Tex. Sammy here is Mr. Dang's nephew, as I mentioned. He's learning how to play American football, aren't you, Sammy?"

The boy nodded solemnly. He was tall and slender but starting to fill out.

"He'll be trying out for the football team come spring," Rupert added.

"Pleased to meet you," said O.B., addressing the men.

The two Vietnamese barely looked up and continued to sit patiently in the boat.

"Well, these two gentlemen showed up at my place this morning and said they wanted to talk to the Texas Ranger. They asked me if they could trust you and I told 'em they could," Rupert declared, looking the Ranger in the eye to stress the point. "They don't have a lot of confidence in local law enforcement, and for obvious reasons, they don't want Bao or his gang to find out they're talking to anybody with a badge."

O.B. nodded. "Fair enough," he said.

"They said they've got something you might be able to use," continued Rupert. "I don't know the details 'cause Mr. Dang, he's not the talkative sort, and Sammy's along to translate what his uncle says."

Rupert nodded to Sammy who said something to his uncle in Vietnamese. The old fisherman stood up, pulled a small cassette tape from his pocket and handed it to O.B. He looked at the Texas Ranger and began to speak rapidly and vigorously in Vietnamese. After he finished he sat down and grunted something to his nephew.

"My uncle says that Nguyen Ngoc Bao is a bad man," the boy began, not making eye contact. "He says that he was a bad man in our old country and he is a bad man here in our new country." Sammy paused, then continued. "He says that when a cat steals a piece of meat, we chase it. But when a leopard takes a pig, we stare wide-eyed and say nothing.

"That is a proverb in Vietnam," the boy added apologetically. "My uncle uses them a lot. He also says that he is tired of being bullied by men like Bao and he feels ashamed that our immigrant community lies on the shore like jellyfish, doing nothing. He says that the tape he gives you is from a telephone answering machine that his wife bought for their business. He says the tape will help you."

O.B. blinked and looked at Rupert, then he looked back at the boy. "What's on the tape?" he asked.

Nu Dang apparently understood this because he answered O.B. directly. Sammy translated.

"He says it is one of Bao's lieutenants on the phone making threats, then Bao himself."

"Making threats?" asked O.B., wondering if a recording of a phone conversation in Vietnamese would carry much weight in a Texas court of law.

The old man nodded fervently and elaborated. His nephew cleared his throat and spoke again.

"Yes, threats to my uncle, threats to his family, threats to his boat. Many threats. Disgraceful insults." The uncle threw in a final comment and Sammy dutifully translated. "He says the Colonel thinks he is still in Vietnam in time of war and that he can do anything he wants."

"Why did Bao threaten you, Mr. Dang?" asked O.B.

Sammy translated again. "My uncle says that Bao wants to make trouble for him because he refuses to respect the fishing territory that he was assigned. And for being insolent."

"For being insolent?"

"You listen tape!" said the old man, pointing at the cassette in O.B.'s hand. "Listen tape!"

O.B. looked down at the tape and then addressed the old Vietnamese fisherman, slapping the tape against his open palm. "I'll do that, Mr. Dang. Thank you for coming forward with this information. And thanks to your nephew for the fine translation." He looked at the boy. "You speak pretty good English."

The boy almost smiled but caught himself. "Thanks," he mumbled.

"Nothing but straight 'A's since he's been enrolled in our schools is the way I hear it," added Rupert. "Young Sammy here will be valedictorian of the high school if he keeps it up."

O.B. nodded. "Well, good luck to you, Sammy." Then he thought to ask, "Are the Pirates gonna do any good this year?" Football was always an appropriate topic of conversation in Texas.

Sammy pursed his lips thoughtfully before answering. "Maybe next year," he said. "We lost fourteen starters from last year."

"A rebuilding year," Rupert explained. "Anything else Sergeant Hadnott? Before we shove off? I know Mr. Dang would like to get back to his boat. He's a feisty old rooster but he he'd just as soon not be seen talking to a Texas Ranger, if you know what I mean."

O.B. agreed and thanked the men again. Rupert started the engine and the old fisherman decided to make one last pronouncement.

O.B. and Rupert waited for the translation, which Sammy had to think about before he spoke.

"My uncle says that you must catch the bear before you sell his skin."

———

CHAPTER 30

"How the hell did you get a shrimp boat through these shallows, Charlie?" asked Jake as he carefully maneuvered his Bertram over a shell bottom reef in Ayers Bay. "I've never seen the tide this high and I'm still skimming the bottom here."

Raul was perched on the bow intently studying the shoreline, hoping to be the first one to spot the outriggers of the *Ramrod*. Charlie leaned out over the boat's flying bridge, scanning the surrounding marsh with binoculars and growing more despondent by the minute. For four hours they had been searching for the shrimp boat.

Earlier that morning Marisol had dropped Charlie off at Jake's boat in Rockport Harbor. He had agreed to let her use his truck so she insisted he take the stolen bicycle for transportation. "Try not to look suspicious," she'd said with a forced smile. Their ardor of the previous night had cooled considerably and neither one of them knew quite what to say to each other. It had been an awkward morning.

"Jake, I think the storm pushed half the water in San Antonio Bay through here," Charlie replied. "The *Queen Mary* could have floated these bays."

"Didn't you say Bao's crew boat went down just before you ran aground?" asked Jake.

"Yeah. The best I can figure, that would've happened right back there somewhere," he said, pointing to a spoil bank about a hundred yards behind them, "Near Snake Island. It must have gone down in the deep water in the Intracoastal. Otherwise, we should've seen it."

"Or somebody already salvaged it," Jake suggested.

"Maybe," said Charlie.

Jake guided his boat back into the Intracoastal channel and increased his speed. "One more pass, Charlie?"

Charlie remained silent, not wanting to quit. A few minutes later Raul cried out excitedly from the bow. "Look Charlie, this is where we crawled, *recuerdas*? I remember the post with the white sign." He pointed to a piling that poked out of the marsh at a 45-degree angle. A broken white board was bolted to the post, which currently served as a perch for a brown pelican.

"I remember because I think, if the wind blow that post over, it blow us over for sure!" Raul said, laughing.

Jake let his eyes follow the path that Charlie and the boy must have used to crawl to the observation tower that rose in the distance, barely visible, hundreds of yards away. What a horror that must have been, he thought. But Charlie wasn't interested in reliving their hurricane ordeal; he looked the other direction, calculating where the shrimp boat would have run aground in the marsh before the storm forced him and Raul to abandon it.

"Let's anchor over there, Jake. At the mouth of that lake," said Charlie. "I think it's time to get our feet wet." His voice sounded tentative; he was afraid of what they would find.

But it was far worse than what Charlie had feared. They had expected a foundered and capsized—but salvageable—boat. But the *Ramrod* lay one hundred feet from the natural shoreline of Mustang Lake, a blackened husk resting on its side in the tall marsh grass. The metal outriggers, cable rigging and masts were scattered across the scorched remains, collapsed where the heat had weakened their supports. Trawling nets had melted into tar-like globs over the surface of the deck. A bitter, acrid smell filled the air.

The sight of the burned-out wreck made Charlie physically sick. He felt violated as he looked at the ruins of the vessel into which his family had put so many thousands of hours of backbreaking work and so much—admit it, he thought—love. It was the last remaining tie to his family and he wasn't prepared for the emotion that washed over him. The loss cut deep.

"Jesus H. Christ," mumbled Jake.

Charlie tentatively poked around the boat, which had not yet cooled from the intense fire. Jake instinctively left him alone. After several minutes, Charlie motioned for Jake, who still gawked at the smoldering trawler, to come closer.

"Check it out." Several sets of footprints were imprinted in the mud around the boat.

"Somebody was awfully interested in your boat, weren't they?" Jake commented. His nostrils flared as he sniffed the air. "Gas. I smell gas."

"Not diesel?" asked Charlie.

"No. Gas. Somebody used gasoline to torch your boat, Charlie. Would have suited them fine if you'd still been aboard, I'd reckon."

The group kicked around the wreckage for another half hour, then deciding there was next to nothing to salvage, slogged back to Jake's boat.

No one talked on the trip back to Rockport. Charlie was solemn and brooding. Raul also maintained his silence from the prow of the Bertram, but he delighted in a pod of porpoises that led them across Aransas Bay almost to the harbor.

Why worry? he told himself. Charlie would figure something out. Just like Johnny had always done. They would find another boat to work together. Everything would be all right.

The porpoises watched Raul with bright, intelligent eyes as they glided effortlessly through the water in front of the boat, their curious expressions and mysterious smiles reflecting Raul's buoyant optimism.

Jake dropped Charlie off at the Rockport Pier where Charlie had left his Schwinn bicycle leaning up against a piling early that morning. Jake agreed to transport Raul back to Shady's for safekeeping.

"It's the best place for you to be right now, *chavo*," Charlie insisted. Raul was still suspicious someone might ship him back to Mexico. "All the Big Red you can drink."

"You come back for me?" asked the boy.

"*Por supuesto*, kid" he answered. He almost called him *sobrino* (nephew) but didn't. *You're gonna have to tell him sometime*, he thought. But at present, Charlie was not in a magnanimous frame of mind.

He thanked Jake again and climbed onto the bike. Even though he had no particular destination, he pedaled away from the pier with great deliberation. He needed the physical exertion. He needed to *do* something.

As he vigorously pumped the pedals his mind swirled with visions of the *Ramrod*, a smoking wreck, lying charred and desecrated on the muddy bank of the lagoon. *Okay, so maybe I was wasn't going to stay and work it*, he thought, but the old shrimp boat contained many of his most precious family memories.

An agitated succession of these images bubbled up through Charlie's consciousness—images of Dubber sitting on the back deck, heading shrimp, wearing his trademark Greek sailor's cap; images of Johnny as a boy, working and playing with Charlie on the boat; and images of Johnny later, as a man, standing with Raul in the wheel-house, the sea breeze ruffling their identical curly blond hair. There was also a disturbing image of Johnny floating face down in the salty water somewhere out in the Gulf.

He pedaled furiously along Fulton Beach Road, feeling anger, guilt and remorse, trying to outrun the corrosive sensations that clouded his head. He rode in the general direction of Rattlesnake Point, for lack of a more productive destination. Oblivious to his surroundings, Charlie focused only on the pavement immediately in front of him until something, some cue—maybe the rhythmic clanging of the shrimp boat rigging in Fulton Harbor, maybe the smell of decaying fish and shrimp wafting from the processing plant—made him slow down and look up.

When he saw Bao's tan Lincoln Continental parked alone in front of Sea-Tex, he leapt off his bike and was striding for the entrance of the building before he was aware of what he was doing. He pulled back the temporary plywood entrance and then crashed through the double-hinged door at the back of the retail area. No one was in the processing area but he heard voices from the second floor office. He bounded up the stairs and walked straight into the tiny, cluttered office. Bao sat behind the desk, speaking on a shortwave radio.

Charlie stood in front of Bao panting with exertion and rage. The Colonel's eyes widened momentarily and then he calmly reached under the desk and produced a pistol, which he laid on the corner of the table. Heavy steps could be heard coming up the stairs outside the door and Bao's lieutenant, Ho Dac, crested the landing and burst into the room. Charlie recognized him as the same thug who had almost thrown Raul into the water. Probably the same man who had stabbed him on the *Ramrod*. As the man rushed him, Charlie instinctively threw a right cross that connected with his jaw.

Ho Dac staggered backwards onto the landing, holding onto the doorjamb to keep his feet and to gather himself for a counter attack. The sound of the hammer cocking back on a .38 caliber handgun stopped the fight cold. Bao barked an order to his lieutenant and he backed off a step, never taking his murderous eyes off of Charlie.

"You burned my boat, you fucker," Charlie uttered throatily, his voice choking with emotion.

A half smile crossed Bao's face. "I don't know what you're talking about. What I do know is this. Ho-Dac and I walked into my office and discovered an intruder—a looter, we thought. I felt threatened and I shot the intruder dead. Isn't that the way you saw it happen, Ho-Dac?"

The chunky man nodded quickly, his eyes eager with anticipation.

Charlie's fervor for revenge, or at least his ardent desire for some sort of cathartic release from the storm of emotions bottled up inside him, cooled quickly as he realized how precarious his situation had become. He was making this way too easy for the son of a bitch.

"This is the second time that I have caught you trespassing on my property, and this state is very clear about the rights of property owners and the defensive use of firearms."

Charlie struggled to concentrate as he stared into the barrel of the handgun. "Bao, before you go all OK Corral on me, would you mind telling me why you keep trying to kill me, what?...three times?"

His mouth was dry, full of chalk. Bao's face betrayed nothing, except, perhaps, a trace of predatory anticipation. "Is it just because you wanted the *Ramrod*, and I wouldn't give it to you?" he asked. "Hell, you've got a hundred shrimp boats already."

Bao lowered the gun slightly. "You are much like your brother. Arrogant, meddling, and much too ambitious for your own good."

"Shit, no one ever accused me of being ambitious. And meddling in what?" Charlie asked. "In your little Vietnamese chain-gang? Showing them free movies? Or is because I was trying to take a few cans of food from your little clubhouse in Mesquite Bay? Come on, Bao! Shooting me for that is a little...excessive, don't you think?"

"I prefer to think of it as efficient. Like your brother, you are an irritant...and just as easy to remove."

Charlie felt a chill. Maybe Marisol had been right all along. He looked Bao in the eye. "What happened to my brother, Bao?"

The Colonel shrugged. "Your brother boarded one of my boats. To render assistance I'm sure he'd say. My boat carried a special cargo, and he discovered it. From my point of view, it looked like an enemy action. I acted accordingly."

Charlie grew rigid. Bao noticed the change in Charlie's demeanor and he continued with relish, taking joy in the pain he inflicted.

"As my enemies or competitors are apt to do, he met with an 'accident'." Bao regarded Charlie with icy equanimity. "As will you...." He pointed the gun a Charlie's heart. "...momentarily. As for the half-breed, he will simply disappear, and everyone will assume he's returned to Mexico.

"When you both are dead, that will be the last of the Sweetwaters, won't it? Unless you or your brother have produced more bastard children that I don't know about."

Charlie had a very visceral notion of rushing Bao, wrapping his hands around his scrawny throat and choking the life out of him before he bled to death from the gunshot he himself expected to receive in short order. If it was going to end like this, he would by God go down swinging. But the unmistakable sound of a voice from outside the office stopped him.

Colonel Bao and Ho-Dac heard the voice too. They were motion-less, listening. Ho-Dac raised his hands as if to say, *what's the play here?*

"Hello?" came a man's voice from below. "Colonel Bao? Are you up there? Hey, Ho-Dac!" the friendly voice called up. "Is the Colonel up there, too?"

Charlie heard the man clomp slowly up the stairs. In through the door walked Sheriff Huckabee.

"There you are, Colonel," he began, "I saw your car outside and I thought we could settle that business about ...oh, sorry, I didn't know you had company." Then he noticed the gun that Bao had pointed at Charlie. He stopped abruptly and looked at both of them. "What's this about?" he asked nervously.

"Sheriff, I found this intruder in my office going through my desk. I caught him committing a crime."

"That's a lie, Sheriff," Charlie countered. "I came up here to talk to Bao about a...boat accident." What could he reveal to Huckabee that would change anything? Rupert had as much as said the sheriff ate at Bao's trough. It was enough that Huckabee happened along when he did. It undoubtedly saved his life.

"What boat accident, Charlie?" asked the sheriff. "What's this about a break-in?"

"Nothing," Charlie answered, turning to leave. "We worked it out." He brushed by the sheriff and the square shouldered Vietnamese and descended the steps, trying to keep his rubbery legs from buckling on the way down. He could feel Bao's eyes on the nape of his neck.

—

When Charlie arrived at the Marina he was still shaking. His brain fizzled like a shorted-out beer sign. He walked in the door and saw Marisol sitting at a table with Miguel.

"What's wrong, Charlie?" Marisol asked with concern. "Even for a *guero*, you're white as a ghost."

"Miguel," he said, "I'll give you a thousand dollars for a drink."

Miguel studied Charlie and then walked into the back, returning with a bottle of rum. He grabbed a glass from under the counter and filled it half way to the top.

Charlie took a huge gulp then slumped in his chair. Marisol and Miguel watched him expectantly. He took a deep breath and quickly recounted the events of the day. Marisol cried when he told her about Johnny's death. But telling the story also helped Charlie recover some measure of equilibrium. And it rekindled the anger he'd felt before—the hot, blind anger that had provoked him into his near fatal run-in with Bao.

Marisol excused herself and went outside. Charlie watched her sit down heavily on the bulkhead. Through the open window he saw tears wetting her cheeks. Miguel went behind the counter and thumbed through one of the Mexican wrestling magazines he was fond of reading, leaving Charlie and Marisol to their own emotions. His was not a shoulder to cry on.

Charlie's mind started working again and he sat very still in his chair, his forearms spread out in front of him on the rough wooden table, his tensed hands resting uneasily on its surface. His eyes gazed out the window, focused intently on a middle distance somewhere out in the bay. The more he thought about what Bao had said, the blacker his thoughts became.

He imagined his brother, floating face down in the gentle Gulf swells, blood from his broken head leaking out behind him into the clear blue water, being carried by the inexorable currents. Killed for rendering assistance.

Miguel Negron approached and stood next to him with the bottle of rum. Charlie didn't register Miguel's presence when he leaned over and re-filled his glass.

A moment later, as if reacting to an invisible alarm, Charlie popped up from his chair. He intended to head for the door, but Negron was still standing next to him and he reached out quickly and grabbed Charlie's arm before he could even push back his seat.

"You plannin' on committin' a crime, you ought to think it through first, 'mano," he said in a low voice. "Believe me, I know."

"There's nothing to think through," said Charlie, startled by the close presence of the Mexican by his side, and in his head. "I'm going to end this now. The bastard's gone too far. He deserves it."

"Every guy I killed needed killin', but sometimes the judge don't see it that way."

"Let go of my arm, Miguel."

"What do you know about killin', *gringo*?"

"What difference does it make? ...Long as he's gone."

"Makes a shitload of difference. One way, maybe the dink's dead, and that cowboy *rinche* has to haul you in for murder, 'cause that's what he does. Raul gets sent back to Mexico. You spend eight to fifteen with somebody like me for a cellmate, getting abused by the prison wolfpack like a blow-up love doll. Another way, maybe the yellow guy's dead, but you're dead too...along with the kid. He's a lot better at killing than you. And then there's Door Number Three."

Charlie glanced down at the scarred right hand that gripped his arm, the word MUERTE written across the back of it in indelible blue ink. "What's the other way, Miguel? What's behind Door Number Three?"

"The other way is that you let me help you. Let me share some of my, ah, expertise on the subject." Miguel rolled the fancy word around in his mouth with relish.

"It's not your fight."

Miguel shrugged. "*Que no?* Marisol's my friend. Johnny was my friend. Even that wetback kid is my friend. It's reason enough. That, and the bar tab you owe."

Charlie looked into Miguel Negron's dark lethal eyes, took a deep breath and nodded. The Mexican released his arm, a white enamel grin of false teeth appearing on his brown face, the first time Charlie ever remembered seeing him smile. It was unnerving.

"*Orale, Carlito.* Now you're starting to use your *cabeza.*" He tapped at his temple with a rough finger. "If you're gonna off somebody, you should never do it when you're all stoked up. Not drunk or stoned, neither. 'Cause then you do it all sloppy and get your ass caught. You got ta have the *sangre fria* if you want to get away with it. You know what I'm saying, *ese?*"

Charlie nodded, wondering if he had it in him to kill a man in cold blood like Miguel suggested. He glanced through the screen door where Marisol sat smoking, alone with her thoughts. He thought about Raul. *I might, just maybe....* He was certainly ready a couple of minutes ago.

"But something you can't do, Charlie. You can't tell Marisol nothin' about this. She's got her official duties, ya know? And I'm one of 'em."

"Okay, Miguel."

"I mean it, *gringo*. This is between you, me and that Viet fucker. Got it?"

"I got it, Miguel."

"Huntsville is a real shithole, and I ain't going back."

Marisol came back through the entrance wiping her eyes. The evening light was starting to fade. "We should get back, Charlie. It's getting dark. Is the bridge open yet?"

"It's still closed to cars and trucks, but they're letting people walk across...or ride a bike across."

"Pump me home then?" she asked with forced cheerfulness.

Charlie felt a strange thrill at her choice of words (or was it apprehension). "Sure thing, *chica*," he said.

Charlie started toward the door. Stopping at the end of the counter he turned around. "Thanks, Miguel."

Miguel shrugged. "*De nada*," and then he added in a low voice, "Happy Day of the Dead."

Charlie had to smile. Sure enough, it was November 2nd, *Dia de los Muertos*. Back in Mexico the kids were eating sugar skulls and wearing skeleton costumes, and the adults burned candles in front of elaborate *ofrendas*, honoring their dead with food, drink and other carnal delights once enjoyed by their dearly departed. Mexico and his life there seemed a million miles and a million years away right now.

———

CHAPTER 31

A knock at the door roused O.B. from his bed at the Sea Gun Inn where he had been laying awake in the dark, thinking. Not expecting visitors, he slid his .357 quietly out of its holster and held it behind him as he went to the door.

"Who is it?"

"It's me, Trinny."

O.B. had to wrestle with this notion for a few seconds.

"From the restaurant," she said insistently, "and the fish house, in Fulton."

He quickly opened the door. In the dim porch light Trinh An Phu stood before him in a knit blouse worn over loose silk trousers. Her long hair was braided down her back. Not nearly so dazzling in his undershirt, white cotton briefs and tube socks, O.B. stood across the threshold from her with his mouth agape.

Trinny giggled. "You not expecting me here are you, Mr. Ranger?"

O.B. struggled to think of any words to say that might be appropriate to the situation. "What..." he started. "How..."

"Please let me in, Mr. Ranger." She looked nervously over her shoulder at the crushed oyster shell parking area and the rows of cabins beyond. The wind had picked up and it thrashed the palms near the building. O.B. looked at his watch—12:30. He realized he was standing in front of this woman in his skivvies, so he ducked inside and began dressing himself as fast as he could. He slipped the gun back in its holster and moved it out of sight.

Trinny closed the door behind her, observing the Ranger with amusement. Once he dressed, she turned on the small bedside lamp and looked around.

For having spent ten days in the motel, the Ranger's room looked like he had just checked in. His clothes were neatly folded in an open box-style suitcase, with two pair of leather boots lined up under the window. A grey-white Stetson and a khaki baseball cap hung on wall pegs. Framed paint-by-number pictures of retrievers and ducks adorned the dark panel walls. Trinny noticed a cassette tape on the table next to some papers.

"Nice room," she said. "You are fastidious Texas Ranger."

Nobody had ever called O.B. Hadnott fastidious before. He wasn't sure what it meant or if it was a good thing or a bad thing.

"Trinny, what are you doing here?" he asked, finally finding his voice.

The girl regarded him carefully before she spoke. "I think you need translator," she answered, indicating the tape cassette. "Unless you learn Vietnamese since I last see you."

O.B. looked over at the tape cassette.

"Nu Dang's wife is friend and neighbor. She tell me about tape."

Sergeant Hadnott wondered about the danger to his potential witness if the tape had become such public knowledge. Trinny sensed his alarm and said, "Don't worry, Mr. Ranger. Nobody know of tape but me and Nu Dang's wife, Lua Xuan. We know if the Colonel find out we have tape, he kill us all straight away."

O.B. nodded, and wondered how safe his hideaway was if Trinny could find him so easily in this out-of-the-way motel room located in a tiny town across the bay from Rockport and Fulton.

"You maybe surprised I find you here, eh, Mr. Ranger?"

At this last display of clairvoyance, O.B. almost resolved to stop forming thoughts altogether.

When he didn't answer, she offered her explanation anyway. "I talk to Vietnamese maids I know work in this town and I ask where tall Texas lawman is staying. They tell me this hotel and give me room number."

"I see," O.B. answered.

"Your room number lucky number. Number Seven, very auspicious. Have you listen to tape?"

"Yeah. I've listened to it." *Couldn't understand a goddamn word of it either,* thought O.B., *no thanks to headquarters, which still hasn't found me a translator.*

"How you understand it?" she asked.

"I, uh, don't."

"Then I help you understand it," she stated authoritatively. She dropped her purse on the table and searched the room. "Where is tape recorder?"

Although still flustered by the presence of the beautiful Vietnamese girl in his room, O.B. had not been totally disarmed of his professional instincts. "Ms. Trinny," he began. "This tape recording could be evidence in a felony criminal case, and I'm not sure it's a good idea to...."

Trinny cut him off. "Phew, Mr. Hadnott! It impossible for you to know who or what is on tape, even if college Vietnamese professor help you. I know local names and local voices. I know what it all mean... I already hear it anyway."

"You already heard tape?" Hadnott inquired.

"I tell you. Lua Xuan is friend and neighbor. She scare to death when she hear tape. Ask me to hear it at once." She let O.B. think about this and then she added, "You be scare too when you hear what Colonel Bao say on the tape."

For the dozenth time, O.B. Hadnott decided to throw away the Ranger manual and improvise his way through this convoluted coastal case. By the time Austin lined up a Vietnamese translator, and sent him what would probably be a very literal typed transcript of the tape, it would be the middle of next week—too long to wait.

Hadnott went to the closet and returned with a small Radio Shack tape recorder and a writing tablet. He invited Trinny to take a seat at the table and pulled out a chair for her. He plugged in the tape and she helped him skip past a long sequence of recorded phone messages and queue it up to the incriminating telephone call. Trinny pressed the play button and started translating in a lovely, confident voice.

Even though the conversation between Nu Dang, Colonel Bao, and Ho-Dac lasted only four minutes, Trinny and Sergeant Hadnott worked for over an hour playing and replaying the message to make sure they had the exact translation and the exact implication of the words.

After they had finished, O.B. sat back and read the transcript to himself one last time. He shook his head in disbelief. "Why would they say something like this if there was even the possibility of it being recorded?" he asked out loud.

Trinny answered. "Bao not suspect poor fisherman have tape machine, or ever dare to record him if he did have," she replied. "The Colonel think he can say and do anything he want to Vietnamese people in Fulton." (She pronounced it "Fur-ton".) "He think he own us, and he know that outside Vietnamese community nobody care what happen to us, as long as it *only* happen to us."

O.B. had to agree with that. Bao himself had said the same thing. Even so, he was surprised that Bao would go into such detail on a telephone. Bao's man talked openly and plainly about "killing Nu Dang and everyone in his family" if he ever crossed the Colonel again. He threatened to "cut off Nu Dang's head and put it in a crab trap" and then put his wife to work as a "pleasure girl" on some of his long-haul gulf trawlers.

When Nu Dang protested to Bao's lieutenant, saying he had no right to do or say these things to him in this country, Bao himself got on the line, reminding Nu Dang that "the police chief and the county sheriff are well paid in bribes and won't even bother to investigate the disappearance of a Vietnamese fisherman, much less a verbal threat."

O.B. looked down at his notes again. He had underlined one line that really grabbed his interest. He asked Trinny once more to confirm the translation.

"So he actually talked about M-20s and RPGs?"

"That is what he said," she confirmed.

"But how do you know if those are the right terms?"

"You forget my old country was at war for my whole life when I live there. Everybody there know the name of these weapons. They as familiar as Kawasaki or Johnny Walker Red."

He read from the transcript. "You fish where I tell you to fish. You transport what I tell you to transport. This week it may be shrimp, next week it may be M-20s and RPGs. You do not have an option."

Trinny nodded. "Yes. This is correct translation. This is the way it is."

O.B. sighed. He really wanted to put this little desperado behind bars. "Trinny, you work for Colonel Bao, at Sea-Tex. You are taking a terrible risk coming here and doing this."

She shrugged. "After I survive the war in my old country, I feel like everything after is, you know, bonus time. I not scared of Colonel Bao."

O.B. was impressed with her quiet courage. He set aside the transcript and the tape recorder and admired the beautiful girl sitting across the table from him. He felt this was as good a time as any to get to know her better.

"Trinny, what did you do back in Vietnam? Was it hard to leave there? And your family, are they here in Texas or still in Vietnam?" The questions tumbled out faster than O.B. intended and he felt a little embarrassed.

Trinny sat back and looked at the Ranger skeptically. Finally she said, "Mr. Hadnott, I like you. I like you since I see you in fish market. You even fight for me in restaurant, but I think you not know who I am or what I am. You see pretty Vietnamese girl and maybe want exotic fling with exotic girl. You not really want to know who I am."

"Try me," said O.B. confidently.

Trinny folded her hands in her lap and looked down for almost a full minute, and when she looked up she regarded O.B. with fierce eyes.

"Okay, cowboy. Here it is. You listen to me very careful. I not want to ever do this again."

O.B. nodded. "Shoot," he said.

"I come from little bit village near Da Nang," she began, "...fishing village. My parents killed in war. My three brother and four sister, I not know...maybe they dead too. I not know which side kill them. It not matter to me. I move to Saigon from countryside when I am fourteen and I work as hostess in dance club, selling taxi dance to American soldiers. War get uglier, Saigon get uglier; I sell other things besides dance to survive. At end of war I escape when Saigon fall, and with money I save working at dance club I catch boat to America. I have no family. I only have me and this new life on Texas coast."

When she finished speaking her glare bore into him from across the table. She lifted her chin as if to challenge him to respond.

O.B. picked up her delicate hand and gently kissed it. Something about this girl's forthright way and her courage to carry on impressed the hell out of O.B. That, and the physical attraction he'd felt for her the moment he laid eyes on her.

She pulled her hand away. "You not hear what I say, Mr. Ranger?"

"Yes ma'am," O.B. answered. "I heard you."

"You not know what dance club is in Saigon, in war time? What girls do there with soldier boys?" she said heatedly.

"I don't care about any of that," O.B. replied assertively, even though he knew he was venturing way off the ranch here. He took a deep breath and moved his head closer to hers.

For a brief moment he thought of Nadine Thaxton, the Odessa girl that Senator Cudihay had snaked him out of. That had been love... hadn't it? Well, it had been something. But nothing like the big sensations welling in him now.

That was the only word—big. He felt like he was being pushed and pulled and submerged in the massive dark tides flowing out into the moonlit ocean outside his door. He had the sensation of being washed out to sea, away from his life as he'd known it, bound for someplace new. He didn't know what unknown shore he had washed up on, but oddly enough, the place suddenly felt like home. Still, it was with no small surprise that the taciturn Ranger listened to the words that next came out of his mouth.

"Trinny. This is gonna seem a little sudden, what I'm going to ask you," he heard himself saying, "In fact, you're probably gonna think I'm *loco*, but...well heck...what I'd like to ask you, Trinny, is if you'd consent to be my wife."

O.B. Hadnott was surprised how much he liked the idea of spending the rest of his life with this woman. His absolute certainty that he wanted this surprised him almost as much as hearing himself pop the question.

When Trinny didn't respond, O.B. wondered for a second if he'd actually proposed to her out loud, or just vocalized it in his head. *Better make sure*, he thought.

"What I'm saying is that I want you to be my wife, Miss An Phu."

Trinny sat back in the wooden chair, dazed, then reached over and slapped O.B. hard across the face.

Yep, she'd heard him alright.

"I...I not know...I not know what to think...I not know what to think, of you! You not hear a word I say? You ask to marry? You think you love me? How could you love me? You see me, what, three, four time? Are you crazy, Mr. Marlboro Man?"

O.B. now found himself back on familiar turf, completely mystified and confounded by the opposite sex. "Yes, ma'am," he stammered. "I heard what you said. And yeah, I guess I do love you. I mean, I know I do. I just thought...."

"You thought what? You think...what you think? That I am easy woman? Or you think I am desperate to marry American lawman? You think I not have other prospect?"

"No," he replied, "I mean yes." O.B. was adrift.

"You think you pity me? Sad story make you pity me?"

O.B.'s mind ground to a halt, the gears hopelessly overheated.

"You not know what you are saying. Maybe you crazy after all."

Trinny stood up and snatched her purse off the bed. She started out the door and then paused, seeming to gather her thoughts. Suddenly she wheeled around, walked briskly up to O.B. Hadnott and kissed him lightly on the lips.

"You think about this some more, Mr. O.B. Hadnott, Texas Ranger. I think about it, too." Then she disappeared out the door. O.B. heard the truck tires crunching over the shells in the parking lot as she drove away.

He lay on his bed a long while before falling asleep, his mind in turmoil, his brain pressing hard against the inside of his skull. "Harder than nine kinds of Chinese arithmetic ..." he mused as he fell off the cliff into sleep.

———

CHAPTER 32

Charlie was awakened by a creaking board on the landing at the top of the stairs. During the three nights he had stayed at Johnny's place on Rattlesnake Point he had learned the sounds of the old pier and beam house—the lone palm that brushed against the southwest eaves, the gurgling and popping of the rusty water heater, the low groan of the building joists as they shifted and rubbed against the pilings, and the warped plank near the front door that complained at the slightest pressure.

Marisol slept beside him in the huge mahogany antique sleigh bed, the only piece of decent furniture in Johnny's dry land home. He could hear her breathing peacefully in the darkness.

Charlie arose slowly and made his way to the door, expecting to open it and startle the raccoon that had been leaving scat on the front deck the past two nights. Just in case, he grabbed Johnny's 16 gauge side-by-side that he'd propped up next to the bedroom door.

He didn't expect to encounter the bulky silhouette of a man that filled the entrance to the door. And he certainly didn't expect the debilitating blow applied to the base of his neck with a quick, powerful karate chop. Charlie crumpled to the ground with a muffled groan, dropping the shotgun onto the floorboards.

"Charlie?" Marisol called out sleepily from the bedroom. The attacker froze, seemingly confused. "Are you okay, *cariño*?" she said a little more urgently.

A man's voice from outside said, "Is someone *else* here?"

Marisol leapt out of bed and raced toward the bathroom; the figure standing over Charlie rushed into the bedroom after her. He caught her by the hair and hurled her against the wall. She rebounded off the wall and threw herself at the intruder, her fingers arched into claws, going directly for his face. The man threw a fist, which glanced off her eye and the side of her head.

Before the man struck her again she rolled off him and lurched toward the front door. She tasted blood and her right ear rang like a gong. At the threshold, she ran headlong into another man who grabbed her in a tight bear hug. She saw his patchy blond beard and long, light-colored hair. His breath stank of marijuana and beer.

"Whoa there, little lady! Where're you goin'?" the man asked. She noted the local accent. "Chill out!" he said, laughing.

Marisol struggled but the man had pinned her arms to her sides. Approximately the same height, they stood eye to eye in the door. He grinned at her and she kneed him in the crotch and then head-butted his face. He bent over double, not knowing whether to hold his broken nose or his aching *cojones*.

"Holy fuck!" he yelped, his nose instantly swollen. The larger man appeared in front of her again. A chilly north wind pushed dark clouds across the sky, but a sudden break allowed moonlight to seep out into the night. Dull green eyes set deep in a flat Asian face regarded her coldly. His expression never changed as his arm sliced through the air, striking a blow to the trapezius muscle at the base of her neck. Marisol collapsed on the ground next to Charlie.

———

The droning of the outboard motor was the first sound Charlie became aware of as he drifted back into consciousness. A distant white noise initially, it intensified until its deafening roar flooded his auditory sense. His brain also registered a throbbing pain in his neck and head. He was cold and wet and unable to move his hands or his feet.

Willing himself out of the stupor, he began to realize where he was—tied up in the back of a small fiberglass boat, probably under a tarp, pounding through a rough bay in the dark of night. He could feel another body close to his.

"Marisol?" he whispered. No answer. He tried again, louder this time. "Marisol?"

"Charlie?" she whispered back. He could hear the fear in her voice. "What are they going to do to us, Charlie?"

"I don't know."

The two prisoners bounced around on the floor of the boat for hours. Occasionally, Charlie would recognize the deep growl of a tugboat pushing a barge through the water. The tug's bright running lights offered a brief glow of light outside the canvas tarp, followed by the sound of its huge diesels. A few moments later the smaller boat bounced as it collided with the wake left by the long heavy procession of barge and tug. He knew he had to be in the Intracoastal Waterway—but traveling which way?

Judging from the way their boat seemed to be riding over the tops of the waves whipped up in the bay by the north wind, he concluded that they were traveling south, traversing the bays that bordered Aransas Pass and Corpus Christi. He remembered passing under the Kennedy Causeway (a sudden hollow echo as the sound of the engine bounced off the bridge above) and finally into the narrow, shallow waters of the Laguna Madre. He hoped the boat pilot, whoever the son of a bitch was, was watching out for the wrack and debris that surely filled the nighttime sea after the hurricane. He and Marisol, bound by the wrists and ankles, would sink like anchors in the dark water if the boat crashed.

At last the pilot slowed and left the Intracoastal. They motored unhurriedly for a while, snaking their way around the numerous reefs and spits of sand that populated the shallow bay. Charlie noticed pale dawn light leaking in beneath the folds in the tarp. Finally, someone killed the engines and silence enveloped the boat.

"Hay-soos! That was one fucked-up boat ride," said the guy with the local accent. "I think my kidneys are leaking blood."

The tarp was yanked away and Charlie and Marisol stared up at their captors. Charlie recognized the big Vietnamese with the broad nose and green eyes holding the tarp. He could see his heavy muscles, even through his work shirt and windbreaker. *Ho-Dac,* Charlie thought, remembering the name Bao had called him. A long red scratch tore across his cheek. At the helm stood another Vietnamese man, less stout but just as dangerous looking. The man pulled out a pair of field binoculars and stood on the seat, surveying the horizon in every direction.

Up at the bow, on the rail of the Boston Whaler, sat a skinny kid in a gray hooded sweatshirt with long, blondish hair and a scraggly beard. Boyish at first glance, Charlie later noticed crow's feet around the kid's eyes and a sun-splotched face, suggesting that he was in his late twenties, maybe thirty. He tried to light a cigarette, cupping his hands in the wind to protect the flame. Behind him stood an elevated wooden fishing shack. He snapped the lighter closed and took a deep drag on his cigarette.

"Morning," he said with a grin, then winced in pain as his nose crinkled.

Charlie could make out a Black Sabbath T-shirt inside the hooded zip-up sweatshirt. The kid's nose had swollen and reddened where Marisol had smashed it with her head. His eyes were showing early evidence of a dandy pair of shiners.

"Y'all look pretty miserable lying down there in your jammies," he said, still grinning. "Sleep tight?"

Charlie wore a pair of Johnny's old flannel pajama bottoms, no shirt, and Marisol had on an oversized Texas Longhorn T-shirt and a pair of cotton panties. She tried to wriggle her shirt down over her thighs but her body was stiff and cold and her hands were tied. She groaned and then glared at the kid on the rail. Through the tangle of her dark hair, Charlie noticed that one eye was swollen and a bruise had begun to spread across her cheekbone.

"What the hell do you want from us?" Charlie asked the big Vietnamese, unable to contain his anger.

"Whoa! Dude's still got an attitude," said the blond kid. "Even though he's all trussed up like an HEB lobster."

Ho-Dac told the kid to shut up, and then he said something in Vietnamese to the boat pilot. The man nodded and slipped over the edge of the Whaler into waist-deep water. He waded up close to the fishing shack, dragging the boat to a rotting piling jutting out of the water and secured the lines. He climbed the shack's tilted wooden ladder, unlocked a heavy padlock and pushed open the door.

From the boat, Charlie studied the flimsy shack. Judging by its good condition he figured they were far enough south of the hurricane landfall to have missed the brunt of the storm. Suddenly Charlie realized where they were. He and Johnny used to fish the shallow turtle grass and mud flats in this part of the Laguna Madre when they were younger, often spending the night in one occasional unlocked fishing shack or another. The locals called it the Graveyard because fish would sometimes school up in the saltwater holes and die when the tides fell and the blistering summer heat evaporated the water. He shivered involuntarily.

He also remembered that the area was very remote, and that the likelihood of being discovered out here any time soon was accordingly pretty slim. Kleberg County, which lay to the west, was an unpopulated stretch of the vast King Ranch. Most of the boat traffic was about four miles west of them in the artificial land cut that extended the Intracoastal Waterway through the mudflats to Port Mansfield.

Ho-Dac pulled a knife out of his pocket, sawed through the duct tape on their ankles and motioned for them to stand up. He left their hands bound together in front of their bodies. As they struggled to move their legs again, he motioned for the blond kid to jump down and help them stand.

Leading Marisol up the ladder into the shack, the local kid made a point of grinning back down at Charlie as he followed her up the ladder, peeking under her jersey as she climbed in front of him. Marisol stopped and turned around, assaulting the guy with a look and a muttered Mexican curse that discouraged him from looking up again.

Before Charlie entered the shack, he paused at the top rung and surveyed the surrounding area. The wind was still up and heavy gray clouds scudded across the sky. The bay was choppy and drab. The dim morning light revealed a pale horizon and he could barely make out the silhouettes of a few neighboring fishing shacks that perched over the water, ghost-like in the distance, too far away for anybody to see or hear them. A rough poke from behind and he entered the shack through a hinged door.

Once inside, Ho-Dac looked at Charlie and Marisol and pointed to the wall adjacent to the door.

"Sit," he said.

After re-taping their ankles the Vietnamese men returned to the boat. Charlie watched them through the open door, standing in the waist-deep water, talking.

"*No entiendo*, Charlie," Marisol said softly. He turned his head and looked at her—scared, defiant, battered and beautiful all at once. Charlie tried to reassure her with a wan smile, and then he turned to the white guy squatting on his haunches on the other side of the small shack.

"Now what?" Charlie asked him.

The blond kid shrugged. "Beats me. Ask them." He motioned toward the door.

"They call the shots?" Charlie asked. "You work for them?"

"I don't work for nobody," he said testily. "They just needed a...." He caught himself. "Dude, just leave it alone."

"A boat? They just needed your boat? Is that it?"

"I said leave it alone," he said a little louder, raising up from his haunches, stepping toward Charlie. Then he glanced nervously at the door and sat back down, wearing his surfer boy smile again.

These Vietnamese scared the kid. It was a feeling Charlie could relate to.

"Pretty tasty little *senorita* you got there." He looked approvingly at Marisol, whose eyes narrowed in anger.

"Why you *hijo de la*...." Marisol started to push herself to her feet but Charlie nudged her back down and shook his head.

"You ever fished the Laguna before?" Charlie asked.

"Some," the blond guy replied, turning his attention to Charlie, a little intimidated by the volatile young Mexican girl and glad to be diverted by the change in the conversation.

"I used to, but it's tough to get here from Port A," said Charlie.

"Yeah," the kid agreed, "that's why I mostly stick to the jetties, or fish the surf on Mustang Island. Long as it's close to the beer and the bikinis." He winked.

"Nice scenery, alright," Charlie said, trying to sound amiable.

"Fuckin' awesome."

The kid kept bobbing his head up and down idiotically at Charlie like he was his new best friend, and then he risked another glance at the girl. "Hey, I bet y'all are freezing your asses off." Charlie' shirtless torso was almost blue and goose bumps covered the girl's arms and dark, shapely legs. "All I got to give ya is this sweatshirt," he continued, pulling off the garment and tossing it over at the captives, "but it's better than nothing."

"Thanks," said Charlie, covering Marisol with the sweatshirt. Outside he heard the voices of the Vietnamese men rising and, although he didn't know a word of their language, he could detect some anxiety, some discord, in their conversation. Then it occurred to him. *They weren't supposed to grab the girl.*

"Y'all didn't expect to find two of us at the house, did you?" Charlie ventured.

The blond kid shifted his glance away from Charlie.

"You were expecting just one guy...me, but instead you found two of us. And now y'all don't know what to do about it, do you?"

"You probably need to shut up is what you need to do," the kid replied.

After a few moments of silence Ho-Dac looked into the shack. Satisfied that his prisoners remained as he had left them, he addressed the blond kid.

"You stay here. We back soon. Don't leave. Don't talk. Watch them." He slid a .22 caliber handgun across the floor. It had worn tape on the butt and rust on the barrel. "Watch them," he repeated. "They move, you shoot." He slammed the door shut and left.

They heard the outboard on the Whaler; the hum of the motor grew fainter until silence filled the shack. Charlie noticed that the north wind had started to lie down and that the sound of the waves lapping gently against the pilings below had replaced the whistling of the wind. If the front had blown through, Charlie reasoned, then the sun would soon be out. Then the murky, churned-up water would start to clear and the fisherman would start fanning out from the marinas and boat docks into the surrounding bays and estuaries. He hoped that some of them would pass their way. What he and Marisol could do in that eventuality, however, seemed far from certain.

The shack was a simple 8' x 12' plywood structure, framed out by 2 x 4s and raised approximately eight feet off the water by eight-inch rough cedar piers—a utilitarian structure constructed by serious fishermen who used them to sleep and to cook in when they weren't outside fishing. Charlie estimated that the nearest marina was around thirty miles away at the far end of Baffin Bay, the probable destination of the Vietnamese.

"Your friends going to Riviera Beach?" Charlie asked, breaking the silence.

"How the hell do I know?"

"I just figured since it's your boat, you'd have some say in the matter."

Surfer Boy sulked against the wall.

"I didn't see a radio on your boat," Charlie continued. "So I guess they needed to find a phone." The blond kid tried to ignore him.

"To call Colonel Bao, I suspect," Charlie added nonchalantly.

This got the kid's attention. He shot a quick look at Charlie, noticeably anxious.

Marisol chimed in. "I wouldn't think Bao's going to be very happy when he finds out y'all kidnapped a woman," she said with a sardonic smile. "Especially one carrying a Texas Department of Criminal Justice badge."

Charlie winced. *Shit!* It makes sense. They would have found her badge if they went through her purse, and now they weren't sure what to make of it...or what to do about it.

"Look, chick!" said Surfer Boy. "I'm not part of this. I just happened to have a boat and these guys paid me a few bucks to use it for a while." Marisol's predatory smile unnerved him.

"So you've worked for Bao before?" asked Charlie.

The kid furrowed his brows. "Dude, you ask too many fucking

questions. You need to shut the fuck up is what you need to do."

"Sorry," said Charlie. "We're not trying to piss you off. We're just trying to understand what might happen next." He waited a few minutes before he continued. "You got a name?" he asked.

The kid eyed him suspiciously. "Why would I tell you my name?"

"Because it's not gonna matter," said Charlie.

"What do you mean it's not gonna matter?" he responded a moment later.

Charlie shrugged. "It's not gonna matter because when those guys get back they're going to kill us."

Marisol turned her head toward Charlie, her eyes wide at hearing the words voiced out loud. But she knew Charlie was right. There's no turning back once you kidnap a law enforcement officer. Her mind began to work furiously. She knew, as did Charlie, that their lifespans could be measured in the time it took the Whaler to return from the nearest marina.

Surfer Boy tried to laugh off this comment but it didn't convince anyone. "Ain't nobody gonna get killed, dude," he declared.

"No?" said Charlie. "If Bao told his boys to pick up Charlie Sweetwater—that would be me—and take him all the way out here, out to this remote spot in the middle of nowhere...what do *you* think they had in mind? A fishing trip?

"And what do you think Bao will tell his men to do with us—all of us—once he hears how they screwed up and kidnapped an extra hostage...a hostage with a badge?" Charlie let the question hang in the air. "They'll be back here with orders to shoot us in the head and dump us in the bay."

"Well it ain't my problem," answered the kid nervously. "I'm not involved. You mess around with a guy like Bao and you get what's comin' to you."

"First of all," Marisol said heatedly, "we never *messed around* with Colonel Bao."

Surfer Boy forced another smile. He looked like he was trying to convince himself that everything was going to work out. "Whoa, hey, I don't care, lady. And like I said, I'm not...."

"And second," she interrupted, "you are involved, *dude*. No way

Bao's going to leave a witness to a murder, especially if the witness is a stoner blabbermouth like you. You're nothing but a loose end—an *expendable* loose end. You'll be floating in that Laguna same as us, probably with water in your lungs after they drown you. And later the *Guardia* or some crabber will find your boat, capsized or with a hole in it or something. Just another unfortunate boating accident out in the Gulf."

They watched the idea enter Surfer Boy's empty brainpan and rattle around in there. His face twisted up and for a moment it almost looked like he might cry.

"Bullshit!" he yelled. "You don't fucking know anything. I'm just a guy with a boat making a delivery. No big mystery. End of fucking story."

"Right," Charlie reassured him. "They probably didn't have any of their own boats available—only your boat would do. They'll come back soon, apologize for the inconvenience and we'll all get back in your Boston Whaler and head to the house. Then y'all will drop us off back in Copano where you picked us up, right? And you and Ho-Dac and his buddy will have a few brewskis and maybe roll up a couple of fatties and laugh about it. One merry fuckin' mix-up."

"I ain't listening to you two no more." The kid stood up abruptly and went out, slamming the door behind him. They heard him outside, his flip-top lighter popping open and closed while he chain-smoked cigarettes on the tiny landing outside the door. A half hour later he came back in and sat down, leaning his head back against the wall. He cast an angry look at Charlie and Marisol and emphatically waved his gun at them, reminding them who was in charge. For a long time there wasn't a sound except the occasional slap of a mullet on the water or the cry of a gull. Surfer Boy's eyes started to droop and after a while he fell asleep.

———

CHAPTER 33

Charlie and Marisol awoke from a light sleep the instant they heard a distinct splash in the bay. The sound was very close to the shack. Marisol raised her head from Charlie' shoulder. A moment later, they heard another unmistakable *plink* as a second fishing lure hit the water almost directly below them. Surfer Boy was still asleep, his head leaning against the wall, snoring gently.

Marisol looked anxiously at Charlie. He straightened up and pulled his knees to his chest, planting his feet firmly on the floor. Someone down below shifted on a boat and banged the hull. This *did* wake the kid up. Sitting up quickly he blinked away the sleep and listened intently.

One fisherman reeled in a line and another splashed a cast into the water underneath the shack. Surfer Boy turned toward Charlie and Marisol and pointed his gun at them, shaking his head to discourage them from making any noise.

Then a young boy's voice, "I don't think there's any fish under there, Dad."

"Cause you scared 'em away, you idgit," came another boy's voice, this one a little older.

"Nuh-uh," the small voice protested. "You don't know that."

A moment later: "I'm not a idgit, you butthead."

"You gotta sneak up on 'em if they're hiding in the shadows. Why do you think Dad poled us over here instead of using the motor?"

"Go ahead and pull in your lines. We'll try another spot," said an adult voice. After some clumping and shuffling in the boat the little one spoke again.

"Hey look, Dad. This shack's unlocked. Can we go up and check it out?"

Surfer Boy stiffened. The voices weren't fifty feet away, and in the still air they sounded like they were right underneath them.

"Yeah, Dad. You said next time we find one unlocked..." said the other boy.

"Okay, sure, I guess," replied the father. "Let me pole over closer first." They heard knocking and splashing as the boat pushed closer to the ladder and the boys moved to the bow, readying to grab the ladder to the shack.

Surfer Boy scrambled to the door and pulled it open. He crouched in the doorway, his right arm obscured from below behind the plywood door. His right hand pointed the pistol at Charlie and Marisol.

"Afternoon, guys," he said as casually as he could manage. The surprised fishermen looked up at the man who had suddenly appeared from inside the shack and was now squatting in its entrance.

"Afternoon," the dad said warily. "Kinda startled us there. We thought the place was empty."

"Naw. I'm here. I was just taking a little nap. You kind of surprised me too, sneaking up on me like that."

"Well," replied the dad, "we certainly didn't mean to do that. Not seeing a boat we figured nobody was here."

"Just me," the blond kid said. "I'm waiting for my friends to get back with the boat. They left to get us some more beer."

There was a pause. Charlie imagined the two boys holding on to the ladder, poised to climb up and explore the shack, their dad standing on the stern of the boat with the push pole.

"Oh," said the dad. The blond kid leaned back from the partially open door and looked over at Charlie and Marisol, still directing the gun in their direction. He turned back to the fishermen, smiling.

"You know," the dad continued, "I got a couple of cold ones in the cooler here if you need something to tide you over."

"Yeah?" the blond kid replied, expectantly.

"Yeah," answered the dad. "To make up for us waking you up like we did."

"I'm thinking that'd be sweet right about now, dude." But as soon as the kid said it, Charlie could see him trying to work out the logistics of retrieving a can of beer from below without revealing his gun or his prisoners. A cooler lid creaked open followed by the tumble of ice as the man extracted a beer. "Hey, you know what?" Surfer Boy said awkwardly, "On second thought, maybe I better not. I'm actually trying to quit."

"I thought your friends went to go get more beer?" said the man in the boat.

"Bait. I said they went to get us more bait. But thanks all the same. I appreciate the offer, dude."

"Sure," the man said suspiciously. "No problem. Come on boys. Shove us off and let's get moving."

Marisol looked urgently at Charlie, who also realized their opportunity would pass if he didn't act quickly. Mentally, he had already measured the distance between himself and the door and he tried to visualize his next move.

The structure moved slightly as the boat pushed off from the ladder. Surfer Boy was waving goodbye when Charlie launched himself off the floor from his sitting position, executing a half aerial turn so that the broad part of his back hit the partially open door at the end of his lunge.

The door slammed into the kid, knocking him first against the doorframe and then out the opening and into the air. Charlie heard a chorus of yells—Surfer Boy as he crashed into the bay, and also the boatfull of fishermen as the human projectile sailed over their heads into the water.

Charlie rolled over and struggled to his feet. He hopped over to the door and pulled it open with his bound hands. Below he saw Surfer Boy struggling to stand up in the waist-deep water. Ten feet away, in a faded green jon boat, two red-haired boys and their dad stared at the thrashing, cursing, bleeding figure in the bay. The blond kid continued to curse and sputter and Charlie realized he was searching for his gun, which must have fallen in the water with him.

"Ah-hah!" he yelled triumphantly, holding the dripping revolver in the air, his back still turned to the shack. The pawnshop gun probably wouldn't fire after falling into the bay, if it could ever fire at all, but Charlie didn't want to take the chance. Balancing himself on the landing at the top of the ladder he leapt feet first into the air. As Surfer Boy turned around, the heels of Charlie' feet caught him square in the chest, knocking him backwards with such force that the gun flew into the air and his head snapped forward so violently that three teeth broke off at the base when his jaws clapped together.

Charlie hit the water flat on his back and slammed onto the hard sandy bottom. When he stood up, gasping for breath, the blond kid was floating face up in the bay, dead or unconscious from the flying body blow. The red-haired kids hadn't moved from the bow of their boat, watching the action with open mouths. Their dad slipped over the edge of the boat and waded toward the floating body, looking at Charlie warily.

"Are you okay, Charlie?" Marisol yelled anxiously from the door of the shack. The red-haired boys' eyes swung up to the dark, wild-haired girl wearing nothing but a short jersey and a pair of undies, bound at the wrists and ankles with silver duct tape. They concluded that this was, hands down, the coolest fishing trip they'd ever been on.

"I think so," Charlie replied, then to the fisherman who pulled the blond kid toward his boat, "Did I kill him?"

The fisherman ignored him as he heaved the body into the boat and began mouth-to-mouth resuscitation, stopping a couple of times to dig some broken teeth out of the kid's mouth. A few minutes later, Surfer Boy started coughing and sputtering, finally throwing up what seemed like a bucket of salt water onto the deck of the jon boat.

The fisherman turned to Charlie. "Where do we start?" he asked.

"Well, I'll take that beer," Charlie replied. "If you're still offering." The sudden turn of events made him giddy. He almost laughed out loud, but he thought better of it. From this guy's point of view the situation would have seemed pretty murky.

"That *gabacho* over there and two Asian thugs kidnapped us last night from our house on Copano Bay," Marisol began, much to Charlie' relief. "The two thugs left in that guy's boat." She pointed her bound hands toward the wet figure groaning on the floor of the jon boat. "Probably getting instructions from their *jefe* about what to do with us, which most likely is to kill us." The fisherman looked down at the blond kid and then at Marisol.

Charlie said, "I know all that's a little hard to believe, but ask yourself—would we make this shit up?"

"Watch your language in front of the boys. Why would they want to kill you?" the fisherman asked. He wore battered khaki pants, a windbreaker over a white double-lined fishing shirt, and a faded orange cap. His tan, weathered skin and no-nonsense fishing rig indicated that this was not his first trip out on the water with his boys.

"That would be a longer story," Charlie replied, this time allowing himself to smile. "Any chance you might cut this tape off us Mr...."

"Grant. Captain Joe Grant. And this is Sean and Little Joe." The boys nodded their carrot-topped, freckle-faced heads at Charlie as a greeting. They were quiet and wary, not sure if all the surprises were over yet.

"Joe Grant," Charlie laughed. "I thought you looked familiar. You have a guide business out of Port O'Connor right?"

"What's left of it," he answered. "Not much business to be had this soon after the storm, so I told the boys, let's go fishin'."

"The school's blown down, too," added the younger boy helpfully.

"I'm Charlie Sweetwater, I live...."

"Sweetwater?" the Captain interjected. "You kin to Rupert Sweetwater?"

"He's my uncle."

Now it was the Captain's turn to smile. Still grinning, he jumped back into the water and cut the tape around Charlie's and Marisol's wrists and ankles. As he worked, he told them about how he had known Rupert for years, and how much he respected him and how much he loved Shady's, "the last great bar-baitstand-honky-tonk and authentic fisherman's hangout left on the Texas coast."

"Dad?" the older boy's voice interrupted his dad's paean to Rupert and his legendary establishment. "The drowned guy's gettin' up." Neither Charlie nor Joe had noticed Surfer Boy's shaky re-entry into the vale of tears. He leaned weakly on his elbows, his shaggy head sunk down on his chest.

"Fuck me nekkid!" he said thickly. "Wha' happened?" He leaned over and promptly threw up again. He sat up unsteadily and looked around trying to re-orient himself.

Marisol regarded the sorry spectacle at her feet. "You still want to play tough?" she asked contemptuously. He looked up at the raven-haired woman with the troubling eyes. He did not want the flying ninja guy or his pissed-off looking girlfriend to inflict any more pain on his aching body. He sat down compliantly in the boat, looking like a sad, dumpy little boy who had just learned that the party wasn't for him.

"They're gonna come back soon, *du*...you guys. And we don't wanna be here when they do." He reached in his mouth and pulled out a tooth, looked at it morosely and tossed it over the side of the boat.

"What do you mean 'we' don't want to be here?" asked Captain Joe.

The kid looked at Joe then back at Charlie and Marisol. "What y'all said about them probably coming back to kill you guys, and then kill me, too? Well, I think you're right about that. I just want to get back to Sharkey's Beach Club in Port A, man, and have me a bucket of cold ones. This shit's not for me." He winced from the pain of the cold air on the stubs of his missing teeth and huffed and puffed through his broken nose. He was done.

"When'd they leave here, Charlie?" asked the Captain.

"About two hours ago. I figure they went to the nearest marina to find a phone."

"Two Oriental guys in a Whaler?"

"Yeah. They work for a guy named Colonel Bao out of Fulton."

"I've heard of Bao," Captain Joe said, stripping off his windbreaker and tossing it to Charlie. "The guys in the boat were heading towards the marina at Riviera Beach. Which means they'll be on their way back by now."

"Which means we need to haul ass," added the blond kid. Captain Joe prepared to shove off with a new sense of urgency.

"Why shouldn't we leave *your* ass here?" asked Marisol. "Why should we trust you not to rat us out first chance you get, *pinche ratón*?"

The two red-haired boys continued to regard Marisol with fear and amazement. They were of an age to still be a little bit scared of girls to begin with. Surfer Boy looked hurt by the accusation. "I swear on my mother that I wouldn't do nothing like that," he pleaded. The broken teeth caused him to lisp: "Ah thweah on mah mutha ...." The two boys snickered. Marisol rolled her eyes.

"I don't think he'll try anything, Marisol," said Charlie. "He knows they'll kill him if they catch up with him, and us." Charlie had met hundreds of these ne'er-do-well beach bums in his lifetime. Mostly just rootless stoners attracted by the siren song of the beach scene when they were young and stupid, they never quite made it up the next rung of the ladder. Old and stupid was usually how they ended up.

"What's your name?" Marisol demanded.

"Billy Donathorn," he answered. He had trouble getting the consonants out through his busted nose. "But everyone calls me Billy D."

"Well, Billy D.," she continued conversationally, "I feel I should tell you that if you do one more thing to displease me, I'm personally going to gouge out your eyes and feed 'em to the crabs."

Billy D. involuntarily raised his hands to his eyes and rubbed them.

They piled into the jon boat and Captain Joe cranked over the outboard. Bao's men would return through Baffin Bay before getting on the Intracoastal to return to the shack, and Captain Joe hoped to make it past the mouth of the bay before Bao's men saw them.

Once the heavily loaded jon boat cleared the shallows, he opened up the little 40 hp Evinrude and coaxed the boat to a plane out on the channel's calm water. The cold front had blown through and now it was a crisp, brilliant, blue-sky day.

In Baffin Bay one of the boys spotted a boat approaching in the distance and looked back anxiously at his father. Joe gave the tiller to his older son and helped arrange the three refugees under some army surplus ponchos. Charlie, Marisol and Surfer Boy reluctantly lay down in the bottom of the wet, fishy boat.

"Sucks, doesn't it, Billy D.?" said Marisol.

"You got a real mean streak in you, lady," he said forlornly.

"*Aún no has visto nada, pendejo*," she replied darkly.

"Huh?"

"You ain't seen nothing yet, *dude*."

Captain Joe slowed the boat to a more reasonable speed for a leisurely father-son fishing expedition, which also kept the ponchos from blowing off. They passed not sixty feet from Bao's men who looked at them long and hard.

"Just keep watching ahead, boys," Captain Joe instructed his sons. He wasn't sure what he would do if these men turned on him and his boys.

Soon the Whaler was out of sight and Joe announced that the coast was clear. Charlie yelled back that the bad guys had a pair of binoculars on board and it would be better to put a little more distance between them. Once out of range, the three emerged from the ponchos and Captain Joe opened up the throttle once again.

"You have enough gas to make it to Rockport?" Charlie screamed over the roar of the motor.

Captain Joe pointed to a hatch under his seat. "Got two more tanks underneath. We'll be fine." Charlie gave him the okay with thumb and forefinger.

Midway through Corpus Christi Bay, they spotted a boat bearing down on them in the distance, the splash from its bow flying fifteen feet into the air as it plowed through the swells in the deep-water bay. Charlie and Billy D. peered into the distance. "I think that's my boat," said Billy D.

Charlie cast a worried look at Captain Joe. They must have discovered the empty shack and put two and two together, thought Charlie. Joe looked down at the throttle and shook his head, signifying that the boat didn't have any more to give. They watched as the faster boat continued to gain on them. Charlie hadn't expected them to make up the distance so quickly.

Nearing the entrance to the Aransas Cut, the Whaler was close enough that Captain Joe and Charlie could see the faces of the two Vietnamese men. No way they could reach Port A ahead of them.

Without warning, Captain Joe whipped the bow of the jon boat to port so sharply that Billy D almost toppled into the water. Charlie had anticipated the abrupt change in direction. He knew where they were going. It offered their only chance of eluding the faster boat.

The jon boat roared past Dagger Point through a narrow straight and into the intricate archipelago of reefs, small islands and spoil banks that permeated Redfish Bay. Once through the straight, the jon boat veered hard to starboard, following the contours of a narrow string of islands covered with tufts of cord grass and agave. Marisol and the boys turned to look back anxiously at Captain Joe, their hands gripping the gunwales of the jon boat.

The Whaler had also found the cut at Dagger Point and pursued them at full throttle over the shallow grassy flats. Billy D. pivoted around on the bench seat and cupped his hands to his mouth.

"Where the hell you going, dude?" he yelled. "This is fucking craze...!" But before he could finish, Captain Joe spun the boat around to starboard again, through an impossibly narrow slot between two mangrove islands. Billy D. fell into Marisol, planting his face on her knee. She didn't lift a hand to help him as he struggled to right himself. Charlie noticed Billy's already battered nose was bleeding again.

Back in deeper water, Captain Joe opened up the throttle and sped around a solid knob of land at the end of an archipelago.

A short time later they heard the high-pitched scream of the Whaler's outboard behind them as the prop grounded out in the shallow mud when it attempted to cross the straight that Captain Joe had just traversed. That would buy them a least a minute or two, Charlie figured.

Rounding the small island, they could see a bleached cluster of wooden buildings rising up on a scrubby island about a mile away. The Shady Boat and Leisure Club. Charlie hoped like hell that Uncle Rupert was home. And that Vita still kept the old cut-down 12-gauge under the bar.

———

CHAPTER 34

Captain Joe wasted no time maneuvering his jon boat into one of the Ransom Island boat slips. The two red-haired boys jumped onto the storm-damaged finger pier and scurried to throw lines over short creosote pilings while Charlie helped Marisol out of the boat. Captain Joe grabbed a short metal bat from his bag of gear. "For sharks," he told Charlie as he hopped onto the pier.

The group dashed down the sandy path towards the big pier and beam building. Over the tops of the sand dunes Charlie noted at least three boats tied up at the ferry dock on the other side of the island. He recognized the flying bridge of Jake Jacoby's Bertram among the boats.

"Hey, I know this place," said Billy D. "This is a great beer joint."

Marisol whirled around to face Billy D., who instantly regretted opening his mouth.

"Listen, Billy Dickhead," she said. "You say one word, or do one thing inside this place that puts us in harm's way," she jabbed a finger at his chest for emphasis, "...and I swear to God I will cut you into chum with a dull knife."

Billy D's eyes widened and he took a step back. "Jeez lady, I won't do nothing. I'm not a bad guy," he complained. But Marisol was hurrying to catch up with the boys.

"Let's go, Billy," said Charlie from behind him.

Sean and Little Joe were the first two through the swinging screen doors of the Shady Boat and Leisure Club, followed by their sandy-haired dad wielding his metal bat.

"Hey-Ho, it's Captain Joe!" bellowed Rupert from behind the counter, "...and his young protégés." About a dozen patrons sat at the bar or around tables watching a TV hanging from a ceiling bracket. The Dallas Cowboys were opening a can of whup-ass on the Washington Redskins. Tucker Adderly was there, as well as Pete Jackson and Bob and Peggy Story. Jake Jacoby walked across the room, sipping on a can of beer and holding a Big Red for Raul, who was reading a comic book at one of the tables.

"Why the long faces?" Rupert continued, noticing the fishermen's grave expressions. The door swung open again and in walked Marisol, barefoot and wearing the Longhorn jersey. *That* got the attention of the male patrons in the bar. Billy D. and Charlie followed her in.

"Rupert," Charlie began. "We, ah, have a big problem."

Charlie quickly explained to everyone what had happened and what was getting ready to happen. "I expect they'll be here in about two minutes," he finished. "And I'm telling you, these two guys are bad asses."

Vita came around from the kitchen in time to hear Charlie. Without hesitation she suggested that the bedraggled group get out of sight and into the small business office behind the bar counter.

"Are these guys armed, Charlie?" asked Rupert.

Charlie looked at Billy Donathorn. "Billy?"

Billy D. looked down at his ratty wet tennis shoes. "Yeah. I expect at least one of 'em has a pistol," he said sheepishly.

"Enough talk," Vita broke in. "Into the office." She put her hand over little Joe's red head and steered him into the room behind the bar. The others followed. "Raul!" she yelled. Raul jumped. "You get in here too."

"Is the phone working, Rupert?" asked Charlie, before going in the office.

"Still out," he replied. "But the ship-to-shore works."

"Good," said Charlie. He paused at the beaded door and addressed Vita and Rupert. "Sorry to bring trouble to your place."

Rupert raised his hand in protest. "Don't worry about it son. You did the right thing."

"Smart move if you ask me," said Tucker.

"Listen y'all," Charlie said, "If they start waving guns around, don't try to be heroes. If they find us, let 'em take me. I'm the one they're after. Then call Sergeant Hadnott."

"Let's see how it goes, Charlie," replied Vita as she shoved him behind the beaded curtain.

Inside the small room lay scattered papers, nautical charts, assorted shells and other maritime souvenirs. A mounted tarpon hung on one wall next to a black and white photo of a younger and leaner Rupert with his big hands on the shoulders of two young boys holding a three-foot Wahoo between them—Johnny and Charlie Sweetwater. All three fishermen wore big smiles.

Back in the main room, Vita passed out instructions. "Okay, sports fans," she said, turning to the group of seated patrons, "the rest of you get back to what you were doing—*like nothing has happened.* Y'all think you can do that?" Heads nodded and they started drinking beer and watching the ballgame once more. *Oscar candidates all the way around*, thought Vita.

Rupert walked over to the TV and turned up the volume on the game. Danny White had just hooked up with Drew Pearson for another touchdown pass and Dallas led the Redskins, 28-14.

As the Cowboys lined up to kick the extra point, the big blocky Vietnamese man pushed open the screen door very slowly and stepped halfway inside the great hall of Shady's. Ho-Dac carefully surveyed the room, marking any doors or exits where someone could hide or flee. A few heads turned away from the TV and looked over at him, but everyone appeared to be absorbed in an American football game on the television set. A handsome, middle-aged woman addressed him from behind the bar.

"Either come in or get out," she said. "You're letting in flies."

Ho-Dac saw no sign of his former captives but he felt certain they were around because the jon boat he'd been chasing was tied to the dock and he had seen them on that same boat not ten minutes ago. He stepped inside the door and motioned for his associate to follow. A mangy yellow dog appeared from beneath a table, growling.

"You want something?" said the woman behind the bar.

"No," he answered. "We're lookin' for someone who came in here."

"And who would that be, mister?" she asked.

"A man and a girl, and maybe another man and some kids."

"My, that's a lot of someones," Vita replied. He waited for her to continue. "But if you don't see them in this room, then I guess they aren't here."

He saw the burly, red-faced man turn around and stare at him coldly. Another big fellow, an old guy sitting at the bar, also looked at him in a very unfriendly manner. Same with the weathered-looking man smoking a hand-rolled cigarette, sitting next to a woman with tall blond hair. He was about to leave, not seeing who he was looking for and not unfamiliar with these chilly receptions from the locals. *Screw the racist American bastards*, he thought. He hated them and he hated their country.

Then he remembered Bao's instructions: "Don't come back here until it is done." He'd nabbed the right man last night, as he'd been told, but taking the parole officer woman had placed him on Bao's shit list. Now he had allowed them to escape. In his fifteen years of service to Colonel Bao, he had personally carried out the executions of six former colleagues when they got too far up on the Colonel's shit list—four in Vietnam before 1975, and two in this country since.

He rolled his shoulders to feel the reassuring weight of the .38 Ruger tucked inside his jacket. He needed to think this out. He felt unsure about the wisdom of shooting up an American bar. In Saigon, he wouldn't think twice about it, but in America things were different, especially when it involved white people, or when it involved people with badges. On the other hand, if the man and the girl were hiding on the premises, which he was almost certain they were, he couldn't leave without them. He, better than anyone, knew there was no going back if he failed the Colonel again.

Ho-Dac sat on a barstool and picked up a menu, which had only five items typed on the page—Eggs, Waffles, Hamburger Basket, Shrimp Basket, Chili. "I want a beer," he said. He had taken a stool directly across from the bead curtain hanging over the office door. Hiding unseen in the darkened room, the group could see the Vietnamese man not twelve feet away. The other Vietnamese man hung back near the entrance.

Without asking Ho-Dac his preference the woman behind the bar pulled a beer out of a cardboard case and placed it in front of him.

"How much?" he asked.

"A dollar."

He pulled a bill out of his pants pocket and set it on the counter.

The woman didn't pick it up. He noticed the beer was not even cold. The ball game droned on from the television and Ho-Dac studied the faces of the patrons as a man from one of the teams on the television ran almost the full length of the field. The announcers and the crowd in the stadium, wherever it was, seemed to be quite excited by this event, but Ho-Dac noticed that none of the spectators in the bar reacted at all. This seemed very odd to him. *They're hiding them*, he realized, *the lying bastards*.

Not one to waste time deliberating, Ho-Dac decided to get down to business. He'd fucked around with these white fishbellies long enough. He turned around and spoke to his associate, Le Loi, who grunted and began walking between the tables towards the other side of the main room. Ho-Dac noticed the hateful eyes that followed Le Loi as he made his way to the restroom signs marked "Inboard" and "Outboard."

"Can I help you with something?" the old guy with the big ears and big forearms asked as Le Loi walked toward the back of the building.

"My friend is going to use your toilet," said Ho-Dac. A few seconds later Le Loi emerged from the bathrooms and began opening doors on the side of the building—doors that led to broom closets, a store room, the kitchen pantry, and a couple of guest rooms.

"Hey," yelled, the old guy. "Those are private rooms." He rose from his stool.

"Please sit down," said Ho-Dac firmly. He relished the surprise on everyone's face when they turned around and saw him pointing his pistol at Rupert.

"Whoa there, mister! You mind telling me why you're wavin' a gun at me?"

"This will take only a few minute. We find what we are looking for and then we leave."

"And what is it you're looking for again?" asked Rupert.

"I think you know."

Le Loi continued searching the rooms one at a time while the Anglos in the bar watched Ho-Dac and his gun. It didn't take long for him to finish searching all the rooms that connected to the main building. From the other end of the bar, close to Rupert, he signaled that there was no sign of the fugitives. In Vietnamese he informed Ho-Dac that there was an exit off a storage room where they could have escaped.

"We go take a walk and look in some other building," Ho-Dac said to Rupert, who he assumed owned the place. Then his eyes narrowed. He belatedly noticed the inconspicuous, bead-covered door behind bar—the entrance leading to the office where Charlie, Marisol and the others crouched in the darkness. Captain Joe clenched his steel fish bat and instinctively moved in front of his boys. "But first, I want to see behind that curtain...in that room."

"Oh, there's nothing back there," said Vita lightly. "Just a closet to store beer and soda pop. You know—closet?"

Ho-Dac started to get off his barstool to walk around behind the bar. Then the front doors swung open and Juan Estrada sauntered in, followed by Rupert's dog Mingus.

Ho-Dac swung around and reflexively pointed the gun at Juan.

Juan flinched. "Hey, that's a gun!" Mingus emitted a low growl. "Why are you pointin' it at me?" He looked to Rupert for clarification.

"These two men seem to think that some people they are looking for are hiding here on the island," Rupert explained. "And this gentleman has decided that a gun's gonna make these people magically appear."

Juan scrunched up his face. "Huh? Well, who is he looking for, Rupe?"

Rupert shrugged. "The gentleman didn't say."

"Well, I seen Captain Joe and those red-headed boys of his runnin' up here from the south docks a little bit ago while I was out cleanin' my boat. Looked like Charlie and some other folks was with 'em too. I came over to tell 'em hi."

Ho-Dac smiled. Enough of this shit. *Closet, hell*, he thought.

Juan wondered why everyone inside Shady's was looking at him like he'd farted—everyone except the Vietnamese guy, who grinned crookedly. What happened next confused Juan even more. Before the Vietnamese guy could completely turn around on his barstool, Vita grabbed the huge cast iron skillet from the stovetop and executed a two-handed major league swing to his head. The five-pound skillet connected with his face with a bone-crunching smack, lifting Ho-Dac off his stool and onto the floor at Juan's feet. Back in the office, Billy D. winced in instinctive sympathy.

Across the room Le Loi ran to assist his pan-faced friend, but as he passed by the bar Rupert rose up and planted one of his Popeye forearms across his mouth, clothes lining him flat onto his back. Not even the Cowboys' defensive enforcer Randy White could have done it better. Neither one of the two Vietnamese moved after that.

Juan watched the dogs, Mingus and Ringworm, sniff at the big unconscious Vietnamese man. Then he looked up and saw Charlie emerge through the beaded curtain, followed by a beautiful dark-haired girl, then Captain Joe and his boys, and finally a scraggly blond guy.

"Could somebody please tell me what's going on?" Juan pleaded.

"Juan," said Jake, "you are dumber than a junebug on a string, but I'll be go-to-hell if you didn't help us out of this jam."

"What jam?"

Vita came around from behind the bar, carrying the loaded 12-guage she kept under the bar. "Juan," said Vita, "These two guys work for that Colonel Bao that we were talking about a few days ago, and they were hunting for Charlie and Captain Joe and the rest of them. They were upset 'cause we wouldn't tell 'em where they were hiding."

"And of course *you* did tell 'em," added Jake.

"Well, how was I to know they was looking for them?" Juan objected.

"I hate to break up the Spanish Inquisition here," Rupert interrupted, "but I think we ought to tie these two boys up and call up our Texas Ranger friend."

"Good idea, Uncle," Charlie responded.

"I not sure we'll have to tie up this one," said Juan, looking down at the inert body at his feet. "He don't look so good."

"Is he dead?" Tucker asked.

"You knocked the holy shit outta that guy, lady," Billy D. felt compelled to add.

Vita came over and examined the splattered face. "He'll live. I think I just broke his nose, some teeth and maybe his jaw. I don't think I cracked his skull." Billy D. shuddered, now knowing of at least two women who could kick his ass if they ever had a mind to.

As Vita doctored (and hogtied) the Vietnamese thugs, Charlie and Rupert radioed the DPS office in Aransas Pass. The duty officer agreed to relay the message to Sergeant Hadnott right away. Marisol accepted Vita's offer of a bath and a change of clothes in Rupert and Vita's big house behind the main building. Captain Joe and his boys decided to head for home, which at present, after the hurricane, meant a two-room rental over in Port A. Joe said they'd had enough excitement for one day. Besides, the football game was over. Before they left, Rupert treated them to free cheeseburgers and a cold drink of their choice. Captain Joe left with a six-pack of Pearl under his arm.

"Now what, Charlie?" Rupert asked later.

"I don't know, Uncle. Bao sent those two guys to kill me, I'm sure of it. And they would've killed Marisol too if Captain Joe hadn't happened along."

Rupert shook his head in disbelief. "Charlie. I'm not sure you should be going back to Fulton just yet."

"I agree, Rupert. I'm thinking maybe we ought to hang out here for a spell."

"Wise choice, son."

"What about Surfer Boy over there?" asked Vita. Billy Donathorn sat alone at a table watching *The Love Boat* on the television, finishing off his fifth can of Miller Light and nursing his injuries. He looked like a whipped mongrel pup.

"Leave him for the Ranger," said Charlie.

CHAPTER 35

O.B. Hadnott received news from the DPS radio dispatcher that a Mr. Charlie Sweetwater and Miss Marisol Cavasos were safe and unharmed after reporting that they had been forcibly abducted the previous night. He also learned that local citizens at the Shady Boat and Leisure Club were holding three men—two Vietnamese and an Anglo—for questioning on Ransom Island on suspicion of assault and kidnapping. He managed a half smile when he heard that "medical assistance would be required for two of the alleged kidnappers."

It was time for Sergeant Hadnott to call headquarters to report on his case. To his Field Captain, he recounted the evidence that had been assembled against Colonel Nguyen Ngoc Bao—a criminal past in a foreign country, lies about his relationship to the U.S. corporation he secretly owned and operated, death threats, and allusions to arms dealing on a recorded telephone conversation (in Vietnamese), possible involvement in a kidnapping, and incriminating (verbal) indications from several people (one now dead) about Bao's illegal activities.

"Not bad", said the Captain, "but not enough."

Sergeant Hadnott had to agree. He thought wistfully about the early days of the Texas Rangers when he could've walked into

Bao's fish house, smacked the little bastard upside the head with his revolver and drug him behind his horse to the hoosegow. O.B. Hadnott, mired in the 20th century, sighed.

"Anything breaking on the Pomade case?" asked the Captain. "That bein' the original reason you're down there, and all."

"No, sir. But if Bao or any of his people had any involvement, I expect that at least some of the Vietnamese fisherman around the harbor will know about it. There don't seem to be many secrets among that group."

"Will any of those people talk to you? Last I heard, you said most of them didn't even speak English."

O.B. thought of Nu Dang and Sammy, and he thought of Trinny. His mind had been weighed down almost unbearably by last night's exchange with her. He had not slept well. "I think so, Captain. Some of 'em anyway."

The Captain snorted. "Well, see what you can get from the alleged kidnappers. Maybe they're ready to give up their boss."

"Yes sir, Captain."

"Say, Sergeant?"

"Sir?"

"There's somethin' else. I just got the damndest phone call from the District Attorney of Travis County, down in Austin. Said a Cajun fella called him this morning and started dropping the names of a bunch of POIs you talk about in your reports. This fella sounded about halfway crazy, but the details he mentioned got his attention. Especially when he told him a Texas Ranger had also been snooping around.

"I didn't get the whole story, but it appears to involve Bao and Senator Cudihay. Said that whole business about the Senator's aide getting shot was some kind of put-up job gone wrong. I wonder just how far Cudihay might be mixed up in some bad bidness."

"Yessir, Captain," said Hadnott. "It occurred to me, too."

He'd avoided trying to tie Cudihay to Bao, as much as he'd had his suspicions. Mentioning a powerful sitting state senator as a Person of Interest in an ongoing criminal investigation was tantamount to career suicide, as any rookie cop could have said. But now that the Captain had brought it up....

Hadnott felt an involuntary surge of anger and anticipation. "We rode out the hurricane together, sir. Beyond that, I don't have anything concrete." O.B. tried hard to keep his voice level, even though the possibility of kicking a board up Cudihay's ass made him feel like a kid on Christmas Eve.

"Well, the DA in Austin asked me to ask my point man—you—whether there's any substance to these allegations and then to call him back. He said he's gonna meet up with this Cajun fella later this afternoon to see if there's anything to the guy's cock-and-bull story. Step lightly, Sergeant. I don't have to tell you these politicos have mighty thin skins and, like it or not, they write our budget. But keep an eye on our elected friend. Shit, it shouldn't be hard, judging by the cable news. Just look for the nearest TV camera."

"I'll see what I can dig up," said O.B.

"You do that and then get your ass back to West Texas. That whole goddam place down there sounds crazier than an acre of snakes."

—

That afternoon in Austin, Neon Leon Guidry found himself in the dead-solid last place he ever hoped to wind up: staring out the window at a view of the state capitol building looming over the shoulder of the District Attorney of Travis County. The DA was wrapping up a convoluted question. Dragging his mind back to the here-and-now and away from the paranoid visions of incarceration he had been envisioning, Leon shifted in his government-issue chair and astutely replied, "What's dat, ya honor?"

The district attorney, a career politician whose shark's eyes betrayed an otherwise placid demeanor, sighed. "Mr. Guidry, you and Mr. Hebert..."—he mis-pronounced L.C.'s name "Hee-bert"—"are here in my office eating up the time and money of the good citizens of Austin and Travis County only because I received a call from a captain of the Texas Rangers in Lubbock. He confirmed he has an officer on detached service down on the coast who says he's knee deep in bad guys. And that those self-same bad guys are mixed up with one of your old running buddies, who just happens to also be a state senator. And the said Senator is endeavoring to extort money from you for unnamed but presumably nefarious purposes. Have I about got the picture?"

"That's right," said L.C. Hebert, jumping into the conversational gap. He couldn't help noticing that Leon looked about as nervous and unhappy as a dog shitting peach pits. "Sir, the Senator is involved with some extremely bad people...people that might've killed a state employee, that, um, Mr. Pomade cat...as well as threatening us. I did me some digging and found out that your office is in charge of investigating mal, ah, feasance and ethics and whatnot in the capitol. It doesn't seem to us that Senator Cudihay is exactly all covered up with ethics."

"So I'm supposed to open an investigation on a sitting state senator on the say-so of a guitar player and a...." The DA eyed Leon dubiously.

Leon shifted again. "Dat would be 'small businessman,' ya honor."

"Stop calling me that. You know how a fairy tale begins, 'Once upon a time...'? Well, a Texas fairy tale starts out, 'You ain't gonna believe *this* bullshit...' And frankly, that looks to be what we have here, gentlemen."

He pointed a fountain pen at L.C. accusingly. "All you've given me is Mr. Guidry's testimony that a sitting senator threatened him with trumped-up criminal charges if he didn't come up with a trunkload of cash," said the DA. "And that this senator has a mutually beneficial relationship with some immigrant fisherman down on the coast."

L.C. could feel it slipping away. "Don't forget the Texas Ranger," he added quickly. "He's down there investigating this Vietnamese character for good reason. And he's investigating this gangster's activities and passing the information back to his captain. Who called you."

"That still doesn't give me anything I can take to an Ethics Committee, let alone a grand jury." Still, the DA had to admit to himself, their story piqued his interest. The Capitol was full of characters, elected and otherwise, who would crawl a mile through a sewer to fuck an alligator. Even among that low-rent crowd, he thought, Llewellyn Cudihay stood out. Had Moses ever met Cudihay, he would have had to come up with a whole new batch of commandments.

The district attorney was nothing if not a savvy reader of the public mood. The electorate was gearing up for one of their periodic spasms of revulsion over the shenanigans of the sleazy shitheels who were supposed to be tending to the people's business at the capitol. The gag reflex of the Great Unwashed usually manifested itself at the ballot box in a throw-the-rascals-out bout of reform, which inevitably proved inadequate and short-lived. Still, a crusading DA with a crooked senator's scalp on his belt might be just the thing for party officials looking for a fresh face to run for, say, lieutenant governor or state attorney general. Stranger things had happened.

"Yessir," replied L.C. "But that's the thing. If the money that the Senator extorts from ol' Leon here goes to Colonel Bao—the guy the Ranger is investigating—then you can charge Mr. Cudihay with funding an ongoing criminal enterprise. Not to mention conspiracy to commit Mr. Pomade's murder if you can prove the Senator knew Bao was going to shoot up his party. And that *is* something a grand jury can look at...."

Neon Leon looked at L.C. in semi-stupefied awe, as though he were watching a parrot speak Chinese. "I thought ya told me ya majored in bidness administration?" he said. "Where you gettin' all dis 'criminal' stuff, you?"

"I clerked in a law office one semester," L.C. said with a shrug. He was enjoying turning the tables on his street-hustling cohort. "And I did a little time brushing up at the University of Texas law library yesterday."

The DA regarded the pair with weary skepticism. *But*...he thought, *but*...

"There might be something there," he reluctantly agreed. "But the money trail would have to be airtight, the Texas Rangers would have to sign off on the whole deal and Senator Cudihay would have to agree to testify about any alleged crimes this Colonel, ah, Bao might have committed."

———

CHAPTER 36

Llewellyn Cudihay could not believe his eyes. The stainless steel handcuffs that encircled his wrists gleamed in the overhead fluorescent lights. There was a gleam, too, in the eyes of the tall, laconic Texas Ranger.

"You're shitting me!" he said in stunned disbelief.

"No, Senator," replied the Ranger with barely-concealed satisfaction in his voice. "I shit you not."

"You can't arrest me...I'm about to go on *television*!"

"I had in mind more of a perp walk," said O.B. Hadnott. "I betcha we could round up a few TV cameras for that."

Cudihay had been changing into a clean shirt in the back of the two-room mobile home he had been using for an onsite office. His regular quarters in a Rockport strip mall had been smashed and flooded by the hurricane.

The Ranger had come marching in, identified himself, announced his intention to arrest the Senator and promptly slapped the bracelets on him. Cudihay didn't know whether to spit or whistle "Dixie." Which was just the way O.B. Hadnott wanted him.

They had it all on film and tape, Hadnott explained. The Senator, the duffle bag full of money (provided by the Travis County district attorney's office), the clandestine meeting between Cudihay and two sinister-looking Vietnamese characters purporting to be representatives of Colonel Bao. The exchange....

"You're bankrolling the Colonel in the furtherance of assorted felonies and misdemeanors," Hadnott said. "That's way the hell against the law, slick."

The Ranger didn't feel the need to explain to Cudihay at that particular moment that the Asian "gangsters" to whom he had turned over the marked and sequentially numbered money Leon Guidry had supplied to him were in fact Trinny's friend, Nu Dang, and his nephew, Sammy.

Nu Dang wanted nothing to do with either the police *or* the bad guys. Part of his attitude was ingrained culturally, part just plain-ass common sense. But Trinny prevailed on him in rapid-fire Vietnamese, appealing to him on behalf of his wife and family, warning him that Bao and his men would certainly make good on their threats if he wasn't stopped. The first step was to call Cudihay and schedule a "rendezvous."

And that was how Nu Dang and Sammy, against both their better judgments, found themselves standing in the alley next to the Sea-Tex fish processors at two in the morning dressed in hooded sweatshirts ("Rockport Pirates" emblazoned on the back) and pulled-low gimme caps, waiting for the sweaty white man in the gabardine suit to haul a ponderous duffle bag out of the trunk of his Cadillac and muscle it over to them.

During the transaction Cudihay seemed discombobulated and pretty well scared shitless. It was a long way from the rooftop Petroleum Clubs and smoky backslapping good-ole boy backrooms where he usually operated.

Neither Cudihay nor the reluctant couriers noticed a beat-up van with smoke-tinted windows parked across the street. It contained, among other things, one tired, sweaty, but otherwise cheerful Texas Ranger. "That's right, you fatass...," Ranger Hadnott whispered to himself as he adjusted the manual focus on the camera and snapped off a rapid series of black and white photos, "...hand 'em the bag. Thaaat's a good boy..." A tape recorder with a directional mic pointed out the window spun silently.

The ominous silence of "Bao's men" unnerved the Senator. But

Nu Dang didn't speak English and Sammy was trying not to laugh. Cudihay didn't know that, of course. He dropped the duffle bag at the men's feet, muttered "For your boss, Colonel Bao," and scuttled back to his vehicle.

It was the last leg of the money trail. Officers of the Ranger Company in Austin had already documented the "payoff" from Leon to Cudihay. Now Hadnott could testify that the Senator delivered the same cash bankroll to people he believed were allied with Col. Bao.

Up until a few minutes ago, Cudihay had preserved the façade of a hard-working public official (never mind that his actual public service had never been more than a façade). The morning after making the drop he'd scheduled a press conference to brag on himself and tout all that he, personally, had done to bring relief to the storm-wracked populace of his district. Then the fucking Texas Ranger walked in and shut the door behind him....

O.B. had had his fun. He pulled out a ring of keys and dangled them in front of the Senator tantalizingly. "Here's what it is. We're going to walk out of here all smiles," said Hadnott. "Past your staff, out the door, and you can have your press conference. No handcuffs." He was satisfied he'd utterly terrified and demoralized the Senator; the knowledge gave Hadnott a warm and fuzzy glow of pleasure.

Cudihay knew he was on a short leash. He had the dawning sense that the gravy train had come to the end of the line. If the law didn't hang him out to dry, Bao would. It was time to start thinking about making the best deal he could manage.

Hadnott unhooked him and grinned a big grin at his new best friend. The warmth of the smile was mitigated considerably by the blue-norther chill in the Ranger's pale eyes.

Hadnott slapped the Senator on the back. Real hard. "Here we go, *amigo*." Cudihay massaged his wrists and began to sleepwalk towards the office door. "Say, Cudihay," asked the Ranger as the Senator reached for the doorknob. "Do you by any chance recall a supper club in Odessa called the Oil Patch?"

Cudihay stopped, goggle-eyed, preoccupied. "Ah...Odessa?...No, I don't, ah..."

"How about a girl named Nadine Thaxton? Pretty girl. Not real worldly, though. Not like you."

The Senator screwed his eyebrows together in thought. "Nadine? Sounds like some kind of truckstop waitress....How the fuck should I know someone named Nadine?"

Hadnott shoved Cudihay through the door. "Just wondering," he murmured.

—

Nguyen Ngoc Bao watched the Senator's press conference on a portable beat-to-shit black and white television in the beat-to-shit warehouse space at the back of the Sea-Tex building. Normally, the room would have been thrumming with chattering Vietnamese fish packers, sorting shrimp and icing down the day's catch. But the electricity was still off along the docks in the aftermath of the storm, which meant no refrigeration for the catch, which meant no packers. Plywood still covered most of the warehouse doors and windows. The big room was hot, steamy and empty. Well, not entirely empty— two men, burlap sacks concealing their features, sat tied to a pair of upright wooden chairs.

Bao had the sound on the battery-powered television turned off. He thought he might throw up if he heard the sound of that fat bastard's voice. The plummy oratory, the salacious, good-ole-boy accent. The wheedling, insinuating tone that felt like someone slipping their oily tongue inside his ear.

Bao hated the voice, hated the pale, slug-like figure of the Senator (and hated most white people, for that matter), and hated that he had to cajole and equivocate and take half measures. In Vietnam, thanks to the political and legal immunity he enjoyed, he had been able to be bold, decisive...and ruthless.

Here, he had to tiptoe around the police, most of who were deplorably honest (the local sheriff being a notable exception). But they were ineffective, and constrained by the fantastic legal niceties of the state from matching his methods in kind. It was a flabby, inefficient, weak-willed system, but it still constrained him.

Where was the fucking *money*? God damn it. Bao fixed on Cudihay's televised image with lethal avidity. The spineless dog said he had the cash, ready to deliver. Then nothing since last night. Bao knew he had to reach out to him, but he could hardly do so while the

Senator was keeping such a highly public profile.

Bao took another sip of cold, bitter coffee and lit another cigarette. He had lost almost ten pounds since the night of the hurricane and looked less like an omniscient crime lord than one of the skeletal *Día de los Muertos* piñatas the Mexican children clobbered with sticks this time of year. Mexican children....

The Mexicans....

The only people that Bao loathed and feared more than the Anglos were the Mexicans. The *narcotraficantes* with whom he had forged a treacherous alliance put him in mind of the renegade Hmong and Meo tribesmen he'd dealt with in Laos and Cambodia—barely one generation out of the jungle, utterly amoral and as naturally pitiless as barracudas. Sanchez had finally called him to set the time and place for the rendezvous. So little time!

The Americans could only send him to jail, but Bao tried not to speculate on his fate if he was not forthcoming with the Mexicans' money in very short order. They would not forgive two fuck-ups. Not them.

One of the increasingly frequent black moods of fatalism and outer-directed rage began to wash over him again. His vision narrowed and everything seemed etched in red. His head began to pound and his breath rasped in and out of his throat.

"God curse all Mexicans," he grunted. He turned to the two men bound to upright wooden chairs behind the television in a corner of the warehouse. The burlap sacks over the men's heads puffed in and out as they breathed shallowly, fearfully. They froze, as though subliminally aware of Bao's sudden scrutiny.

"God curse all lackeys and traitors, too," Bao snarled. He stalked over to the trussed pair and jerked the sack off the head of one of the men.

Blinking, blinded by the sudden light, Ho-Dac craned his neck up to regard his boss. Flickers of fear jittered in his swollen green eyes.

———

"I'm on break!" Trinh An Phu took off her apron and hung it on a coat hook inside the kitchen of Charlotte Plummer's restaurant. The owners had hooked up a generator and the local hangout was almost back to normal after the hurricane, although the regulars were still getting a lot of mileage recounting the barroom brawl that had reduced the dining room to a shambles a couple of days previously.

"Okay, Trinny, but don't wander far. The lunch crowd's gonna be comin' soon and dem shrimp ain't gonna peel demselves." Leona, the head cook and arbiter of all things in the kitchen, nodded at the big gunnysacks of fresh Gulf-caught jumbos on the stainless steel countertop. *Thank God for the shrimp boats the storm had spared*, she thought.

Trinny waved in acknowledgment. "Later, gator," she said merrily, pleased with the new slang she'd added to her patois.

Walking across the oyster-shell parking lot, she decided to cruise over to the nearby Sea-Tex warehouse. Payday at Sea-Tex had been two days before the hurricane, but what with working two jobs, Trinny didn't always manage to pick up her check promptly. The warehouse manager was accustomed to rat-holing her check in his top desk drawer for whenever she could drop by. Even though the warehouse had closed for repair since the storm, just maybe somebody would be there.

She ducked down the alley behind the restaurant and walked a block towards the marina where the shrimp fleet docked.

Just as it had at every idle moment, her mind turned to the Texas Ranger's extraordinary proposal. Her imagination ran up against a blank wall once again. O.B. Hadnott had attempted to explain about the West Texas landscape he called home—the intimidating expanse of sky, the red rock canyons that carved up something he called "the Caprock," the flat, hallucinatory vastness of the equally incomprehensible "Llano Estacado," whatever that was. (Trinny couldn't begin to even pronounce it.)

It would be cold that far north. And the dryness, my God. Hardly any lakes and rivers to speak of, let alone an ocean. Trinny's whole life had been defined by strips of land bordering green and blue continents of water. Now here was another continent, where water held no sway. And so far away ("Later, gator") from her friends who had also become her family.

On the other hand, the lanky, woefully out-of-place lawman was offering her the only glimpse of security she'd ever known. What would it be like to have a roof over her head that was truly hers? To not have to depend on the capricious whims of the ocean and the weather? To live without fear of parasites like Colonel Bao?

What did she *really* want? *I'll think about it tomorrow,* she decided yet again, as she lifted the edge of a plywood sheet and pushed her way through the front door of the Sea-Tex warehouse.

Normally, a long display case showcased the shrimp, redfish, trout and dolphin for customers wanting to take home a sack of fresh seafood. She always made a point to ladle out the ice into snowy mounds and carefully position the fish, taking care to make an attractive arrangement. Today, however, the refrigeration was still out, and the big case sat empty. No customers, so sorry.

The manager's office was behind the case and through a swinging wooden door. As she rounded the corner behind the display case, Trinny glanced through the big Plexiglas window that offered a view of the warehouse—the plastic was scratched and scuffed and clouded with humidity but angular shafts of light shot through exposed rips in the warehouse windows and roof, illuminating the dusky interior. She squinted a bit, and then she froze, as though she had just walked up on a water moccasin.

The glass was nearly opaque but she could see clearly enough to spy Colonel Bao advancing on two men tied to chairs, hoods concealing their heads. And she could hear Bao's voice.

Bao removed the hood and backhanded Ho-Dac savagely. "Idiot!" he hissed. He spoke in Vietnamese. "A woman! A woman with a badge. You find it in her purse and then you still take her? She couldn't see you in the dark...she hadn't seen you when you knocked her unconscious. Yet you still take her?"

Ho-Dac shook his head, mumbling thickly through a split lip, blood running down his chin. "Lines still down...no radio...Couldn't call you to check first. I called later. I called later to ask..."

Bao slapped him again. Ho-Dac's face, already scarred by Vita's skillet, sprouted a fresh welt. "Texas Department of Corrections. Is that where you want me to go? To one of their prisons? Maybe you want to run things now, hey?"

"They...they were both in the house. We were told to grab the man in the house, that house. We did as you told us. As we always do..."

Ho-Dac was terrified. He knew he was staring his own death

in the face. He'd served as Bao's enforcer, and even executioner, on two continents. He understood what the rail-thin colonel was capable of. But always before, Bao had been icy and dispassionate in inflicting punishment or vengeance. The raving, sweating, disheveled figure raising his hand to strike him once again looked like...a madman.

"And you let them both escape. Sweetwater is still free...and the others...also free," Bao snarled as Ho-Dac's head snapped backwards at the force of another blow. "And you follow them to a bar, make a spectacle of yourself. Get arrested...."

Bao detested being in anyone's debt, but he had had to humble himself in the early morning hours, had had to stand in supplication in front of the desk of the oily county sheriff and cajole—practically beseech!—Huckabee to release his men into his personal custody. Afterwards, the paperwork, Huckabee assured him, would be "misplaced"—for a certain gratuity to be arranged later. He all but licked his lips, the fat parasite.

Bao had frog-marched Ho-Dac and his hapless companion, Le Loi, into the deserted alley behind the police station, where a panel van waited. The doors opened and the two men found themselves facing the business end of a shotgun held by a white man. Before they could protest, Ho-Dac's and Le Loi's hands were bound behind them, rags stuffed in their mouths, the medic's bandages ripped from their faces and hoods jammed down over their heads.

As soon as it was done, Bao paid the white man off. Just another thug, a skinny cracker with Confederate flag tattoos and a crystal meth habit that kept him looking for any quick and dirty job that came his way. Bao had told him he was collecting some gambling debts. He just wanted to throw a scare into the two welshers; no one would get hurt.

Bao sent the man on his way and climbed behind the wheel. This he would tend to personally. Like he should have done with Sweetwater, the one man outside his inner circle that might know about the upcoming drug deal.

Now, in the warehouse, his frustration and rage came to a rolling boil. Behind him, the Senator mouthed away silently on the television. There wasn't a sound or a soul in the warehouse (except for

Trinny, peering over the wooden transom below the window, petrified with fear).

Paralyzed though she was, she could hear him clearly, his voice a malevolent hiss. "Taken to jail! The one night I needed two reliable men! I was counting on you both to meet that slug-bellied politician to pick up his money. A half million dollars! If I arrive at Matagorda tonight with only half the money the Mexicans are expecting, I'm a dead man. A dead man...."

Bao's hand was sore and swollen from the beating he had dealt out to Ho-Dac. It wasn't enough to satisfy him, to quell the surging anger and fear that gnawed at him. Not nearly enough.

Bao took two steps back, drew his .38 revolver from his waistband and shot Ho-Dac between the eyes. The force of the big slug blew out the back of his head and knocked the bound figure onto the floor, chair and all.

Le Loi, beneath his hood, began to scream behind his gag. Bao turned to him and snatched the hood off his head. Le Loi's eyes rolled madly in terror. Bao removed the gag and his captive erupted with a torrent of screams, invective and nearly incoherent curses.

Bao's eyes narrowed. "You talk too much," he said. He grabbed the back of Le Loi's chair and dragged it over to the long stainless steel sorting table that ran from the conveyor belt to the harbor at the end of the building. Gasping for breath, Bao tipped the helpless man forward. As he opened his mouth once more, Bao jammed his jaws down on the edge of the table. Le Loi looked as though he were taking a bite out of the long metal tabletop.

With all of his strength, Bao struck the back of Le Loi's skull with the heel of his hand. Le Loi's shriek was nearly lost in the crackling, shattering sound of his teeth and jaw as they disintegrated.

Bao dragged him back. Blood smeared the edge of the sorting table and Le Loi's ruined face was almost unrecognizable. His mouth was a red and black hole from which blood poured. Tiny shards of his teeth were still visible poking up out of the red meat of his jaw.

Outside the window, in the front of the warehouse, Trinny curled in a ball, catatonic with fear. She prayed Bao would not hear or see her. *I've got to get to the Ranger*, she thought over and over hysterically.

He was the only one who could protect her. She had to tell him what she'd seen and heard. But what did "Matagorda" mean? Maybe he would know.

Fortunately for her, Bao was at the far end of the building, dragging the chair, with a groaning, bleeding Le Loi still tied to it, out through the big rolling door and onto the private dock behind the warehouse. He glanced around the harbor and then, with a last grunt of effort, Bao turned the chair and pushed it off the pier. The whimpers and cries of his lieutenant ended in a splash below the pilings.

It took some time, though later Trinny could never have said how much, before Bao finished dragging Ho-Dac's body into the walk-in cooler and hosing his blood and brain matter off the floor. He wiped down the bloodstained sorting table and turned off the television (*As the World Turns* having replaced the Senator's press conference). Finally, giving a last glance around, the Colonel exited through the building's side door, climbed into his panel truck and drove away.

At last, hardly daring to breathe, Trinny raised her head and summoned the courage to dart out the front door and back to the restaurant, where Leona read her the riot act for taking "half the damn day" for her break.

"Hey! Where you going, girl?" Leona yelled from the kitchen. "I need you for the lunch...." But Trinny didn't hear the rest of it. She had already snatched her purse off the coat peg and dashed out the side door to her truck.

CHAPTER 37

Trinny waited until she got to O.B. Hadnott's door at the Sea-Gun Inn before she fell to pieces. The Ranger sat in his jockey shorts and a T-shirt, completing a report about the incident at Shady's, when a light, frantic tapping on the door intruded on his concentration.

Recalling the last time he had heard that knock, O.B. took a moment to pull on his gabardine trousers and a pearl-snap shirt. He opened the door and Trinny fell into his arms, crying and chattering in a frantic mixture of Vietnamese and accented English. Her eyes darted around the tiny room, as though seeking unseen enemies.

Because O.B. didn't have any more idea than the man in the moon what to do in such a situation, he simply held her and stayed quiet. Which, as it happened, turned out to be the right thing to do after all.

He escorted her to the swaybacked couch in front of the television and eased her down, holding her all the while. Not that he had a choice; Trinny clung to him with all the strength and tenacity she could muster.

Finally, he began to pick up salient details as Trinny's hysterical crying jag ran its course. There had been a shooting...no, an *execution*...two men...bound and blindfolded. Bao—out of control, screaming. Like a demon. "Now, he find *me*, he find me, he kill me, too...." She was babbling, but O.B. managed to make out something about Matagorda and money and planes and Mexicans.

Then Trinny said something that commanded all his attention: "Tonight." She said. "Tonight it all happen." The money, Bao, Mexicans.... Whatever it was, it was coming down tonight. O.B. knew he was going to have to hurry. But there was the little matter of the terrified woman in his arms.

Hadnott rocked her in his arms instinctively, making shushing noises. "Now, honey, no one's going to find you. And no one's going to hurt you. I promise."

As pleasant as it was to cradle the small, warm female bundle in his embrace, even a female as clearly terrified as this one, his mind began to shift gears as habit and training took over.

A material witness to a double homicide...Hadnott thought to himself what he dared not confirm to Trinny. She was right; Bao most certainly would kill her if he even suspected his deeds at the Sea-Tex packinghouse had been overseen and overheard.

Bao certainly had nothing to lose now. Senator Cudihay was ready to give a statement attesting to the Colonel's criminal enterprise and his involvement in the murder of Neddy Pomade. Charlie Sweetwater could testify about the kidnapping by Bao's employees— slightly ambiguous evidence, but certainly enough to throw a spotlight onto Bao and his crew. There was the tape of Bao and his lieutenant harassing and threatening Nu Dang and his wife—maybe inadmissible, but that would depend on how good Bao's slimeball lawyer was. Then there were Bao's two soldiers, cooling their heels in the Rockport jail. With a little come-to-Jesus persuasion, Hadnott felt certain he could entice them to....

Stupid, he thought. *You ought to go back to Paducah and chase sheep rustlers, you numbskull....*Suddenly he knew exactly who Bao had capped at the warehouse. He had no doubt that the man on the night desk at the Aransas County Sheriff's office would have a sudden attack of amnesia regarding just who, precisely, might have bonded Ho-Dac and Le Loi out in the early morning hours. And, no doubt, the accompanying paperwork had evaporated, too.

Never mind. The murders trumped everything. If Hadnott could get a warrant—and he didn't have any doubts about that— he felt certain a forensics team could find enough evidence to put Bao in the warehouse at the time Trinny said. Presumably, the body of the second man was still washing around under the Sea-Tex pier. Trinny had seen Bao drag the victim out of the warehouse door to the wharf, and heard the splash. Now, if only Bao was still hanging onto the gun....

He realized Trinny was speaking and forced his mind back to the here-and-now.

"...What?" he said belatedly.

"I say, even if you Texas Ranger, how you gonna get this bad, bad man? You put on your six-gun, ha? Everyone around him end up dead."

"We're gonna get him, Trinny—that I can promise you. But first we have to make sure you're safe."

He had given voice to her worst fears. She began to come apart again. Even her English began to slip away. "No safe! Not in Rockport! No place safe for Trinny!"

"Did he see you, Trinny? Do you know if Bao saw you before you ran?"

She stopped crying and looked down, concentrating. A moment later she looked up and shook her head. "No, I not think so." She took a deep breath. "I not think so," she repeated.

"That's good. But just in case, I think it might be better if you don't stay at your own place tonight."

"But where?" she asked anxiously. "Where do I go?"

"Well, ah..." Hadnott couldn't quite believe the errant thought that was fluttering around his Panhandle-simple brain. "Well, ah, there might be a place...."

He took her shoulders, turned her to face him, waited until her panic attack subsided.

"Miss An Phu," he said formally. "Do you remember what I asked you, here in this very room, not two days ago?"

"I remember," she said and then, with a wan attempt at humor, "I been a little busy since then."

Hadnott smiled. "Well, I meant it then and I mean it now. I want us to get married." He gestured around the cheap, tawdry room. "I kinda wish we were in Paris, France—or hell, even Dallas—and I was on my knee with a big ol' diamond, but this will have to do." He picked up the ring-pull tab from an empty can of Pearl beer and slipped it on her finger.

"That how you keep me safe?" she said dubiously. "Marry me and take me off to Lubbock?" (She pronounced it "Rub-ock," which O.B. found infinitely endearing.)

"No," Hadnott said, then hastily, "I mean yes, yes, we'll get married and go to Lubbock, if you want. But what I meant was... what I was getting around to was...." He felt like a tall, gangly boy at the Starlighters Dance Club again, trying to work up the nerve to ask the homecoming queen for a foxtrot. He hadn't enjoyed the tongue-tied feeling then, and the sensation hadn't improved any with the years.

Trinny managed a smile at the tall Ranger's obvious discomfort. *He's about as smooth as the soldier boys back home,* she thought. *Just another lonely man a long, long way from home.*

"What I meant was, if we were gonna get married, uh, eventually...soon I hope...." Hadnott looked around at the awful paintings, the bare light bulb hanging from the ceiling, the wheezing, dripping window unit, the hot plate with the cans of Wolf Brand Chili, Ranch Style Beans ("They're Husband-Pleasin'!"), the jar of Pace Picante Sauce and a box of saltine crackers that constituted Hadnott's pantry and, lastly, the sagging queen-size bed.

"Well, um, maybe you could stay here." Asking a gal to spend the night in your room, even without any hanky panky on the menu, was a *big step* by O.B.'s traditional way of thinking. No female since Nadine Thaxton had ever spent a night in his room before. "This is the last place Bao would ever look for you, and you'd be safe here." She looked around the room indecisively.

He decided to level with her. "Look, this isn't over. Bao is out there and he's a danger to you and everyone around him, and that's the God-honest truth. And when we do arrest him, you're going to have to testify. You'll have to look him in the eye and tell a jury what you saw today. You're gonna have to be brave Trinny. But I'll be there with you.

"Then, if you still want to, when this is over, we can go away together and leave all this behind us."

Trinny felt more lost than anytime since she had left Vietnam. There was no more home in Rockport, that was certain, as long as Bao remained free. The ocean, her small circle of refugee friends, the other waitresses at the restaurant—that was all she knew of America. Anyplace else—especially this "West Texas" a thousand miles away—seemed as remote as Mars. Suddenly, she felt stubborn and mulish.

"Hey, Mr. Marlboro Man," she said hotly. "You think you take me to Rub-ock just like that? We one happy family, eh? How you think I fit in at the, the, ah, country crub? You think blonde ladies, other Ranger wives, invite little Vietnamese girl to come make cookies and drink highball? I think you been drinking too much your gut-rot whiskey!

"*This* is my home! My friends here, my job here, the ocean here. You and I together, well, maybe...."

She tried to soften her tone, seeing the stricken look on Hadnott's face.

"Maybe even married," she said more gently. "But this West Texas, this 'Rrano Estacato'? I don't know...I don't know...."

The room seemed very small all of a sudden, and O.B. didn't seem to know what to do with his hands. He had the sudden conviction he had a big piece of spinach stuck between his teeth.

Trinny smiled, a small and elusive smile. The emotional catharsis had left her wrung out and weary. She leaned over and kissed the startled Hadnott softly on the lips.

"So okay. We get the bad guy, like in cowboy movies. Kiss girl, ride into sunset. Everybody cheer. But I not stay here alone. Not while you go after outlaw. I go with you."

"Trinny you can't...," he saw the terror coming back in her eyes. "Okay," he said gently. "How 'bout this? I'll follow you into town, and then...." He paused, considering the options. Trinny waited expectantly. "Trinny, if you won't stay here, and if you think you're up to it, probably the *best* thing you can do is go back to work at the restaurant—just like normal. You stick to your routine. You think you can do that?"

Trinny took a deep breath. "Yes. I can do that," she said. "You are right. Just normal day. Beside, if I no show up for lunch shift, Miss Leona will fire me for certain. Then I be up...."

"Shit creek?" O.B. offered.

"Yeah," she smiled, more broadly and kissed O.B. again, more emphatically. "We have same creek in Vietnam."

She gathered up her things, touched up her makeup in the small vanity mirror and opened the door. She looked both ways down the deserted second-floor motel balcony. *She's still scared,* thought Hadnott. *And to tell the truth, I don't blame her a bit.*

"Don't leave the restaurant alone," he said out loud. "Get one of your friends to walk home with you. Don't worry, Trinny, we'll work it out."

She looked up at him, smiling. "We work it out. That what we do, have always done. Work it out. You make good Vietnamese, Mr.

Marlboro Man. You put the Colonel in the jail and then we talk about that other thing."

And with that, she turned and left.

O.B. followed Trinny into town and watched her disappear into the restaurant, then headed for the DPS office. Within the hour, he was on the telephone with his captain at the Ranger barracks headquarters of Company C, in Lubbock. The first blue norther of the winter had blown into the Panhandle the night before and it was colder than a well-digger's ass, the captain said, just by way of making conversation. The quail hunting was good, but the dog-ass Texas Tech Red Raiders had dropped a game to the TCU goddamn Horned Frogs. "How anyone can root for a team named after a horny toad beats the hell out of me," the captain complained.

O.B. filled in his captain on the latest developments, including Trinny's startling testimony and his own conclusion that Colonel Bao would meet with Mexican narcos tonight.

"Sergeant Hadnott, you listen to me, if we want a sure-fire conviction on this case you're going to have to keep an eye on that immigrant gangster. Don't let him or that money out of your sight. Find out where this meeting is and make sure you get the drop on Bao. I'll help you coordinate backup. You got all that, Ranger?"

"Yessir," O.B. answered.

"You follow that fucking money!"

"I understand, Captain."

Then he heard his voice uttering words he would never have imagined when he picked up the telephone:

"Captain, ah, sir...? I was wondering, ah, when this is all over, do you think we might be able to discuss if there might be an opening at, um, Company D?"

"In Corpus Christi?! Are you outta your mind?" his captain barked, and his displeasure and disbelief came across clearly from the frozen South Plains.

"Sergeant, I'm sure I don't have to tell you that Company D has jurisdiction on the Texas coast. You've expressed exactly how delighted you are with that little corner of Eden several times during the course of this assignment, with some very colorful language. And now *this*? Are you going native on me, Sergeant Hadnott?"

"Ah, no sir," O.B. replied smartly. "That is, I don't think so...That is...Well, I just thought I'd ask."

"O.B.," said the captain, not unkindly, "You're so country you probably piss bobwire and shit footballs. You've bitched and moaned about that waterlogged, godforsaken country, as you call it, ever since you got down there. West Texas is home. Have you got your mind right, Sergeant?"

Hadnott straightened up and looked out the window of the DPS office. A bougainvillea bush waved languidly in the ceaseless Gulf breeze. Behind it a blue heron stood rigid on the balcony railing. In the distance the masts and rigging of the big gulf shrimp boats in Conn Brown Harbor were silhouetted against the seaward sky.

"Yes, sir," he replied, with a sudden clarity he hadn't felt since he'd arrived on the coast. "I've got my mind right."

———

CHAPTER 38

With the Ransom Island ferry back in service, Marisol decided to hunt down a working phone in Aransas Pass so she could check in with her office. Charlie insisted on going with her.

"Bodyguard?" she asked.

"Male escort service," he replied. "Reasonable rates."

Raul tagged along as well, arguing that the comic books he wanted to buy would improve his English. "The Bat Man, he is very smart," Raul explained. (Though secretly he thought Robin the Boy Wonder was a bit of a *maricón*.)

Standing in a payphone booth outside an Exxon station near the harbor, Marisol told her sympathetic supervisor why she had over-stayed her vacation...had to help some Fulton friends put their homes and lives back together after the storm. Such ruin! Such devastation! She felt she just had to pitch in.

Most of it was true, of course. She left out the barroom brawl, the gunplay, the kidnapping and the assault and battery. No use going all *telenovela* on the guy. "*Hasta luego*, then," said her supervisor. "But hurry back—all the bad guys miss you." She hung up, puffed a breath of dismissal, and then dug into her pocket for another dime.

She phoned Miguel to report about her recent adventure in the Laguna Madre.

"Miguel, are you still there?" she asked. He hadn't responded after she finished recounting her tale.

"Yeah. I'm here."

After another pause Marisol said, "Miguel, what's going on in that head of yours?"

"Just thinking."

"Thinking what, exactly?"

"Just...thinking," he said.

"Listen, Miguel," Marisol said forcefully. "That Texas Ranger is all over this thing now. And he's got the resources and the authority to do something about it. Don't you be getting any ideas about jumping in, okay? Don't...do...anything."

Miguel picked up a beer bottle cap that lay on the bar and idly bent it in half, his knuckles popping out like walnuts as he squeezed, the tattoos on the backs of his hands seeming to swell. His flat obsidian eyes gazed toward the Fulton Harbor. His first thought after hearing Marisol's kidnapping story was to grab an ice pick and march over to the Sea-Tex and push it through Bao's ear, but he checked himself, remembering his own advice to Charlie a few days ago.

"You know that Bao or his guys woulda killed you out there on the Laguna," he said. "Still will if they get the chance."

"I don't doubt it," Marisol agreed, remembering Ho-Dac's lethal expression at Shady's when the gun-toting thug zeroed in on the bamboo office curtain and the refugees that crouched behind it in the dark.

The bartender puffed his breath out in frustration. "*Oye chica*, now's prob'ly a good time for you to take your little butt back to Austin. I just learned there's gonna be some more serious shit going down around here pretty soon." He knew he shouldn't be talking about the things he'd heard, but Marisol was the closest thing he had to a friend. She needed to know.

"Huh?" she said. "What are you talking about, Miguel?"

"A guy came in here earlier today. I used to know him back in... the old days. I dunno who was more surprised to see who. I told him I wasn't in the life anymore. He said that's okay, he was just passin' through. Said he's on his way to Corpus to pick up some merchandise.

Said a local player was meeting a bunch of badass narcos at a place not that far from there, at Mata...Matagrande? Something like that."

Marisol pushed open the phone booth door and motioned to Charlie to come over. She covered the phone receiver with her hand. "Charlie, do you know of a place called Matagrande? Not too far from Corpus?"

"Matagrande Key? Yeah, I know it. It's a long sandy strip of nothin' by Baffin Bay, close to where we were day before yesterday," he answered. "Why?"

"Miguel thinks that's where Bao's drug deal is taking place... tonight." She put the phone to her ear. "Miguel, did he say Matagrande Key?"

"Yeah. I guess so," he replied. Marisol nodded yes to Charlie.

Charlie raised his eyebrows pensively. "Makes sense. That part of the bay is way off the beaten path...and there's nothing on the mainland near there but a bunch of King Ranch grazeland, maybe a *vaquero* or two. You could land a small plane without anybody seeing, easy. Ideal spot for Bao to meet his suppliers."

"Miguel. Are you sure about this?" Marisol said into the phone receiver.

"I'm just tellin' you what I heard," he said. "But I'm guessing we're talking *mucho dinero* on this deal. This guy that came in, he's pretty way up in the Syndicato. Had a junior *carnal* taggin' along with him."

"No wonder Bao's so serious about removing any...loose ends," said Marisol. "And he's convinced Charlie's a loose end."

"Take him to Austin with you, then," said Miguel. "You like the *gringo*, don't you?"

"I'll think about it Miguel," she answered quietly. "But in the meantime, you promise me you'll stay out of this."

"You're the boss," he said.

After she hung up the phone she discussed options with Charlie. He immediately rejected the idea of leaving.

"Goddammit," he said, "We're supposed to be the good guys. For crissakes, we got our own personal Texas Ranger on call, don't we? Let's give the information to him, the whole bucket of snakes. He might decide to shoot Bao just to keep from filling out the paperwork on all this shit."

"Not a bad idea," Marisol agreed. "You think that *gabacho* is up to it? I think he's scared of the water, maybe. Big boots, big hat. I don't know...."

"He'll have help. Helicopters, SWAT teams, whatever he needs. Let them handle it. But..." he looked earnestly at Marisol, "...if Bao's little rendezvous is tonight, we need to let Sergeant Hadnott know about it, now."

"You're right," she agreed, "But I won't mention Miguel's name. You either. I don't want him connected to any of this, in any way."

An hour later, O.B. Hadnott had spoken with Charlie and Marisol and coordinated a plan to intercept Bao that included local DPS agents, the Coast Guard, the Kenedy County Sheriff's office and representatives from the Houston-based DEA. "We got this from here," he told Charlie. "You guys take the night off. You've sure enough earned it."

━━━━

CHAPTER 39

Colonel Bao tossed two heavy duffle bags over the stern, where they landed with a thud on the crab-slick deck of Nu Dang's shrimp boat. Both Nu Dang and Sammy recognized one of the bags instantly. It was the same bag they'd collected from the fat politician—and the same one they'd handed over to the Texas Ranger. Now it lay like a carcass smack-dab in the middle of Nu Dang's boat. They'd never expected to see the bag again—and the sudden appearance of Bao shocked them.

"I need your boat," Bao said in Vietnamese. "We are going for a ride." His tone was flat and non-negotiable. It wasn't a request.

Sitting cross-legged on the boat deck, Sammy looked at his uncle with alarm. Nu Dang yelled at the intruder, "You have no right!"

The Colonel was in no mood for debate. All day long he'd anxiously awaited the bank transfer from his Cayman Island accounts, and for the money promised to him by Senator Cudihay, which finally materialized in a dumpster behind the Sea-Tex fishhouse. An anonymous phone call—it sounded like it could have been Cudihay's voice—told him the location of the duffle. Now it, along with all the cash he'd been able to scrape together by liquidating his local and offshore accounts, lay bundled up in a pair of canvas bags on the deck of the boat.

Assembling the narcos' money had taken all day and time was running out. Everything had to be ready for his appointment with the Mexicans. Bao didn't even want to *think* about what would happen if it wasn't.

Heading straight for the rendezvous was out of the question. Somebody, probably that meddlesome Texas Ranger, had ordered one of Rockport's patrolmen to watch him, and other law enforcement agencies might be monitoring his activities too. He couldn't simply whistle up one of his own surviving boats and make straight for the barrier island rendezvous, no matter how anxious he was to transact his business. He needed a decoy. Had Bao paid any attention to American sports (although a big fiberboard sign on the Rockport Pirates' high school stadium read "Sea-Tex Marine Proudly Supports the Pirates!"), he would have called his plan an end run.

Easing his Lincoln Continental up to the entrance of Fulton Harbor, Bao recognized the marked Rockport PD patrol car in the parking lot of Charlotte Plummer's restaurant. The cop—who Bao knew vaguely from his previous interaction with the local flatfoots— was far from RPD's best and brightest, but he was probably sitting behind the tinted window scanning the outer harbor area with binoculars. He was about as subtle as a ten-foot tall pink flamingo.

God damn it, thought Bao. He was tired, filthy, paranoid and strung out on coffee, cigarettes and raw nerves and he'd just recently killed two men. He was unraveling, he could feel it. He hated making decisions when he was like this. But he had to do something, and quick.

Before the policeman could spot Bao's distinctive car, the gangster put his automobile into reverse and jammed the big car into a concealed space between a bait shop's big refrigerator unit and the hull of a dry-docked oyster boat. From that angle, Bao's eyes lighted on the hull of Nu Dang's trawler, *New Hope*.

My harbor, my boat, he thought. The usually calculating and methodical Colonel Bao would not have ordinarily considered a sudden impulse to hijack a boat at random. But that Colonel Bao wasn't running the show now.

Bao exited the car and walked to a pay phone on the side of the boarded-up bait shop, still out of sight of the oblivious cop, and fished a dime out of his pocket. He gave the man on the other end of the line crisp instructions about meeting him in Port Aransas with a speedboat. From there, in his own boat, he could proceed to the meeting with the Mexicans. There was still time.

He quick-walked back to the car, eyes jittering in every direction. He pulled his revolver out of the glove compartment and stuck it in his waistband under his jacket. Then he opened the trunk and hoisted two heavy canvas duffle bags over his shoulders and set off down the pier for Nu Dang's trawler.

Nu Dang stood up and was attempting to shoo his unwanted trespasser off his boat when the Colonel whacked him across the temple with an open hand. Nu Dang fell over the crab traps and landed next to Sammy, who watched Bao with calm contempt.

"You, boy, go start the engines," Bao demanded in Vietnamese. Sammy rose to his feet and stood face to face with Bao. Off-season weight training for the football team, a healthy diet of all-American cheeseburgers, and surging teenage hormones had put some meat on the boy. He was almost a head taller than the Colonel and maybe twenty pounds heavier. But none of that trumped the oily blue steel revolver that Bao jerked out of his waistband and pointed at the boy

Without taking his cold eyes off the boy, Bao addressed Nu Dang, who slowly picked himself up off the deck. "Uncle, do you want to watch me blow your nephew's head apart? Is he the brains of this family? Let's find out."

Nu Dang started to respond but Sammy raised his palms in submission and started for the wheelhouse.

The Colonel picked up the duffel bags and followed Sammy into the cabin, crunching a fugitive blue crab under his shoe as he crossed the deck.

As Nu Dang unloosed the lines from the dock pilings he didn't see his wife, Lua Xuan, who was walking toward the pier. She, however had seen Bao jump aboard their boat and strike her husband, and she had seen the pistol. She stood anchored to the concrete bulkhead, panic-stricken, two brown sacks of groceries clutched to her chest.

As the *New Hope* motored through the Fulton Harbor jetties toward the bay, Lua Xuan dropped the groceries into the oily water and ran for her car.

———

CHAPTER 40

Charlie lined up his shot and punched the eight ball into the corner pocket. With O.B. Hadnott and seemingly half of South Texas law enforcement running interference for him, he felt like he'd been given a new lease on life.

"Hey waddaya know? Another lucky shot!" he said. "That makes it, what? Three games to nothing?"

Captain Joe Grant replaced his pool cue in the rack and sat down on a bar stool at Hooper's, one of the oldest bars in Port Aransas and looking every minute of it. "I don't understand, Charlie," said Joe. "I've got a pool table in my house, or used to anyway, and you whipped me like a rented mule."

"Exceptional hand-eye coordination, my man," Charlie replied. "And genetics."

"Yeah, that's it for sure," Joe answered. "Genetics."

"The blood of kings runs through my veins," Charlie continued, holding his pool cue like a scepter. "Or so my momma told me when I was just a pup."

Marisol came walking back from the bar with a glass of char-donnay. She whistled briskly and snapped her fingers, "Here, King;

here boy!" Charlie laughed. So did Captain Joe.

Joe cocked his head inquisitively at Charlie, one eye squinted closed. "Rupert told me that the original Sweetwater arriving on these shores was kicked out of England to relieve overcrowding in the jails. And for giving the Lord Mayor's daughter the clap." Joe's mouth was a little looser when his boys weren't around.

"Well, they put kings in jail, too," said Charlie.

"When they didn't chop their heads off," added Marisol.

"But once your royal namesake set foot on this continent," Joe continued, "he became just another homeless, tempest-tossed refugee—the wretched refuse washed up on our teeming shore. Same as tar balls and old crab trap floats."

"Carlito, you're just another wetback when it comes down to it," said Marisol, concluding her take on the illustrious Sweetwater pedigree.

Charlie sat down beside Marisol and gave her a wounded look. "So, you don't like boat people? ...Or *mojados*?"

"I don't know. Let me see your papers, mister. And I'll decide whether or not to send you back to Mexico." They all laughed some more and then Joe raised his longneck beer to Charlie. "Anyway, cheers, Your Majesty. I guess that since you won and I lost, I've got to buy the next round?"

"Damn straight," said Charlie. "Pay homage to the King of Hooper's."

Charlie drained his bottle and caught the attention of the waitress. "*Dos mas, por favor*," he shouted over the din in the bar. He placed his pool cue in the rack and they moved to a table near an open deck overlooking the docks of the Port Aransas Marina. The white flags of the bait shops were snapping in the wind and water slapped against the underside of the finger piers. Everyone took a drink or two. Marisol listened to Charlie and Joe trade more ribald speculations about their respective ancestries. Normal life began to seem plausible again.

Marisol finished her wine and stood up. "You boys can discuss your philosophies without me for a minute. *Yo me voy al baño.*" She made her way towards the ladies' restroom labeled "Gulls" on the door (a sign reading "Buoys" was nailed to the men's door.)

Joe sat back down. He'd risen from his chair when Marisol stood up, the way his mama had raised him. After Marisol walked away he turned to Charlie. "I'm glad I ran into y'all tonight, Charlie. I had to get outa that one-bedroom place we're staying at right now. I was bouncing off the walls, cooped up in there with two over-amped boys."

"Yeah, I was ready for a hiatus too, man," Charlie remarked. "I needed some distance from this Bao thing. Handing the whole deal off to the Texas Ranger made me feel like the weight of the world's off my shoulders."

Joe nodded in agreement. "Well, I'm glad that Ranger stepped up. Let him tend to the Colonel." he said.

"No shit."

"You think he'll be able to catch him?...Bao?"

"One riot, one Ranger," Charlie answered with a shrug. "Anyway, he says he's got help coming in. Big as this is, they'll have the National Guard, the Aggie Corp of Cadets and the Rockport-Fulton marching band working on the case. My only job is to keep Raul and Marisol outta harm's way for awhile."

"After what's happened to y'all, I still think going to Austin would have been a good idea," said Joe. (Charlie had filled him in on every-thing.) "Farther away from Fulton, farther away from Bao."

"Well, we'll be safe over at Rupe's place. You know the Colonel won't send any more of his men back to Shady's. Not after what happened there a couple of days ago."

Marisol came out of the ladies' room and wandered over to study the jukebox. Both men cast a glance her way.

"That's quite a girl," Joe said appreciatively. "My youngest boy calls her Wonder Woman."

"She's something all right," Charlie agreed. "I can see why my brother liked her so much." Charlie's cheerful veneer fell away for a moment and Joe watched him make interlocking rings of condensa-tion on the table with the bottom of his beer bottle. Hadnott and his Mounties might catch Bao, but it didn't seem likely he'd ever answer for Johnny's death. Charlie's good mood sloughed off like dead snakeskin.

The waitress dropped a couple of cardboard coasters on the table and placed three sweaty longnecks on top of them. "Three bucks," she said. Joe handed her a five.

"So what are your plans now, Charlie?" Joe asked. "I guess you'll have some insurance money comin' to you for the *Ramrod*. You gonna try and start fresh?"

"Oh, I don't know, Joe," said Charlie. "I'm not real good at making plans. The more you get to know me, the more you'll know I've got a great future behind me."

Marisol put a quarter in the jukebox and, after due deliberation, punched in songs by Neil Young, Freddy Fender and L.C. Hebert. She made her way back to the table.

"I got you a beer," said Charlie. "They're out of that cheap wine you were drinking."

"Thanks," said Marisol. "I guess it's time I showed you boys how to drink, anyway."

After a moment Joe started chuckling to himself.

"What?" asked Charlie.

Joe turned to his two companions. "I'm just remembering how Vita knocked that guy out back at Shady's."

A wide grin crossed Charlie's face, and then he threw back his head and laughed. "No shit! I thought she'd killed him. That frying pan was as big as a trash can lid. It must have weighed ten pounds, easy. And then Rupert...." Maybe some belated battle fatigue was setting in. His mood swung again. Johnny wouldn't want him to brood. "...he swings his big hairy arm around like a sailing boom and, *Bam!*" Charlie gasped for breath between howls of laughter. "I swear to God, he lifted that other guy *off* the floor before he dropped!" Charlie swung his arm horizontally and let it fall palm forward onto the table with a smack. Joe grabbed his beer to keep it from toppling off the tabletop. He was laughing too—big, cathartic belly laughs.

Marisol giggled. "Neither one of the guys moved for twenty minutes," she said.

"So to hell with going to Austin!" Charlie proclaimed. "Here's to Uncle Rupert, Aunt Vita and the entire cast and crew of the Shady Boat and Leisure Club. Not even the Ringling Brothers can compare." They raised their beers to Shady's and tipped them back.

Charlie's' perspective regarding the last two weeks was changing.

He realized that when he wasn't getting shot at, stabbed, or kidnapped, that his little adventure in Texas was producing some unexpected serendipities. Like reconnecting with his old friends at Shady's. Like discovering he had a blood nephew he never knew he had. Like Marisol. He was even starting to get a taste for the pucker-inducing danger he'd endured. He remembered a quote by Winston Churchill, something to the effect that there was nothing more exhilarating than to be shot at without result.

Charlie picked up his beer, drank to the old English bulldog, and they clinked bottles again. "We shall fight them on the beaches..." he intoned, and then couldn't remember how the rest of the speech went. "Sons of beaches," he said, stifling a belch.

———

CHAPTER 41

Lua Xuan caught up with O.B. Hadnott as he walked out of a U-Totem located near the bridge between Rockport and Fulton. She still shook from fear and rage after seeing Bao hijack her husband and nephew. In a cacophony of Vietnamese, pidgin English and pantomime, she finally managed to make Sergeant Hadnott understand what had happened. O.B. immediately radioed the lookout posted near the harbor to watch for any movement from Colonel Bao.

"Templeton, this is Sergeant Hadnott," he growled into the radio. "Come in."

"Yeah, Sergeant," said a crackly voice. "This is Templeton." Zeke Templeton was on loan from the Rockport Police Department. O.B. was not thrilled with his temporary recruit but he figured any idiot could sit in a squad car and watch a bunch of shrimp boats for an hour or two. Follow the money, his captain had ordered.

"What the hell's going on over there?" O.B. demanded.

"Well, everything's normal, as far as I can tell, Sarge." There was a pause and O.B. Hadnott could visualize the cop scanning the harbor from his car. "Just the usual stuff," he added. O.B. had never been called "Sarge" in his life.

Then O.B. narrowed his eyes. "Templeton, are those dishes I hear in the background?"

"Uh, well, yes sir, I popped into Charlotte Plummer's for a quick bite." O.B. winced. "...And there's a pretty fair view of the harbor from up here, at least if you're sitting in one of the booths near the..."

"Templeton!" Hadnott interrupted. "Did you happen to notice one of those forty-foot trawlers leaving the harbor a few minutes ago?"

There was silence on the other end of the radio. O.B. couldn't stand it any longer. He knew the answer he'd get. He switched off the radio and shook his head. "What a sorry excuse for a peace officer," he muttered.

"Miss Xuan," he said (he pronounced it "Zan," as close as he could get). "I'll get your family back. And I'll get the Colonel too. Don't worry. If they're heading south like you say, I might be able to intercept 'em. I believe I know where they're going." He patted her clumsily on the shoulder. *But right now*, he thought, *I gotta figure out how to get a boat and get my ass on the water, pronto.* The team assembled by Ranger Headquarters would be heading for Kingsville right now, the closest town to the drug rendezvous.

He was discouraged to learn the DPS had no immediate access to watercraft, but he quickly learned that the Texas Parks and Wildlife Department did. A couple of quick calls by the department switchboard operator led him to the Rockport Harbor. He had to pull rank to compel the two TPWD game wardens to meet him there. Since Lana they'd worked long hours to transport food, water and medical supplies to victims of the hurricane (more storm-tossed refugees) and they were not overly thrilled to be chasing down a local Vietnamese troublemaker at the end of a very long week.

Although O.B. had managed to override his fear of getting back on the bay, he was unprepared for the kind of contraption the TPWD boys presented for transportation. He approached the airboat warily.

"Where do I sit?" he asked.

The game wardens both enjoyed the flatlander's uneasiness. If he wanted to go on a boat ride, then by God they'd give him one he wouldn't forget. Texas Ranger badge or not.

"I'm afraid you'll have to stand in front of the propeller back there," explained Officer Emilio Rodriguez. "You can hold onto the seats up front. Sorry we've only got two; but I sit in one seat and Officer Harrison here sits in the other one. He's the pilot. We removed the front bench seat so we could haul more supplies over to Port O'Conner and other communities hit by the hurricane. We weren't planning on joyriders." Harrison barely suppressed a smirk.

Hadnott was stooped over, halfway between the boat and the dock. He straightened up and froze the two young game wardens with a flat and fearsome gaze.

"You two men listen up," said Hadnott sharply. "This is the furthest thing from a joyride. Two people's lives might be in danger and the man who has them has already killed at least two others. I want you officers to see to your sidearms and get this transport under way right this minute. Don't make me repeat myself."

Properly chastened, Harrison warned the Ranger not to get his hands or any clothing too close to the prop cage. "That's an airplane propeller back there, Sergeant, powered by a 500 horsepower air-cooled Lycoming aircraft engine. And that blade turns at 2500 rpms. It'll suck the shirt off your back and shred it into a million pieces. An arm too."

O.B. reluctantly boarded the airboat, stashed his Stetson in a compartment up front, and positioned himself behind the game wardens, standing spread-legged and gripping the back of the two seats with white-knuckled fingers. For all his no-nonsense façade he was inwardly terrified. He might get chopped into trotline bait before he had a chance to drown. Outstanding.

As they eased away from the dock, he scrutinized the airboat anxiously, looking around him like a wild animal caught in a spring-door trap. When they cleared the jetties and entered Aransas Bay, Harrison stepped on the gas and O.B. feared his eardrums would explode from the noise. He tapped Officer Rodriguez on the shoulder and stuck a finger in his ear. Rodriguez grinned as he grabbed a set of heavy-duty ear protectors and handed them back to the Sergeant. They'd had no trouble selling Ranger Hadnott on the life jacket when they shoved off, but he'd initially refused the ear protection. Macho had its limits.

The western sun hovered near the horizon, streaming amber light through the last sliver of sky not covered by the heavy grey clouds that were blowing in from the northeast. The bay was getting rough and O.B. tried to ignore the waves that washed over his boots. His mind tried to work out the physics of the flat-bottom vessel as it skated over the surface of the water at an alarming speed.

The tremendous jet of air directed behind them by the five-foot propeller created a frothy wake in its path. O.B. reasoned that the tall vertical prop-rudders more or less pointed the boat, and it appeared that Harrison could move them laterally by grabbing a long rudder stick that reached up from the floor. There were no brakes, no seat belts, and no protection. From what O.B. Hadnott could gather, he was riding on a sea-borne bottle rocket.

They blew through Redfish Bay travelling straight through the shallow grass flats and *over* the small sandy islands. The high-powered airplane boat machine (O.B. wasn't sure what to call it) was perfectly suited to the multiformity of the marsh. Twenty minutes passed and they saw no sign of Nu Dang's boat.

Reaching the mouth of Corpus Christi Bay, Harrison lifted his foot slowly off the gas and the airboat slowed and settled into the water. He removed his ear protectors and turned toward Sergeant Hadnott. "If they left Fulton in a shrimp boat thirty minutes before we hit the water, I don't think they couldn't have made this bay before us. Any idea where they might be going, Sergeant?" he asked.

O.B. shook his head. "Huh?" he yelled much too loud. Officer Harrison pointed to the ear protectors, which O.B. removed. Harrison repeated the question. Attenuating his voice O.B. replied, "Like I said, I think he's heading out to meet the Mexicans for the drug deal. He's got a whole lot of cash with him. I figure the drugs will either arrive by water or by air. Some place called Matagrande Key. Near Kingsville, and Baffin Bay."

Rodriguez and Harrison thought about it. Finally Rodriguez said, "That doesn't make any sense, Ranger. There's not enough water in that part of the bay for a shrimp boat to draw, especially around Matagrande Key. They must be heading somewhere else, and they've been trying to decoy us. Maybe we should circle back towards Port Aransas through the ship channel. Since they're in a shrimp boat they could be trying to make it to the Gulf via the Lydia Ann Channel—plenty of places in the Gulf to rendezvous for a drug deal—or they could continue towards Corpus...or they might continue on down to someplace more accessible in the Laguna Madre. But Matagrande Key?" Rodriguez scratched his head. "I don't know."

"Wherever it is," said Harrison, "I think they're still behind us. And we'll either run into them in the channel, or we'll find 'em docked up ahead in Port A, or...," he paused, "...or they're already out in blue water."

"Does this boat go out there?" asked Sergeant Hadnott.

"In the Gulf? Not on a day like this," answered Rodriguez. "We'd likely be swamped as soon as we cleared the jetties. And you wouldn't want that."

O.B. agreed that he wouldn't.

"Well," declared Sergeant Hadnott, "Let's try the channel."

Harrison nodded and fired up the bottle rocket again. Five minutes later they encountered Nu Dang's shrimp boat in the channel.

Officer Rodriguez and Sergeant Hadnott unholstered their weapons as Officer Harrison eased the airboat towards the trawler. Hadnott saw only one person on the boat and it looked like Nu Dang. As the vessel slowed to a standstill, Nu Dang exited the cabin and waved his skinny arms frantically.

"Is he armed?" asked Rodriguez, sighting his gun on the Vietnamese boat captain.

"No, that's Nu Dang," Hadnott replied. "He's okay. But watch out for another Viet guy, not the kid, but an older guy, real skinny. He should be considered armed and dangerous."

When nobody else appeared on deck, O.B. was perplexed. Nu Dang still waved his arms, yelling something unintelligible in Vietnamese.

"There's supposed to be three guys on board," O.B. said in a low voice. "I don't see anybody else. Move closer."

Harrison moved the airboat closer to the shrimp boat and when it became apparent that Nu Dang was alone they tied off to the stern and Hadnott boarded the boat. Gun in hand he searched the vessel, stern to bow, with Nu Dang following along behind him, chattering in Vietnamese the whole time.

"Goddammit, Nu Dang! If you'll stop your jabbering for just... one...second," O.B. shouted. When Nu Dang finally settled down, O.B. tried to sort out the situation. It took five long minutes for him to understand that Bao had forced Nu Dang to pull in at the Port Aransas public docks, and that the Colonel had jumped ship with his duffle bags, boarded another boat and headed out the jetties for the Gulf, heading north, the opposite direction from Matagrande Key. Sammy had been forced at gunpoint to go with him, and instructed Nu Dang to motor for the city of Corpus Christi on the other side of the bay. O.B. guessed that the Colonel threatened to kill Sammy if Nu Dang didn't do what he said. He feared, but didn't tell Nu Dang, that Sammy was probably dead either way.

O.B. scratched his head. He had no idea where Bao was heading now. He considered going after them in Nu Dang's boat but he realized it would be too slow to catch anybody in the Gulf. He'd been tricked by that little yellow bastard, and he'd lost his advantage, not to mention almost a half million dollars of the State's money.

Rodriguez and Harrison felt bad for the Texas Ranger now. Rotten luck. "Um... Sergeant," said Rodriguez, "We'd be glad to take you back to Rockport, or we can drop you at the Port A Marina, in case you want to poke around and ask some questions. At any rate," he continued, "we need to be getting back before it gets too late, and too rough." The wind had increased since they'd left Rockport Harbor and there were whitecaps on the bay.

O.B. Hadnott stared blankly at Officer Rodriguez. He felt utterly defeated. He'd let his suspect get away. That wasn't supposed to happen to a Texas Ranger. That wasn't supposed to happen to *him*.

"Sergeant?" Rodriguez said.

O.B. looked down at his waterlogged boots and soaked khaki pants. "I guess Port Aransas would be fine," he muttered.

When Nu Dang realized that nobody would chase after Bao or try to rescue his nephew he started ranting again, obviously not happy with the way things were shaping up. O.B. climbed down into the airboat and Nu Dang never stopped berating him. His voice echoed inside O.B.'s head until the prop noise drowned out all other sounds.

—

Idling alongside the public pier in Port A, Rodriguez reached inside the metal storage box near the bow of the airboat and retrieved Sergeant Hadnott's Stetson. Some marine oil streaked the crown of the immaculate silver-belly hat but when he tried to rub it off it only made the smudge bigger. He handed the hat up to the Ranger. Hadnott grimaced.

"Sorry we weren't able to catch this guy, Sergeant. You want us to call this in to the Coast Guard?"

"No. I appreciate the offer," O.B. said slowly. "I'll make the call from here. It's still my case." *But probably not for much longer*, he thought to himself, remembering the five hundred thousand dollars of taxpayer money motoring around in the salt water, out of sight, out of his control.

O.B. grabbed his hat and thanked the men again, then walked toward the fuel pumps and the Marina dockside store. Maybe somebody saw something. Maybe the store had a working phone. But finding the Marina closed for the day he simply sat down on a guano-covered piling and let the chilly wind wash over his face, feeling disconsolate and lowdown. (What was he going to tell the Captain? What was he going to say to the team in route to Kingsville? What was he going to say to Nu Dang's wife? And to Trinny?)

By and by, O.B. noticed that gusts of wind carried fragments of music from across the marina cove. He raised his head and saw warm light pouring out of a tin-roofed building crowned by a large hand-painted sign that said *Hooper's Place*. He'd have to call the Captain and the DPS barracks on the mainland and confess his failure; the beer joint would certainly have a phone. And, he realized, that wasn't all.

O.B. was not one to indulge in self-pity. In fact, he considered it a deplorable weakness in a man, but at that moment he decided that more than anything else in the world, he wanted, he *needed,* a stiff drink—something to help clear his head. Something to fortify him for the call he was going to have to make to his Captain.

———

CHAPTER 42

Just twenty minutes earlier Colonel Bao's own 26-foot Grady White pushed off the Port Aransas T-Head and motored slowly through the jetties toward the Gulf.

The Colonel looked around him and formulated a check list:

TWO WELL-ARMED ESCORTS ☑
(He was rapidly depleting his Vietnamese henchmen, and he made a mental note to control his temper next time he wanted to kill another one);

ADEQUATE FUEL ☑
(They assured him the tanks had been filled in Aransas Pass);

MONEY FOR THE MEXICANS ☑
(He nudged the duffel bags at his feet with the toe of his shoe);

STORAGE SPACE FOR THE MEXICAN'S HEROIN ☑
(Under the vee-berth cushions in the forward cabin);

HOSTAGE ☑
(Sammy squatted just inside the doorway of the sunken galley below where Bao stood).

The boat swap and a hostage were precautionary steps. Even though the Mexican *jefe* had called to confirm the exact location and time of the exchange only that morning, and even though no one appeared to have noticed his departure from Fulton Harbor, he was taking no chances. Colonel Bao felt in control for the first time in days. He could easily dispose of the hostage later. He glanced down at the boy.

"Are you comfortable young Nu Than Sa'ng?" asked the Colonel, speaking to Sammy in Vietnamese.

Sammy ignored the question.

"Tell me, Nu Than Sa'ng—Sang, the name means bright, you know—do you only answer to your foreign name?"

Sammy raised his eyes to the Colonel's and shook his head. "Sammy *is* my name."

"A fool's name for a foolish boy."

Bao eyed the boy with sudden speculation. He *did* need some fresh blood in the organization. And something inside him craved corruption and defilement.

"Do you understand that you could make a fortune working for me? America is indeed the land of opportunity. When I own those neglected shipyards over in Palacios, my boats will be designed by smart engineers—Vietnamese engineers—to hold vast amounts of well-hidden contraband.

"You could be part of this, Nu Than Sa'ng. And you would see that stolen foods taste the best, to use one of the Vietnamese proverbs your uncle is so fond of."

"I don't think my uncle uses that proverb," declared Sammy in perfect English, with a hint of Texas drawl. "But one of his proverbs I do remember," he continued, this time in perfect Southern Delta Vietnamese. "One worm may damage the whole soup." Then back to English, "Colonel, I would rather flip burgers at a Dairy Queen for the rest of my life than work for you."

Bao's face hardened and he pulled his head out of the galley. He braced his hands on the console as the Gulf swells begin to pitch the boat when they exited the jetties. The pilot pushed the throttle forward and the boat roared northward into the Gulf. Colonel Bao glanced down briefly and then savagely kicked Sammy square in the face with the heel of his shoe, knocking him unconscious. The boy fell backwards into the darkness of the cabin.

—

Normally, O.B. Hadnott instinctively cased a room before selecting a seat in a restaurant or tavern, but when he walked into Hooper's he walked straight up to the bar.

"Double Jack Daniel's, no ice," he demanded of the barkeep. "And a phone. I've gotta make a call."

"The drink I can do you for," answered the bartender, "but the phones are still out." The Ranger stared at him blankly. "Storm," the barkeep explained. "Sorry."

The bartender returned and set the tumbler of brown whiskey on the bar. O.B. fixed his eyes on it like it was a diamondback rattler. He hadn't touched hard liquor for many years—not since Nadine had jilted him, in fact. He vaguely recalled a period of drunkenness and despair while he holed up in a hunting camp trailer in Stonewall County. He had had an uncomplicated agenda back then: for days he drank, he stared at the campfire, he drank some more.

He howled at the moon and sang Hank Williams cheating songs— badly. He drunkenly contemplated ways and means of stuffing Cudihay's body down a lonely wellhead out in the brush country. He unloaded his service revolver at a jackrabbit, a coyote, a buzzard, a horny toad, a prairie dog and even a high-flying Braniff 707 traveling from Dallas to San Francisco. Clean misses, all. He passed out, he woke up and he drank some more. After it was over and he went back to work, he vowed he'd never get on the outside of that much whiskey again.

In Hooper's, as the standoff with the whiskey continued, O.B. tried to not to believe he would always be star-crossed when it came to women. "I promised Trinny and that other lady I'd put the Colonel behind bars," he reminded himself. He'd had the Colonel in his sights, and he'd missed him. "I never should've asked that moron Templeton to help me stake out the Colonel. Now...no Colonel, no money, no girl —bad luck, just flat ass bad luck." O.B. imagined himself busted down to state trooper, sitting alone in his squad car on West Texas Hwy. 84, nabbing speeders on the Gawd-forsaken stretch of blacktop between

Snyder and Post. He reached for his glass.

"Uh, Sergeant Hadnott?" said a voice over his shoulder. O.B. swung around and saw Charlie Sweetwater standing behind him, holding a pitcher of beer and three mugs.

"What are you doing here?" O.B. asked.

"I'm having a beer," Charlie replied. "Me and Captain Joe and Marisol are sittin' over there by the window."

O.B. blinked and looked off toward the window.

"Sergeant?" Charlie began carefully, "What are *you* doing here? Didn't you and your men have an, um, appointment with Colonel Bao tonight?" Charlie sensed that something was not right with the Texas Ranger.

O.B. slowly swiveled his head back around to Charlie. "He...he got away," he replied distractedly.

"Got away!" Charlie tried to contain his concern. "But the drug deal is tonight! He meets the Mexicans tonight!"

"Yeah, well, I'll be damned if I know where that'll be."

"It's not Matagrande Key? Like Marisol said?"

"Evidently not,"

"Fuck," Charlie muttered under his breath. He regarded the Sergeant skeptically. "Where's your team, Sergeant Hadnott?"

"Wrong location. Too shallow. Bad luck."

"Sergeant Hadnott," Charlie said firmly, trying to get the Ranger's full attention. "Would you mind coming over and tellin' Captain Joe and Marisol what you just told me? It'd be more private over there." He had noticed that several heads around the bar leaned in their direction.

O.B. shrugged and then slid off his barstool, whiskey in hand. He halfheartedly followed Charlie to the table where he explained the situation to the others.

"We met Nu Dang's boat heading up the channel towards Corpus Christi," he began, gazing out the window. "He was alone. Bao took his nephew. The game wardens told me that the water around this Matagrande Key was too shallow to float a shrimp boat."

"It was a decoy." All eyes turned to Marisol. "The shrimp boat was a decoy," she repeated. Charlie and Joe nodded in agreement.

O.B. seemed to be focused on his whiskey as he rotated the glass slowly on the table.

"Sergeant?" asked Marisol. "How could Bao have gotten away? I mean, where are your...resources?"

O.B. looked up. "On their way to Kingsville, from Houston."

"But didn't you tell us back in Key Allegro you were going to have Bao's boats watched, and the harbor too?" Charlie asked.

"Turned out my watchman had his eyes on a Fisherman's Platter instead. If it hadn't been for Nu Dang's wife spotting Bao, we wouldn't have any idea where he is." It sank in on him again. "And sure enough, we don't. Bao seems to have handed us our asses."

"I bet he doubled back..." said Marisol, "...and probably switched boats."

O.B. pulled at his ear and sat up, as though awakening from a trance. "Let's assume he switched boats and took off again," he said. "That means he's still got the money and Nu Dang's nephew, Sammy."

"So, if not Matagrande Key, then where?" Joe posed the question they were all thinking.

Charlie slapped his palms down on the table with a crack like a pistol shot, scaring the shit out of half of the bar.

"Matagorda!" he said. "Hell, it was staring us in the face. Marisol said they'd doubled back—and she's right."

"Matagorda?" asked O.B. "Trinny said that word, but I didn't understand what she was trying to tell me."

"It's an island, another barrier island, *north* of Rockport. About twenty miles north. Used to be a bombing range for the military until a millionaire bought it and fenced it off to everybody. It's deserted. There's an old Army Air Corps runway still there, on the south end. It's a perfect place for Bao to meet a plane!"

"I'll be go to hell," said O.B. in dawning wonder.

Joe whistled. "Well, if they're in a half-decent boat, and they left right at dark they'll be at Matagorda inside of an hour—if they're going to Matagorda."

"I think they are," said Charlie. "Where else could they go? They didn't head toward the Laguna and Baffin Bay, and the Parks and Wildlife guys would've seen them if they'd headed back towards Rockport in the bay, which doesn't make any sense anyway. I think they headed north, towards Matagorda. Nu Dang said he saw them turn north outside the jetties."

O.B. had already decided on a course of action. "What's the fastest way to get to this Matagorda Island?" It may have been just a hunch, but it was enough to bring out the Ranger in O.B. Hadnott once more.

Charlie sat back in his chair. "Well, that could be a problem, Sergeant. Normally you could drive over to Port O'Conner. It's a one-horse town just a stone's throw from the north end of Matagorda Island. A private boat ferries you the short hop across to the other side. Bird watchers use it to go over and look for the Whoopers. But, it would take way too long to drive there."

"And the roads and the ferry were hammered by the hurricane," Joe added. "I live there. No telling what kind of shape they're in."

"I know some guys in Fulton that would probably loan us their boat," Charlie continued, "But it's a thirty-minute drive just to get there, and that's *after* we take the Port A ferry to the other side. Then it's another thirty minutes on the water to get to Matagorda."

"Couldn't he use Rupert's skiff? The one we came in on?" asked Marisol.

"Naw," said Charlie. "It's too small. And with that little 10-horse outboard it'd take forever to get to over there. And we can't call Rupert or anybody else to bring us a boat because there's still no phone service here. Joe, what about your jon boat?"

"I bent the prop during our high speed rally through the bay the other day," he said. "It's at the shop getting repaired."

O.B. knitted his brow in concentration. Where the hell was he going to find a boat? Couldn't he just commandeer one? *Why the hell not,* he thought. *I'm a Texas Ranger in hot pursuit of a villainous son-of-a-bitch.* As he pondered his options he looked up and took in the growing crowd of people that was filling Hooper's Place. A moment later he grinned.

Charlie, Marisol and Captain Joe exchanged puzzled looks. They'd never seen Ranger Hadnott smile before.

"Folks," O.B. drawled. "I think we've found ourselves a motorboat."

Charlie and Joe followed Sergeant Hadnott's gaze and saw Billy Donathorn playing foosball in the game room annex of the bar.

"Billy D!" laughed Joe. "Oh, he's gonna love seeing us again."

"That's for sure, fellas," declared the Sergeant. "We had a long talk after I picked him up on Ransom Island the other day. I'd never seen a guy actually wet his pants in an interrogation before. Let's go see how Mr. Donathorn and his motorboat are gettin' along."

"Of course, Cap'n Joe and I are going with you, Sergeant," Charlie insisted. Marisol looked at him in surprise.

"Damn straight we are," Joe rejoined.

"And I'll stay here and call in the cavalry," Marisol appended. "We've all got a stake in this."

O.B. Hadnott paused and considered his options. No way could he find Matagorda Island by himself...not in a boat, not in the dark. The Coast Guard was out of position at present with no way to call them back. And even if he could reach the TPWD boys again—they certainly knew the terrain—they would be less than enthusiastic about going on another wild goose chase.

The Ranger inhaled deeply and then looked long and hard at the three willing volunteers sitting at his table. "Y'all know we're playing for keeps here." The three of them nodded.

"Yep," they said in unison.

"Then consider yourselves officially deputized," he declared, solemnly.

O.B. Hadnott squared his hat on his head and stood up. He raised his shot glass in a toast and smiled. A predatory and disquieting smile. "Now let's go get that fucker."

The rookie deputies gulped their beers and stood up to leave. O.B. hesitated a moment, narrowing his eyes at the amber-colored whiskey still in his hand. He set the still-full tumbler down on the table and then turned and strode resolutely toward Billy D.

———

CHAPTER 43

It was raining in the Gulf, so Charlie hunched down behind the salt-crusted window on Billy Donathorn's Boston Whaler. Sergeant O.B. Hadnott stood to one side of the steering console, enduring the rough seas and the stinging rain with stoic resolve. He glared fiercely ahead, bending his knees and gripping the rail to steady himself as the small craft pitched on the waves. The adrenaline pulsing through his body mitigated his seasickness.

Marisol had watched them cast off from the dock at the Port A marina. They'd had time for a quick war council before Billy D reluctantly surrendered the keys to his boat. The three men agreed that Marisol should take the skiff across the channel to the DPS bunker in Aransas Pass and try to rally the troops and re-direct them from Kingsville to Port O'Connor. She also agreed to inform Joe's wife that he'd be a little late for dinner.

"Sergeant, do you really think they'll listen to me? Why would they?" she'd asked, dubiously. "A Mexican girl in an old dinghy?"

"Use my name, Miz Cavasos," O.B. had replied. "Tell those DPS boys it's my considered opinion that a major drug deal involving the prime suspect in a double homicide will transpire at this Matagorda airstrip tonight. Most of these officers are still involved in hurricane recovery, but they also know about my case, and they can contact the Coast Guard and the Houston team and give 'em the new information. The DPS boys will be able to free up a few warm bodies if you tell them it's an officer-in-distress situation. Tell 'em the Ranger said to come a-runnin'."

Inside, O.B. felt far less confident. Bao had already snookered him once tonight. What if he doubled back again to a meeting place they had no inkling of?

"Tell them...hell, tell them it's my best guess and I need help," he said finally. "I'll take the responsibility."

Marisol reached up impulsively and hugged the taciturn lawman, much to his discomfiture. She kissed Captain Joe on the cheek and gave Charlie an *abrazo* that nearly cracked his ribs. Then, without another word, they climbed into Billy D's beat-up Whaler and sped away.

The roar of the Mercury outboard changed pitch each time the boat bounced over a large swell. Captain Joe piloted the boat through the choppy seas, keeping an eye on the magnetic compass mounted on the console, maintaining a northeastern course for Cedar Bayou.

Billy D hadn't put up much of a fight. What could he say? O.B. reminded him of his precarious position as an accessory to kidnapping, a serious felony in the state of Texas, subject to some real hard time in Huntsville, "You'd be a popular prom date for some pretty bad *hombres*," Sergeant Hadnott added for effect. Then Charlie reminded Billy that a favorable court testimony from him and Marisol might keep him out of the correctional facility. That is, if he wouldn't mind loaning them his boat for a few hours. Captain Joe just wanted to know how much fuel was in the gas tanks and if the compass was accurate.

Billy D., a strip of medical tape holding his broken nose together, watched morosely as the trio pulled away from the Port Aransas pier. It was not at all the night he had imagined for himself—namely, a few beers at Hooper's, then an evening of flounder gigging in the mud flats behind Mustang Island. He trudged back into Hooper's where he spent his last ten dollars on a pitcher of draft beer and shot of cheap tequila.

—

The low clouds and light rain reduced visibility considerably, but just to be safe Joe turned off the running lights when they reached the mouth of the Cedar Bayou cut. The airstrip lay on the southern end of Matagorda Island, about two miles from where the cut joined Mesquite Bay. Snaking through the creek-like bayou, the three men scanned the darkness for lights and listened for voices or the sound of an engine.

Even in the darkness, Charlie noticed that the hurricane had reshaped the channel dramatically. It was deeper and wider than before. He thought about how nice it would be to come back here for a little recreational fishing. It was high time he showed Raul the art of fly-casting into a school of hungry bull redfish. Johnny would have wanted that.

On entering Mesquite Bay, Captain Joe turned north towards Bray Cove, which allowed him to approach the airstrip under the cover of the twisting marshy waterways that bled into the island from the bay. He and Charlie figured Bao would anchor up closer to the mouth of the Cedar Bayou channel, probably tying up to the pilings that marked the old fish camp on Matagorda. *That's what I would do*, Charlie thought—the quickest and easiest route to the airstrip, the quickest exit to the Gulf.

When the water became so shallow that the idling prop dug into the sand, Joe cut the engine and locked the outboard into its raised position by hand. Charlie moved to the front of the boat and grabbed one of the three-pronged flounder gigs to pole the boat quietly through the water. Joe pushed the boat from the stern with the other flounder spear.

Winding through the narrow channels in the saltmarsh, O.B. couldn't tell north from south or wet from dry—it was a maze like nothing he'd ever seen before. But he could spot the Grady White's bimini top, its white shape silhouetted against the dark sky not fifty yards ahead of them. Charlie and Joe saw it too, and they quietly guided the Whaler into a narrow cut, all but invisible in the tall reedy grass surrounding them. *So Bao chose the stealthy approach, after all,* thought Charlie. *You're sneaky, Colonel, but so are we.*

O.B. hooked a long leg over the gunwale and motioned to Charlie and Joe to stay put and be quiet. He figured he'd spent more than enough time these past couple of weeks riding in boats. He was ready to be on dry land. On dry land he was a skilled and lethal Texas fucking Ranger. But before he'd taken two steps in the inundated marsh, the mud sucked off one of his boots. He cursed silently and groped around for a moment in the darkness for his missing boot. Undeterred, he continued wading through the intertidal grass towards the runway, trying not to think about what stingrays, snakes and carnivorous fish might be fixing to gnaw on his sock-clad toes.

Charlie and Joe looked at each other, wondering what to do. Finally Charlie slipped quietly into the water and starting moving toward Bao's boat, moored in the distance. Joe shrugged and followed. They both stopped when they heard the unmistakable sound of a prop engine plane approaching in the distance. Charlie tapped Joe's arm and motioned toward the boat and the silhouette of a man emerging from under the bimini to search the sky for the plane. They couldn't make out who the man was, but they could see the rifle he cradled in his arms. They wondered if Sammy was alive and if he was aboard.

Charlie touched Joe on the shoulder then tapped a finger to his own temple, a signal that he had an idea. Joe could see his white toothy smile illuminating the darkness. Whatever tricks Charlie had up his sleeve, Joe decided he was in. Bao's men had threatened his boys, and now the Colonel was conducting his wicked business practically in his backyard. Only last week Joe had taken his boys fishing near this very spot. He smiled back at Charlie and followed him back to Billy D's boat.

O.B. had heard the plane engines too. He crouched behind a groundsel bush near the runway and watched, and waited. A light mist had replaced the rain and the temperature had dropped. But O.B. was not mindful of the cold, the sodden clothes on his back, or the one stocking foot. He was focused on two men standing on the runway. The one waving a flashlight at the incoming plane had a gun slung over his shoulder. O.B. was quite sure that the other one carrying the two canvas duffle bags, was Colonel Bao.

The twin prop Beechcraft Super King circled the Matagorda runway and then made its landing approach. A few minutes later it taxied to the end of the runway where Bao and his lieutenant awaited. The Mexicans kept the engines running even as the hatch opened and the stair ladder unfolded to the ground. One, then two, gunmen descended from the plane and stood on either side of the ladder until a third man, wearing a blue guayabera, joined them on the cracked concrete runway. The plane's bright runway lights illuminated Bao and his subordinate on the tarmac. One of the Mexican gunmen used a battery-powered floodlight to scan the grass and scrub around them. O.B. ducked his head as the bright light passed over his position.

Meanwhile, Charlie and Joe retrieved Billy Donathorn's improvised flounder rig from the back deck of the Boston Whaler and lowered it into the water. The rig was a homemade contraption that consisted of a waterproof spotlight fastened to a ski pole, which attached to a 12-volt battery nestled into a Styrofoam float. A fisherman would pull the floating battery behind him as he waded through the shallows, using the powerful light to search for the pan-shaped flounder that hid in the sand, and the gigging spear to pin the fish to the bottom. Flounder-gigging was to sportfishing what the Funky Chicken was to classical ballet, but almost every local fisherman on the Coastal Bend kept a flounder gig setup in his boat or the back of his pickup.

Charlie had thought of another use for the spotlight. Their movement drowned out by the noise of the plane engines, he and Joe waded as close to Bao's boat as they dared and planted the rusty light pole into the mud bottom, aiming the darkened light at the boat. They squatted in the submerged grass and studied the activity on the nearby tarmac.

The pilot shut off the plane's engines and the Mexican in the guayabera walked toward Colonel Bao, a big smile on his dark face. When the man reached Bao the two of them briefly shook hands. The Mexican peered into one of the canvas bags and started to grab for the handles, but Bao pulled back the bags. "First, I would like to test the merchandise, Mr. Sanchez," he said, motioning toward the plane.

The smile on the Mexican's face disappeared for an instant then returned. "Very well, Colonel," he answered. "If you insist." He turned quickly and walked back to the plane, disappearing into the hatch. A moment later he descended and stood at the base of the ladder. Soon a series of tightly bound packages dropped from the door, where one of the gunmen stacked them into a neat pyramid on the ground.

One of the Mexicans brought a package to Colonel Bao, who slit the plastic and placed a pinch of powder to his tongue. He nodded his approval and the Mexicans gathered the wrapped bricks and stacked them in front of Bao on the tarmac. The man in the blue guayabera approached Bao again.

"Since we are being so trusting of one another," he said, "I think I will count the money you owe me." He reached for the bags and for a moment they simultaneously held the handles. *"Con su permiso?"* said Sanchez with a forced smile. "After all, it is I who should be suspicious...considering the problems with your previous payments.

Attempted payments, I should say." He gestured toward the bag and added. "I assume these funds will compensate me for the first delivery, *and* for the merchandise at your feet?"

"It is all there. As we agreed," Bao replied. He hid his apprehension well. It helped a little knowing that less than a hundred yards away the man he'd left on his boat, which was veiled in the darkness of the marsh, had the head *narco* sighted in the crosshairs of his night scope. Bao released the bags and the Mexican squatted down and began removing stacks of bills and laying them out on the runway. While one of his men held the light, Sanchez counted the bound packages of cash, picking packets at random and thumbing through the bills. He didn't bother to examine all the bundles, just enough to satisfy himself.

A jumpy silence suffused the group and everybody felt tense and jittery. "Everybody," as it happened, included a mature whooping crane roosting in a hollow of matted spartina grass between Ranger Hadnott and the tarmac. The unusual commotion followed by the sudden quiet finally unnerved the creature beyond endurance, and it found that it could hide no more. When the gigantic snow-white bird unfolded its magnificent seven-foot wingspan and ascended like a ghastly apparition, bugling its prehistoric screech as it rose, O.B. was sure he'd never seen a creature so immense or heard a call so astonishing. It scared the bejesus out of him, and he instinctively pulled his service revolver and aimed it at the rising bird, but somehow he managed to stop the hammer at half-cock position.

One of the Mexican *pistoleros*, however, let loose a burst from his Ingram MAC-10 and shot the bird dead. The whooper crashed to the ground with a thud.

That did it. Bao's lieutenant was sure the Mexicans were firing at him so he returned fire, hitting one of them in the shoulder, but not before the Mexicans sprayed a round of bullets back at him, piercing his leg below the knee. The wounded Vietnamese limped back toward the boat, firing as he retreated. Meanwhile, Bao's man on the boat began loosing rounds from the marsh towards the plane, hitting the injured Mexican enforcer again, this time in the belly.

Sergeant Hadnott flattened himself on the ground as bullets whistled above him, blowing the tops off the shrubs and tall grass. Out in the marsh Charlie clipped the light cables to the battery, activating the spotlight and enveloping Bao's boat and the gunman on the bow in a sudden flood of bright light. The Mexican's automatic fire immediately shifted away from Sergeant Hadnott to the spot-lit boat that had suddenly appeared on the bay shore. The startled gunman discharged a few rounds in the general direction of Charlie, Joe and the flounder lights, and then directed his fire back at the Mexicans.

During the chaos neither Sanchez nor Bao had moved. Still squatting on the tarmac, Sanchez looked up at Bao and they glared at each other in mutual suspicion and disdain. The Mexican started stuffing packets of money back into the canvas bag but he stopped when Colonel Bao pulled his .38 out of his jacket. Sanchez rose slowly.

"You will not live very long if you continue to do business this way, Colonel Bao," Sanchez said calmly.

"I should never have trusted a spic," Bao replied. "I had hoped you would be different from the Americans." He raised the gun to arm's length and put it to Sanchez's head.

His eyes filled with hatred, the Mexican *narco* snarled at the Colonel. "*Chinga tu madre... pinche macaca.*"

"Fuck you too, you mongrel bastard," Bao answered, then he pulled the trigger, blowing off one side of Sanchez's head.

O.B. had retreated behind a small berm, and when the barrage of bullets moved elsewhere he rose carefully to assess the situation. Bao's wounded gunman staggered toward the water dragging his mangled leg behind him. One of the Mexicans knelt at the base of the airplane ladder, firing rounds at the light that had somehow material-ized out in the saltmarsh. (*Where did that come from?* O.B. wondered.) The other Mexican appeared to be wounded, dragging himself towards the plane, leaving a bloody trail behind him. The third Mexican lay crumpled on the tarmac in a pool of blood and bright light. Above him stood Bao, a gaunt figure holding a smoking pistol.

Bao was desperate but not suicidal. The drugs and the money lay at his feet—*right there*—illuminated by the lights of the plane, but he knew his pistol was no match for the Mexican's automatic weapon, which would be turned on him any second. Not enough time to gather the packets of cash or the bricks of heroin, either one. He cast a despairing glance at the booty, then, howling with rage and frus-tration, turned and ran for his life. At the edge of the darkness, O.B. glimpsed Bao running northeast towards the Gulf of Mexico.

The airplane pilot cranked over the engines as soon as the shooting started and now engaged the propellers, preparing to take off. The Mexican with the AK47 pulled his gutshot *compañero* up the ladder as the plane pivoted on the airstrip, closing the hatch just as the engines reached full throttle. The powerful air stream from the propellers toppled the pyramid of heroin and scattered the packets of money and the near-empty canvas bags off the tarmac and into the darkness, blowing them over the lifeless body of the *narco* Sanchez.

Sergeant Hadnott, blinded by the blowback of dust and gravel, fired a few shots at the plane as it rolled down the runway and lifted off the ground and then pursued Bao's crippled lieutenant as he limped towards the spot-lit boat in the bay. When the Vietnamese turned to fire at Sergeant Hadnott, O.B. shot him in the chest, killing him instantly.

The Texas Ranger continued toward Bao's boat, figuring *(hoping)* that the Colonel would circle around. A couple of bursts of automatic fire shattered the flounder light and the bay shore became dark and silent. O.B. slipped into a narrow channel and moved warily toward Bao's boat, taking care to keep his gun above the chest-high water. He stopped when he heard the sound of an ignition turning over, and then the rumble of an outboard engine very near to him. Too near. O.B. peered into the darkness trying to locate the boat.

The outboard engine revved to a high-pitched roar and O.B. struggled to see over the tall vegetation bordering the creek. Without warning, the bulrushes parted and a white V-hull burst through the water, the motor screaming as the pilot attempted to plane out the boat in the constricted channel. O.B. tried to dive out of the way but the edge of the hull clipped the side of his head and threw him onto the bank. He attempted to stand but lost consciousness and toppled over into the mud.

From Billy D's Whaler, Charlie and Joe watched the boat fly past them like a shrieking ghost as the pilot attempted to reach Cedar Bayou and then the safety of the Gulf.

"He'll never make it," said Joe. Sure enough, five seconds later they heard the outboard groan as the prop hit dry land, followed by a banging and crunching noise when the boat flipped and crashed on a reef. After that, silence.

Finally, Joe spoke. "Shall we take a look?"

"Man, that sounded terrible," said Charlie, reaching under the console for a flashlight. He turned to step out of the boat then paused and reached down for one of the three-pronged gigs lying on the deck. "Just in case," he said. Joe grabbed the other spear and followed Charlie into the water.

The boat lay on its side on a small reef, its nose partially submerged in the bay. Charlie shined the flashlight over the deck, looking for bodies, but the boat appeared empty so he began to search the surrounding area. He heard a groan from inside the cabin so he leaned in and shined the light through the door. Sammy was sprawled out between a vee-berth cushion and the fiberglass hull.

"Sammy! Are you okay?"

Sammy groaned again and opened one eye. The other eye was purple and swollen shut. A half smile appeared on Sammy's face. "Hey, it's you," he said weakly.

Charlie stood up and yelled, "*Oye*, Joe. It's Sammy. I think we need to get him to a doctor."

"Okay, Charlie," Joe replied, "We can take this guy too...unless I decide to stab him first."

Charlie found Joe on the other side of the reef, standing over Bao's lieutenant, holding the trident spear to the prostrate man's throat. The man's leg was twisted at a terrible angle and his mouth was leaking blood.

"He's banged up pretty good but I get the feeling he'd still try and put a knife in my back if I turned it to him." The Vietnamese glared up fiercely at Captain Joe.

"I'll go get some rope and we can tie him up," Charlie suggested. "Can you keep Uncle Ho engaged until I get back?"

"I was born to gig," Joe said solemnly.

Once Bao's man was trussed up and tossed onto the back deck of the Whaler, and Sammy was arranged on a stack of cushions on the bow, Charlie grabbed the torch and lowered himself into the marsh to search for Sergeant Hadnott.

"Careful, Charlie," cautioned Joe. "The Ranger may not be alone."

Charlie held up his gig. "Don't worry man. I'm armed and dangerous." He waded off toward Matagorda.

Twenty minutes later Charlie returned, burdened down by the Texas Ranger he had draped over his shoulder in a fireman's carry.

"Is he okay?" asked Joe as he helped pull the unconscious man aboard.

"Maybe. There's a nasty gash on his head but his breathing and pulse seem normal."

"He caught a bullet?"

"I don't think so," replied Charlie. "I didn't find him on the island. I literally stumbled over him not forty yards from here on the bank by the channel. I'd almost given up on him."

Joe examined the Sergeant's head wound. "Something clobbered him good."

"I think that boat ran over him. One of Bao's goons was lying dead on the ground nearby and I think Sergeant Hadnott put him down and then got keelhauled by the boat."

"Jesus," said Joe. "It's a wonder he didn't drown."

"No shit," said Charlie, ripping a strip of fabric from the bottom of his T-shirt and binding the bleeding wound on Ranger Hadnott's head. Charlie arranged him on the deck next to Sammy.

"Charlie, whaddaya say we get this sea ambulance back to civilization?" said Joe.

"Excellent idea," Charlie replied. "That okay with you, Sammy?"

Sammy smiled weakly and gave the thumbs-up sign, then he eased his head onto the sea cushion and closed his eyes.

"Hey, Charlie," asked Joe. "You didn't happen to see the Colonel out there anywhere did you?"

"No, man. No sign of him. But I did see three bodies: one of Bao's guys, a Mexican, and one very dead Whooping Crane."

"A Whooper?" asked Joe, surprised.

"Yep. Don't ask me how," he replied, climbing over the gunwale of the boat.

Captain Joe shook his head and climbed into the pilot's seat to crank over the engine. "That's a goddamn shame," he muttered. "About the Whooper, I mean."

"Yep," said Charlie.

Joe shoved the shifter into gear, and prepared to ease the Whaler through the water toward Cedar Bayou. "This has been one hell of a day!"

You don't know the half of it, brother man, Charlie thought to himself. When Captain Joe turned around to pilot the boat, Charlie reached over the side and hauled in the second burden he'd discovered on the island.

———

CHAPTER 44

Charlie awoke in Marisol's upstairs room at the Tarpon Inn. He listened to the trade winds rattle the palm fronds outside the door and wondered if he hadn't somehow dreamed the whole thing. Then he noticed the indentation beside him where Marisol had laid and decided that, nope, it was real life its ownself. *I could get used to this*, he thought drowsily.

The screen door opened and Marisol walked in carrying a breakfast tray from the hotel and one of those little cardboard caddy doodads containing two cups of coffee and some sausage biscuits from the mini-mart. Tucked under her arm were several newspapers.

"Hey, it's Rip Van Winkle."

Charlie yawned. "How long have I been asleep?"

"Well, you came in late. Then you pretty much fell into bed and haven't moved since, as far as I can tell." She set the coffee and tray on the bedside table and dropped the papers on Charlie's belly.

"The curse of the workin' man," said Charlie picking up the stack of papers. Marisol made him scoot over on the bed so she could read over his shoulder.

The papers from Houston, Dallas and Corpus Christi all led with the same story—Shootout in the marsh! Guns! Drugs! Money! A

Texas Ranger. Dead Mexicans and Vietnamese of various shadowy reputes. Investigations ongoing. No mention of Bao's whereabouts. Charlie and Joe were acknowledged only as "local fishermen". Hadnott had agreed to keep their names out of it.

Below the fold, but still on the front page, was a story under an Austin journalist's byline: "Grand Jury Indicts Coastal Senator." Llewellyn Cudihay was going up on charges of embezzlement, extortion, contributing to an ongoing criminal conspiracy and aggravated mopery, as well as criminally negligent manslaughter for his part in Neddy Pomade's death. An accompanying photo showed the Honorable Senator doing a perp walk outside the Travis County courthouse, his seersucker jacket covering his porcine head. The sight gratified Charlie and Marisol immensely. (O.B. Hadnott, wrapping things up from a hospital bed in Corpus Christi, smiled a rare smile as he gazed on the same picture in the *Caller Times*.)

The *Rockport Pilot* featured none of these sensational developments on *its* front page, of course. With the Ducks Unlimited Fundraiser & Wild Game Banquet only two weeks away, there was nothing to be gained by making Rockport and Fulton look like downtown Beirut except to scare off the tourists. And nobody wanted that.

A little while later, after the newspapers had been read, Charlie set down his coffee and looked playfully over at Marisol who sat in a stuffed chair near the bed, and made what was, for him, an overtly romantic overture. "Hey, baby," he said. "How 'bout you get those biscuits in the oven and your buns in the bed!"

Marisol smiled. A glorious sight. "How could a girl resist an offer like that?" she answered. "But first, you tell me what you've been up to these past couple of days. I haven't seen you much. My *brujita's* intuition tells me you're up to something."

"Ah, the Lasso of Truth."

Marisol looked puzzled.

"It's from a comic book I bought for Raul," Charlie explained. "*Wonder Woman*. She had a magic lasso and anyone she caught with it was forced to obey her and tell her the truth."

"This Wondrous Woman was Mexican, wasn't she?"

"I wouldn't doubt it for a moment."

"Then spit it out," she demanded playfully.

Charlie grinned his coyote grin. "Well, Wondrous Woman...as it turns out, your intuition is correct. I have been up to something."

Marisol waited expectantly. Charlie leaned back and clasped his hands behind his head, savoring the moment. "Well?" she said, tossing a crumpled napkin at him. "Obey me!"

"I was in Corpus Christi a lot of that time," Charlie began. "I went on a little spending spree."

"Spending spree? What are you talking about Charlie?"

"Well, let's see...First, I talked to an immigration lawyer about making Raul a legal resident. It shouldn't be too hard with the blood test and everything. The lawyer said that with permission from the boy's grandparents, I can also become his legal guardian."

Marisol's eyes widened. "He'll like that. But what...."

"Hold on girl, there's more," Charlie interrupted. "Then I went to a bank and set up a nice college fund for the boys." He started counting on his fingers. "Let's see, there's Raul, Captain's Joe's two boys, Sean and Little Joe. And then of course there's Sammy Dang," Charlie said. "Anyway, every one of 'em will probably follow in their daddy's footsteps and end up being a fisherman, but I'm a big proponent of over-educated fishermen.

"And last but not least, there's the new shrimp boat I bought. I found it for sale at the Corpus boat docks."

"A shrimp boat, Charlie? Why..."

Charlie raised his hand. "Let me finish," he said. "She's a beauty too. A little bigger than the *Ramrod* with a solid teak hull, passable diesel engines, and a beautiful galley. With a little boost from the insurance money, she can be outfitted and ready to work in no time." Charlie finished and watched Marisol with delight.

She was gratifyingly shocked, and thoroughly mystified. "Charlie," she said slowly. "What are you saying? Are you planning on...staying?"

"I've been doing a lot of thinking. This is my home, Marisol. I just never realized that I was homesick until recently."

A brief smile formed on Marisol's face and then she wrinkled her brow inquisitively. "But the money? Where did you get the money for this...spending spree?"

"Just a little souvenir I picked up while I was tramping around looking for our Ranger friend in the marsh," he said. "That Mexican aero-plane blew the dope and Bao's money all the hell over Matagorda Island when the *narcos* split. One of the moneybags was snagged on a palmetto bush not too far away from our unconscious friend. Like Moses in the bulrushes. I counted it out the next morning—there was a little over $200,000 inside."

"But why didn't you mention it to me? Or to anyone" she asked, flabbergasted.

"Need to know basis," replied Charlie. "Besides, I thought you might want to um, give it back...you know, to the Ranger, or to the DA."

"Charlie, you hurt my feelings."

"After I dropped Joe and Sammy and our drug-dealin' prisoner on the mainland, I went back out there with the DPS boys to help them make sense of the crime scene. Who was shooting from where and what-all. Money and dope were scattered all over the place. I would've picked up some more of that green stuff but by then the island was crawling with state troopers and Coast Guard swabbies.

"The cops recovered the dope, the state money that Hadnott had fronted Cudihay, and *most* of Bao's drug money. Of course, they'll never miss what they can't find. As far as yours truly is concerned, the cash is the ill-gotten gains of a nefarious criminal enterprise, and therefore falls under the Law of Salvage. But...you being a badge carrying officer of the TDCJ and all, maybe you think I should give it back?" Charlie looked at Marisol solicitously. Marisol's eyes danced with amusement.

"Give it back, my ass."

Charlie clapped his hands together. "Haw! That's my true blue accomplice! And you know what? I think I'll have enough left over to fix up the place at Rattlesnake Point, too. Maybe get a new couch and kitchen dinette set."

"But what about Mexico?" she asked. "What about your home and your business in Mexico?"

"My partner agreed to buy me out. It's a nice place for a visit in the dead of winter—I'd really like to show it to you sometime—but I'd rather *live* here."

Marisol's face softened. "I think I like that idea, Charlie," she said tenderly. "Both of them." *Maybe I'll look into that opening at the Aransas County DA's office after all*, she thought. She was just about to join him in bed when they heard footsteps pounding down the longleaf pine balcony. A perfunctory knock then the door to the room flew open and Raul came bursting in, grinning like a jack-o-lantern. He held a sack in his hand.

"I bring you breakfast tacos, Charlie!" he said breathlessly. "Hurry and eat the taquitos and then we go catch the fish in the surf...."

Charlie caught the sack of foil-wrapped breakfast tacos and laughed.

"The bait, it is in the truck of Mr. Joe," Raul continued excitedly. "He say that the fish they are biting *bery* hard right now. Sean and Little Joe are in the truck too. Waiting...on you!"

They heard more steps coming down the balcony and Captain Joe stuck his head in the door. "Am I interrupting anything?" he asked cheerfully.

"Just catchin' up on the news," Charlie answered.

Joe chuckled. "Pretty cool stuff, huh? Did you see the part about the 'two local fishermen'?"

"Saw that," said Charlie. "We're heroes, sort of."

"Well, all's well that ends well, right?"

Charlie agreed. "Except that Bao's still alive, and...at large."

Joe shook his head, "No, man. You didn't see the Rockport paper?"

Marisol picked up the paltry local rag again and Joe showed her the small item at the bottom of the inside back page, part of the police roundup, below the tide charts and the local high school football scores: "Suspect Sought in Businessman's Slaying."

Apparently, a local entrepreneur in the Vietnamese fishing community, one Nguyen Ngoc Bao, was found dead in the back office of a boathouse he owned in nearby Port O'Conner. The local constabulary was investigating. They definitely suspected foul play; the deceased was found with a rolled-up Mexican wrestling magazine jammed down his throat. The County Coroner ruled it death by strangulation, noting that it must have been protracted and quite terrible.

"*Christ*," murmured Charlie.

"Frontier justice," said Marisol with ill-concealed satisfaction.

They looked at each other, both thinking the same thing. "I suppose our friend Miguel has an alibi for the last day or two," Charlie said quietly.

Marisol nodded. "He's a law-abiding citizen, right? Wouldn't hurt a fly." *If he did it, I hope to God he covered his tracks*, she thought.

"Right." Charlie agreed. *It could have been the narcos, or one of Bao's own guys*, he thought. *Sure. Maybe.* "*Sangre fria*," he remembered Miguel telling him.

Marisol looked up at Captain Joe. "But how did Bao get off the island?"

"There's a dirt road," said Joe. "It's not much, but enough to follow on a moonless night. From the eastern end of the island it's only a hop and a skip over to Bayucos Island and then a short swim across the channel to the mainland. The water's not much more than three or four feet deep most of the way. Maybe he made his way across via the oyster reefs and spoil banks. Or stole a dinghy. Who knows? The main thing is, somehow he made it to Port O'Connor where he thought no one could find him."

"But someone did know where to find him," said Marisol.

"Yeah," Charlie said. "Someone."

Charlie thought of Bao for a moment, stumbling through the night down the long, bladed dirt road that led to an illusory refuge. Broke, busted, welted by the clouds of insatiable mosquitoes that infested Matagorda, a hunted man who must have known that karma had him in its sights. For a second, he almost felt sorry for the poor bastard. The moment passed.

Joe interrupted their thoughts. "Anyway, Charlie, it's time to get your lazy bones out of bed! We drove by Mustang Beach on the way over here and I saw some guys taking trout out of the surf hand over fist. The beer and tackle are already downstairs in the truck. Come on, man! Let's go rip some lips!"

"*Sí*, rip some lips!" said Raul excitedly. "*Vamanos, Tío...ándale!*"

Charlie liked being called uncle. Yesterday he had told Raul he was Johnny's son. The boy couldn't have been happier, although he admitted he'd suspected it all along.

Charlie sat up and swung his feet to the floor, "Okay, okay. I'm coming." He looked up hopefully at Marisol. "You in?"

Marisol popped up out of the chair. "I'm in," she said. "Why not? And who knows? Maybe I'll teach you boys a thing or two about surf casting." Raul and Joe high fived and exited the room. Marisol grabbed Charlie by the hand and yanked him to his feet. "I'm all in," she said smiling.

Charlie smiled back. "I was kinda hoping you'd say that."

CHRISTMAS EVE...AT RANSOM ISLAND...

With his eyes closed, L.C. Hebert rips through a guitar solo on an up-tempo version of "Bad Luck Shadow" by Johnny Otis. His new Grammy award sits on top of his amplifier. He carries it everywhere, in a velvet Crown Royal sack, like a charm. ("Don't let nobody tell you different," Leon Guidry had told him the day after the awards ceremony. "That goddamn thing will look great on the hood of a new Cadillac!") The perspiration on his face glistens in the bright lights, and as the horns pick up the chorus, L.C. slowly opens his eyes to the packed room, and smiles.

No one can deny it. Shady's is hopping tonight. The music washes over the crowded dance floor and splashes against the faded beadboard walls. The tables and chairs are bunched up along the perimeter of the big room to make more space for the dancers. On an improvised plywood stage a six-foot woofer releases bass breakers that rattle the beer bottles and ripple the amber content of countless cups and glasses.

Multi-colored Christmas lights crisscross the rafters and illuminate the whirling bodies that stomp, strut and shuffle over the worn pine floor. Pot luck dishes line the bar—everybody has pitched in: huge bowls of u-peel-'em shrimp, long platters of steamed blue crabs, and stacks of sliced sausage and boiled corn. More exotic fare is intermixed with these Gulf Coast staples: Vietnamese-style salted fish, Bánh Bao dumplings, grilled meatballs, and assorted plates of wraps and spring rolls.

It has been a long time since live music and dancing rocked the weathered old building. Behind the bar, with his back to a bubbling cauldron of gumbo, Rupert Sweetwater is beaming. Vita walks up and thumps Rupert on the ear, reminding him not to forget to refill the crockpot on the bar with gumbo. Before walking away she leans up and kisses her husband on the cheek. Rupert guesses that she's forgiven him for his earlier full-throated declaration to one and all that tonight the drinks are on the house, by God.

Juan Estrada stands motionless before the dumplings, trying to figure out if geometry and physics will permit him to fit maybe just one more on his already heaping plate. Tucker Adderly stands impatiently behind him, prodding Juan in the back with an over-filled plate of his own.

Bob and Peggy Storey sit on barstools, swiveled around to face the stage. Peggy's hair rises in an impressive, immobile beehive. She claps enthusiastically, while her hard-faced husband surveys the dance floor like he's searching for the guy who kicked his dog.

Seated at a table near the back door, Raul, Sean and Little Joe construct a tabletop tower out of saltshakers and ashtrays. Their tower crashes down when Raul fails to balance a final beer cap on the apex of the three-foot creation. They look up quickly to see if Vita is watching them, and then gather the scattered items so they can start again.

Out on the dance floor Captain Joe twirls his wife, then catches her as she executes a graceful backwards dip. Jolly Jake Jacoby scoots across the floor with Melba from the Palm Harbor Marina, who is quite fetching in her scarlet, low-cut party dress.

Sammy Dang had summoned the nerve to ask a Rockport High cheerleader to accompany him to this much-anticipated Ransom Island event and he holds the pretty girl gently in his arms, focusing hard on his lead. The purple orchid pinned to her dress matches the color of the half-circle bruise that still remains under Sammy's eye. His uncle Nu Dang and Aunt Lua Xian sit in a cluster of tables occupied by a large group of their Fulton Harbor friends. They are chattering and making toasts in Vietnamese, enjoying themselves to beat the band. The Chus are dancing as best they can while holding their baby boy, Shady, between them.

Off in a corner of the room, Billy Donathorn is playing—and losing—to Pete Jackson at the long sawdust-covered shuffleboard table.

In the middle of the dance floor throng, O.B. Hadnott clings amorously to Trinh An Phu, his eyes closed and a faint smile on his face. Trinny's hand reaches high to rest gently on O.B.'s shoulder, a brand new engagement ring shining from her finger. He is on leave, awaiting the paperwork that will reassign him to the Corpus Christi Ranger barrack that oversees the Gulf Coast. He wears a new silver-belly Stetson and looks every inch the Marlboro Man.

Charlie and Marisol are dancing too. They laugh as they attempt a Lindy Hop double swing turn. Rupert Sweetwater hoots from behind the bar when they get tangled up and he spryly bounds onto the dance floor. He taps Charlie formally on the shoulder, bows to Marisol and then whisks her off into the crowd.

Charlie sighs and watches them as they disappear into the mass of gyrating dancers, until he locks eyes with Leon Guidry who stands by the corner of the stage, his arms crossed, puffing on a vile plastic-tipped Roi-Tan cigar. Leon smiles his crooked smile and nods his head at Charlie—a validation of the spectacular triumph of the first annual Johnny Sweetwater Tribute and Christmas Ball. L.C. Hebert's fee has gone up exponentially since he won his Grammy. Leon made certain of that. But in a fit of short-lived and surely-to-be-regretted magnanimity, Neon Leon has announced that his star client is playing for the door. Plus a chartered fishing trip for the band, courtesy of Rupert and Jake Jacoby.

The smoke from Leon's cigar drifts up into the rafters where the spinning ceiling fan grabs it and blends it back into the reverberant, super-heated air of the room. Much of the music and smoky warm air escapes through the propped-open wooden louvers and spills out onto the wooden portico surrounding the building.

The music streams out over the sand-and-shell ground that marks the boundaries of Ransom Island, past the newly-patched finger piers that jut out from the land, and past the rusty outriggers of the Fulton-based trawlers that are moored to pilings. The music and lights pour out across the still water and the supratidal islands of cordgrass, glasswort and wolfberry that float above the tidal flats of Redfish Bay.

On this calm, cold night on the Texas Gulf Coast, a bright moon etches the diverse features of the salt marsh in hyper-realistic detail. In the shallow depths of the bay a towering Whooping Crane stands motionless on one long spindly leg in the submerged grass beds. It watches with interest the ruffling water emanating from a pod of tailing red drum that feeds near the grassy shore. The finger mullet scatter to escape the hungry reds, but one fish swims too close to the Whooper and in a flash the bird stabs it with its multi-colored beak. With the fish wriggling in its bill, the crane ascends into the air, its long neck extended, its slow deliberate wingbeats carrying them toward the rising moon and the great Gulf of Mexico.

THE BY-GAWD END.

ABOUT THE AUTHOR

Miles Arceneaux is the storytelling alter ego of Texas-based writers Brent Douglass, John T. Davis and James R. Dennis. The inspiration for the story comes from roots that run deep on the Texas Coast and from the characters, stories and experiences absorbed there along the way. *Thin Slice of Life* is Miles Arceneaux's first novel.

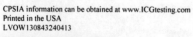
CPSIA information can be obtained at www.ICGtesting.com
Printed in the USA
LVOW130843240413

330681LV00002B/5/P